Lynda La Plante was born in Liverpool. She trained for the stage at RADA and worked with the National Theatre and RSC before becoming a television actress. She then turned to writing – and made her breakthrough with the phenomenally successful TV series *Widows*.

Her novels have all been international best-sellers. Her original script for the much-acclaimed *Prime Suspect* won awards from the BAFTA, British Broadcasting and the Royal Television Society as well as the 1993 Edgar Allan Poe Writer's Award.

Lynda La Plante has been made an honorary fellow of the British Film Institute and was given the BAFTA Dennis Potter Writer's Award 2000. She was awarded a CBE in the Queen's Birthday Honours list in 2008 and inaugurated into the Crime Thriller Writer's Hall of Fame in 2009.

Visit Lynda at her website: www.laplanteproductions.com

Follow her on Twitter @LaPlanteLynda

Lynda La Plante

SILENT VICTIMS

A PRIME SUSPECT NOVEL

SIMON &
SCHUSTER

London · New York · Sydney · Toronto · New Delhi

A CBS COMPANY

First published in Great Britain by Reed Books, 1994
This edition first published by Simon & Schuster UK Ltd, 2013
A CBS COMPANY

3 5 7 9 10 8 6 4 2

Simon & Schuster UK Ltd
1st Floor
222 Gray's Inn Road
London WC1X 8HB

Simon & Schuster Australia, Sydney
Simon & Schuster India, New Delhi

www.simonandschuster.co.uk

A CIP catalogue record for this book is available
from the British Library

Paperback ISBN 978-1-47113-550-7
Ebook ISBN 978-1-47111-495-3

This book is a work of fiction. Names, characters, places and incidents
are either a product of the author's imagination or are used fictitiously.
Any resemblance to actual people, living or dead,
events or locales, is entirely coincidental.

Typeset in Bembo by M Rules
Printed and bound by CPI Group (UK) Ltd, Croydon, CR0 4YY

SILENT VICTIMS

Preface

When I was commissioned to write *Prime Suspect* for Granada Television, I had no notion that it would change my life. I had been very successful writing a series called *Widows*, but it had not resulted in offers of work that I felt excited about. The plot of *Widows* pivoted on four men attempting a dangerous armed robbery, and all died when the explosives held in their truck exploded. They left four widows, who discovered the detailed plans and decided they would audaciously attempt to pull the robbery.

My meeting at Granada was to see if I had any other project they could consider. Due to offers coming in that were all similar to *Widows*, I decided that the best way to approach the possible commission was to find out exactly what the network was looking for, rather than pitch one or another of my ideas. I was told they were actually looking for a female-led police drama, but they did not want her to be in uniform.

'*Ah, I have been researching exactly that, and have some great material in a treatment,*' I LIED! But when I was asked what the title of this proposed new show was, out came, and with no forethought, the title *Prime Suspect*.

I knew this was a great opportunity, and with nothing actually written, I had to launch into research to prepare a treatment for a possible series. I was fortunate enough to meet Detective Chief Inspector Jackie Malton. She was attached to the Metropolitan Scotland Yard murder squad, and had risen through the ranks from uniform to become one of only three high-ranking female officers. By the time I had completed a story line and treatment, we had become friends. The friendship continued as I gained a commission to write the series *Prime Suspect*.

Via Jackie, and her eagerness for me to 'get it right', I went to my first autopsy. I spent time in incident rooms, pathology labs, and forensic departments. She was a never-ending source of encouragement and in many ways Jane Tennison was created via Jackie's constant desire that for once a woman was portrayed within the police force in a realistic way. She would read every scene, make corrections and suggestions with anecdotes appertaining to her own career. She was a complex woman and had been subjected to discrimination throughout her career. As I rewrote and polished up the scripts she became quite emotional because I had acted like a sponge listening and inserting sections that she didn't recall telling me about.

The moment *Prime Suspect* aired on British television it created incredible critical acclaim. I had to fight for a number of scenes to be retained. Producers were concerned that I had written an unsympathetic woman, but I refused to change, explaining over and over that this was a character based on reality. When she examined a victim she didn't, as they wanted, show emotion but retained a professional distance. To make her ambitious was yet again not wholly acceptable, but I persisted, and again I was helped by being able to introduce Jackie Malton.

Helen Mirren was unafraid of the role and added a strong quality to the character. She was the right age, she was still a very attractive woman and yet her believability never faltered.

The books cover *Prime Suspect 1, 2, 3 . . .* and they mean as much to me as the television show. Sadly with all good things, sometimes the powers that be have their own agendas and only these three books represent my voice. I only ever wrote three episodes, and three books. The learning curve from being a writer for hire, which I was on *Prime Suspect*, became the next major change in my career. I formed a production company, so that enabled me to produce my own work, cast, edit, and choose the directors. That said, although I have produced and written numerous series, I don't think there will ever be one as close to me as *Prime Suspect*.

Sincerely,

Lynda La Plante

Chapter One

The colour slide of a naked female corpse flashed up on the screen. The girl was about seventeen, with long blond hair trailing over her white shoulders. She had once been very pretty. The projector clicked and the screen was filled with a close-up of the girl's head. The ligature, a piece of fencing wire, bit deeply into the soft flesh of her neck. Her once pretty blue eyes were swollen, blood filled, bulging blindly towards the sky. Her tongue protruded like a fat purple worm.

The audience in the darkened lecture hall didn't stir. Trained not to display emotion and hardened by experience, the homicide officers, police medical teams, and Pathology scientists sat in silent rows, enduring the grisly peep show. Hardened or not, experienced or otherwise, some stomachs churned. A few of the younger men felt faint, nauseous, or both. The voice of the lecturer didn't help. Jake Hunter went remorselessly on, the catalogue of human depravity and perversion made even more chilling by his educated Boston drawl.

'So far, apart from a recent case in the United States, known serial killers have all been male, almost all white, often unusually intelligent or extremely cunning. Most victims are female, usually young women, whose death – as you see here – is frequently accompanied by violent sexual assault. Invariably there is evidence of torture and mutilation. A number of cases have involved homosexuals.'

Another slide flashed up. A full-face close-up of a swarthy, dark-haired, unshaven man with piercing, crazed eyes separated by a bony blade of nose. His thin, veined neck was cut off by a nine-digit mug-shot ident code.

'Richard Trenton Chase, the Sacramento "Vampire Killer,"' Hunter went on. 'Arrested for seven murders.' The slide changed. 'Note his own handwriting, taken from a scrawled message left at the scene of one of his crimes. *Catch Me Before I Kill More, I Cannot Control Myself.*'

Hunter turned to the audience. He was of medium height, with an athletic build that filled out his expensively tailored tweed suit. Under it he wore a button-down cream shirt with a striped silk tie. If the suit marked out his fashion sense as transatlantic, the brown cowhide boots with stirrup trim were strictly Dallas by way of Fifth Avenue.

Hunter went on, 'Later, I'll come back to the clues the handwriting gave as an insight to the killer's personality.'

He hadn't spotted Tennison. She'd arrived late, quite deliberately, and was standing by the door, her short hair a honey-blond blur in the flickering darkness. It rather amused her, Jake not knowing she was there, although they had already met twice during his lecture tour of England. Observing him secretly in the reflected glow of the screen gave her a tiny flutter of excitement, part nerves, part sexual danger.

His short brown hair was a little more flecked with grey, especially noticeable at the neatly trimmed sideburns, yet the bastard was still as ruggedly handsome as ever. His eyebrows were sun bleached, standing out against his tanned, craggy features. Had she aged as attractively? She still got her share of looks on the street, workmen whistled at her from scaffolding, but inside she sometimes felt like the Wicked Witch of the West. That was the job. A woman in a man's world. Required, *expected*, to handle the daily dish of crap and not flinch.

So she wasn't surprised, as she'd noticed on entering, to be the only woman present. She'd been the only female Detective Chief Inspector in the Murder Squad, at her previous posting at Southampton Row. About to move to Vice on the northern perimeter of Soho, Jane Tennison had no doubt that she'd be the senior female officer there by several light-years.

'Mass murder is the quintessential American crime,' Hunter told his attentive audience. 'Virtually unheard of a century ago, it has now become almost an epidemic. We are coming through a phase where males in the thirty-to-fifty age group are more brutal, more violent, than ever before. I have no doubt that these mass murders have a contagious element . . .'

They were listening silently not out of politeness or boredom, but because Jake Hunter spoke with the authority of hard-won experience. He had lived through it, been there on the front line. As a consultant to the New York Police Pathology and Forensic Research Unit, he was one of the world's top-ranked experts in the field; not only had he studied in depth the theoretical and historical background, he had witnessed the terrible bloody fact firsthand. He had been at the forefront in pioneering the technique of psychological profiling, now used by police forces in the United States and Europe. His books had become standard texts for the training of homicide officers, and were also required reading for students and academics specializing in criminal psychology.

In recent years he'd turned to fiction, producing three best-selling novels, two of which were under option to Hollywood studios. His latest book, however – and the reason he was here, lecturing to colleges and promoting it to a wider public – was nonfiction, a distillation of his many years' experience as a leading criminologist in the country that had patent rights on the concept of serial murder.

Another slide flashed up.

'George Henard executed' – Hunter repeated the word in his soft drawl – '*executed* twenty-three people, aiming point-blank volleys to their heads before turning the ...'

He stopped short, seeing Tennison, and paused, eyes blinking. Tennison gave him a warm, slightly mischievous smile.

'... before turning the nine-millimetre semiautomatic gun against his right temple for one final shot. What we cannot believe,' Hunter said, winding up to his chilling conclusion, 'is that the world is full of people with the potential to do this.'

Someone had done something singularly unpleasant to little Connie. He was a slender, pale, waiflike creature with loose, curly red hair that in sunlight was imbued with a golden sheen. He was lying on a sagging sofa in the flat of a drag queen named Vernon – or Vera – Reynolds who at that precise moment, 9.35 p.m., was floating in a mauve spotlight dressed as Marlene Dietrich singing 'Falling in Love Again' in a husky, tremulous baritone.

Connie tried to raise himself. His luminous dark brown eyes were muzzy. The cloud of auburn hair tumbled over his white forehead, but his beauty was marred by the dark stain of dried blood, like a slug's trail on his smooth cheek, where it had oozed down from the sticky gash on his right temple.

Again he tried to get up, failed, fell back. There was a racing blue edge of flame on the carpet. It touched the sofa and climbed the wrinkled cover. The flames turned to orange, their bright reflection twinkling in Vera's spangled and sequined gowns on the rack in the rear alcove.

The peacock feathers on another gown wafted in the updraught as the fire took hold. Half the room was ablaze, engulfing the sofa and the young boy so quickly that it sucked all the air from his lungs, leaving his scream stillborn in his raw throat.

The rack of gowns caught fire. Feathers and charred bits of chiffon wafted upward in a writhing cloud of smoke. The curtains went up. The paintwork on the frame of the closed window bubbled and peeled off. The entire living room and cluttered tiny kitchen of Vera Reynolds's shabby little flat were now ablaze.

With the sound and fury of a small but powerful bomb, the window blasted out into the night. The explosion shattered the peace of the six redbrick blocks of the flats. Burning debris showered down into the paved courtyard three floors below, setting alight a line of washing.

Already, from somewhere across the city, came the wail of an ambulance siren.

*

He'd find that bastard! Jimmy Jackson swung the old mid-night-blue Merc into a side street near the canal, the headlights making oily smears on the wet cobblestones. He gripped the wheel tightly, his scarred, pockmarked face thrust forward, his slitted eyes hot and mad, peering through the cracked windshield. His thick, fleshy lips were drawn back against his teeth. Where the fuck was the little turd! Sure bet that Fletcher was down here with the dregs, another homeless, snotty-nosed kid living in a cardboard box with winos, dossers, and sewer rats for neighbours.

Jackson spotted a movement. He snarled a grin and stamped on the big brake pedal. Next second the door was flung open and he was out and running, tall and mean in a studded leather jacket and torn jeans, knee-length biker boots ringing on the greasy pavement.

The terrified kid had taken off, heading for the iron bridge over the canal. But each of Jackson's thumping strides was equal to three of Fletcher's. He caught up with him by the edge of the canal that had the carcasses of bed frames, bikes, and supermarket carts sticking up from its putrid surface. Reaching out a clawed hand, Jackson grabbed the kid by the hair and yanked him to a skidding halt; the act of doing it, the thrill of power, gave him something close to sensual pleasure.

The kid was babbling with abject terror. Jackson stooped over from his lean yet muscular six-foot height and smacked him in the teeth. He hit him again with both barrels, left fist, right fist, to forehead and jaw. The kid squirmed on the ground, one grimy hand with bitten nails forlornly held up to ward off more punishment.

Jackson raised his fist.

'Dunno ... dunno where he is!' Fletcher screamed through his bloody mouth. 'I dunno where he is – I swear!'

Jackson took a pace to one side and kicked him in the groin. The steel toe cap went in with a satisfying *solid* thunk. He pushed his spiky mop of hair back with both hands. The kid might not know after all, but then again he might. Jackson needed a bit more convincing. He reached down for him.

Fletcher screamed, 'No, please ... I dunno, I swear! Please don't, don't ... PLEASE DON'T HURT ME!'

Small groups of people in nightclothes were standing on the balconies watching the fire crews at work. Some of the crowd had babies and toddlers in their arms. Hoses from three tenders snaked up the brick walls and over the concrete balconies to the third-floor flat. The fire was out, just a plume of dirty grey smoke eddying from the blackened, blasted-out window and wafting away on a northerly breeze.

A patrol car, siren off but with lights flashing, sped into the courtyard from the main road and stopped with a squeal of brakes, rocking on its suspension. Two uniformed officers, bulky, square framed, leapt out and ran towards the stairway. A slighter figure, round shouldered and rather hunched, wearing a shapeless raincoat that should have been given to Oxfam years ago, climbed out and shambled after them. He paused to look up to the window. The bright flare of arc lamps, set up by the fire crews, illuminated the balcony like a film set. Detective Sergeant Bill Otley sniffed and pinched his beaked nose. The call on the closed police band had reported at least one body. Not strictly his line, but Otley was in the habit of poking his nose in where it didn't belong.

Taking his time, as he always did, Otley went up the bleak stairwell. On the third-floor landing, pools of water everywhere, he glanced around, sharp eyes in his narrow, intense face missing very little. He appeared intense, Otley, when he was reading the *Mirror*'s sports page or watching the weatherman on TV. As if he was suspicious of everybody and everything, seeking out the guilt, the real motive, behind life's innocent facade. Life wasn't all that innocent, he knew damn well; everybody was guilty of something.

'Some of the tenants want to know if it's safe to return to their flats,' said a voice from within.

'Keep everybody clear,' the fire chief replied. 'We're checking the flats immediately above and below . . . '

The ambulance attendants were bringing out the body. Just the one. Otley stood a couple of feet inside the tiny hallway watching as they lifted it onto a stretcher and covered it with plastic sheeting. Curious position. The heat of the fire had petrified the charred, spindly black bones into what must have been the corpse's physical attitude at the moment of death. Arms stuck out like rigid sticks. Legs bent, feet curled underneath. The skull was a shapeless knob of sticky tar.

Otley pressed himself to the wall to let them pass.

'Anybody got an ID on it?'

'You jokin'?' one of the ambulance attendants said, manoeuvring the stretcher through the front door. 'Can't even tell if it's male or female yet!'

Otley grinned. He let them go and stuck his head into the living room. The arc lamps made stark shadows of the firemen and the two uniformed officers rooting about in the wreckage.

The fire chief gestured. 'Can somebody get duckboards on the balcony landing?'

Otley retreated through the hallway. As he went out he heard one of the uniformed officers say, 'The flat belongs to a Vernon Reynolds. Lived alone. Aged somewhere between late twenties and early thirties . . .'

Otley pinched the hooked tip of his nose and descended into the gloom of the stairwell.

'I thought it might be nice to eat in the room tonight,' Jake Hunter said. He was lounging in the passenger seat,

one arm draped casually along the back of Tennison's seat
as she drove him to Duke's Hotel just off St James's Street
where his publisher had booked him a suite. A cheroot
dangled from his lips. He had the expansive air of an actor
winding down after a performance. But then he always
felt easy in the company of Jane Tennison. She felt easy
with him too, though sometimes she wondered why the
hell she should.

It had been ten years since his last trip over here.
That was when they first met, and when they had their
affair that became a long-term relationship. Long term
in the sense of the seven months and fourteen days they
had lived together in Jane's Chiswick flat. As a Detective
Sergeant with the Lambeth Met, she had attended a
course at the Bramshill Officer Training College where
Jake was visiting lecturer. She was unattached, and so
was he. Drinks in the bar one evening plus an almost
instantaneous mutual attraction had led, naturally and
inevitably, to their becoming lovers. At thirty-four years
of age she was no starry-eyed innocent virgin. Jake, two
years older, had been married in his twenties; his wife
had died in a car crash before they had celebrated their
first anniversary. But when they embarked on their affair,
neither of them had realized what they were getting
into. And when they did, it was too late to do anything
about it.

Sooner or later, however, an awkward fact had to be

faced. Jake was due to return to the States, to take up his consultative post with the New York Police Pathology and Forensic Research Unit. Jane was in line for promotion to Detective Inspector – something she had been fighting tooth and nail for – and had the chance of taking charge at the Reading Rape Centre. There was no middle way, for either of them. They were both committed to their careers, and both deeply in love. Impossible to reconcile the two. Jake had gone home, Jane had got her promotion and moved to Reading.

Since then, nothing much. Postcards, a few telephone calls, one birthday card – from her, carefully worded, to his office. End of story, until three weeks ago, when the flame had been rekindled.

Tennison was aware of his scrutiny, gentle, rather amused, and concentrated all the more on her driving.

'I thought it went really well tonight,' Jake said. Not bragging, just a simple statement of fact. 'Better than last Tuesday. It felt more relaxed, don't you think?'

'Oh, you always impress me,' Tennison said, with just a touch of mockery, though it was true, he always did. 'How long will you be away?'

'Two weeks.' His publisher had fixed up nine speaking engagements and double that number of signing sessions from Brighton to Edinburgh; a punishing schedule. 'You are coming with me?'

Tennison hesitated. Then she gave a firm shake of the

head. 'I've been meaning to tell you. I'm starting this new job ...'

'Aahhh ...' Jake blew smoke at the windshield, nodding sagely. He might have expected this. In fact he had. 'Are we still going back to the hotel?' he asked, keeping his voice neutral.

'Yes,' Tennison said evenly, without a pause. 'Just for a drink.'

Mike Chow, the senior pathologist, and his three assistants in their long green plastic aprons and white wellington boots prepared the corpse for the autopsy. Lying on the stainless steel table, the body had been straightened to a more natural position. The blackened sticks of arms rested straight by its sides, the legs had been uncurled from their defensive foetal crouch.

'Okay,' Mike Chow said, poking at the charred scraps of fabric with a steel spatula, 'we'll get the clothes cut off and see what's left.'

A police photographer moved around the table, taking flash shots from every angle. One of the assistants began to snip away, delicately stripping off the burnt clothing with his gloved fingers.

The pathologist leaned over, taking a close look at the corpse's head. A few singed strands of reddish-auburn hair could be seen still clinging to the grey knob of skull. Impossible to tell, though, whether it was male or female.

Mike Chow picked up his clipboard, flicked over a page. He blinked through his glasses. 'Could be a . . .' A frown clouded his face as he turned to stare at the body. 'Vera stroke Vernon Reynolds. What's that supposed to mean?'

They'd eaten a late supper, surprisingly good by hotel standards, in Jake's suite. A bottle of vintage Chateauneuf-du-Pape to go with it, and two large brandies with their coffees. Jake was sprawled on the bed, waistcoat undone, his tie pulled loose from his unbuttoned collar. He still wore his fancy cowhide boots, which far from detracting from it, added to his aura of total well-being.

Tennison stood at the small table next to the window, leafing through one of the twenty copies of Jake's book stacked on it. There was a bookstore display unit with a blowup of the dust jacket and several glossy photographs of Jake at his most seriously thoughtful. One of these took up the whole back cover of the book Tennison was hold-ing.

She read the blurb inside the jacket and glanced up, smiling.

'You've taken four years off your age!'

Jake lazily swung his legs down and got up, flexing his shoulders. He wasn't abashed. 'Serial killers are big business.' His voice was a little slurred at the edges as he made a flippant gesture towards the pile of books.

'Help yourself. Well, they were big business – last year! I think I missed the gravy train.' He gave her a look from under his sun-bleached eyebrows. 'Story of my life.'

'Can I?' Tennison asked, holding up the book.

'One? Just one?' Jake came across and picked up a pen. 'Take one, you get eight complimentary copies,' he threatened, waggling the pen.

Tennison rested her arm on his shoulder as he leaned over to write. She smiled as she read the dedication. Very personal, but not so intimate – or incriminating – that she couldn't proudly show it off to a close friend or two. She gave him a hug.

'Thank you.'

Jake took her hand in both of his. 'Why don't you come with me?' The wine and brandy may have gone to his head, but she knew he was serious, not just fooling around.

'I don't want to get hurt again,' Tennison said quietly.

'Again? That doesn't make sense.'

She swallowed. 'Jake, there wasn't anyone else before . . . you know.' Ten years on, the memory hadn't faded, though she had exorcized the pain, or so she thought. 'Just it was going too fast. It was such a big decision.'

'Then why didn't you talk it through with me?'

'Because if I had, you would have made the decision for me.'

15

He raised an eyebrow, watching her intently. 'Would that have been so bad?'

'There's no point in discussing it now,' Tennison said, withdrawing her hand. She turned away.

'There might not be for you, but there is for me. I wanted to marry you. I wanted to have kids with you, you know that.' His voice rock steady now, befuddlement swept away. 'Don't you think I deserved more than a kiss-off phone call . . . "I'm sorry, Jake, it's not going to work."' He gave a slow, sad shake of the head. 'You never gave it a chance.'

Tennison spun around. She said in a tone of sharp accusation, 'I didn't know you wouldn't come back.'

'What did you expect me to do? Come running after you?' He spread his hands helplessly. 'You said it was over, then you hung up on me. Now you're doing the same thing. What are you so afraid of?'

'This is a bit ridiculous.' Tennison clenched her fists impotently. If only she'd acted sensibly, like the mature woman she was, and stayed well away. If only she didn't still fancy him like crazy. 'It was all a long time ago, and it isn't the same now.' If only! 'I shouldn't have started seeing you again . . .'

'So why did you come tonight?' Jake asked softly.

'Maybe I just couldn't stay away from you,' she said, avoiding his eyes.

'Just stay tonight,' Jake said, softer still. 'Then I'll go on my tour, you go . . .' He gestured.

'Vice. I'm heading a Vice Squad.' Tennison was looking anywhere but at Jake, yet she was keenly aware of his approach. Her stomach muscles were knotted with tension. His fingers gently touched her shoulder, turned her towards him. Slowly he put his arms around her and drew her close. His warmth, his nearness, the musky odour of his aftershave mingled with tobacco smoke, took her breath away. She made no attempt to resist.

'I mustn't,' she said, her grey-green eyes looking up directly into his. He touched her cheek. 'I mustn't.'

Chapter Two

Already, before 9.30 a.m., Commander Chiswick had twice tried to get through to Superintendent Halliday, and no joy. This had better be third time lucky. Tall but rather stooped, with receding grey hair, Chiswick stood at the window of his ninth-floor office at New Scotland Yard, phone in hand, gazing out across Victoria Embankment towards the Thames, barely a ripple on its sluggish, iron-grey surface. A mass of low dark cloud threatened the rain that the morning's forecast had said was imminent.

He straightened up and his eyes flicked into hard focus as Halliday, finally, came on the line.

'It's public.' Chiswick's tone was clipped. 'John Kennington's formal resignation accepted due to ill health. That's it. No option, so I've heard – case dismissed.' He listened, breathing heavily with irritation.

'I've only just been told. I'll see you there, why not? We'll have to go, otherwise it'll look suspicious . . .'

He glanced sharply over his shoulder as his personal assistant tapped at the door and came in, a sheaf of opened mail in her hand.

'Good,' Chiswick said impatiently into the phone. 'I'd better be on my way over to you now. Your new DCI should be there any minute.'

He banged the receiver down and headed for the door. His assistant held up the mail, but he walked on, ignoring her. His gruff voice floated back as he went out.

'Call my wife. I have a dinner tonight. Ask her to send over my dinner suit.'

His assistant opened her mouth to remind him of something, but too late, he was gone.

When he'd worked with the Murder Squad at Southampton Row station, Bill Otley was known to everyone as 'Skipper'. The name travelled with him when he transferred to Vice at the Soho Division on Broadwick Street. One of the longest-serving officers on the Metropolitan Force, yet still a lowly sergeant, his personal problems, his bolshie attitude, but even more his solitary drinking had held him back. His wife Ellen had died of cancer of the stomach eight years earlier. They'd always wanted children, never been able to have them. His marriage had been very happy, and since her death it seemed as though all warmth and light and joy had been wrung out of Skipper Bill Otley. He lived alone in a small terraced house in the East End, shunning emotional entanglements. The job, and nothing but the job, held him together, gave some meaning to what was otherwise a pointless existence. Without it he wouldn't have thought twice about sticking his head in the gas oven.

Now and then the notion still occasionally beckoned, like a smiling seductress, usually when the moon was full or Chelsea had lost at home.

Leaning back in his swivel chair, a styrofoam cup of coffee with two sugars on the desk by his elbow, Otley jerked his leg, giving the metal wastebasket a kick that clanged like a gong. Everybody looked around. The full complement of Vice Squad officers was here, ten of them male, and five women. The WPCs acted as administrative support staff, as was usual in the chauvinist dinosaur of an institution that was the British police force.

'We supposed to sit here all morning?' Otley demanded with a sneer. The team was gathered to be formally introduced to their new DCI, Jane Tennison. Five minutes to ten and no Tennison. Otley was pissed-off, so of course he had to let everyone know it.

Inspector Larry Hall walked by, cuffed Otley on the back of the head. Hall had a round, smooth-skinned face and large soft brown eyes, and to offset this babyish appearance he went in for sharp suits and snazzy ties, a different tie every day it seemed. He was also prematurely balding, so what hair he had was cropped close to the scalp to minimize the contrast.

He addressed the room. 'Right, everybody, I suggest we give it another five' – ignoring Otley's scowl – 'and get on with the day's schedule. We need an ID on the body found in the burned-out flat last night.'

'Voluptuous Vera rents it.' Otley gave Hall a snide grin. 'But it wasn't her. It was a kid aged between seventeen and twenty.'

'Working overtime, are we?' Hall ribbed him. But it wasn't overtime to Otley, as everybody knew. He was on the case day and night; probably dreamt about the job too.

'I wouldn't say she's overeager to get started,' Otley came back, always having the last word. Turning the knife in Tennison gave him special satisfaction. He'd never liked the ball-breaking bitch when they'd worked together on the Marlow murder case at Southampton Row, and nothing had changed, he was bloody certain of that.

He finished his coffee at a gulp, and instead of hanging around waiting like the other prats, scooted off to the morgue, a couple of blocks and ten minutes' brisk walk away, north of Oxford Street.

Mike Chow was in the sluice room, removing his mask and gloves. He dropped the soot-blackened gloves in the incinerator and was filling the bowl with hot water when Otley put his head around the door.

'What you got on the barbecued lad?'

'I'll have to do more tests, but he had a nasty crack over his skull.' The pathologist looked over the top of his rimless spectacles. 'Legs and one arm third-degree burns, heat lacerations, rest of the body done to a crisp.'

Otley tilted his head, indicating he'd like to take a gander. Nodding, Mike Chow wiped his hands on a towel and led him through into the lab. He pulled on a fresh pair of gloves.

'We've got an elevated carboxyhaemoglobin – blood pink owing to high level of same.'

Otley peered at the remains of the skull on a metal tray on the lab bench. He then took a long look at the illuminated skull and dental X-rays in the light box on the wall. Glancing over his shoulder, mouth pulled down at the corners, he gave Mike Chow his famous impression of a sardonic, world-weary hound dog. 'Bloody hell . . . looks like someone took a hatchet to him!'

Shit and corruption! First day in her new posting and she was over an hour late. After spending the night at the hotel she hadn't arrived back at her flat till nearly ten. She'd freshened up, grabbed her briefcase, and battled with the traffic. Even the Commander had beaten her to it. He was waiting to show her around, make the introductions, though fortunately he seemed too preoccupied with something else to show any displeasure.

Tennison tried to keep pace with Chiswick as he strode along the main corridor, shrugging out of her raincoat and trying not to get her feet caught up in her briefcase.

'Bomb scare, so all the traffic was diverted, and then my battery ran low, so I . . . ' It sounded pathetic and she knew it. 'Sorry I'm late.'

Chiswick didn't appear to be even listening. He pointed to a pair of double doors with frosted panes, not breaking his stride. He seemed to be in one hell of a hurry. 'That's the Squad section office. You have a good hard-working team assigned to you.'

Tennison nodded breathlessly.

He turned a handle, pushed open a door to what Tennison first took to be the cleaners' broom closet. Bare wooden desk, one metal-frame chair, dusty bookshelves, three filing cabinets, a small plastic vase with a wilting flower.

'If you want to settle yourself in . . . ' Chiswick was already moving back out, leaving her standing there on the carpetless floor. 'I'll see if Superintendent Halliday has made arrangements. He's right next door.' The Commander pointed to the wall, painted a mixture of old mustard and nicotine.

He went out and closed the door.

Tennison dumped her briefcase on the desk, sending up a cloud of dust. There was an odour she couldn't identify. Dead cat maybe. A rickety blind covered the window. She raised it, hoping for some light and space. It rattled up and she stared out at a blank brick wall.

She turned and said, 'Come in,' at a tap on the door. There was a scuffling sound. With a sigh, Tennison went to the door and opened it to find a red-faced uniformed policewoman weighed under a stack of files and ring binders. Tennison stood aside and watched as the pudgy, rather plain girl with short dark hair staggered in and deposited the files on the desk, sending up more dust.

'You are?'

'WPC Hastings. Norma. I was instructed to bring these to you.'

No 'ma'am'. Were things that casual around here, or just plain slack?

Tennison folded her arms. Take it slow and easy, don't jump the gun. 'Do you have a listing of all the officers on the squad?'

Sweating and flustered, WPC Hastings frowned. 'Didn't you get one this morning?' She had large, square teeth with a gap in the middle.

'I've just got here,' Tennison said, breathing evenly, trying not to get irritated, though she already was. 'If you could do that straightaway, and arrange for everyone to gather in the main office.'

'Most of them are out.' Norma shrugged. 'Would you like a coffee?'

'No, just the list,' Tennison said patiently.

The girl went off. Tennison gazed around at the four walls. This had to be a joke. This wasn't April 1st, was it? She looked through the files, then tried the top drawer of the desk. It came out four inches and stuck. She tried the next one down and that stuck after only two. She kicked it shut, making her big toe sting, and the air blue. What kind of stinking shit-hole was this?

Superintendent Halliday was a neat, fastidious-looking man with short fair hair and pale blue eyes fringed by blond lashes. Not puny, exactly – he was nearly six feet tall with bony shoulders that stretched the fabric of his dark grey suit – but not all that robust either, according to Tennison's first impression. From the moment she entered his large, spacious, nicely decorated corner office (right next door to her rabbit hutch!) he kept glancing at the gold Rolex on his freckled wrist. She hadn't expected the welcome mat, but at least he might have shown her the courtesy due a high-ranking officer who was about to take over the Vice Squad. Damn well would have too, Tennison reckoned, if only she'd been a man.

'I want you to give Operation Contract your fullest and immediate attention. I know it'll be a new area for you, but I am confident your past experience will be an added bonus.'

All the feeling of a talking clock, Tennison thought. As if he'd rehearsed it in his sleep. She had no idea what Operation Contract was. She thought about asking, and then decided not to give him a stick to beat her with by displaying her ignorance. She nodded to seem willing.

Halliday tapped the desk with manicured fingers. 'It is imperative we get results – and fast. There's been enough time wasted.' He shot his cuff and glanced at his watch yet again.

'As yet I have not had time to familiarize myself with any of the cases ...' Tennison was distracted as WPC Hastings entered without knocking. Halliday showed no signs of noticing her presence. Norma draped a black evening suit in a cleaner's bag over the back of a chair and went out.

'... the cases I will be taking over. But, er – Operation Contract I will make my priority.'

Halliday stood up. 'Good.' He stuck his hand out. Tennison shook it. 'The team will fill you in on our progress to date.' Another swift glance at the Rolex. 'I was expecting you earlier.' Small wonder he could remember who she was, Tennison thought, leaving his office.

Sergeant Otley flicked the sugar cube into the saucer. He did it twice more, leaning his head on his hand, elbow on the table. Observing him with heavy-lidded, soulful eyes, hands twisting nervously in her lap, Vera arched her neck, her Adam's apple rippling like a trapped creature. Inspector Hall stood with casually folded arms near the door of the interview room. He was interested, and secretly amused, to see how the Skipper would handle Vernon stroke Vera Reynolds. There was the vexed question of gender, for a start.

'I told you . . . I did the show and then went out for a bite to eat with some friends.' The reply was half-whispered, yet it wasn't a lisping, camp voice.

Offstage, Vera wasn't dragged up like some transvestite queen. There was no secret about who and what she was, but she chose to dress plainly and conservatively, favouring a simple blouse in dusky pink, a straight dark skirt, and leather sling-back shoes with low square heels. A few rings and a string of purple beads were the only bits and pieces of jewellery. Under her wig and make-up, in fact, Vera had rather a strong face, Hall reckoned, with good bones; though the mouth, shapely and sensitive, was a dead giveaway.

Otley flicked the sugar cube. 'And you don't know who was in your flat?' he inquired in his usual drab tone.

Vera gave a little shake of the head.

Hall put his hands on the back of Otley's chair and leaned over. 'Vernon,' he said, not unkindly, 'if I go out and leave somebody kippin' in my place, I wouldn't be stupid enough to say I don't know them. I mean, that is stupid, isn't it?'

Vera threw up her hands, the knuckles red where she'd been kneading them. She swallowed hard, the Adam's apple doing a double gyration. 'It could have been any number of people – you see, it was well known I leave a key on top of the front door ...'

Otley made a sound, a kind of muffled snort. He sighed and shook his head, crumbling the sugar cube between his long hard nails.

'About seventeen years old?' Hall said. 'Reddish blond hair ... ring any bells?'

Vera bit her lip, staring down at the table. Then a tight, rapid shake of the head. She was steeling herself for the next question when she was saved by Norma's face at the small glass panel in the door. She tapped and stuck her head in.

'Fire team would like Mr Reynolds as soon as possible. There's sandwiches and coffee served in the Squad Room. Can you get everybody mustered, same as this morning, for twelve-thirty sharp?' Norma waggled her dark unplucked eyebrows at them. 'She's here.'

While Inspector Hall escorted Vera Reynolds out and put her in the charge of two uniformed men, Otley followed Norma along the corridor to Tennison's office, which at the moment was minus Tennison. The Skipper peered in, an evil grin on his face, watching Norma in the dim, dusty cubbyhole trying valiantly to wrench open one of the desk drawers. Norma looked up, perspiring.

'She won't like this,' Otley gloated, rubbing his hands.

'She's not here, Sarge. Nor should you be,' Norma said pointedly.

Otley cackled.

Tennison capped her fountain pen with a decisive click and stood up. She tugged her suit jacket straight at the front and came around the desk to face them. The Squad Room stilled. Not very tall, under five feet five, her honey-blond hair cut in a swath across her forehead, she seemed rather out of place in a room of hulking men; all but one of the women police officers were taller, even if they didn't have her rounded, sensual figure.

The tension in the hot, crowded room was almost palpable. Tennison certainly wasn't relaxed, and neither were they. A new Detective Chief Inspector heading Vice might spell all kinds of trouble, and already she had two strikes against her. Her reputation as a tenacious round-the-clock obsessive who worked her team to the bone, and the fact that she was female. Even the WPCs were wary of that.

Fingers laced together at her waist, feet braced apart, Tennison let the silence gather for a moment. She wanted control from the start, and was determined to have it.

'So . . . please accept my apologies. Not got off on a very good footing on my first day.' Small smile. Let them know you can afford it. 'I will obviously need everybody's cooperation, and I would also appreciate it if . . .'

She caught a movement as Hall slithered in. He gave her a weak, apologetic smile and she returned a curt nod. He grabbed a sandwich from the cafeteria tray and it was halfway to his mouth when Tennison said:

'It's Inspector Lawrence Hall, yes?' He nodded, mouth open, sandwich unbitten. 'Well, let's you and me start off on the right footing, shall we? If I ask everyone to be at a place at a certain time, and only unless you have a good excuse . . .'

'I'm sorry,' Hall interrupted, 'but I had to arrange for Reynolds to be taken over to the Fire unit. I was waiting—'

'Is Sergeant Otley with Reynolds?' Tennison asked sharply. Hall hesitated. 'Yes,' he lied. 'You know about the fire, do you?'

Tennison nodded, slowly folding her arms. 'Why is this fire and the boy of such interest to you, or this department? I know Vernon Reynolds. I know what he is, but that isn't against the law.'

'Well – one – it was on our patch. And in the area we have been targeting, Euston and St Pancras, on Operation Contract. The dead boy was possibly a rent boy.' Hall glanced towards the door, wishing Otley would show up.

'Vernon was probably taking a few quid for letting them use his place.'

'Has he admitted that?'

Hall shifted uneasily under her gaze. Where the fuck was Otley? 'No, ma'am . . . well, he's not likely to, is he? He's saying he doesn't even know who was in there.'

Tennison scented that matters were spinning beyond her control. Nip it in the bud. No mavericks on her team. She said briskly, 'I'd like a full report on this fire business and then I will tell you whether or not this department wishes to continue with the investigation. Our priority is Operation Contract.'

Hall stared at his feet. The other officers, munching sandwiches and slurping coffee, exchanged looks. First morning in and she was throwing her weight around. This was going to be a load of fun, they didn't think.

With a curt nod of her head, Tennison indicated that work should continue. The officers turned back to their desks, to their mounds of paperwork, reaching for phones. They were all aware of her scrutiny: new regime, new boss, and they were being required to pass muster.

Tennison beckoned to one of the WPCs standing in a small group next to the wall-length filing section. She came over, a tall, striking girl with frank, open features and friendly blue eyes.

'What's your name?'

'Kathy.'

'Can you give me a brief rundown on the operation?'

WPC Kathy Trent led her over to the large board. 'I've been trying to question as many of the kids as possible.' She smiled diffidently, eager to help.

Tennison watched closely as Kathy took her through it. She still hadn't got a handle on this Operation Contract thing. The board was crammed with information. Under 'TOMS' – police slang for female and male prostitutes – a long list of names and locations: Waterloo Street, Golden Fleece, Earls Court, Euston Station, Stars & Stripes. Farther along, headed 'OPERATION CONTRACT', photographs of young boys, some of them no older than eleven or twelve, with video stills of supermarket checkouts, tube station platforms, mainline station concourses. More typed lists of targeted locations – cafés, coffee shops, street markets, soup kitchens, cardboard cities – spotted in different colours. Tapes led from these to a huge map of central London with corresponding coloured pins. A duty rota of officers on surveillance was marked up in black felt-tip, with dates, times, and frequency, all cross-referenced to file number such-and-such. At first sight it seemed to be an efficient and comprehensive operation, well planned, rigorously executed.

'Most of the older rent boys are carrying pagers, portable phones, so our team – four of us, ma'am – concentrate on the younger ones skiving around Soho.'

Kathy pointed to a sheet marked up in coloured felt-tip, a blizzard of asterisks, arrows, code numbers. 'We staked out the Golden Fleece, Euston Station, Earls Court ...'

Tennison nodded, content for now to listen and learn, get some kind of grip on it.

'Our problem is that when the kids are actually out on the street, they've already accepted the lifestyle.' Kathy didn't sound sad, simply resigned to reality.

Over by the door, behind Tennison's back, Sergeant Otley sneaked in, made a rapid gesture to Hall. The Inspector scuttled over.

'You've been with Reynolds and the Fire team,' Hall said under his breath, tapping his nose.

'I haven't.' Otley grinned. 'I've been up at Records and we got ...'

He pulled Hall behind the half-open door as Tennison glanced their way.

' ... boy is Colin Jenkins, known as Connie.'

Otley punched Hall's arm. He then made a show of arriving for the first time, all innocent, to be met face-to-face by Tennison, who'd marched smartly over.

'Sorry I'm late, ma'am,' said Otley with a straight face. 'But I've been seein' if I can get your drawers loosened.'

Everybody heard but nobody laughed.

Tennison stood with her back to the window. On the other side of the desk piled high with three-inch thick files, Otley waited, sardonic grin absent for the moment. He'd had to deal with this slit-arsed bitch before, and knew what to expect.

The room was still in an almighty mess, though WPC Hastings had managed to find her a desk lamp that worked and two more straight-backed chairs with the varnish worn through to bare wood. For the moment, Tennison had more important preoccupations.

'Right, Sergeant, I am not prepared to take any crap from you, or stand by and let you stir it up. So let's clear the air.' Tennison jerked her head, eyes hard as flint. 'Sit down.'

'Judging by the state of the rest of your office I don't think I should risk it!' Otley pulled a chair forward and sat down, an uncertain half smile hovering on his face. 'Joke!'

'If you don't want to work with me, I can get you transferred.'

Otley studied his thumbnail. 'I was out of line at Southampton Row, but, that said' – he shrugged – 'I know you did a good job.'

'Thank you,' Tennison said, her sarcasm like a saw's edge.

Her last case with the Murder Squad had been a racial and political minefield. Teenage half-caste girl dug up in the back garden of a West Indian area seething with antagonism against the police. Despite this, Tennison had stuck to the job like a terrier with a bone. Tracked down and collared a young white bloke with a sickening, sadistic streak who liked taking photographs while buggering his schoolgirl victims.

Otley was looking anywhere but at Tennison as she moved a stack of files from her chair and sat down. She stared at him a long moment, letting him sweat a little, and then flipped open the green cover of a file. She tapped the report.

'I have a lot of catching up to do, so, come on ... are you going to help me or not?'

'I got an ID on the boy in the fire at Reynolds's place,' Otley volunteered. He took a folded sheet from the pocket of his crumpled suit. 'He was a runaway, fifteen years old. Colin, known as Connie, Jenkins. All the state-run homes have their kids' teeth checked on a regular basis and filed on record—'

'What's this boy got to do with Operation Contract?' Tennison asked bluntly.

There were connections here she couldn't make. Otley and Hall seemed to be running some cowboy operation of their own. Plus there was an undercurrent in the department; she'd sensed it right away. Not unease exactly, more a kind of apathy. Lack of motivation. She had to get to the bottom line of all this before the whole bloody mess swamped her.

She strode along with Otley to the Squad Room and up to the board.

'It was supposed to be a slow start to a massive big

cleanup.' He swept out his hand. 'All the areas targeted were those specifically used by rent boys.' A glance at her under his brows. 'It's Halliday's obsession.'

'Yes . . . And?'

'That's what it is – cleanup operation.'

'So what's the big deal? Why has it been taking so long?'

'Because it's a bloody cock-up – if you'll excuse the pun!' Otley said with some heat. 'The Guv'nor before you got dumped. Somebody had to take the blame.'

Tennison saw a chink of light. The entire room, while ostensibly working, was taking in every word. Kathy and Norma were sitting at their VDUs, staring at the green screens. Otley was about to go on, checked himself, and looked towards Inspector Hall. Hall came up and the two men swapped some kind of coded message.

Hall turned to Tennison, keeping his voice low.

'Ma'am, a few of us think the same way. There was a leak, word got out. No gamblers, no boys on the streets.' His tone turned bitter. 'We spent weeks getting ready for a big swoop, all hush-hush . . . came out empty-handed. Surveillance trucks, uniformed and plainclothes officers – it was a fiasco. It had to be a leak but Chiswick and Halliday keep on pushing it.'

Tennison looked at Otley standing a few feet away, head sunk on his shoulders, flipping through the pages of a report that just happened to be on the desk.

Under the force of her gaze he raised his eyes. 'I'd say, now, the buck stops with you.'

She knew that. It was the sly curl of his lip she didn't like.

Chapter Three

'So we stop, and old John looks at this unattended vehicle, he looks at me, we're both wet behind the ears, and I said, "What do you think?" There it was, parked without lights in the middle of this copse on a housing estate in Cardiff . . . '

Chief Superintendent Kernan paused, smiling down at the man seated next to him at the top table, the 'old John' in question. Kennington, receding silver hair brushed back, distinguished, with a supercilious air, returned the smile. He puffed on his cigar, smiling and nodding at the great and the good gathered for his farewell dinner in the banqueting room of the Café Royal. Every senior-ranking policeman on the Metropolitan Force was here. These were colleagues he had worked with, served under, commanded during the nearly forty years of his rise to very near the top of the heap.

Several judges were in attendance, not one under sixty-five. Barristers who'd defended against him, prosecuted with him. Pathologists, forensic scientists, doctors, one or two people from the Home Office, a junior Minister, and a sprinkling of sober-faced top brass from the security services whose names and photographs never appeared in the newspapers.

Kernan took a sip of brandy before continuing. In spite of his apparent joviality, the puffy, pasty face with its mournful hangdog look seemed painfully at odds with his black tie, starched shirt, and black dinner suit. Leaning forward, hands splayed on the white tablecloth, he spoke into the microphone.

'So we drive across the copse. Midway across we get bogged down in the mud. So we get out and radio for assistance.'

Grins and nods from the rows of tables stretching down the long elegant room, chandeliers reflecting in the gilt-framed mirrors. Everyone relished a good cock-up story.

' . . . a Panda was just passing, so they followed us across the copse – and they got bogged down about ten feet away from us. Next came a Land Rover. They got as far as our patrol car. So there we all were . . . and John says, maybe we should check out this abandoned vehicle. So we wade across this bloody bog, and find a note pinned to the windshield. "GONE FOR HELP. STUCK IN THE MUD."'

Thumps on the tables. Flushed faces guffawing. Everybody having one hell of a good time, getting better by the minute so long as the free booze kept flowing.

Three seats down from Mike Kernan at the microphone, Commander Chiswick took advantage of the laughter to mumble into his companion's ear, 'Sweep it under the carpet job. Now I've been warned to keep it there ...' He met the other's wide-eyed gaze, nodding meaningfully.

Kernan had consumed three large brandies while on his feet, and his speech was getting slurred. He now poured another treble, ready for the finale. 'So I would like to propose my toast, and to give my very good wishes for a happy, productive retirement – to John Kennington. Gentlemen! Please raise your glasses!'

There was a gulping silence while everyone drank, and then a loud buzz of animated chatter, ribald comment, and hee-hawing laughter. Plump hands beckoned urgently to the waitresses, beavering around in their short black dresses and white pinafores. The speeches were only halfway through, a powerful incentive to get three sheets into the wind by the shortest possible route.

Kernan stood back from the microphone. He then remembered and swayed forward, bending over to speak into it. His voice boomed like a station announcer's, bringing winces and bared teeth.

'Gentlemen ... please may I ask your attention for Commander Trayner.'

Kernan shook hands and slapped backs on his unsteady return to his seat next to Superintendent Thorndike. He flopped down, belching, grinning at everyone for no other reason than he was half-pissed. Thorndike pursed his lips. He didn't approve of such behaviour in a senior officer. He didn't actually approve of Kernan full stop, even though it was Kernan who had wangled him the post of Super at Southampton Row. It should have gone to Kernan's next in line, his senior detective Jane Tennison, but Kernan, a founding member chauvinist pig, wasn't going to stand for that. So prissy boots Thorndike got promotion and ball-breaker Tennison got dumped.

At the microphone, Trayner was burbling on about more good old days with good old John Kennington. This time it was Manchester, not Cardiff, from where Trayner had some very happy memories, and some not so great ones. ' . . . and John here brings a Tom into the station. He was writing up a charge sheet, listing drunk and disorderly, abusive language, and – as the lady in question was stark bollock naked at the time . . . '

Kernan leaned in Thorndike's direction. His eyes were gone and his breath enveloped Thorndike like a toxic cloud.

'Why don't we just give him his watch, eh, and piss off home? Eh?' He guzzled some more brandy. 'Unless there's a cabaret – eh? Is there a cabaret?' He squinted at Thorndike, whose thin wrists stuck out of his starched cuffs like celery sticks. Prim and proper, he was like some-body's bleeding maiden aunt, Kernan thought sourly. Never had really took to the man, but then Mike Kernan didn't take to the human race in general.

'You not drinking?' he asked suspiciously. He reached for the brandy bottle and poured Thorndike a whopper. 'Bill Otley's with the same squad, did you know that? With Tennison – Vice Squad!'

Kernan laughed loudly, coinciding with the general laughter at something Commander Trayner had said. He pushed the glass across.

'Have a drink! This is going to be a long night!'

Thorndike hesitated, but finally took a sip. Keep on his good side. Never know when you might need him.

'. . . if you think I was pissed,' Trayner was saying, building up to the punchline, 'wait until you see what's inside the greenhouse!'

Not having a clue what the story was about, Kernan banged the table, joining in the laughter and applauding like a maniac, bellowing, 'More! . . . More! More!'

Edward Parker-Jones tilted the boy's head to the light and examined his face. Bruising around the forehead and left cheekbone. A diagonal gash extending from his ear down to his jawline. His lower lip was split and had dried into a crusty scab.

'What am I going to do with you, Martin?' Parker-

Jones sighed. 'Look at you! Have you eaten today? You haven't, have you?' He ruffled the boy's hair. 'Do you want some soup? Cup of tea?'

Martin Fletcher twitched his thin shoulders in a shrug. He was reluctant to even open his mouth. The beating he'd taken from Jimmy Jackson the night before, down by the canal, had scared him to quivering silence, his gut churning as if he were riding a roller coaster, jumping at shadows. He'd spent the rest of the night curled up in a shop doorway, whimpering. Today he'd wandered the streets, a forlorn lost figure in a grimy windcheater and jeans ripped open at the knees, his toes sticking through his trainers.

The recreation and advice centre run by Parker-Jones was the only refuge he could think of. It was an oasis of warmth and comfort – a hot drink and a bite to eat – before slinking back to the streets for the night. But it wasn't safe even here. That bullying swine Jackson some-times showed his ugly, pockmarked face, on the prowl for some poor kid who owed him money, or a favour, or who Jackson just might want to beat the shit out of for the sheer fun of it.

Parker-Jones put his arm around Martin's shoulder and led him through the reception area, where a few lads were idling the time away gazing listlessly over the notice board. Jobs, hostel accommodation, personal messages, dubious offers of help by phone.

'Go and sit down and I'll get Ron to bring you something in.'

He had a deep, resonant voice that went with his neat appearance and confident personality. A tall man, broad in the chest, late thirties, Parker-Jones carried himself as someone of authority: an organizer, intelligent and decisive. His black hair, parted in the middle, flopped over his ears when he was in a hurry, giving him a rakish look that was somewhat at odds with his image of a solid rock in a shifting world.

'Did you call home?' he asked Martin. 'You promised me you would at least call your mother. Do you want me to do it? Martin?'

Martin shook his head and wandered off into the TV lounge. Broken-down armchairs and two old sofas were grouped around the set, and there was a shelf of dog-eared paperbacks, some jigsaws, and board games. The walls were a sickly purple, with green woodwork. It was empty at this hour; between seven and eight was usually quiet, which was why Martin had dared take the risk.

On the way back to his office, Parker-Jones called out to a scruffy black kid with a hearing aid, wearing a back-to-front baseball cap, 'Ron, get some hot soup for Martin Fletcher, would you?'

The black kid dropped the duster and metal wastebasket he was carrying and went over to the alcove where a copper urn with a brass tap bubbled and spat, steam jetting out of the top.

Otley came down the narrow wooden stairway from the street, the shoulders of his raincoat stained dark with drizzle. The advice centre was on his beat. It was situated just off Brewer Street in Soho, at the bottom of a cobbled alley that during the day was crowded with market traders, selling everything from fruit and veg to lampshades, toilet paper, and bootleg records and tapes. The doorway was directly opposite the neon-lit entrance to a strip club. Farther along, a couple of shops stayed open until past midnight, catering to the soft porn magazine and video trade.

Otley knew about the hard Swedish and German stuff in their back rooms, for selected clients only, but he let it ride. The perverts had to go somewhere. Better they got their jollies that way than molesting the young and vulnerable.

'Bit quiet tonight, isn't it?' Otley said.

The three boys loitering at the notice board looked him up and down with sullen eyes. No one spoke. Hands in his raincoat pockets, Otley glanced around at the peeling mustard-coloured walls with posters tacked up for rock concerts long gone. The carpet was a dank green, greasy and black with the tread of many feet. The wall opposite the reception counter was bare brick, steam pipes near the ceiling, huge Victorian radiators jutting out into the passage. To the left was the games room, which had a pool table and a football table with wooden players; to the right, past the office door, the fluted glass panels of the TV room. Otley thought he saw a rippling shadow move inside.

He said casually, 'Any of you know Colin Jenkins? Nicknamed Connie?'

The door marked 'E PARKER-JONES – PRIVATE' opened, and Parker-Jones came out. He spotted Otley at once and marched straight over.

'What do you want?' Dark eyes under thick black eyebrows staring hard. 'If you are looking for a specific person, why don't you ask me?'

Otley remained unruffled. He'd been stared at before. 'You know a lad called Colin Jenkins?'

'Yes. Red-haired, about your height. Nicknamed Connie.'

Otley nodded slowly. 'Used Vera Reynolds's place. I need to ask some of the boys about him.' Parker-Jones was about to say something, but Otley went on in a monotone, 'He's dead. He was on the game, wasn't he?'

'Are you telling me or asking me?' Parker-Jones drew himself up to his full height. 'Is this official? I've already discussed this with an Inspector ...' He frowned and snapped his fingers. 'Inspector Hall. I really don't understand why you and your associates persist in coming in here ...'

His indignation was wasted on Otley, who had strolled

off in the general direction of the television lounge. Ron came from the corner alcove with a plastic cup of soup. Parker-Jones took it from him and hurried past Otley into the lounge, still complaining in his fruity, rather portentous voice.

'You people make my job and the social services work exceptionally difficult. I attempt to get these boys off the street, give them a place they can come to – and I am continually harassed, as are the boys.'

He held out the cup of soup. A tousled head poked up from behind an armchair. A nail-bitten hand reached out.

'They are not in my care, they come here of their own free will. They come here because this is one of the few places they can come to.' He sounded righteously outraged, as if he had been accused of something, his reputation besmirched.

Otley stood in the doorway watching as Martin Fletcher took the soup in both hands. The boy looked up at Parker-Jones, his bruised and battered face breaking into a wan smile. Parker-Jones ruffled his hair and smiled back, the steadfast rock in an ugly, shifting world.

Tennison pushed through the glass double doors into the corridor leading to the Pullman lounge at Euston Station. She checked her appearance in a small hand-mirror, flicking her hair into place with her fingertips. The stewardess behind the glass door pressed the entry release buzzer.

Tennison entered the thickly carpeted room, the din of the station below hushed behind triple glazing and velvet drapes. She looked around nervously. The stewardess held out her hand, presumably for a first-class ticket.

'I'm just meeting someone here.' Tennison returned the stewardess's smile with a small embarrassed one of her own. 'I don't have a—'

'It's okay, she's with me.'

Jake Hunter threaded his way through the deep comfortable armchairs grouped around low tables. The lounge was almost empty. The stewardess dimpled at his smile, and he led Tennison across to his table. She put her briefcase by the chair and unbuttoned her raincoat.

'I've never been in here before. Mind you, I don't usually travel first class. Thank you,' she said, as Jake helped her off with her coat. She hadn't dressed to please him, though the dark red linen jacket and charcoal grey pencil skirt made her feel slim and attractive, and she was glad she wore it.

They sat down. Jake drew his armchair closer.

'I've got about an hour before my train, but I just wanted to—'

Tennison interrupted, speaking in a rush. She was still flustered. 'I'm glad you called. I wanted to talk to you. There's a case I'm working on.'

Jake caught her arm as she reached for her briefcase.

'I don't want to talk about any work, Jane. I just

didn't think we, or I ... could walk away without, without ...'

He sighed and sat back, rubbing his chin, as the stewardess appeared beside them with the drinks menu.

'Whisky and soda, please,' Tennison said, ignoring the card. She watched the stewardess go, and then took a good look around. 'I'm very impressed. I didn't know this was even here.'

Jake leaned forward and took her hand. She thought of pulling away, but didn't. He had to have his say, and she couldn't stop him. Did she want to? Good question. If only she knew herself.

'Jane, we've got to talk, because, I ...' She realized he was nervous too. It was a struggle to get the words out. 'Jane, I'm married and I have four kids ...'

'I know,' Tennison said calmly. 'It's on the flyleaf of your book.'

'Yeah!' Jake sounded almost angry. He leaned closer, his voice low and urgent. 'But what isn't is the way I feel about you. What I've always felt about you.'

'No, but you wrote that in the front of the book.'

'Can you just be serious, just for a second, for Chrissakes!'

'There's no point.' She repeated quietly, 'There's no point.'

'Then why did you come?' Jake asked stiffly.

'I just wanted to ask you your opinion about something

I'm working on.' Tennison glanced away from him. His eyes were like lasers on her cheek.

'I don't believe you.'

The stewardess placed Tennison's drink in front of her, along with a napkin and dish of peanuts. Jake took the bill and nodded his thanks.

Silence then, while Tennison stared at her untouched drink. She said, 'I knew you were married. I shouldn't have stayed.'

'Why did you?'

'Because . . .' She gave a tiny vexed shake of her head. 'Because you wanted me to. Don't—' She held up her hand as he tried to speak. 'I wanted to, Jake. I wanted to be with you.'

It was hell to handle, and the only way she knew how was to make light of it, kill the feeling with fake humour.

'I've always been a glutton for punishment, maybe that's why I'm so good at my job. I've got that, you've got a family – perhaps we've both got what we wanted. If I haven't, then I've no one else to blame but myself.'

Jake sighed miserably. 'What a mess.'

'No, it isn't,' Tennison said briskly, 'because we'll do what we agreed. We won't see each other again. You'll get on the train, and in the meantime . . .' She reached down for her briefcase.

Jake turned his face away from her, but she could see

his throat working. 'I love you,' he said, hardly moving his lips, and took her hand, holding it tightly.

'Yes, I know,' Tennison said softly.

Jake let go of her hand. He took a huge breath and turned back to look at her. 'So . . . what's this case you're working on?'

Larry Hall looked up from the computer as he heard the door swing. Otley was standing there, hair plastered to his forehead, hand on the shoulder of a puny kid with terrified eyes in a face that had been through the mangle.

'I want an interview room and somebody to take a statement.'

It was 7.43 by the clock on the wall of the Squad Room. Hall frowned. 'You're not down for tonight, are you?'

A couple of officers were working a few desks away. Otley lowered his voice. 'This lad knows something, but he's scared.' He nodded towards the corridor. 'Come in with me?'

Hall took his jacket from the back of the chair and slipped into it, automatically adjusting the knot in his tie. He looked at Martin Fletcher, then tugged the lobe of his ear. 'Hey, Bill, how old is he?'

'I think your boy was already dead,' Jake said, studying the pages of the autopsy report spread out on the table. There were some grisly morgue photographs that Tennison had shown him and quickly tucked back into her briefcase. She leaned forward, her clasped hands resting on her knees.

Jake indicated a paragraph. 'Says here that the fluid taken from the blisters showed no sign of vital reaction.'

Concentrating hard, Tennison tried to put the pieces together. 'So, if the fire wasn't accidental, he was murdered? . . . Is that what you're saying?'

Muted chimes rang out. '*The train on platform thirteen is the eight p.m. Pullman Express to Liverpool, calling at Watford, Crewe . . .*'

'What does "pugilistic attitude" mean?' Tennison asked, fretting.

'Arms held out, legs flexed.' Jake thought for a moment. 'It's caused by the coagulation of the muscles on the flexor surface of the limbs . . . so the body could look as if it was in a sitting-up position.' He raised his eyebrows. 'Jane? I'll be back in London next week, and maybe—'

'No, we agreed, no more meetings.' Tennison shuffled the pages together and closed the file. 'That's your train.' She put the file in her briefcase and snapped the locks. 'Don't call me again, please.'

Jake picked up his bag. He dropped it and fished in his pocket for change. Tennison got up and took the bill from his hand. 'I'll get this. You'd better go.'

He looked down at her gravely and put his hand on her

shoulder. She did what she promised herself she wouldn't, but she couldn't help it. She took his hand and pressed her lips to it.

She could still taste him when he'd gone, turned abruptly and walked out, while she stood staring at nothing. She sat down for a moment and then went to the window. He was striding across the concourse to platform 13. Suddenly he stopped, turned quite slowly, and stared up, his fair eyebrows standing out against his tanned face.

Tennison saw him move on and watched his tall figure until it was lost to sight, beyond the barrier. She came away from the window. The stewardess was clearing the table.

'Ah . . . I'd like another whisky and soda.' Tennison felt as if her insides had been scoured raw. She managed a smile. 'If that's okay.'

'For he's a jolly good fe-ellow, for he's a jolly good fe-ellow, for he's a jolly good fe-el-low! And so say all of us!'

Mike Kernan wasn't singing. He was staring, bleary-eyed, watching them sing their stupid heads off. Chiswick. Trayner. Halliday. All the rest at the top table, up on their hind legs, bellowing away. And John Kennington, slightly flushed, holding the velvet presentation box, that haughty smirk on his lips.

In Kernan's book, Kennington wasn't a jolly good

fellow at all. Far from it. Did he have a tale to tell, if only he felt like telling it . . .

'I'm out of here.' Kernan pushed his chair back. He tried to stand and fell back. 'Can't take any more of this crap.' He leaned over, almost in the lap of Thorndike, who gazed at him with naked disapproval. 'Somebody should ask him to start the cabaret,' Kernan said, nodding, wagging his finger. 'I saw him at the Bowery Roof Club . . .'

Thorndike's attention sharpened. 'The Bowery what?'

Kernan had made it to his feet, swaying. He tapped his nose. 'Keep this out of it . . . but you see that iron-haired bloke, Judge Syers, top table? Ask him if he can get you a membership. "Iron" being the' – he belched – 'operative word. G'night.' He staggered off.

Iron? Thorndike pursed his lips. What did that mean?

The singing had finished. A slow applause started as Kennington stepped forward to the microphone, holding the velvet box in one hand and a gold pocket watch in the other. He raised an eyebrow, beaming down at them.

'Gentlemen . . .' He waited for the applause to die away. 'Gentlemen, tonight is a sad, very sad occasion for me, but you have made it a night I will never forget.'

They were on their feet, applauding, none more vigorously than the iron-haired judge. Thorndike never missed an opportunity. He'd wheedled his way nearly to the top of the greasy pole, currying favour, playing the smiling sycophant, but there was some distance to go.

He took advantage of the applause to sidle around, finding himself very conveniently at the judge's elbow. 'Excuse me ... it's Judge Syers, isn't it?'

Judge Syers turned and stared at him, cold probing eyes under bristling grey brows.

'We met at a lodge dinner,' Thorndike lied smoothly.

Judge Syers seemed to think this not impossible. He gave an almost imperceptible nod of his iron-grey head. 'What's your name?'

Cutting through the smoke, the mauve spotlight picked out the face of Marlene Dietrich. Huge dark eyes, a gash of red for the sultry mouth. Thin arcs of eyebrows against an alabaster forehead. Silvery blond hair framing high cheekbones and the rouged hollows beneath. The spotlight widened to reveal her tight, skin-toned dress, figure-hugging from neckline to her ankles. Sequins gave off glittering sparks so that she seemed to shimmer like a cloud of dazzling light.

> 'Falling in love again, never wanted to
> What am I to do
> I can't help it ... '

Vera swayed hypnotically on the small stage against a backdrop of silver satin drapes. Her arms floated like pale slender reeds, nails sharp as talons, teardrops of blood. Her low throaty voice caressed the words like a hand stroking fur, inviting, suggesting, seducing.

Below the stage, small lamps in the shape of tulips glowed on the gold lamé tablecloths. The close-packed faces were blurs in the dim light. Some were focused on the stage; Vera Reynolds was a hot act, one of the most popular with the members. Other faces – older, lined, jaded, belonging to men in muted, well-cut business suits – were constantly on the move, eyes roaming the darkness, searching for that special someone.

Half past midnight. The Bowery Roof Top Club was reaching its peak.

Thorndike followed Judge Syers out of the lift into the small lobby on the ninth floor. A handsome young man with a thin moustache that curved down to a pointed beard, his sleek ponytail looped into a bun, sat behind the reception desk. He was checking names and numbers on a screen. Through the doors, Thorndike heard a husky voice singing, 'Falling in love again, never wanted to . . .'

He was secretly thrilled. He'd never before entered such an exclusive establishment. The place reeked of power and privilege, even if the decor wasn't to his taste. In fact it was rather vulgar, in an expensive way, Thorndike decided. Heavy tapestries of silver and gold adorned the walls. Pillars of vine leaves in wrought iron, painted gold, supported tubs of exuberant foliage. Large mirrors framed in gilt reflected the heated exotic splendour. Thorndike didn't quite know what to make of it all; he'd certainly never seen anything like it.

He stared, blinked, and pursed his thin lips in a prudish pout. That marble statuette – good God! A full-size male nude, the anatomical detail leaving nothing to the imagination. He quickly averted his gaze.

'Member and one guest,' the receptionist said, pushing the book forward. Judge Syers stood aside as Thorndike signed.

The act was just finishing. They came through into the bar, and Thorndike got a glimpse of a blond head bowing low, arms gracefully extended, acknowledging the applause. The air was thick with smoke and heavy with perfume. The little flutter of apprehension he felt became stronger as he gazed around. What struck him most forcibly was the height of the women. Many of them were over six feet tall in their spiked heels. Gorgeous, slender creatures in sparkling evening gowns, exquisitely made up, with manes of wavy hair cascading over their shoulders, silver blond, molten red, raven black. Their dresses were cut away in the most revealing places, except there was nothing to reveal. In fact, Thorndike decided, goggling, they looked like women and they moved like women, only more so. His apprehension escalated into dry-mouthed panic.

There were boys too, some of whom looked no older

than sixteen. Their hair was slicked back, glistening with gel. They wore black leather jackets over white T-shirts, with tight jeans fashionably faded at the knees and crotch.

The bar was crowded with respectable city types, middle-aged and older, in close conversation with the willowy, preening creatures and the young boys. Thorndike seemed to recognize a face here and there, and blanched at the thought that if he knew them, they might know him.

He followed Judge Syers down the four steps from the bar area to the tables clustered around the stage. The judge knew practically everyone, the way he was nodding and smiling. Then Thorndike spotted the look-alike Marlene Dietrich on the far side of the room. She pushed through the crowd towards them, silvery-blond hair gleaming in the smoky light. She came straight up to Judge Syers, a head taller, placed her hand on his arm, and leaned over to whisper in his ear.

Thorndike backed away. He looked around, eyes swivelling, panic rising in his chest. A tall graceful creature with flowing red hair, sharp painted nails, and a low-cut gown revealing a chest as flat as an ironing board winked at him.

Thorndike stumbled up the steps and fled.

'It was an accident,' Vera Reynolds said in a low, frightened voice. Her grip tightened on the judge's arm. 'A terrible accident.'

She glanced nervously over her shoulder. He was there in the bar, as usual. He was looking straight at her. Vera shuddered. She couldn't make a move without Jackson knowing about it.

Judge Syers was reaching for his wallet. 'I'm sorry. If there is anything I can—'

'No.' Vera held up the palms of both hands, whitened by constant applications of lemon juice. 'No, I don't want money,' she protested. She half-turned. 'I'd better go and change.'

Judge Syers watched her threading through the crowd. He went up into the bar. He nodded to one or two people, and gradually worked his way around the intimately chattering groups. A tall elegant man with snow-white hair, leaning on a cane, was deep in conversation with a paunchy balding man of similar age, late sixties. Frampton was a Member of Parliament, and in common with most MPs he liked the sound of his own voice. Those within ten feet had to like it too, given no choice.

'It is a bloody outrage!' Frampton's watery eyes bulged. His nose had been broken in a public school boxing match, and the years of booze had covered it with a maze of tiny broken blood vessels. 'They are saying that the leak sent four times the permitted amount of radioactive dust into the atmosphere. Claims by the government that this could not harm people or the food chain are simply a cover-up!' He thumped his cane. 'I fully intend to raise the matter in the House.'

Kilmartin sipped his drink, nodding.

'Greenpeace campaigners have been targeting the place for years,' Frampton went on heatedly. 'To state that a Chernobyl-style disaster could not happen here is rubbish!'

Smiling to himself, Judge Syers moved to the bar. He ordered a gin and tonic, then indicated Frampton and Kilmartin with a nod of his head. The barman set about fixing the drinks.

Farther along the bar, a cigarette hanging from his mouth, Jackson squinted through the smoke at the judge. His biker gear had been replaced by a hip-length leather jacket, designer jeans, and Reebok trainers. As Judge Syers turned, Jackson lazily looked away.

The music started up as another act came on. This time it was a Bette Midler look-alike in army uniform, burning red hair, six-inch silver heels, a high bust like two melons under a blanket, blasting out 'Boys from the Backroom'.

'If one of the biggest nuclear reprocessors for nuclear warheads in the world can have a leak, no matter how small, it means their security and safety rules must be monitored more closely . . . '

'You're in good voice as usual,' Judge Syers said. 'Are you well?'

'Terrible,' Frampton boomed. He waggled his stick. 'I've got ruddy gout. First time out in weeks.'

They shook hands. The barman placed their drinks down. Judge Syers lit a cigar and puffed it into life. The three men raised their glasses. 'Cheers!'

Judge Syers watched Bette Midler strutting her stuff for a moment. He stared into his drink. 'Colin Jenkins is dead.' Frampton frowned over his brandy glass, rather puzzled. 'I think he called himself Connie,' the judge said quietly. He looked at Frampton. 'We should talk . . . '

The three men moved off, Frampton limping, towards a curtained doorway leading to the members' private bar.

Jackson watched them go, cold as a snake. He turned then, his fleshy lips curving in a dead smile as Vera Reynolds moved slowly up the steps and came to stand beside him.

Chapter Four

Piece by piece, the Fire team had reconstructed the sitting room of Vera Reynolds's flat. The charred furniture had been replaced in its exact position, according to the drawings made by the team and the fire brigade immediately after the blaze had been put out. Sections of fabric from the burnt-out sofa had been salvaged and draped over its blackened frame; the scorched covering still bore the clear outline of Connie's body.

A cool breeze blew in through the glassless window frame, weak beams of morning sunshine showing the ravages of the fire in every grimy detail.

'The paraffin heater was found here.' Ted Drury, heading the Fire team, squatted on his haunches, pointing to the white plastic tape in the shape of a cross on the sodden, ashy carpet. 'Right by the settee. Not – as described by the owner-occupant – on the far wall.'

A second cross of red tape marked the location of the heater, as stipulated by Vera. His colleague, also attired in waterproofs and green wellington boots, took notes. A Polaroid camera was slung around his neck.

'Cold that night, so the boy lies down ...' Drury pointed. 'Maybe has moved the fire closer, from there to here.'

'No, it was found with the ridges facing away from the settee.' His colleague laid the smoke-blackened paraffin heater on its side, demonstrating. 'If he had moved it to get warm by, the heater would have been the other way around.'

They both turned as footsteps scuffled through the debris in the hallway. Vera Reynolds stood in the doorway. She stared around, ashen-faced, her lower lip trembling. Her friend Red was with her, a mop of curly dyed red hair bright as a flaming beacon, long legs, and a firm little rump in tight blue jeans. They carried black plastic rubbish sacks filled with pots and pans and other kitchen utensils.

Vera gave a tiny squeal and reached down.

'Please don't touch anything in the room,' Drury warned her.

'It's my photograph album,' Vera said, anguished. It lay open on the carpet next to the sofa, its edges buckled and scorched.

Red put her arm around Vera's shoulders, hugging her.

'Don't look – just don't even look. You're insured. Keep on saying to yourself, "I am insured."'

Vera gazed at the rack in the alcove where all her lovely, beautiful, gorgeous evening gowns had been, fighting back the tears. Red led her out. 'You'll have to have every carpet replaced. The water's done more damage than the fire!'

The two fire officers looked at each other. Odd to think that pansies had the same feelings as normal folk.

Tennison called the first briefing for 9.30 a.m. Except for two or three officers who were out checking statements, the entire Vice Squad, Soho Division, was assembled in the Squad Room. After the tension of the previous day, the atmosphere was markedly more relaxed. People lounged around drinking coffee, wisecracks were bandied about, snatches of laughter, general good humour. Tennison thought she might even get to like working here.

'Is there anyone on the squad who has had any past dealings with Colin Jenkins?'

Kathy passed over a sheaf of reports that she'd winnowed out concerning boys of Connie's age.

'He might have been picked up a few months back, maybe more. We rounded up a lot. I can't find the report on him, but I'm sure that a Jenkins – I think it was a Bruce Jenkins – was interviewed with a probation officer, as he was underage.'

'What's this advice centre?' Tennison asked, leafing through. A whiff of cigarette smoke floated by, and she had to battle against the temptation. Did the urge never, ever let up?

'One of the places we targeted,' DI Hall said. 'I've already been there. The guy that runs it—'

Otley chimed in. 'Mr Parker-Jones. States he hadn't seen our Connie for months.' And if you believe that, his tone said, I'm a dead ringer for Richard Gere.

'Has it been confirmed yet whether the fire was arson or accidental?'

Hall shook his head. 'Don't know. Fire team are still working on it.'

Everyone straightened up a little, took their feet off desks, as Superintendent Halliday walked in. 'Want to run over a few things,' he said brusquely. Tennison nodded. She was on her way, following him out, when she heard Kathy saying to Hall, 'Guv, there was an emergency call placed at nine-fifteen, night of the fire. Caller did not leave his name.'

'What emergency call?' asked Hall.

Tennison paused at the door.

'Somebody called an ambulance.'

'An ambulance?' Hall frowned. 'For Reynolds's address? Get the emergency services to send over the recording.'

Tennison hurried along the corridor, catching up

with Halliday as he passed her open door. Norma was labouring mightily, logging the stacks of files and placing them on the shelves. Soon it might start to resemble an office.

Halliday turned to Tennison, rubbing his forehead. He looked distinctly green around the gills.

He said, 'Last night a lad called Martin Fletcher was brought in – Otley will explain the circumstances – but the last thing we need is any aggro from Social Services about questioning underage kids without legal advisers.' He shot her a warning look, then his face creased with pain. 'Christ, I've got a headache ...'

Kennington's farewell bash was taking its toll. Serves you bloody well right, Tennison thought with satisfaction.

'I'd like you to set up meetings with the British Transport police, get to know all the centres and halfway homes in our area. I'd like us to try for another swoop on those areas we've targeted.'

'Sir, this boy in the fire, Colin Jenkins,' Tennison said as Halliday walked on to his office and opened the door. 'According to the team he was on the game!'

'Well, he isn't anymore, so he's one less to worry about.' Clutching his head, Halliday went in and slammed the door.

Norma looked up as Tennison came smartly in, heels rapping. She didn't need smoke signals to know that a storm was brewing. Tennison sent her off to get Martin

Fletcher's file, and when she returned her boss was pacing the small space between the desk and window. Still pacing, Tennison quickly scanned through the file, and then snatched up the phone. Norma kept her head down, literally, sorting out the files.

'DO Tennison. Extension seven-eight, please.' While she waited, fingers drumming, she spotted some Post-it memo slips stuck to the blotter and attracted Norma's attention.

'There were three messages. The Fire team, Forensic department, and someone called Jessica Smithy. She's a journalist. Said she is doing a piece on rent boys—'

'What paper is she from?' Before Norma could answer, Tennison said into the phone, 'Would you please ask Sergeant Otley and Inspector Hall to ...'

There was no need, as Otley tapped on the door and stuck his head in. Tennison banged the phone down. Hall followed the sergeant in.

'That's it, Norma,' Tennison said. 'Out, thank you.' She waited until the door had closed and came around the desk, brandishing the file.

'What the hell do you think you're playing at – *no!* Don't interrupt!' Otley shut his mouth as Tennison glared at him. 'Last night, according to the roster, *you* were not even on duty – but last night the pair of you interviewed a Martin Fletcher, correct?' She opened the file, glancing down at the yellow slip paper-clipped to the top sheet.

'When later interviewed by his probation officer, a Miss Margaret Speel, she noted that this same Martin Fletcher had extensive bruising to his face, arms, and upper neck . . .'

'Wait, wait,' Otley said, shaking his head rapidly. 'We brought him in like that!'

'*Don't* interrupt me, Bill.' Tennison's eyes blazed. 'This same probation officer has subsequently filed a complaint against this department – which, in case you two had not bloody noticed, *I am head of*.' Her voice sank to a dangerous whisper. 'Martin Fletcher, you idiots, is fourteen years old!'

Otley swore under his breath and flopped down into a chair, a hand covering his eyes. Hall stayed on his feet, goggling.

'Oh, man – he swore under caution he was seventeen. He said he was seventeen . . .'

'And as such he should have been allocated a lawyer, a probation officer, or an appropriate adult,' Tennison went on relentlessly. She tossed the file on the desk and folded her arms. 'So, which one of you wants to start?'

Otley looked up at Hall, who coughed and as a nervous reflex smoothed down his tie, a garish swirl of reds, pinks and purples.

He said, 'There's a known heavy, beats up on the young kids. Jackson, James—'

'So? Get to the point.'

'He picks up the young kids, the really young ones, in and around central London – Euston, Charing Cross—'

'I know the stations. Go on.'

Hall blinked his large baby-brown eyes. 'Martin Fletcher was one of his boys.'

Otley's fists were clenched on his knees. With a great effort he kept his voice under tight control. 'Reason I brought Martin in was because I reckoned he might help us get a handle on Connie, why he was in that flat.'

'We just wanted to talk to him about Colin Jenkins,' Hall added. 'Then he starts to tell us about Jackson.'

'The bastard plucks 'em off the station,' Otley said, 'takes them out, gives them food, offers a place to stay – that's it, he's got them.' His mouth twisted in his long, haggard face. 'Keeps them locked up. Not just boys, it's very young – only the very young – girls as well. He drugs them, keeps them dependent.'

Thoughtfully, Tennison went back around the desk. She leaned her knuckles on the edge.

'Did Martin Fletcher tell you all this? Or is it past history?'

'We've sort of known about the scams,' Hall said, 'but we can't get any of the kids to name Jackson – he was one of our main targets. We don't know where he holds the kids, but Fletcher, he admitted—'

'Just hang on a second.' Tennison's narrowed eyes

flicked between them. 'What do you mean, "holds the kids"? Kidnaps them?'

'No, they go with him willingly,' Otley said. His voice had a raw, ugly edge to it. 'And then once he's got them – that's it. We're talking about kids as young as twelve and thirteen ...'

'None of the kids will talk. We've had him hauled in on numerous occasions, we've even got as far as getting charges compiled against him, but the statements are always withdrawn, the kids are terrified of him, they won't go against him. So when Martin tells us Jackson beat him up because he wanted to know where Connie was, we reckoned we got something.' Hall gestured irritably towards the desk. 'Have you read my report?'

Tennison straightened up. 'Yes!' She flipped open the buff cover, and began to read out loud.

'SGT. OTLEY: "Where does he stay? Do you know his address?"

FLETCHER: "No, sir."

SGT. OTLEY: "Did he beat up on you, Martin?"

FLETCHER: "Yes, sir, he did."

SGT. OTLEY: "Why did he do that, Martin?"

FLETCHER: "I don't know."

SGT. OTLEY: "Did you know Connie?"

FLETCHER: "No."

SGT. OTLEY: "Come on, Martin, he was murdered."

FLETCHER: "No, sir!"'

Tennison brought her fist down on the page, glaring across the desk at them. 'We do not as yet have any proof that Colin Jenkins *was* murdered.'

Hall took the file, turned it around and thumbed over a couple of pages. He looked up. 'Excuse me, Guv . . .'

'Help yourself,' Tennison said curtly.

Hall read out loud:

'INSP. HALL: "Tell me about Colin Jenkins."

FLETCHER: "I don't know him."

INSP. HALL: "I think you are lying."

FLETCHER: "I'm not, I didn't know where he was, that's why Jackson done it to me . . ."'

Hall looked at Tennison. 'Jackson beat up Martin Fletcher on the same night Colin – Connie – died.' He read on.

'INSP. HALL: "What time did Jackson beat you up?"

FLETCHER: "Eight to nine-ish."'

Hall closed the file and stepped back. During the silence Otley stared at nothing and Tennison tapped her thumbnail against her bottom teeth. 'Have you got a realistic time for when the fire started?'

'Yes,' Otley said, getting up. 'About nine-thirty.' He yanked his crumpled jacket straight at the back. 'Jackson could have done it! Even if he didn't, this could be what we need to get him off the streets so we can get the kids to talk.' He stared hard at Tennison. She thought some more and then gave a swift nod.

'Okay. You get hold of the probation officer and Martin Fletcher, and bring Jackson in for questioning . . . just helping inquiries,' she added quietly, staring him out. In other words, no more bloody cock-ups that would leave her holding the shitty end of the stick.

Tennison wanted to see for herself. Statements, autopsy reports, tapes, photographs told one version of events. They might be true and accurate, but they were one-dimensional, open to interpretation. Nothing like being there, seeing it, smelling it, touching it.

She took Otley along with her to Vera Reynolds's flat. The Fire team was still there, sifting through what remained of Vera's most treasured possessions. A plastic sheet had been taped over the window to keep out the draught. Even so it was cold, the air acrid with the lingering smell of smoke that seemed to enter every pore, making Tennison's eyes sting.

'Body was found here, on the settee.' Drury showed her, his gloved hand tracing the outline of Connie's body on the singed fabric. 'This is, or was, a paraffin oil heater, and the seat of the fire.'

He pointed to the white cross on the carpet.

Tennison crouched down for a closer look, lifting the tail of her beige Burberry raincoat to prevent it getting soiled. 'Was it an accident?'

'No.' He was very definite. No pussy-footing around.

The man knew his business, and his confidence gave her a lift. 'The heater was pushed or kicked forward. And there are signs that paraffin had been distributed around the room, probably from a canister of fuel that we found by the door.'

'So somebody started the fire,' Otley murmured, stroking his jaw.

Tennison leaned over to inspect the covering with its ghostly imprint of Connie's last few seconds alive. No longer just a poor dead lad, she thought; now he was the subject of a possible murder inquiry.

'If you stand by the fireplace, for example, and say you trip ...' Drury acted it out for them. 'There's an arm-chair, a footstool, a coffee table, but none would indicate the victim had fallen. Coming from the opposite direction ... if he had, say, fallen against the heater, then he wouldn't have been lying that way around. His head would be at this end.'

Tennison pictured it in her mind. It was as important to know what hadn't happened as what actually had. She thanked him with a smile and stepped onto the duckboards leading outside. In the Sierra Sapphire, heading for the morgue, she asked Otley if anything had been found in the flat that might be a possible weapon.

Otley sat in the passenger seat, not wearing his seat belt as she'd asked him to. 'Yes, taken to the labs,' he said,

rhyming them off. 'A heavy glass ashtray, a pan, a walking stick handle, er . . .'

'Any prints on them?' Otley shook his head. 'What
about Vera Reynolds? She in the clear?'

'Time of the fire he was on the catwalk in a tranny
club.' Otley looked across at her. 'He still insists he didn't
know the boy. You want to talk to him?'

'I suppose so.' Tennison sighed, gnawing her lip. 'But if
Connie was killed, it won't be down to us to sort it.'
Seeing her murder inquiry vanishing over the horizon,
she said, 'We won't get a look in.'

Like a kid who's had an ice cream snatched from
under her nose, Otley thought. It should have made
him feel gleeful, her disappointment, but somehow it
didn't.

'DCI Tennison's gone walkabout,' Halliday said darkly
to Commander Chiswick. 'Nobody knows where she
is.'

Chiswick closed the door and tossed the report onto
Halliday's desk. 'It's just official, the fire – it wasn't accidental.'

'Well, in that case it's nothing to do with us, is it!' A
smile broke over Halliday's pallid features. Maybe now he
could shake this blasted hangover. He sat back, relieved.
'Thank God!'

'Make sure she understands that this is the Vice Squad,'

Chiswick told him stolidly, spelling it out. 'Any other crimes are forwarded to the correct departments.'

'We might have a bit of a problem. The boy was earmarked in Operation Contract, could be a tie-in, but I'll have a word . . .'

'You'd better,' Commander Chiswick said, his face stern. 'I don't want her – us – to have anything to do with this murder, so reallocate the investigation.' He wagged his finger. 'And tell her, Jack, she has no option.'

Chiswick went out, leaving Halliday delicately massaging his temples with his fingertips.

They arrived at the morgue a few minutes before two-thirty, and were about to enter the laboratory when Tennison received a call on her mobile. She waved Otley on and listened to Norma relaying her messages.

'Right. Okay. Did he leave a number?' Tennison couldn't get to her notebook fast enough, so she wrote the number on her hand. 'Anything else?' She listened impatiently. 'Again? Just tell her I am unavailable, or put her onto the press officer.'

She zapped the aerial back and strode into the white-tiled laboratory. Otley was standing with Craig, a scientist with the Forensic team, before a large, oblong lab bench with a white plastic worktop. Pieces of burnt remnants from the boy's leather jacket, trousers, boots, and underwear were pegged out and separately tagged. There was some loose change, covered in sticky human soot, and sections of what had been a leather wallet, calcified in the heat so that it crumbled to the touch.

'Just official, the fire wasn't accidental,' Tennison informed Otley. 'What's all this?' she asked, sticking her nose in and watching Craig poking with a glass rod at a hard wad of blackened paper that was crumbling to greyish ash.

'Money. Or the remains of it. We've still got some under the microscope, but it's quite a lot.'

'Like about how much?'

Craig was squinting at it through horn-rimmed glasses, wrinkling his hairy nostrils. 'At least five hundred, could be more.' Using the glass rod as a pointer, he took them through the display. 'The clothes, all good expensive items. Quality footwear. We've got a label from his leather coat, it was Armani . . .'

He moved on, and Tennison said in a quiet aside to Otley, 'Martin Fletcher didn't say anything about money, did he? You think this is what Jackson was after?'

Otley shrugged. Money hadn't even been mentioned.

Farther along the bench, Craig was pointing to some crinkled bits of glossy paper. 'These are sections of pho-tographs, all beyond salvaging, but they were stuffed inside his jacket. And these scraps of paper, all charred, I'm afraid. Possibly letters . . . hard to tell.'

'This is it?' Tennison said, surveying the worktop.

'Yes, this is all that's left of him,' Craig said.

On their way out, Tennison said quietly to Otley, 'Get Vera brought in again.'

Inspector Larry Hall and WPC Kathy Trent were cruising Euston Station in reverse, so to speak. They weren't looking to be picked up, they were planning to do the picking up – when they found him. To a casual observer they would have appeared just like any other young couple waiting to meet someone. Hall wore his dark navy car coat over his double-breasted blazer, and Kathy had on a loose, deep purple trenchcoat and black suede ankle boots.

Already they'd walked the full length of the concourse at least a dozen times. As each train arrived and the passengers surged up the ramp from the platform, they stood midstream, scanning the wave upon wave of faces rolling towards them.

At ten minutes to three, with Hall starting to fret that they were wasting their time, he got a call. He inclined his head, listening intently, and then spoke into the small transceiver inside his turned-up collar. 'Is it him? Sure? Okay, we're on our way.'

He set off, Kathy walking briskly beside him. 'Jackson's hanging around platform seven.' He held out his hand, and Kathy slapped it. 'You owe me a fiver!' Hall said, grinning. 'I said Euston, you said Charing Cross!'

The Liverpool train had just pulled in. Jackson was

sitting on the metal barrier at the top of the ramp, eating a burger. He looked quite relaxed, waiting, it seemed, like several others, for the arrival of a friend. His eyes roamed over the passengers: businessmen, families, older people with their luggage on a cart, but he wasn't interested in any of them. Then he spotted a young boy, fourteen, perhaps fifteen, scruffily dressed, carrying a cheap suitcase tied up with string. Jackson tossed the burger away and slid down. Wiping his mouth, he watched the boy coming up the ramp. He sidled to his left, getting into position to intercept the boy as if by chance.

Hall and Kathy, and a third plainclothes officer, moved in slowly, threading their way through the stream of passengers.

'Hi, how you doin'?' Jackson was all smiles, a friendly face in a strange, hostile environment. 'Do I know you?' The boy gave a little nervous smile, shaking his head. 'You from Liverpool? You know Steve Wallis?' Jackson patted his shoulder reassuringly. 'I'm not the law, just waitin' for a friend. You got somebody meetin' you? First time in the Smoke?' Jackson stuck a cigarette in his mouth and offered one to the boy. 'Hey, man, you want a drag?'

As the boy reached to accept it, Hall stepped between them, nose to nose with Jackson. Jackson fell back a pace. He half-turned, nearly colliding with the third officer standing right behind him. Hall muttered a few words in Jackson's ear.

Her arm around his shoulder, Kathy said to the boy, 'Have you got somebody meeting you, love?'

The boy shook his head. He looked past Kathy and got a glimpse of the two officers walking off with Jackson between them, merging into the crowd.

Otley came into the interview room with a tray of canteen teas in proper cups and saucers. He slid it onto the desk between Tennison and Vera Reynolds. Norma was sitting next to the wall, plump black-stockinged legs crossed, taking notes. She looked bored to tears.

'Vera's admitted that she knew Colin.'

'Connie,' Vera corrected Tennison. Her head was bowed, her long pale hands with the manicured nails clasped tightly in the lap of her leather skirt. She wore a loose halter-neck knitted top, coloured bangles on her bare arms. 'He didn't like his name, sometimes he called himself Bruce.'

Tennison made a note on her pad.

'Bit butch for his kind, isn't it?' Otley said, standing with legs apart, sipping his tea.

Vera turned her face to the wall.

Tennison's patience was running short, but she summoned up some more. 'Vera, the sooner this is all sorted out, the sooner you can leave.'

'On the other hand, if you killed your little feathered friend,' Otley said, 'then you'll be caged up – with no make-up bag in sight.'

Tennison looked at Vera over the rim of her cup. She glanced up at Otley, who rolled his eyes. They waited.

'If it's proved to be arson . . . ' Vera's voice was croaky; her eyes red-rimmed. 'I mean, if somebody did it, does that mean I won't get the insurance?' Her brow puckered as if she were about to cry. 'Oh, God . . . all my costumes. I don't know what I'm going to do.'

'Never mind your costumes, Vera, what about Connie?' Otley's patience was running shorter than Tennison's. 'Who do you think set light to him?'

'I don't know.' Staring at the desktop, fingers plucking at the baggy sleeve of her knitted top.

DI Hall tapped on the door and looked in. Otley went over, and Hall whispered to him, 'I've got Jackson and the probation officer waiting to see . . . ' He nodded at Tennison. 'And Martin Fletcher's being brought in.'

Tennison was making one last try. 'Vera, if you are protecting someone, then you had better tell me. You have already lied to us, wasted our time . . . ' She looked across at Hall. 'Five minutes.' Then back to Vera. 'Why did you lie about Connie?'

Norma looked at Hall, cross-eyed. She tapped her watch, blowing out her cheeks. He grinned and went out. Tennison leaned her elbows on the desk, waiting. Otley stood holding his cup and saucer, waiting. He glanced impatiently at his watch. Vera took a long time lighting a cigarette. She blew out a great gust of smoke, then, as an afterthought, hesitantly offered the packet.

'I've given up,' Tennison said.

'I've tried, I've had the patches.' Vera smiled weakly. 'I've got patches for hormones, nicotine – my arse looks like an old pub table. I even tried the chewing gum. How did you give up?'

'With great difficulty.'

Norma's mouth sagged open as she watched the pair of them. She looked at Otley, who gave her a snide wink.

Tennison pushed the loaded ashtray across. 'You had better help me, Vera, I am losing my patience. Why did you lie?'

'I wasn't lying – about knowing him. Nobody really knew him. He was very gentle, very beautiful. He wanted to be a model. A professional model,' Vera insisted, making sure Tennison understood the difference. 'He used to answer the ads . . . '

Tennison glanced up sharply and glared at Otley as his sigh exploded in the quiet room. She rapped her knuckles on the desk. 'What about James Jackson, Vera?'

Vera drew deeply on her cigarette. 'He's an animal, should be caged.'

'Did Connie have someone looking after him? Say Jackson?'

'You mean like a pimp? No, the older boys don't have them, really. Not like the Toms.'

The *bing-bong* of the chimes came over the wall speaker. 'Sergeant Otley to main reception please.'

He looked to Tennison, and at her nod left the room.

'I would help you, you know that,' Vera said slowly, as if, with tremendous effort, she was forcing the words out of herself. 'I always have in the past. You're . . . you're not like the others, and I've always appreciated the way you speak to me—' She broke off to suck in a lungful of smoke. 'But – I can't help. Maybe . . .'

Tennison counted silently to five. 'Maybe what?'

'He used the advice centre, for letters, I know that.' She stubbed out the cigarette. 'Edward Parker-Jones runs it.'

Tennison's hand reached towards Vera's, but instead of touching it she picked up the ashtray and tipped it into the wastebasket. Abruptly, she stood up. 'Norma, will you show Vera the way out.' She tore the sheet from her notepad. 'And check out this. Give it to Kathy.'

Tennison went into the corridor, leaving the door open. She stood there, grinding her teeth. She was annoyed with Vera and bloody angry with herself. She found it difficult to concentrate, and her insides were jumpy. Was she coming down with flu or what? She wasn't in top form, and knew it.

Otley strode up. She faced him wearily.

'Martin Fletcher's now in reception, and the probation

officer's with him. I think you need to have words with Martin, and before Jackson.'

Tennison nodded abstractedly, trying to get her train of thought back on the tracks. Vera appeared, clicking her handbag shut, followed by Norma, who pointed along the corridor. 'Down the staircase and right ...'

Kathy hurried through the double doors from the opposite direction. 'Guv, there's a couple of messages – that reporter again, Jessica Smithy. I've told her to contact the press office but she's really pushy, insists she wants to talk to you. So does Superintendent Halliday, and there's ...'

She was interrupted by the loitering Otley, who'd gone beyond fed up to plain pissed off. 'Guv? How do you want to work it?'

Tennison waved Kathy away. 'Leave them on my desk,' she said sharply, tiredness nagging at her. Kathy looked hurt, but Tennison couldn't be bothered. 'I'll talk to Martin first,' she answered Otley.

Having set off for the stairs, Vera was back, clutching her bag, in a distressed state.

'You are going the wrong way, Vera,' Tennison said with the forbearance of a saint. 'The main exit is back down the corridor.'

'I wanted to talk to you!' Vera burst out, on the edge of panic hysteria. 'You see, if it gets out that it was me who told you ...'

'You didn't tell me anything, Vera,' Tennison said, tight-lipped.

Vera suddenly flinched. Her eyes grew large and round. Terrified, she stared past Tennison to where Jackson was being escorted towards them by Inspector Hall and a uniformed officer. Backing away, Vera whispered hoarsely, 'Don't you let this go, don't stop. Please, don't let this go, you dig deep, don't let it go . . . '

Jackson had seen her, and Vera saw that he had. She kept on backing away, and then turned and scurried off. She looked back, once, at Tennison, naked fear in her eyes, and vanished down the staircase.

Otley stood aside as Jackson was taken into the interview room. He waited by the door, watching Tennison dithering in the corridor.

'Where's Martin Fletcher?' she asked irritably.

'Room D oh six,' Otley said, and when she dithered some more, he said loudly, as if she were deaf or stupid, 'It's the one next to the coffee machine!'

Tennison took three paces and stopped. '*Where's the bloody coffee machine?*' she said through gritted teeth, but the door had closed.

Halliday came through the double doors. He went past at a clip, not breaking his stride. 'Colin Jenkins. Can you get me the full case records to date?'

'Yes, sir,' Tennison said. 'Where's the coffee machine?'

'Make sure you get everything to me ASAP. That's

firsthand, Chief Inspector,' Halliday said over his shoulder. 'I don't want anything sprung on me. That understood? I'll be in my office . . . ' He disappeared around a corner, his voice floating back, 'Downstairs on your right.'

Stumping down the stairs, Tennison made a silent screaming face.

Chapter Five

Martin Fletcher's bruised face had matured over the past twenty-four hours. The blow on his forehead had ripened into a huge purple swelling. His cut lip was an angry puffy red. The gash on his cheek had crusted over, weeping yellowish pus. A plug of bloodstained cotton was stuck up his left nostril.

Head sunk between his shoulders, he sat in the interview room, smoking, continually flicking at the filter tip with a gnawed-down thumbnail. The ashtray had overflowed onto the tabletop. Nearby, the unwinking red light of the tape recorder glowed like a tiny ruby.

A uniformed officer stood by the door. Next to Martin sat his probation officer, Margaret Speel. She was in her early thirties, neat and unfussy in a light grey suit, with an oval small-boned face and frizzy black hair cut in severe bangs just above her eyes. She leaned towards him, bowing her head to be on a level with his.

'You understand the question, Martin? Now, we're all getting tired, we've all been here a long time . . . '

Tennison looked up from the report in front of her. It was after six in the evening, it had been a hectic yet frustrating day, and under the harsh strip lighting she knew that she must have looked like a worn-out old hag. She certainly felt like one. She tried again.

'Martin, last night you talked to Sergeant Otley and Inspector Hall, and you told them that the man who attacked you—'

'No! That was words put in me mouth.' Martin sniffed loudly. 'I never told nobody nuffink – and that is the Gawd's truth.'

Tennison ploughed on. 'You also said that the man's name was Jackson and that he specifically asked you if you knew where Colin Jenkins was—'

Again Martin jumped in. 'No – I never said that – never.' He took a swift drag, his fingers trembling, showering ash everywhere. 'What happened was . . . you know that escalator top of King's Cross Station? I was comin' down, me coat got caught like, and I fell forward.' He ducked down to demonstrate. 'I hit me head on the stairs, and then, when I got up, I fell over again and hit me nose. Nobody hit me.' He stared at her, one eye swollen and bloodshot.

'So you lied to the police officers who questioned you?' Tennison said quietly.

'Yeah, I suppose so.' He grew bolder. 'Yeah, I lied 'cos . . . 'cos I'm underage – I mean, they really scared me like, and . . .'

'Martin, did you know Colin?'

He glanced sideways at Margaret Speel and then took another deep swift drag, a single plume of smoke issuing through one nostril.

'Yeah, not like – well, red-haired bloke, wasn't he? Quentin House, he was there wiv me, now he's burnt like a crisp!' Due to his cut lip his grin was lopsided, showing the black gap of two missing front teeth. 'That's a joke goin' round – Quentin Crisp, famous poofter . . .'

'Have you ever had sex with a man?'

'Me? Nah!'

'What about a blow job? Ever been paid for doing that?'

Martin shrugged. 'Few times, when I'm broke like, but I'm not into that. I got other means of employment.' He was sounding cocky now, starting to brag.

'Such as?'

'Breakin' and enterin', nickin' cars, radios. Beggin' – do a bit of that.' He smirked. 'Sell my life story to the newspapers.'

Tennison looked at Margaret Speel, whose expression remained exactly the same: in fact hardly any expression at all, apart from a slight cynical twist of the mouth, that must be part of the job description, Tennison thought.

Martin was laughing. 'I can nick a motor, go for a joyride, an' you lot can't do nuffink!'

Tennison snapped her notebook shut.

'You listen to me, Martin. You think you can play games with us, lie to us, and it's all a joke. Well, it isn't. Colin Jenkins has no one to claim his body, no one to bury him.' Tennison stood up. Martin wouldn't look at her. 'Nobody cares about Colin Jenkins but us.'

Absolutely seething, Tennison went up the stairs and strode along the corridor, muttering to herself, 'I have just about had enough of this bloody place – kids can run riot over us without—'

Otley was leaning against the wall outside interview room D.03 having a smoke. He eased himself into his usual round-shouldered slouch as Tennison stormed up.

'—Is Jackson in here?' she snapped, jerking her thumb.

'He denies knowing Martin Fletcher,' Otley said.

'And Martin Fletcher denied his entire statement! Can we hold Jackson on attempting to pick up that boy at the station?' Otley shook his head. 'So we've got nothing on him ...! No prints from Vera's flat?' Otley shook his head. 'Nothing off the possible weapon?'

'Nope, nothin',' Otley said, still shaking his head.

For just an instant Tennison seemed to deflate before

his eyes. Then she rallied, straightened up, took a deep breath, brushed a hand through her hair, and jabbed her finger at the door. Otley pushed it open.

She had expected Jackson to be a nasty piece of work and she wasn't disappointed. What she hadn't expected was his overweening confidence bordering on insolence. He was sprawled back in the chair as if he owned the place, long legs splayed out, leather jacket undone, blowing smoke rings into the thick blue haze that filled the room. Cigarette stubs floated in the cups of cold coffee on the table. He couldn't be bothered to look up as she entered, heavy-lidded eyes in the long, pockmarked face glazed with boredom, scruffy mop of hair sticking up in spikes. He leaned back, blowing another lazy smoke ring.

'Open the window,' Tennison rapped out to Hall. 'Shut the door,' she told Otley. Jackson sniggered. Bossy bitch.

She whipped around on him. 'And you, take that smile off your face! Because I am going to book you and send you away, Jackson, for a very long time.'

Jackson looked at Hall as if to say, *Where the fuck did you dig this twat up from?* He looked at Tennison and then dropped his eyes to the Marlboro packet he was turning slowly over and over. He said in a calm, controlled voice, 'What am I supposed to have done?'

'One – you were caught approaching a juvenile. Two – attempted murder of another juvenile, Martin Fletcher, and three – that you did on the night of the seventeenth murder Colin Jenkins.'

Jackson stubbed out his cigarette and rose to his feet wearing a pained, crooked smile.

'SIT DOWN!!'

Sighing, he dropped into his seat. Still amused, he watched the manic Tennison dragging out the vacant chair with a clatter, picking up the laden ashtray and banging it into the wastebasket. She threw it down on the table, turning to Hall. 'You've read him his rights?' Then to Otley, 'Sergeant, has he given you his contact number for his brief yet?'

She sat down opposite him, scanning his statement sheet, cheeks slightly flushed. 'What's your address?'

'Flat four, Addison Lane Estate, my mother's place . . .'

'And your full name is James Paul Jackson, yes?'

'Yes, that's my name.' He turned the packet over slowly, as if it were a tricky, delicate operation.

Tennison went down the sheet. 'Unemployed . . . arrested . . .' Hardly audible, she read on. 'No charges, no charges, no charges . . . you are very well known to the Vice Squad, aren't you?' She closed the report. 'You've been very lucky until now,' she said, smiling, the boss congratulating a promising recruit before dumping on him from a great height. 'Because obviously we couldn't formally charge you until we had interviewed Martin Fletcher.'

The smile vanished. Hard-eyed now, she let the silence hang.

Jackson looked at Hall, then at Tennison. He opened the packet and eased out a cigarette. Slow and deliberate, with a steady hand, he picked up his lighter. The phone rang. Hall reached for it and had a whispered conversation.

'I never touched Colin Jenkins,' Jackson said, sucking the smoke deep. 'I wasn't even there. I wasn't at Vernon Reynolds's flat full stop.' He sighed, shaking his head, still very full of himself. 'End of questions.'

'But you admit that you attacked Martin Fletcher on the night of the seventeenth—'

'I was at the advice centre,' Jackson stated calmly, flicking ash. 'Ask Mr Parker-Jones, he saw me there. There was also a kid called Alan Thorpe, and I got three or four more witnesses to prove I was there.' Again the heavy sigh, glancing around the room. 'This is ridiculous, waste of time.'

'Why did you want to find Colin?'

'I never found him. I admit though, I was looking for him. Martin must have told you that. I was looking for Connie, but – I – never – found – him.'

'Advice centre,' Tennison said, making a note. 'Why were you looking for Colin Jenkins?'

Jackson closed his eyes momentarily and opened them the barest slit, staring straight at her. 'He owed me some money.'

'How much?'

'Couple of hundred.'

'Couple of hundred?' Tennison said, eyebrows raised. 'But you are unemployed! That's a lot of money.'

'Yes, that's why I wanted it back.' Jackson rubbed his unshaven chin and leaned forward. 'Look, I'll be honest with you.' He cleared his throat, big confession coming up. 'Sometimes I ... do the odd trick, I mean work is really hard to come by, you know? And my mum, she gets behind with the rent ... so, I blow a few blokes, an' I don't like it when some kid nicks my dough.'

Tennison laced her fingers together and stayed silent. She wasn't going to waste an ounce of breath on this kind of bull. She heard another of Otley's long-suffering sighs. Hall leaned over and murmured that the Super wanted to see her in his office.

'I'm not going to lie about Martin,' Jackson said, waving his cigarette about carelessly. 'I guess I just lost my temper. You tellin' me he's gonna press charges? Martin? No way.' He was staring at her, tugging his earlobe, as if he was trying to figure something out. 'Like you said, it was a lot of money ... '

Tennison said nothing. He sounded brash and cocksure, right enough, but she sensed that underneath the swaggering bravado he was getting rattled. Good. Get him rattled some more.

'I'm not sayin' anything until I got a brief. Because

you . . . ' Finger jabbing, fleshy lips twisting. 'You're not listening to what I'm sayin'.'

Very businesslike, Tennison collected her things together and stood up. She said to Inspector Hall, 'I think Mr Jackson should be taken to the cells until we have, as he has requested, contacted his brief, and we have verified his alibi for the night in question.'

'Right, let's go through your witnesses,' Otley said. 'Names, Jackson.'

Tennison went out. Hall looked to Otley, patting his tie. She was sailing bloody close to the wind. She'd nearly charged him with murder without a shred of real evidence.

Jackson was making a brutal job of stubbing his cigarette in the ashtray. He glared up at Otley. 'What's her name?'

'One dead rent boy, Chief Inspector, is not going to bring the entire department to a standstill, is that understood?'

Halliday stood with his hands stuffed in his pockets, looking out onto a darkening Broadwick Street. It was the vacant hour, lost in no-man's-land between the exodus of the office workers and the first stirrings of Soho nightlife.

Tennison was taken aback. 'I wasn't aware of any standstill—'

'Just let me finish, please.' Halliday swung around, an abrupt movement that betrayed his edginess. Usually neat to the point of fastidiousness, his tie was slightly askew and his short fair hair was ruffled as though he'd been combing his fingers through it. He placed his pale, freckled hands on the back of his swivel chair. 'As Colin Jenkins's death is now a homicide, I suggest we hand it over—'

'But we have ...'

'—to the correct department.'

'But we have a strong suspect in custody,' Tennison protested. 'And far from any standstill, we are making progress. The reason I am interested in Jackson is because of the direct link to Operation Contract.'

The Superintendent released a small sigh. 'Go on.'

'Jackson's well known to Vice, and has in actual fact been questioned on numerous occasions. If he did murder Colin Jenkins, I think it will act as a strong lever for more information.' She hesitated, knuckles tapping her palm. 'There's also an advice centre that keeps cropping up, run by a man called Edward Parker-Jones.'

'Operation Contract at no time initiated an investigation into Edward Parker-Jones ...'

'I wasn't contemplating any investigation into Mr Parker-Jones. But he is my suspect's alibi, and the longer we have Jackson locked up, the easier it'll be to question the kids.' Tennison was furious with herself that she sounded to be pleading, and didn't know why the hell she should have to. 'Look, you did say that my priority was Operation Contract ...'

'All right,' Halliday conceded. He rubbed his forehead and swung the chair around to sit in it. 'Just keep me informed if there are any new developments.'

Tennison nodded and left the office. Halliday sat down, drumming his fingers. He stared at the closed door for a moment, picked up the phone and started to dial.

As Tennison closed the door to Halliday's office, Kathy came up.

'Guv, have you got a second? You asked me to check back if Colin Jenkins had been brought in. Well, he was – but he used the name Bruce Jenkins, charged with soliciting.'

'So who did the interview?'

'Sergeant Otley. But it was almost a year ago, and he was underage, so a probation officer took over from our department. I've traced her,' Kathy said, 'but she's not much help. She's sending the report in.'

'You remember anything about him?' Tennison asked.

Kathy shook her head glumly. 'No, sorry . . .'

She went off, leaving Tennison gazing dully at the dark green wall opposite. She felt totally drained. Her brain had seized up, and she felt unable to connect one coherent thought to another. She started to drag herself back to her office next door when she heard Halliday talking on the phone, his voice faint but distinct.

'. . . how can I tell her to back off something if it has

a direct link to the bloody job she was brought in to do?'

Tennison looked up and down the corridor and leaned in.

'If she isn't suspicious now, she would be if I pulled her off it,' Halliday said, sounding exasperated. After a pause he went on, 'She knows nothing, because I'm sure of it. We'll just make damned sure it stays that way.'

The receiver went down and rapid footsteps thudded on the carpet. Tennison made it to her door just as Halliday's door opened. She nipped in and gently pushed the door to with her fingertips, seeing him pass by through the crack. She clicked the door shut.

Otley had been on the bevvy the night before. His gaunt face was greyer and even more deeply lined than usual, eyes like piss-holes in snow. Nonetheless he was enjoying himself. He kept sneaking wicked little grins at Hall, whose return smile was rather lukewarm.

It was the 9.30 a.m. briefing in the Squad Room, and the entire team – with the exception of DCI Tennison and WPC Kathy Trent – was assembled, paying close attention to Commander Chiswick. Halliday was there, the Colin Jenkins autopsy report and forensic lab reports on the desk in front of him. There was also a new face. Otley recognized him as Detective Inspector Brian Dalton – dark, tanned, with sleepy brown eyes that had the women turning somersaults, Otley reckoned. A real handsome bastard.

So Otley's delight was twofold. Chiswick was holding court while Tennison was conspicuous by her absence (maybe she hadn't even been *told*!) and new people were being drafted in, probably without her knowledge. At any rate, something was going down, Otley gloated, and the old cow would hit the freaking roof when she found out.

'The deceased, Colin Jenkins, was, according to the Path reports, unconscious when the fire took hold.' Chiswick had a pedantic, monotone delivery, better suited to reading the weather forecast. 'This is verified by the low amount of smoke inhalation, indicating very shallow breathing. But his death was due to carbon monoxide poisoning, therefore we are treating the case as murder ...'

Otley folded his arms, hugging himself, as Tennison came in, followed by Kathy. Halliday nodded a greeting to Tennison, who went to stand beside him.

'... as it is clear from the fire reports that the fire was not accidental, but an act of arson. We all have a backlog of cases,' the Commander said, looking towards Tennison. He didn't nod or smile, he just looked. He faced the front.

'... and my own feelings concerning the murder and its obvious complexities are that we keep it inhouse. So I'd like this case brought to a conclusion as fast as possible, and have requested backup to assist Detective Chief

Inspector Tennison's inquiry from CID AMIT area seven-stroke-eight.'

AMIT 7/8 was the Area Major Incident Team, based at New Scotland Yard, which covered the Soho, Piccadilly Circus, and Leicester Square beat.

'Thank you,' Chiswick said, and a buzz of chatter started up.

Otley nudged DI Hall. They both watched, Otley with undisguised glee, as Tennison stalked out, face like a storm cloud.

She was halfway along the corridor when Chiswick and Halliday appeared behind her, following on at an even pace. When she was a reasonable distance from the Squad Room, Tennison halted and turned, facing squarely up to Halliday.

'I do not, at this stage, need any assistance. I already have a strong suspect.'

'James Jackson,' Halliday muttered to Chiswick, 'earmarked in Operation Contract.'

'I would also appreciate it,' Tennison said crisply, getting it off her chest, 'if I were to be informed before the squad of any further decisions connected to the Colin Jenkins investigation.'

DI Dalton ambled up, tall, dark and handsome, with an engaging grin. Otley's head poked through the Squad Room doors, wearing a devilish smirk, relishing every moment.

'Ah, I'm sorry, Jane, I didn't have time this morning to introduce you.' Halliday extended his hand. 'This is one of your new team, DI Brian Dalton. Brian, this is Chief Inspector Jane Tennison.'

'Good morning,' Tennison said without so much as a glance at him, and went into her office.

She busied herself for an hour with a mound of paperwork. The mind-numbing chore brought her anger down from white heat to a dull smouldering red. Why in heaven's name she hadn't developed an ulcer was one of the unsolved mysteries of the age. Or had a nervous breakdown. But she was saving that for her three-week holiday.

Norma kept her supplied with coffee, and at eleven o'clock DI Hall came to her office with the tape sent over from the ambulance emergency service. All such calls were taped and kept for a period of months. They listened to it several times, straining to hear through the whining distortion and crackling electronics; also there was music and pinging noises in the background, which didn't help.

'*I want to report an accident. It's flat five. I need an ambulance. I want to report an accident. It's flat five. I need an ambulance ...*'

'Call logged at nine-fifteen p.m.,' Hall said.

Tennison rewound the tape. 'Recognize the voice? It's not Vernon, is it?'

Hall shrugged. It could have been King Kong.

As they were replaying it, Brian Dalton knocked and came in, and leaned against the wall, supported by an outstretched arm, one ankle crossed over the other, studying his fingernails.

'Didn't leave his name?' he said, when it was finished.

'Of course!' Hall said, beaming brightly. 'We're just replaying this because we like the sound of his voice!'

Tennison started the tape again. She turned it off when Otley put his head around the door. 'Jackson is now with his brief, Guv!' He pushed the door open, holding his wrist up, pointing at his watch.

Tennison went into the corridor, nodding at Otley to come with her. Dalton followed. Tennison gave a sweet smile. 'Just stay put a minute,' she said, and firmly pulled the door shut on him.

She moved a small distance along the corridor, then leaned against the wall, head bowed, inspecting the worn carpet. Hated that colour, even when it was new. Sort of snot-green.

'Bit overqualified, isn't he?' Otley said, jerking his head.

Tennison's head came up fast. 'You interviewed Colin, alias Bruce, Jenkins. What happened, Bill? Did it slip your mind?' He blinked a couple of times, and Tennison really tore into him. 'Here am I trying to get a handle on the boy, and you, you – interviewed him!'

Otley looked at the ceiling. A cord of muscle twitched in his hollow cheek. Here we go again. Ball-Breakers Inc.

He said, 'I had a two-minute conversation with him, just after I first came here. I didn't remember it until Kath told me ...'

'And? Is that it? Was he intelligent? Was he dumb? Was he cheeky? Where was he picked up? Was he caught in the act? What was he doing? I presume you did question him. He was soliciting, wasn't he?'

It was Otley's turn to inspect the carpet. 'He was just ... very young, quiet.' Small shrug. 'Very quiet.'

'Take Dalton with you. I want Martin Fletcher brought back in.' Tennison's face was stony. 'I presume you can remember who he is.'

She walked off and Otley trudged back to get Dalton and do the bitch's bidding.

With his brief present – Mr Arthur, a short squat little man with a sweaty bald head, wearing a threadbare suit and scuffed brown suede shoes – Jackson seemed more inclined to talk. The cockiness was still there, the indolent sprawling posture, the sneering fleshy lips, the chain-smoking. You can't touch me, I'm fireproof: he might have carried it around with him as a neon advertising sign.

Tennison and Hall listened, not interrupting, getting as much down on tape as was possible in the time. Time was the problem.

'... and there was another kid, Kenny Lloyd, he was there. And – oh yeah, Driscoll. Dunno his first name.

Disco Driscoll, and Alan Thorpe, Billy Matthews, they was with me, from ... ' He sucked on the Marlboro, held the smoke in, let it explode through his nostrils. ' 'Bout half eight onward, at the advice centre.' He wagged his head, lips pursed. 'Played some pool, watched TV ... I told you this, I told you about even Mr Parker-Jones being there.'

'Well, we will check out these witnesses, but until then you will remain in custody,' Tennison said officiously. A fair and honest copper playing it by the book.

Mr Arthur was agitated. His false teeth weren't a perfect fit, and his speech was accompanied by constant clicking and a spray on the sibilant consonants. 'But my client has clearly stated to you that on the evening in question he has not one, but *five* witnesses, and you were given their names last night!'

Tennison said primly, 'Mr Arthur, until we are satisfied that these witnesses can verify that Mr Jackson was where he said he was ... '

She looked up at Otley, who had just entered the room and was beckoning to her. She went over to him while Mr Arthur's querulous clicking voice kept on complaining.

'What about these other charges? I mean, you have held my client for nearly twenty-four hours. If there are other charges to be levelled at my client, then we have a right to know exactly what they are.'

Otley said quietly in Tennison's ear, 'Nobody can trace Martin Fletcher. He was in the Bullring last night, Waterloo underpass this morning.'

'The probation officer, Margaret Speel, doesn't she know where he is?' Otley shook his head. Tennison ground her teeth. This bloody investigation was falling apart at the seams. She poked her finger into Otley's chest. 'Then you'd better get out and find him! Find every one of Jackson's alibis and wheel them in. All of them!'

She turned back to Jackson, who was lighting a cigarette from the stub of the last one. Cocky little prick. 'Take him back to the cells,' she said to Hall.

Jackson grinned at her. He said to his brief, 'How long can they hold me here?'

'What time did you bring my client in?' Mr Arthur asked Hall, almost bouncing up and down in the chair. 'The exact time, Inspector . . . ?'

Tennison glanced back from the door, then made a swift silent exit.

She went directly to the Squad Room. One of the team was writing up the names of Jackson's alibi witnesses in black felt-tip on the board: ALAN THORPE. BILLY MATTHEWS. ?? DRISCOLL. KENNY LLOYD.

Kathy was showing Norma some holiday snaps. 'Not got any work on, girls?' Tennison asked.

Kathy hesitated, then passed one over for Tennison to see. 'They're my kids.' She exchanged a quick guarded glance with Norma; neither of them had worked under a female DCI before – hardly surprising when they were rarer than duck's teeth – and they weren't sure how to take Tennison.

'I was just saying that after each one I've got to start all over again.'

'What do you mean?'

'Maternity leave,' Kathy said. 'Back I come and everyone's changed over. I'm shuttled here and there.'

'Your decision though, isn't it?' Tennison said, flicking through the snaps. Two blond-haired toddlers paddling in the sea, the younger one only just past the baby stage.

Kathy bridled. 'No way – I don't know where I'm going to be sent.'

'No, I meant it's your decision to have kids. Norma, do you have any?'

Norma shook her head. 'No, but I'm not married either.'

Tennison handed back the photographs. 'That probation officer for Colin Jenkins, she send over anything?'

Kathy went across to her desk. Norma pointed behind her to the board, a typed list of Colin Jenkins's clothing and possessions.

'He had to have somebody shellin' out. His gear, the Armani jacket, designer jeans. Then there's the money – five hundred quid.'

'Traced to a children's home,' Kathy said, coming back with a wallet-type cardboard folder. 'They've sent a few photographs, just small black-and-white jobs.' She laid them out and glanced through the résumé she'd compiled. 'No family. Taken into care aged three. His mother OD'd a year later, and he was moved from one – two – three homes, a foster home, and then back again.' She held up the sheet. 'That's about it.'

Tennison looked at the smudgy photographs, which showed Connie standing in various groups, children's homes and schools, aged from six to roughly thirteen. A good-looking kid, but terribly solemn in all of them. Small wonder, Tennison thought. What a miserable existence . . .

She glanced around as the Squad Room doors swung open, and got a shock. She stared uncomprehendingly at Haskons and Lillie, standing there large as life: two detectives who'd served under her at Southampton Row.

Tennison stood up. 'What are you doing here?'

Haskons tossed his raincoat down and gave an elaborate shrug. 'You tell us. Thorndike said you needed some backup – so, well, he sent you the cream.'

DC Lillie, the taller, thinner of the two, more easy-going and laid-back than DS Haskons, merely shook his head.

Tennison came around the desk. She wasn't annoyed, she was totally pissed off. This was getting beyond a fucking joke. She jerked her head for them to follow. 'You'd better come into my office.'

They went out. As the doors swung shut, Kathy gave Norma a dig with her elbow. 'Catch the little snide line about it being my decision? Who does she think she is!'

Tennison opened the door to her office and ushered the pair inside ahead of her. 'I'll be with you in a minute.'

She closed the door, not quite slamming it, though she felt like doing so, and stood glowering towards Halliday's office.

'Inspector Tennison?'

She turned, feeling like the place was suddenly teeming with strange new faces. He trotted towards her, slightly out of breath, looking a bit flustered, holding a scrap of paper. 'I'm from Rossington station. DI Ray Hebdon. I was told by Superintendent Halliday to' – he checked the paper – 'report to you.'

Tennison made a sweeping gesture, indicating her office. 'Please, be my guest.' Hebdon went in.

Tennison rapped on Halliday's door. There was a brief pause before he answered, during which she ran both hands through her hair, her simmering temper coming nicely to the boil. She went in, marched up to his desk, and came straight out with it.

'First the male model Dalton. Now it's DS Haskons,

DC Lillie, and a pink-faced nervous type from Rossington station. Could I have an explanation?'

Halliday was partly bent over, peeling a hard-boiled egg and dropping the shell in the wastebasket. A plastic lunch box contained three more hard-boiled eggs. He leaned back in his chair, holding up the peeled egg. 'They sit like lead in the gut.'

'Don't I have a say in the matter? Any choice?'

'Chief Inspector, you have three extra men. Use them.'

'Correction, I have four! Dalton.'

'I know how many, Chief Inspector,' Halliday said testily. 'You wanted to retain the murder inquiry, didn't you?' He bit the top off the egg.

Tennison went to the door. She cast him a dark look under her brows. 'Any more due? Or is this it? They have a few spare dog handlers at Hammersmith!'

Halliday laughed, mouth full of egg. He tapped another on the desk and peeled it, tossing the shell fragments into the wastebasket.

Tennison left the office, hoping he damn well choked on it.

Chapter Six

Otley had nothing personal against Dalton – he hardly knew the bloke – but there was something about the young detective inspector (not a day over thirty-five, Otley judged) that irritated him. Not his good looks: Otley had no personal vanity whatsoever. It was more Dalton's impulsiveness. He did everything at the gallop, instead of taking his time and sizing up a situation. And he had no streetwise sense, not a scrap. That's what got to Otley, the fact that the bloke was deskbound for most of his working life, far removed from the seedy pubs and afternoon drinking clubs that were part of Otley's daily round.

That was it. Otley had placed him. An eager-beaver Boy Scout dressed up as a police inspector.

They parked the car and set off on a tour of the Bullring and the Waterloo underpass. This area, south of the river, between the Royal Festival Hall and the National Theatre, was notorious for the hundreds if not thousands of people who inhabited its concrete walkways, its brick viaducts near Waterloo Station, dossing down in cardboard boxes, huddling near the heating vents, constructing little shelters out of bits of timber and plastic sheeting. Dossers, winos, junkies, bag ladies, the physically sick and the mentally ill, kids on the run from home and institutionalized care, and on the game: the hopeless and dispossessed and forgotten, the new London poor of 1993.

It wasn't Otley's patch, though he knew the area and its floating population of misfits well. Trouble was, a lot of them knew him, so it was difficult to wander about incognito. And in broad daylight, two o'clock in the afternoon, there weren't any shadows to skulk around in, creep up on them unawares.

They walked through the Bullring, a huge concrete bowel wrapped around by a network of roads heading north across Waterloo Bridge and south to the Elephant and Castle. The noise was horrendous, the continuous streams of traffic shattering past overhead. Dalton spied a group of kids in a concrete cubbyhole behind one of the massive arching supports. They were crouched in a circle on the filthy, rubbish-covered ground, empty spray cans, squeezed-out tubes of glue, and broken syringes and needles everywhere.

'We're looking for a kid nicknamed Disco Driscoll—'
Dalton made a grab as they scattered, and collared one.
'Hey – I'm talking to you!' The boy was squirming.
Dalton wrenched the aerosol can from his grimy hand.
'What's this?'

'Makin' a model aeroplane, mate!'

Dalton tried to swipe him as he ran off, and missed.
Otley looked away, hiding a grin.

The squalid brick viaducts of the Waterloo underpass
housed a community of down-and-outs, living in
patched-up shelters tacked to the walls. Groups of them
sat around campfires on the pavements, passing the bottle,
and mingled with the smoke was the sharp reek of meths
and cleaning fluid. It was gloomier here, under the arches,
and the two detectives were able to approach without
being observed. Otley touched Dalton's arm, making him
slow down, and said in a low voice, 'Kid with the lager
cans, that's Kenny Lloyd. What I suggest we do . . . '

He was about to suggest they split up and circle in, one
head on and one behind, blocking the kids' retreat, but
he never got the chance. Dalton was off and away. He ran
fast, charging along the greasy pavement, but the group
Kenny was in, their instinct for self-preservation honed on
the streets, saw him coming and were off in a flash, just
dark blurs disappearing into the gloom.

Otley sighed and shook his head. Where had they dug
up this dickhead from?

Ten minutes later they were sitting in the outdoor cafeteria of the National Film Theatre, overlooking the river.
There was a cool breeze and some ragged cloud overhead,
but Otley was enjoying a cup of coffee and a sticky iced
bun in the fitful sunshine. He broke off a piece and tossed
it to a seagull. At once more seagulls started to swoop
down.

Dalton didn't approve. 'You shouldn't encourage
them – shit all over you.' Otley tossed another chunk.
Dalton turned away in disgust. There was a poster in the
Film Theatre window for Andrzej Wajda's *Man of Iron*.
'Good movie that, have you seen it?' Dalton asked.

Otley's eyes were elsewhere. He was watching three
ragged kids picking up leftover scraps from the tables. One
boy in particular, hustling cigarettes from the patrons,
looked familiar. Otley watched him for several minutes, a
skinny, pathetic-looking specimen in a torn T-shirt, filthy
jeans, and cheap trainers, bare ankles caked with dirt. His
thin, ravaged face was marked and bruised, his mouth
erupting in open cold sores.

'Just going for a leak, okay?'

Dalton paid no attention as Otley rose and casually
threaded his way through the tables. He came up by the
boy's shoulder as he was rummaging inside a trash bin and
said softly, 'Hello, son.'

The boy looked up, pale puffy eyelids and a pair of dark
purple bags. 'It's twenty quid, down the toilets.'

Otley placed his hand on the boy's bony shoulder. 'You just blew more than you bargained for – I'm a police officer.'

'Okay, so I'll make it ten.'

'Hey! Watch it!' Otley was smiling. 'I just want to ask you a few questions . . .'

Warily, the boy took a step backward. His eyes flicked past Otley to where Dalton was heading towards them through the tables.

'It's about that fire,' Otley said, taking out a fiver. 'Heard about it? You know Colin Jenkins? Connie?'

Dalton came up and the boy took off. He barged through the tables, turning chairs over behind him, and leapt the wooden barrier surrounding the eating area, skinny elbows pumping as he hared off along the concrete embankment. Dalton was after him like a shot. Kicking the chairs aside and leaping the barrier, his long legs gained on the boy with every stride.

Otley took his time, going out through the swingbar gate and following after them at his own pace. He saw Dalton reach out and grab the boy by the nape of the neck, they both skidded and went down, the boy punching and kicking wildly. Dalton gripped him by the hair, his other hand under the boy's chin, and the boy sank his teeth into Dalton's hand. Dalton cursed and belted him hard, hauled him to his feet and belted him again.

'That's enough,' Otley said, walking up. 'Back off him . . .'

Dalton gave him another crack before stepping back, sucking his hand. 'Little bastard bit me!'

The boy wiped his bloody nose on his arm, eyes rolling in his pinched face, frightened to death. 'I dunno nuffink, I swear to God, I dunno anyfink . . .'

Joe Public strolling by and taking an interest in all of this made Otley jumpy. He moved close to the boy, keeping his voice low.

'I haven't asked you anything yet. Let's start with your name.'

'Billy,' the boy said, his chin quivering. 'Billy Matthews.'

The three new members of the squad were in Tennison's office, jackets draped over the backs of their chairs, bringing themselves up to speed on the investigation. Neither Haskons nor Lillie was too enthusiastic about the case; why they were here at all was something of a mystery.

'I dunno why we're going to all this bleedin' trouble – nasty little queen,' Lillie complained. 'We got an address for him, for Colin?'

'He's not got a permanent one,' Haskons replied.

'He must have lived somewhere! What about a recent photograph?'

'These are from a children's home,' Ray Hebdon said,

spreading them out. 'Few years old, black and white.' He glanced down the report. 'Not much else.'

Haskons picked up a photograph of Connie, aged about nine, in school uniform, unsmiling. He stared at it and blew out a disgruntled sigh, his broad face with its fleshy nose and heavy jaw set in a lugubrious scowl. 'Was he claiming the dole? Any benefits?'

'No, nothing from the DSS,' Lillie said.

Haskons folded his arms and stared through the window at the brick wall. The phone rang and Hebdon answered it. 'No, she's not. Can I take a message?' He found a pencil and a memo pad. 'Jessica Smithy. What? Yes, I'll tell her.'

Haskons yawned. 'Any vice charges? I mean, he was on the game, wasn't he?'

'Too young to bring charges,' Lillie said. 'In 1988 he was picked up, shipped back.' He studied the school photograph. 'I don't understand, you know . . . what makes a poofter want to screw this scrawny, sickly-lookin' kid?'

'Make our job a damned sight easier if we had a recent photo,' Haskons said with a long-suffering tone.

Lillie tossed over the morgue photograph of Connie's head, a knob of blackened bone, the face burnt off. 'Here you go!' he said, laughing.

Tennison and Hall came down the stairs into the advice centre. The only sign of life was the black kid with the hearing aid, Ron, mopping the floor near the contacts board. Tennison had a quick gander around, peering into the empty TV lounge. Hall wandered over to the corkboard crisscrossed with tape, coloured cards with job notices stuck in it.

'It's usually quiet around now,' Hall said as Tennison joined him. 'Kids don't drift in until early evening.'

Tennison turned to Ron, mechanically mopping. 'Is Mr Parker-Jones here?' At his nod, she said, 'Could you get him for me?'

Ron knocked on the office door, opened it an inch or two and looked inside. Tennison reached past him, and with the flat of her hand pushed the door open. 'Is he in there?'

The desk lamp was on but the office was empty. Everything was neat and tidy, books on the shelves carefully arranged, wire trays on the desk containing invoices and letters.

'Could you see if he's anywhere in the building? I'll wait in here for him.' She showed Ron her ID 'It's important.'

Ron went off, and Tennison gave a nod to Hall, who was at the contacts board, searching through them, jotting down names and phone numbers. He returned her nod and went back to the board, keeping one eye on the stairs as a couple of kids came down.

Tennison went in and pushed the door partway closed.

She went over to the two filing cabinets and tried one of the drawers. Locked. She looked around. On the wall above a thriving rubber plant was a row of impressive framed certificates, elaborately scrolled text and fancy borders. Mallory Advice Center, Maryland. Chicago University Child Therapy Unit. New York Speech and Sign Language Institute. A dozen or so letters trailed after the name 'Edward Parker-Jones'.

She moved around the desk. There was a stack of stamped and sealed envelopes. She flicked through them, checking the addresses. She leafed through the loose memos and the notepad, glanced at the yellow stickers on the blotter. She bent to try the desk drawers when the door was pushed open and Hall made a quick gesture.

Tennison was standing by the bookshelves when Parker-Jones breezed in. His presence immediately filled the small office. It wouldn't have surprised her to learn he was an honorary Southern colonel as well, judging by the framed credentials.

'Can I help you?' He didn't smile but his deep modulated voice was pleasant enough.

'I am Detective Chief Inspector Jane Tennison,' she said, holding up her ID. 'You must be . . . '

'Edward Parker-Jones. Could I see it?' He pointed to her ID. 'Thank you,' he said, handing it back. 'Well? How can I help you, Chief Inspector Tennison?'

He moved around the desk, rubbing his hands, which

gave Tennison the opportunity to exchange a look with Hall. He went out and closed the door, leaving Tennison alone with Parker-Jones, and giving him the chance to sniff around.

Tennison started with a smile. 'I've come about the investigation into Colin Jenkins's death. Could you tell me where you were on the night of the seventeenth of this month?'

'I was here. I was here from six-thirty until at least twelve.'

Tennison's eyes widened a fraction. Neat answer, very pat. 'Do you have any witnesses who can—'

'Exactly how many do you require?' asked Parker-Jones, completely at ease, relaxed and confident. 'I can make out a list.'

'I am interested in the hour between eight-thirty and nine-thirty,' Tennison said.

After a small sigh, Parker-Jones reeled them off. 'Alan Thorpe, Donald Driscoll, Kenny Lloyd, one or two other lads ...'

An identical list, the same familiar names.

'Do you know a James Jackson?'

'Yes.' Parker-Jones nodded. 'Strangely enough, he was here that evening.'

'You have a very good memory,' Tennison complimented him, turning on the charm.

Edward Parker-Jones didn't succumb that easily. 'Not

really. But it is my job to help the social services by keeping some kind of record of the youngsters who come and
go here.' He suddenly remembered, or gave a convincing
performance of doing so. 'Ah – oh, yes ... Billy
Matthews.' He took a desk diary from the drawer and
turned to the relevant date. 'Billy Matthews. He was here
also.'

Tennison watched as he wrote out the list of names,
using a gold-nibbed fountain pen. He had strong hands,
dark hair sprouting from his crisp shirt cuffs to his knuckles, and wore a chunky gold ring with an amber stone on
the little finger of his left hand. He was rather good-looking in a louche way, with dark deep-set eyes, his black hair
swept back over his ears.

Parker-Jones passed the list to her. He sat down; there
was another chair, but Tennison preferred to stay on her
feet.

' . . . yes, Billy Matthews, I arranged for him to see a
doctor. He was found in the toilets here.' Parker-Jones
tightened his lips, shaking his head. 'He's a tragic case.
He's only fourteen, full-blown AIDS. One of the reasons
I remember that evening specifically is that Jackson was in
a particularly aggressive mood. He'd been trying to find
a boy earlier in the day. Martin Fletcher.'

'Why was he looking for him?'

'I really don't know,' he said with a slight frown, and
checked the diary again. 'Martin wasn't here on the

seventeenth but he turned up the following day. In fact . . . a Sergeant Otley spoke to him recently.'

'You said Jackson had been here in the day, so what time did he return in the evening?'

Parker-Jones seemed rather amused. 'Is Jackson a suspect?' he asked, one eyebrow raised. 'Is that what this is all about?' He found her silence just as amusing. 'It was an accidental death, surely? That building's a fire trap, all those old blocks are.'

'I'm sorry, but could you . . .' Tennison cleared her throat. 'Could you please answer the question? What time did James Jackson return here?'

'Around half eight, or thereabouts. He stayed for about two hours.'

'Two hours!' Tennison mulled this over. She slipped her shoulder bag on. 'Thank you very much, Mr Parker-Jones. You know Reynolds's flat?' she asked, going to the door. She turned. 'Just that you mentioned it was a fire hazard, so you must have been there . . . ?'

Rising to his six feet two Parker-Jones said without a flicker of hesitation, 'Of course, Vera is well known by everybody around here. She – he leaves the front door key for friends to pop in. I have always had a good relationship with the Vice Squad,' he said evenly. 'You must be new – correct?'

Tennison smiled thinly. 'Yes, and I really appreciate your help.'

'Most of the kids that come here are wretched – abused, unloved, and friendless. But they do at least come here, and we can maintain contact.' He moved around the desk towards her. 'These children are prey for the perverted. If my centre was to be closed down it would be very sad . . . '

'I am sure you are doing a very good and worthwhile job, Mr Parker-Jones. But I am also trying to do mine.' They faced each other in silence for a moment, and then Tennison said, 'I noticed you have an impressive list of credentials.'

'Thank you.' He was standing close to her. She could smell his aftershave. Violets. She recognized it as Fahrenheit by Christian Dior.

'Just one more thing,' Tennison said. 'Do you keep a record of photographs?'

'Of the boys that come here?' At her nod, he said, 'Good heavens no, be far too expensive.'

'Not even casual snapshots of, say, a Christmas party? Colin, or Connie as he was called, was a frequent visitor here, wasn't he?'

'Yes, he was, but not recently. In fact I haven't seen him for about three months.'

An answer to everything. What with that and his meticulous memory, this was one hell of a cool customer. Tennison pressed him further.

'You have no idea where he was living? Or if he lived with anyone?'

'I'm afraid not. He did leave messages on the notice board, and I think he received letters a few times, but not for quite a while. If you leave it with me I'll ask around and get back to you.'

Tennison smiled perfunctorily and opened the door. Edward Parker-Jones put out his meaty, hairy hand to shake hers. It was left in midair as she turned and left the office.

In the car, while Hall drove, she studied the list in Parker-Jones's beautiful rounded handwriting. Of course it had to be perfect. Mr Bleedin' Hearts Wonderful.

'He's given me virtually the same names as Jackson – we'll have to release him.' She smacked her head back against the headrest. 'Shit! Banged up, at least he couldn't scare anyone from talking to us. And they can't find Martin Fletcher now . . .'

Hall said, 'I've made a list of all the jobs and contacts off the centre's notice board. A lot of "Young Male Models" required. Reads like a Toms' telephone kiosk.'

Tennison perked up a bit. 'That ties in with something Vera said, that Connie wanted to be a model. Good . . . good . . .'

She leaned across and gazed at him admiringly. 'And may I say you are wearing a very positive tie this evening, Inspector!'

Hall's chubby face beamed and he actually blushed.

*

DI Dalton took the tape from his pocket and handed it to Superintendent Halliday. He then stood fidgeting as Halliday walked back around his desk. The room was warm, though Dalton was uncomfortable with more than mere heat. He didn't know why they'd picked him for this. Skulking hole-in-the-corner stuff was never his style.

'Tennison's got the murder inquiry partly because it'd be more trouble to stop her,' Halliday said. He looked directly into Dalton's eyes. 'But it is the murder and only the murder we want investigated.'

Dalton shrugged, shuffling his feet. 'There's nothing else, nothing I've heard. Jackson is still the prime suspect . . .'

'We want Jackson charged,' Halliday said, and lowering his voice for emphasis: 'What we do not want is the investigation broadened. Understand?'

Dalton nodded and started to leave. Halliday said, 'Better go and let the nurse have a look at that.'

Dalton glanced at his hand, wrapped in a handkerchief. Vicious little bastard. He nodded again and went out.

At 5.30 p.m. Tennison fronted the update briefing in the Squad Room. The purpose of this was to acquaint all the team with the day's developments, to coordinate the various activities, and to delegate fresh lines of inquiry. As she spoke, Hall was at the board behind her, writing up the names of Parker-Jones's alibis. It didn't need pointing out to anyone that these tallied exactly with Jackson's witnesses.

Norma took notes, jotting down questions and queries from the floor as well as Tennison's spiel.

'We will stick to the weekly rota as arranged, because we now have' – Tennison gestured to the officers drafted in from AMIT – 'DC Lillie, DS Haskons, and DI Hebdon, and DI Dalton handling the murder investigation.'

The others were present, but no Dalton, Tennison noticed.

'That said, when we have further information for Operation Contract . . . ' A moaning chorus joined in on the word 'Contract'.

'Cut it out, you know Superintendent Halliday is making it a . . . ' Everyone joined in. '*Priority.*'

With a smile, Tennison turned to Hall. 'Okay, can you farm out all the contact numbers you got from the centre? Keep up the links between each investigation.'

The team went back to work. Ray Hebdon pushed through. 'Excuse me, Guv, there was a message from some woman Smithy, from a newspaper. I put her name and number . . . ' His jaw dropped as Dalton walked in. 'I don't believe it!'

A smiling Dalton came up to Hebdon and Tennison. 'Hey! How are you?' His right hand still wrapped in the handkerchief, he held out his left, which Hebdon gripped. 'We were at Hornchurch together,' Dalton told Tennison. 'My God, how long is it? You still playing for the rugby team?'

'Nah, did my knee in, tendons, had to have an op. Bit off track for you, isn't it? I thought you were with Scotland Yard.'

'Yeah, I was . . . but I got transferred here.'

Tennison had clocked the 'Scotland Yard', and she also clocked Dalton's evasive look when he said it. He followed her as she moved to the desk.

'We've traced three, all said they were at the advice centre all evening and Jackson was there. We've not traced Alan Thorpe, but we've got a list of hangouts.'

'Pass them over to Larry, he's just farming out work for tomorrow,' Tennison said. 'And those on tonight can have a search for Martin Fletcher. I want him back in!'

'What's this? What you doin' here?' Otley had entered and was gaping with surprise at Haskons and Lillie. He went over, grinning fit to bust, and cuffed Haskons. 'He got Fairy of the Week at Southampton Row,' he informed the room. 'Five times on the trot!'

Haskons squared up to him, ducking and weaving. 'Watch it, you old poofter.' He jerked his thumb. 'Ray Hebdon – Bill Otley, the Skipper!'

The two men nodded. Otley turned his head to watch Tennison leaving the room. He pinched his nose, giving them all a look. As the door swung to, he said,

'Jackson was released 'bout fifteen minutes ago ... does she know?'

Hall called them to attention.

'Okay, we're trying to find anyone with a recent photo of Colin Jenkins, any known contacts, and where he's been living. Clubs, coffee bars, known hangouts for the rent boys. Who's taking what?'

From the door, Otley yelled, 'As from today we will be awarding the Fairy of the Week award!'

Kathy yelled back, 'Yeah – and we'll award the Prick of the Week. Apparently you're not eligible, as you've been one ever since you arrived.'

Lots of raspberries, honks, and hooting laughter.

Otley gave a universal V-sign and disappeared.

Twenty minutes later, having written up his report, Otley took it along to Tennison's office where she was looking over a large-scale street map pinned to the wall. He dropped the report on her desk.

'The advice centre and Vera's flat.' Tennison pointed to each, ringed in red, where she'd just marked them.

'I timed it,' Otley said, perching on the edge of the desk. 'You could make it there and back in ten minutes.'

The door was open, and Dalton came in, a bandage on his hand. He stood listening, his tanned face impassive.

'So Jackson could easily have done it.' Tennison glanced over her shoulder at Otley. 'But five alibis say he didn't.'

'I reckon we could break down those kids' statements if we had Jackson behind bars. They'd all say he was visiting the Queen Mother if he told them to. He's got to them, it's obvious.'

'It's obvious with Martin Fletcher. I want him brought back in.' She went around the desk, biting the end of the felt-tip pen. 'Parker-Jones ... he's Jackson's strongest alibi. Dig around a bit, but on the QT ...' She gave him a look.

'He's squeaky clean,' Otley told her. 'I think your predecessor had a nose around but came up with nothin'.'

'Oh, he did, did he?' Tennison was frowning and shaking her head. 'Could be just a personal reaction – and there was something about his voice.' She rooted underneath some files, then opened a drawer and searched inside. 'Shit! Where the hell is the tape?' She looked at Otley. 'Did you take a tape from here?'

'No. Is it in the machine?' Otley reached over and pressed the Eject button. Empty. He was conscious that Tennison was staring hard at him, plainly disbelieving.

She straightened up, sighing, and glanced at her watch. 'Don't waste time looking for it now. We'll call it quits for tonight, get an early start in the morning.'

Dalton gave a nod to them both and went out, closing the door. Otley still waited, watching Tennison opening, searching, and banging shut every drawer in her desk. Finally she stood up.

'You didn't take it, did you, Bill?'

'What? The tape?' He shook his head. 'No, why would I do that?'

Tennison suddenly looked weary. She slumped back in the chair, rubbing her forehead. 'Getting paranoid. It'll be here somewhere.'

There was a reason for Otley's lingering presence. Out it came, a touch of asperity in his tone.

'Guv, can you get Dalton off my back? I can't work with him. I could have got a lot more out of those kids – one bit him this afternoon. I nearly did myself,' Otley said darkly.

He was a bastard, Otley, and a chauvinist pig to boot, but she trusted his instincts, because they so often chimed with her own.

'What do you make of him?' she asked.

'Not a lot. Don't know why he's on board, do you?'

Tennison shook her head. With a grunted 'G'night,' Otley left her alone. She got up, arching her back, and stood with hands on hips looking over her desk. She lifted the reports and files and checked everywhere. She peered down the side of the desk and underneath her chair.

She sat down again, and looked at her watch. Yawning, she picked up the phone and dialled. As she waited she drew Otley's report towards her and started reading.

'Hello . . . Dr Gordon's receptionist, please.' She waited,

reading. 'It's Jane Tennison. I'm sorry, but I'm running a bit late. I've got an appointment at six-thirty.' She listened, nodding. 'Great, see you then.'

She dropped the phone down and moved slowly around the desk, the report in her hand, still reading. She stopped dead and stared. She read it again, the bit that had frozen her to the spot.

'Oh, shit . . . !'

Moving fast, she went into the corridor. To the left, outside the Squad Room doors, Commander Chiswick was having a quiet word with Dalton, whose back was towards her, and as Tennison strode quickly up, Chiswick lightly tapped Dalton on the arm, shutting him up.

'Evening, sir,' Tennison greeted the Commander. She turned to Dalton and indicated her office. 'Before you go . . .'

When Dalton came in, a moment or two later, she was leaning against the desk. He'd barely crossed the threshold before Tennison said, 'Has anyone looked at that hand?'

'It's nothing,' Dalton said, bending his wrist to show her. 'I put a bandage over it.'

'I'm sorry, there's no easy way to tell you this.' Tennison reached behind her for Otley's report and held it up. 'Billy Matthews has full-blown AIDS. I think you should get to a hospital.'

Dalton frowned at her, blinking rapidly. 'The bloody

little bastard,' he burst out hoarsely. 'I had to have a shower when we got back. I'll go and see the nurse.' He hadn't quite grasped it, Tennison could see. 'The little shit!'

'I'm sorry . . .'

Dalton went very quiet, staring at his hand. Only now was he realizing the full implications, his tan fading as the blood drained from his face. He looked scared now, dead scared.

'He bit me, he broke the skin, he . . . bit me.' He swallowed and looked at Tennison, his voice quavering. 'Jesus Christ. I was bleeding . . .'

'Go to the hospital, you'll need a tetanus injection for starters.'

Dalton didn't move. He simply stared at her, mouth hanging open, looking about ten years old.

'Would you like someone to go with you? Do you want me to take you?'

'No, no, it's okay . . .' He turned away, holding the wrist of his injured hand. 'I've got my own car . . . er . . . thank you.' He went out and turned right, heading for the stairs.

Tennison emerged from behind the screen, buttoning up her blouse. She took her suit jacket from the back of the chair and shrugged into it. Seated at the leather-topped desk in his white coat, Dr Gordon was making an entry in her medical file, having already prepared the sample stickers for the lab tests. The glass slides in their plastic containers were by his elbow.

'Can I ask – if somebody has full-blown AIDS and bites somebody else, actually draws blood, how dangerous is it?'

Dr Gordon was the same age as Tennison, if not younger, though this had never bothered her. He had a friendly, amiable disposition, which was more important. He looked at her over his silver-framed glasses.

'Very. It's not the fact that the AIDS carrier has drawn blood, but if his blood then makes contact with the open wound . . . human bite is extremely dangerous, contains more bacteria than a dog bite. Full-blown AIDS?' He put his pen down, laced his fingers when he saw how intently she was listening to him.

'Often their gums bleed, it's really dependent on how far advanced the AIDS carrier is, but bleeding gums, mouth sores . . .'

'How soon can it be diagnosed?'

He tilted his head slightly. 'It's not you, is it?'

'No, it's not me.' Tennison sat down, smoothing her blouse inside the shoulders of her jacket. 'I'm fine. Well – a bit ratty, but I put that down to my periods being a bit erratic.'

'Well, it could be the onset of the menopause. We'll get these samples over to the lab, but until I get the results I won't prescribe anything.' Dr Gordon leaned forward, regarding her soberly. 'Your friend should be tested for antibodies immediately, but that will only prove he or she doesn't have it already. I'm afraid it'll take three to six months to zero convert and they should have HIV tests every four to six weeks for the next six months.'

'So it'll be six months before he knows?'

'Afraid so. That's how long it will take to show a positive infection.' He held up a cautioning finger. 'However, full-blown AIDS can take anywhere up to eight to ten years to develop.'

'Thank you very much,' Tennison said, getting up. 'Do you have any leaflets I could take?'

While he found her some she thoughtfully put on her raincoat and collected her briefcase. She turned to him.

'You mind if I say something? "Onset of menopause" may not mean much to you, but it does to a woman. It means a lot.'

Dr Gordon paused, watching her, waiting.

Briefcase clasped in her hands, Tennison was studying her shoes. 'I'm not married, maybe never will be, so it doesn't make all that much difference to me – but I am only forty-four, and ...' She shook her head rapidly, shoulders slumping. 'Oh, forget it!'

'Be a couple of days,' Dr Gordon said kindly, handing her the leaflets. 'I'll call you.'

'Thank you,' Tennison said, stuffing them in her

pocket. 'And thank you for fitting me in. I'm sorry I was late.'

As she got to the door her bleeper sounded. She fished it out and pressed a button. 'Can I use your phone?'

Chapter Seven

In the softening gloom of early dusk the unkempt graves and slanting headstones of St Margaret's Crypt flashed red and yellow in the lights of the patrol car and ambulance parked outside the rusting iron gates. Two uniformed officers were cordoning off the area inside the churchyard with yellow marking ribbons: POLICE LINE – DO NOT CROSS. Arc lamps had been set up. The sudden harsh glare as they were switched on transformed the crypt into a ghastly gothic world of drunken shadows and crumbling statues, broken glass glittering in the long grass.

A motley collection of human detritus watched with befuddled curiosity. Some were crouched on the low broken-down wall, others slumped on the pavement, wrapped in blankets with layers of newspaper inside. Empty wine and cider bottles filled the gutters. Situated between the Bullring and the underpass of Waterloo Bridge, the derelict churchyard was home to a night-time population of summer residents; the winter months were far too cold for sleeping on gravestones, even topped up with Thunderbird wine and two litres of Woodpecker.

Otley was talking to the police photographer when he saw Tennison's Sierra nosing along the narrow cobbled street. She stopped some distance away, leaving room for the ambulance, and wound her window down. Otley went across and leaned in.

'Body was discovered about an hour ago. There's a doctor checking him over now.'

Tennison followed him, stepping over the heaps of rubbish and broken bottles. As they approached the gates a hand reached out, grabbing at her coat, and a slurred voice said, 'Givvus a quid fer a cup o' tea ...'

Tennison stopped one of the policemen. 'For Chrissakes, clear them out of here!' she snapped. 'Get rid of them!'

Lifting the yellow tape for her to bend under, Otley gave a half smile. 'Can't get rid of them, Guv. Each tombstone's an allocated lodging.' He pointed. 'He's over there, by the angel. Some bloody guardian!'

He remained at the tape, watching Tennison moving through the headstones towards a huge white praying angel with a shattered wing, marble eyes raised sightlessly to heaven. Then, with his sardonic grin, Otley went out through the gates and along the street in the direction of Waterloo Bridge.

The doctor had been kneeling on a plastic sheet while he carried out his examination. He stood up, clicked his small black leather bag shut, and moved aside. Tennison peered down. In death, Martin Fletcher looked even pathetically younger and frailer than he had in life – short, brutish and nasty as that had been.

He lay on his back on the pitted tombstone, one leg bent under the other, his arms open wide. His head was tilted to one side, puffy eyelids closed in his chalk-white face, a string of saliva and vomit hanging from his half-open mouth. By his outstretched hand were two cans of lighter fluid and a two-litre plastic bottle of Woodpecker cider, empty.

I never told nobody nuffink and that is the Gawd's truth ...

Tennison had seen all she wanted to. She turned away, thinking that Martin Fletcher must have told somebody something, or he wouldn't have ended up a cold lump of meat on a stone slab, fourteen years of life washed down the drain.

Otley stood at the chest-high wooden counter of the sandwich trailer not a stone's throw from the iron trellis-work of Waterloo Bridge. It was dark now, the patch of waste ground near the trailer dimly illuminated by a sulky fire in an oil drum. A dozen or so kids sat around it, one of them holding a thin shivering mongrel on a piece of string. Cans of beer were being passed around. Somebody had his nose inside a brown paper bag, breathing heavily, then coughing and spluttering as he passed it on.

'You want ketchup? Mustard? Onions . . . ?'

The stallholder held Otley's hamburger in his palm. He pushed a large white mug towards Otley's elbow. 'Sugar in the tea? Milk? Top or not?'

'No top, mate,' Otley said, reaching into his pocket for change. 'An I'll have the rest, but easy on the ketchup, heavy on the mustard.' He plonked a pound coin and fifty-pence piece down and turned to the boy beside him. Alan Thorpe was a fresh-faced kid with jug ears and straight blond hair hacked off in ragged clumps. Otley guessed he was about thirteen.

'Who else was there that night then?'

Together they strolled, Otley munching his hamburger and sipping his mug of tea, towards the group around the fire. On the far side of the trailer, in the vast shadow cast by the bridge, Tennison slowly drew up. She wound her window down. From this distance she couldn't hear, but she could see everything that was going on. Otley saying something that made the blond kid laugh, and Otley laughing too. Otley bending down to feed the dog some hamburger. Otley talking to the blond kid, paying close attention to what he said. And then Otley glancing up and seeing her car, the word 'Shit' as discernible on his lips as if she'd heard him mutter it.

He came across, chewing the last of the hamburger, wiping his fingers on his handkerchief. He gestured.

'Come midnight they're around this place like flies. Does a hell of a trade.'

'The boy that bit Dalton, Billy. Turns out he's got AIDS.'

Otley stared. 'Jesus Christ. How's Dalton?'

'We don't know yet,' Tennison said bleakly. 'It's tough.'

'Yeah, it's tough for Billy too,' Otley said, and she was surprised by the bitterness in his voice. He leaned on the open window and nodded towards the group. 'That was Jackson's third witness, blond boy with the dog, Alan Thorpe.' He belched and covered his mouth with the back of his hand. 'Says he was too pissed to remember who was at the centre the night Connie died, so that's one alibi that's no good.'

'You want a ride home?' Tennison asked him.

Otley hesitated, half shook his head, then changed his mind. As they drove off, the midnight blue Merc with the rusty patches that had been parked under the bridge with its lights off ghosted forward. Jackson slid out from behind the wheel. He stood running his thumb over the rings on his hand, wearing a long, beat-up leather coat that nearly reached his ankles. Pursing his fleshy lips, he gave a low whistle. The kids around the fire turned to look. Jackson whistled again. The dog was released and trotted over to him, trailing its bit of string.

Jackson knelt down, rubbing the dog's head. He looked up, smiling.

'Alan, come here a sec.'

When nobody moved, Jackson stood up.

'ALAN!' The smile wiped from his face, he pointed. 'You! Come here. Don't mess with me, get over here.'

The group of kids shrank away as Alan Thorpe stood up and shuffled across the loose gravel. He was shuffling too slowly, and Jackson made an angry beckoning gesture.

'What was all that about?' Jackson asked softly as Alan came up. And reaching out, Alan shying away a little, Jackson ruffled the boy's hair.

'He wanted to know about Connie,' Alan said, barely audible.

Jackson opened the passenger door. 'Get in, Alan. We're goin' for a little ride.'

'Okay.' Alan moved forward. 'What about me mates, can they come too . . . ?'

Jackson grabbed him by the back of the neck and flung him inside. He smiled. 'Just you an' me, Alan.'

Alan suddenly grinned back, eyes impish in his soft childish face. 'Got a punter for me, 'ave yer?'

Jackson slammed the door.

Tennison turned off Holloway Road into the little street

of neat terraced houses, each with its own few square feet of scrubby garden. Otley lived three doors from the bottom end, where the viaduct of the London to Birmingham mainline blocked off the street.

She didn't expect him to invite her in for a coffee, and he didn't. She wouldn't have accepted anyway. They were reluctant colleagues, not bosom friends. He was strangely on edge. He opened the door but stayed in the car, one leg out. He looked back at her. In the streetlight his eyes were black pits, unfathomable, perhaps unknowable. She didn't know him.

'Your real bastards are the ones that use them,' Otley said. 'Can't get to them though, can you?' Grinning at her, teeth clenched. 'Especially if they got friends in high places. Dig deep enough an' you come up against concrete ... know what I mean ...'

He was out fast then, slamming the door, through the squeaking gate, up the little path, not looking back. As if he'd said more than he should, shown too much of how he really felt.

Tennison drove home, too tired to bother to understand what he had been getting at. A large Bushmills and bed, that was all she wanted. Another day over, thank God.

At 9 a.m. it started all over again. The Squad Room was a cacophony of ringing phones, shouted questions, some foul language, and twenty conversations going on all at once. Updates from the night-duty staff were being passed around. Halliday was at the big notice board with Norma, who was taking him through the various lines of inquiry that were under way. Tennison had one ear to everything that was happening while she listened to Kathy. She felt to be in better shape today, her attention keener, adrenaline buzzing with the noise and activity. Down one day, on a high the next, it was puzzling.

'I've been checking out the cards from the advice centre. One of the so-called photographers was busted a few years ago, so he was quite helpful.' Tennison nodded to show she was listening. Kathy went on, 'He's mostly porn and girly pics, but he put me onto a Mark Lewis . . . ' She passed over a note of the address. 'He specializes in male "beauty" style pictures. I called his number but got short shrift. I think it'd be better for one of the men to have a go. If Connie was trying to be a model he could have used him.'

'Thanks, Kathy.' Tennison gave her a smile and a brisk nod. Halliday was now talking to Ray Hebdon, so Norma was free. 'Any messages?' Tennison called to her.

Hall had gathered some of them together for a pep talk. 'I just want a quick word, okay? Can you keep dealing with as much of that backlog as possible, and those in court today – Please Give Times! Availability!' Lurking smiles as he adjusted the knot in his immaculate tie, lemon and grey diagonal stripes with embroidered fleur-de-lis.

'Right, I want to give you all a serious warning. I know it's been said before, but I'm saying it again – and I'll keep on saying it. Some of these youngsters have full-blown AIDS. They know it! You know it – keep it in your minds. Please, I know you are all aware of the risks, but heed the warnings and the instructions you've all had concerning any form of confrontation. Biting is just as dangerous as one of them stabbing you with a hypodermic needle ...'

Tennison was at the board, Norma at her elbow reading out the messages. The names of Jackson's witnesses were ringed and ticked, a line in red through Martin Fletcher's name. Billy Matthews had a tick and two question marks.

'Oh, and Jessica from the newspaper, she's the most persistent woman I have ever known!' Norma said, concluding her summary. 'She says if you don't have the time to return her calls, she will come in and see you at a convenient time.' The stocky girl shook her head, exasperated. 'But she refuses to tell me what she wants.'

Farther along, Haskons and Lillie were taking notes from the update bulletin board. Tennison said, 'Next time she rings, tell her that unless she tells you what is so important ...' She frowned up at the board. 'The Jackson alibis ... Alan Thorpe was drunk, why the query on Billy Matthews?'

'He doesn't remember where he was that night. We

need to question him again – he might remember!' The inference being that if Norma could have ten minutes alone with him, he damn well would.

Tennison returned to her desk. Otley breezed in and came straight up. He seemed to regard the morning briefing as optional, she thought crossly. Went his own sweet way. But as usual he hadn't been idle.

'Martin Fletcher virtually drowned in his own vomit. His blood alcohol was so high, it could have been bottled! Plus other substances.' He gripped the edge of the desk in both hands, leaning at an angle. His polyester tie, the knot askew, hung down limp and wrinkled. His suit looked as if it had been slept in. 'He'd been sniffing from a gas lighter canister. They said if you'd put a match to him he'd have combusted!'

Superintendent Halliday was standing at the doors, gesturing. Tennison craned her head around Otley to see that she was being summoned. She gave Otley a look, and with a sigh followed Halliday out. Now what?

'So, where are the cream?' Otley drawled, punching Hall on the shoulder. He raised his voice. 'That scruff Haskons and Co.?'

Haskons nudged Lillie, and the pair of them turned from the board with wide grins.

Hall said, 'Their team's checking into a mini-cab firm that's a cover for a hire-a-cab and a Tom-thrown-in. New place just opened, King's Cross.'

'Inventive,' Otley remarked with a sly wink. 'But who drives?'

'You released Jackson? That means his alibis pan out?'

'We're still checking, still trying to retrace all the boys, take them through their statements again,' Tennison told him. All this was up on the board, so why the grilling? There was a hidden agenda here, though she was blowed if she could even hazard a guess.

Tennison spread her hands. 'I didn't have enough to hold Jackson. Pity, because I think the kids are scared of him, covering up for him.'

Halliday leaned back in his chair. 'So Jackson is still the prime suspect?' Tennison nodded. 'And Parker-Jones? You went to see him?'

Again, that note of criticism, censure even, in his voice. It nettled her.

'Yes, is there any reason I shouldn't have gone to interview him?'

'No,' Halliday said curtly. 'Was the interview satisfactory?'

'He was very cooperative—'

She was interrupted. 'Do you think it will be necessary to see him again?'

Tennison put her head forward, frowning. 'I don't understand – are you telling me not to interview my main suspect's alibi again?'

'I saw the case board, you've three boys that gave Jackson an alibi.' He added flatly, 'So stay off Parker-Jones.'

Tennison straightened her spine, getting riled up now. 'Am I in charge of this investigation or not?'

'No. I am. So now I am telling you, back off him and stay off him. You are diverting and wasting time. If Jackson is your man, then get him. Concentrate on Jackson and wrap this case up.'

She knew better than to argue. He was laying down the law, and he had the clout to back it up. This wasn't the moment to have a flaming row. Besides, she had a hidden agenda of her own.

From the reception area Tennison could see over the low partition to where Margaret Speel was talking to a woman with dyed blond hair and a sallow complexion, in her late twenties. The probation office was a dismal, depressing place. The carpet was worn thin and the furniture was scratched and shabby. An attempt had been made to brighten things up with posters, and one corner had been turned into a children's playpen, a few cheap plastic toys scattered around, a little slide decorated with Mickey Mouse stickers. Somehow all this made everything seem even more pathetic. It reminded Tennison of an older woman trying to camouflage the ravages of time with daubs of garish make-up and youthful clothes.

The receptionist was on the phone. She had been on

the phone ever since Tennison arrived, nearly ten minutes earlier. Tennison looked at her watch and tried to attract Margaret Speel's attention.

'Did you look for the signs?' The probation officer's voice carried over the partition, mingled in with conversations from other parts of the room. 'I told you what to expect – if his speech is slurred, eyes red-rimmed. Has he got a persistent cough? Yes? Did you smell it on his breath ...?' She glanced up, raising her hand. 'Just a minute, Mrs Line.'

She came around with her brisk walk, dark and petite, attractive in a pert, almost elfish way. Large thin gold loops dangled from her small white ears. 'Is it Martin Fletcher again?' She gestured to some seats with hideous green plastic coverings.

'No, he's dead,' Tennison said, sitting down. 'He was found last night, drug abuse.'

Margaret Speel sank down beside her. 'Oh, no ...'

Tennison got the impression that the probation officer wasn't all that surprised. She waited a moment, then got straight on with it.

'Do you know a Billy Matthews?' Margaret Speel nodded. 'Is there any way you can get him off the streets?'

'What do you mean, "get him off the streets"?' Margaret Speel said, testily repeating the phrase.

'He has full-blown AIDS.'

Margaret Speel looked plaintively to the ceiling and

back at Tennison, twitching her mouth. 'And just where do you suggest I put him?' She swept her hand out, as if Billy Matthews might possibly doss down on the threadbare carpet. 'Oh, really! You know of one boy with full-blown AIDS, and you want him off the streets. Well – where do I put him? With the rest? Do you know where they all are? How many there are?'

Tennison shook her head, smarting at her own blithe assumption, her own crass ignorance. The probation service had to deal with dozens, scores, perhaps hundreds. She only touched the tip of the iceberg. She got up and started to leave.

'I suggest you contact Edward Parker-Jones, he runs the advice centre.' Margaret Speel was trying to be helpful, but her voice remained brusque. These people waltzed in, knowing nothing, and expected miracles. She was sick to death of it. 'If Billy's there, then I can try and do something for him.'

Tennison nodded slowly. 'What do you think of Edward Parker-Jones?'

She wasn't expecting such a simple question to produce such a reaction. Margaret Speel's eyes blazed fiercely.

'He should be given a medal! It costs one thousand five hundred a week to keep really young offenders in an institution, and more staff than—'

'Did you ever come into contact with a Colin Jenkins – Connie?'

'No.' Her mouth snapped shut.

'Do you know a James Jackson?'

'I know of him but I have never had any professional dealings with him.'

Pick the bones out of that.

Tennison thanked her politely, but Margaret Speel was already striding off, and the Detective Chief Inspector imagined she could see steam coming out of her ears.

Mark Lewis's studio was off the Whitechapel Road, down a maze of streets behind the sooty redbrick Victorian edifice of the London Hospital. It was on the first floor above a Chinese take-away, and something of the exotic oriental influence had seeped upstairs to the photographer's studio, which also housed his office and darkroom.

Lewis minced rather than walked. An ex-dancer, he moved lithely and fast as lightning around the black-draped studio. Haskons and Lillie got dizzy just watching him zoom about the place – setting up his camera, arranging the lights just so, explaining to his model – a young black guy with an oiled gleaming torso, posing on a white pedestal – precisely what he was after with expressively floating gestures and a snapping of the fingers. But he was a professional, and good at his work, with a real feeling for it. There was also a steely quality to him, a certain watchfulness in his brown eyes, a thinning of the soft mouth, as if hinting that what you see is not all you get.

He said he could give them ten minutes. He took them along a narrow passage into his office, the darkroom in one corner behind a plywood partition. It was a large room with a skylight, two of the walls covered in silk hangings with oriental motifs. There were paper Chinese lanterns, glass wind chimes floating in the still air, and brass gongs of different sizes. And under a miniature spotlight, a display of Buddhas, fiery dragons, and mythical Eastern gods.

Next to the darkroom were several large cupboards, a row of filing cabinets, and a desk with a leather, gold-embossed appointments diary.

It all seemed legit. To Lillie, Mark Lewis was exactly as he appeared to be – a poofter photographer with curled hair that was remarkably dark and lustrous, given his age, on the downward slope of forty.

'Red curly hair, about five seven, slim build. His nickname was Connie, real name Jenkins,' Haskons said.

He and Lillie were sitting on the couch. Mark Lewis had too much nervous energy to stay in one spot for long. He was continually on the move, a figure of medium height dressed in a black shirt, open at the neck, and tight-fitting black trousers, black socks, black moccasins.

Haskons produced a photograph. 'This was taken when he was about nine. We're just trying to trace people that knew him, may have known where he lived.'

'No need firing names at me. I don't remember

names – faces yes, I never forget a face. Now I am very busy, but if you can give an idea of the time he came to me, then you can look at all the portfolios—'

He leaned over from the waist to squint at the photograph. 'No. Don't know him.'

'Some time last year maybe?' Lillie ventured hopefully.

Lewis went to the office alcove and returned, thudding down three huge albums onto the mosaic coffee table. Spinning around, he was off to the filing cabinets, plucking out brown folders bulging with glossy prints.

'Don't you keep a record of clients?' Haskons asked. 'Dates of the sessions?'

'Some don't like to use their real name. I am strictly cash up front and cash on delivery – and I pay VAT and taxes,' Lewis said, giving them a direct look. 'I run this as a legitimate business.'

He dropped the folders on the coffee table, and was spinning off somewhere else. They couldn't keep track of him.

Haskons exchanged glances with Lillie. As detective sergeant, Richard Haskons was the senior of the two, but they had operated together as a team for so long that the question of rank never interfered in their working relationship. They both turned to watch Lewis.

' . . . I just take the photographs. If it's for publication, then I charge so and so. If it's for a private collector, then it's between myself and the client.' He swished aside a black curtain masking off the darkroom. 'I print up all the negs, I do everything myself. I am, my dears, a one-man show. I had an assistant once,' he confided, 'but – Trouble, with a big T.' He smiled briefly. 'I'll be in the darkroom.' He went inside and drew the curtain.

The two detectives took an album each, turning the pages.

At full throttle, Shirley Bassey suddenly shattered the peace and quiet, belting out, 'The minute you walked in the joint, I could see you were a man of distinction . . . '

DC Lillie nearly fell off the couch. Haskons was singing along at the top of his voice—

'Hey, Big Spender . . . spend a little time with me.'

After the far-from-veiled warning from Halliday, Tennison was on her mettle. It was the cack-handed way he had gone about it that riled her. Telling her to lay off Parker-Jones was as good as waving a red flag at a bull. The man had as much subtlety as a sledgehammer.

She called DI Hall into her office. She didn't know whether Hall was Halliday's man or not, but she intended to find out.

'If it wasn't Jackson – if I've been going in the wrong direction – then I need another suspect, another motive. And it was just something you said that I'm a bit confused about . . . '

Arms folded, Tennison leaned against the desk, study-ing her shoes. Speaking slowly, as if thinking out loud, she went on, 'If I remember correctly, you said the advice centre had been targeted before I came on board ... did that include Parker-Jones himself?'

'Not the man. It was more his boys. It's where they all congregate, one of the first places for the really young kids.'

Tennison's 'Mmmm,' was noncommittal. 'And was it sort of inferred you all stay clear of him?'

Hall fiddled with the knot in his tie. He wasn't very comfortable, kept adjusting his position in the chair.

Tennison looked at him. 'Larry, if I have to initiate a full-scale swoop – that's kids, Toms, pimps, punters – close down clubs, coffee bars, centres – and I am under pressure to get it under way, and ... ' She bent down to his eye level. ' ... Parker-Jones's name keeps on cropping up.'

'Yeah, but—' Hall's poor tie was getting some stick today. At this rate it would end up as bad as Otley's. 'But we never found anything; look, I know this is off the record, okay? The Chief Inspector before you was warned off. Parker-Jones is a very influential man, got friends in high places, and we sort of backed off him.'

Tennison pointed to the wall. 'And this came from the Guv'nor?'

Hall nodded, chewing his lip.

'Okay, okay ... and then Operation Contract got the green light for the big cleanup.'

'Well, you know what happened – we knew it – waste of time.' Hall was stumbling over his words. 'Chief Inspector Lyall was out, I think he's in Manchester now. I honestly don't think there's anything subversive going on, but ... '

'But? There was a leak?' When he didn't answer, Tennison got up and paced the office. 'Come on, I've checked the charge sheets, nothing subversive? Somebody must have tipped off the punters, never mind the clubs!'

'Off the record, I think we got close to someone with heavy-duty contacts,' Hall admitted, looking at her properly for the first time.

Tennison stopped pacing. 'You got a suspicion?' She brushed a hand through her hair, a faint smile on her lips. 'No? Not even a possible?'

'If I had I'd tell you, honestly.' His babyish round features put her in mind of an eager-to-please Boy Scout. He wasn't Halliday's man, she was convinced: too transparent. She believed him.

'What about you?' he asked her.

Tennison laughed. 'If I had, Larry, I wouldn't be trying to wheedle it out of you. Okay, you can go, and thanks.'

The Squad Room was unusually quiet. Some of the team had gone to the canteen for an early lunch, others were out chasing down leads. An impatient Otley was standing behind Norma, leaning over her as she spoke into the phone.

'Good morning, can I speak to Chief Inspector David Lyall? It's personal, could you say a Sergeant Bill Otley, Vice Squad, Soho . . . yes, I'll hold, thank you.'

Two desks along, Kathy was just finishing another call. 'Okay, yes, I've got that. I'll pass it on.' She put the phone down and called out, 'Sarge?'

Otley went over.

'Sarge!' Norma yelled. 'I've got him coming on the line now . . .'

Otley scuttled back and grabbed the phone off her. 'Go and help Kathy.' He turned his back on her and cupped his hand over the mouthpiece. 'Dave? Listen, mate, I need a favour. Remember when you were here you thought you got something on a bloke—'

'Sarge.' Norma was back. 'Kath's just got a call, tip-off from one of the street photographers. He reckons the guy we may be looking for is a Mark Lewis. Where's your lads, Sarge?'

'Just one second, Dave . . .' Otley turned furiously, jabbing his finger. 'Bloody check the board – go on!' He cupped the phone, opened his mouth to speak, but didn't. He looked up again. 'Mark Lewis? Hang on a second, I think our boys are there now. Check it out.'

Leaving him to his call, Norma went over to the board. Kathy joined her. 'Who's he talking to?'

Norma tapped her nose. 'Chief Inspector here before Tennison . . .'

Kathy scanned the board, then pointed. 'Mark Lewis. They're seeing him this morning.' Her finger moved along, and she was suddenly excited. 'Guv! This Mark Lewis, the photographer we got a tip-off about – he's on the list from the advice centre.'

Otley covered the phone and whipped around.

'Well, bloody contact them!' He muttered into the phone, 'Dave, sorry about this . . . okay, yeah, can you fax me what you sniffed out?' He looked up wearily. 'Hang on.'

Hall was standing there, arms folded, looking peeved.

Otley held the receiver against his chest. 'Well, what was your little private conflab about?'

'Cut it out, Sarge, that's my phone,' Hall said, holding out his hand. 'Is it for me?'

'No, it's personal.' Otley jerked his head. 'Just check over Kath, she's had a tip-off.' Hall sniffed loudly and went around the desk to the board. Otley crouched. 'Dave? As a favour, mate. We're sniffin' around Parker-Jones again, yeah . . .'

Chapter Eight

'There is nothing like a dame ... Nothing in the world. There is nothing you can name that is anything like a dame!'

Shirley Bassey had been replaced by the soundtrack of *South Pacific*, and Haskons sang lustily along. He and Lillie were working their way through the albums. There were hundreds of photographs, mostly black and white, all of them featuring gorgeous young men and svelte pretty boys in various states of undress. The shots of couples were suggestive certainly, but not strictly pornographic.

'Some great-lookin' fellas, they must all work out like crazy,' Lillie said. 'Here, look at this one.'

'Yeah, yeah ...' Leafing through the album, Haskons couldn't be bothered; he'd seen enough naked male flesh to last him a lifetime. Even the show tunes were beginning to bore him. 'I've had worse taken on me holidays.'

'What, kissin' blokes?' Lillie sniggered.

'Piss off! I mean in swimmin' trunks.' Haskons flipped over a page, scowling. 'This is a waste of time. I got some that go back to the seventies. I dunno what we're doing here, why we're here . . . ' He threw out his hands. 'If he did a bit of modellin', so what? What we lookin' for?'

His bleeper sounded. He reached inside his jacket to kill it, and looked around the room.

'You see a phone?'

'Mr Lewis? Can I use your phone!'

Mark Lewis cocked his head. He half-turned from the processing bench. In his left hand he held a thick bundle of ten-by-eight glossy prints, colour and black and white. With his right hand he was feeding them, one by one, into a bath of acid. They fizzed and buckled, turned brown and sank to the bottom in a grey-brown slimy sludge.

He leaned towards the black curtain.

'Be my guest! I can't come out, I'm working on some negs. Phone's on the shelf in the passage.'

He stayed there until he heard Haskons move away, then quickly turned back to the bench and carried on methodically feeding the prints into the acid bath.

*

When Haskons returned he found Lillie examining the lock on one of the large cupboards. Haskons called out, 'Thanks, Mr Lewis!' and said in Lillie's ear, 'That was Kathy. Tip-off. If there was anyone doing the real heavy stuff, then this is our man . . .'

Lillie had taken out a bunch of keys. He selected one and slid it into the lock. It clicked open.

'Hey, watch it!' Haskons whispered. 'We've no search warrant.'

From top to bottom the cupboard was filled with videotapes. Lillie pulled one out and looked at the label.

'He's messing us about. Never said anythin' about this lot.' He showed Haskons the label. '"Adam and Adam." That's original.'

Haskons went over to the darkroom.

'Mr Lewis, we need to talk to you a minute.'

He pushed the curtain aside and peered in. Mark Lewis's startled face craned around over his shoulder. He shifted across, attempting to shield what he was doing. Haskons went in and shoved him out of the way. He saw the photograph Lewis had just dropped into the bath and reached for it.

'No! Don't!' Lewis anxiously paddled the air like an hysterical schoolgirl. 'It's acid, it'll burn your hand off!'

Lillie appeared, in time to see Haskons lifting the print out of the bath with a steel ruler. Crinkling and turning brown, the image was still discernible. A naked, beautiful boy with curly red hair.

They lay on Tennison's desk, a dozen or more of the large colour photographs of Connie in various artistic poses that Mark Lewis hadn't had a chance to dispose of. Otley picked one out at random. It happened to be of Connie bending over, firm round buttocks presented to the camera like two peaches.

Tennison leaned against the windowsill, pushing her cuticles back with the clip of her fountain pen. She said thoughtfully, 'Parker-Jones is regarded as the Mother Teresa of Soho . . . and he's Jackson's alibi.' She scratched her nose with the fountain pen clip. 'There's something that doesn't quite sit right. If Jackson was looking for Connie because he owed him money, why – if we presume he found Connie – why didn't he take it?'

Otley shook his head and tossed the photograph down. There was a tap at the door and Haskons looked in. 'Mark Lewis is in interview room D oh two. We're getting a video room set up, view Connie's tapes.'

Tennison nodded to indicate she'd be right along. She followed Otley to the door. The phone rang. 'You go ahead,' she told him, and reached for the phone. 'Chief Inspector Tennison's office.'

It was Dr Gordon's receptionist. Tennison listened, frowning. 'Is this bad news? Is it the tests?'

She moved around the desk to sit down. She closed her eyes, listening. 'Yes, yes . . . I'll come in. Thank you.'

She put the phone down and sat silently for a moment, rubbing the back of her hand. Snapping awake, she opened the top drawer and took out her diary. Underneath it was the cassette tape she'd hunted high and low for. She took it out and turned it over.

Kathy came in. 'You wanted DCI Lyall's contact number. He's in Manchester.' She put the paper down. 'I think the Sarge . . .' She paused. Tennison was thumbing through the pages of the diary, chewing her lip. 'You okay?'

Tennison banged the diary shut. 'Kathy, you didn't put this tape in my drawer, did you? It's the ambulance call-out tape.'

'No.' Kathy turned to go.

'You don't have a cigarette, do you?' Tennison said.

'No, I'm sorry, I don't smoke,' Kathy said, leaving.

The diary and the tape lay side by side on the desk. Tennison stared at them, pulling distractedly at the neckline of her blouse. She tossed the diary back into the drawer and slammed it shut.

DS Richard Haskons and DI Ray Hebdon were in Taped Interview Room D.02 with Mark Lewis. As the arresting officer, Haskons was having first crack. Hebdon stood watching, arms folded, his tie pulled loosely away from his collar. The atmosphere was close in the small room, and he imagined he could smell Mark Lewis sweating. Or maybe it wasn't his imagination; the photographer was highly agitated, twisting a handkerchief in his heavily veined hands, the nails neatly manicured and coated in clear varnish.

'Go on,' Haskons prompted.

'I last saw him about four, perhaps five days before the fire. He wanted some photographs – not the explicit ones, just some head and shoulders . . . '

'And?'

'He never showed up.' Lewis looked his age now, deep lines etched into his forehead, the skin rough and open-pored on his sagging cheeks. His confident, finger-snapping breeziness had been utterly punctured. His tongue flicked out to wet his lips. 'Look, I was only destroying them because I know he's dead and I just didn't want to be involved.'

The door opened and Tennison walked in. She'd run a comb through her hair, freshened her make-up, and was, outwardly at least, calm and composed.

'DCI Tennison has just entered the room,' Haskons said into the microphone. Tennison mouthed *Thank you*. Haskons continued. 'Did he say what he wanted the photographs for?'

'I assumed Connie was maybe trying to do some legit modelling work. He . . . well, he was a very good-looking boy. Quite a star.'

'When he came to you on the other occasions, when these' – Haskons tapped the three or four photographs on the table between them – 'these were taken, did he commission them himself or did somebody else?'

'Those,' Lewis said, blinking down at them, 'well, he paid for them. I suppose he was going to try for work on spec.'

'Did you ever see Connie with anybody else?'

'You mean apart from the other models?'

'Yes. Did you ever see Connie with anybody?'

'No,' Lewis said, hardly moving his lips.

Haskons pressed him. 'So he always came to the studio alone?'

'Yes, apart from the other people in the session. He was always alone.'

Haskons looked at Tennison, standing alongside Hebdon. She gave the slightest of nods. It wasn't necessary now to imagine Mark Lewis sweating, it was plainly visible, his dark curly hair clinging damply to his forehead. The handkerchief resembled a length of twisted, grimy rope.

'What about the videos?' Tennison asked, closing the other claw in a pincer attack. 'We know what business you are in, Mr Lewis, we know about the videos. Now, was Connie ever seen with anyone else when he came to your studio? I'm not talking about the models – did anyone ever *bring* him to your studio?'

'No, he was always by himself.' Lewis looked up, his eyes shifting from face to face, an abject appeal. 'He was very beautiful, very special, very professional. It was just business—'

'Mr Lewis.' Tennison wasn't moved by any kind of appeal. 'We know you made videos with underage boys.' Meaning, we can throw the book at you any time we like. 'So did you ever see Connie with anyone?'

'Somebody was with him, once,' Lewis mumbled. He cleared his throat. 'No idea who it was, but he paid for the film. Sat watching . . . I'm going back at least a year, eighteen months.'

'How much did this film cost?' Haskons asked.

Lewis wiped his neck with the grimy rope. 'Two thousand.' He swallowed. 'Pounds.'

'Describe him,' Hebdon cut in sharply.

'Who?'

Hebdon leaned over the desk. 'The man with Connie. Describe him. How old for starters?'

'Oh!' Mark Lewis made a vague, fluttery gesture. 'Well, be about late fifties, maybe older. Tall, grey-haired, grey . . . he was all sort of grey, really, pinstriped suit, smart, had a briefcase . . . '

'How did he pay? Cheque or cash?'

'Cash.' Lewis nodded emphatically. 'He had the cash in the briefcase.'

Tennison bent down to have a quiet word in Haskons's

ear. He leaned to one side and whispered back, 'He waived his right . . .'

'So he's made his call, yes?' Tennison murmured, and was assured by Haskons's nod. Mark Lewis watched them with glazed, slightly moist eyes. He visibly jumped when Hebdon said, 'Did he take part in the video? This grey-haired man?'

'Well . . . not physically.'

'What's that supposed to mean?' Haskons said belligerently.

Lewis stammered, 'He s-said what he wanted, t-told me what he wanted Connie to do.'

'Have we got the video?' Haskons asked him.

'Oh, no – that one never even had a copy made. He took it out of the camera. All the others we made came after. Connie got a bit of a taste for it.'

It was the first direct answer he'd given that Tennison actually believed. Everything else had had to be, quite literally, sweated out of him. She said, 'You got an address for Connie? A phone number?' Mark Lewis shook his head. '*No?*' Tennison said icily, pointing at the tape recorder. 'Would you please answer the question?'

'No, I don't know where he lives,' Lewis said meekly.

'*Lived*, Mr Lewis. Connie is dead. How did you contact him when he was alive?'

Lewis stared dumbly at the table, squeezing the wet rag of a handkerchief. The door was pushed open, and Otley beckoned to Tennison. She went over and had a whispered conversation.

With a tight, icy smile, Haskons said, 'We've a stack of your films starring Connie, and you want us to believe you had no way of contacting him?'

'. . . search warrant . . .'

Lewis stared glassily past Haskons's shoulder, having caught Otley's words. He saw Tennison nod to Otley, who disappeared. She came back in and shut the door of the humid, claustrophobic room as Hebdon leaned over the desk, putting his face close to Lewis's.

'Mark, you're getting in deeper. You've just admitted you filmed Connie eighteen months ago. He was still a minor.'

'I – I didn't know how old he was. He told me he was eighteen!'

Tennison barked at him, 'Mr Lewis, how did you contact Connie?'

Dalton tapped and came in. He wanted a word. With a sigh Tennison followed him into the corridor.

'I think you should have a look at it, it's just a home video.'

'Of Connie?' Dalton nodded. 'Okay, we'll take a break in ten minutes.' She looked into his eyes. 'How you feeling?'

Dalton shrugged it off, waggling his hand with the bandage on it. 'I'm fine, no problem.'

She watched him walk off down the corridor. No question about it, he wasn't fine, far from it, and maybe there was one hell of a problem. She went back in. Lewis was hoarse and ragged, squirming in the chair, his collar, his shirtfront, drenched with sweat.

'I'd leave a message and he'd call me . . . I never knew where he lived, I swear.'

He hadn't much resistance left. It was a token effort. Tennison knew they had just about squeezed him dry. But not quite.

'So, if I, for example, saw one of your films, and wanted to contact somebody in it . . . I'd get in touch with you?'

'Yes.'

'Then what?'

'I'd go around to the advice centre and stick up a note for him.'

'Advice centre, which advice centre?'

'One in Soho, near some old flats.'

'Did you get paid for carrying these messages back and forth?'

Rather late in the day, Mark Lewis decided this was an affront. 'No. No, I did not get paid.'

'You just did it as an act of kindness?' Hebdon said, with only the faintest sarcasm.

'Yes.'

Tennison opened the small top window, and then

opened the larger one. The fresh clean air was delicious. 'Do you know Edward Parker-Jones?' she asked, breathing deeply and turning to him.

'He runs the advice centre.' Lewis nodded. 'But I don't know him. He wouldn't approve, you know ...' His eyebrows, as suspiciously dark as his hair, went up and down. 'Very straight.'

Tennison took a pace nearer and asked quietly, 'Why do you think Colin Jenkins was murdered?'

'I don't know.'

Tennison let the silence hang for a moment. She didn't believe him, and she didn't not believe him. For the time being, the jury was still out.

She moved up close to the table, standing very straight, looking down on him.

'Mr Lewis, you were read your rights, and you said that you did not require any legal representation. You were also granted permission to make a phone call, which you did. I now have to inform you that a warrant has been requested for a search to be carried out at your premises, and you will be held in custody until formal charges are presented.'

She tapped Haskons on the shoulder, who rose, tugging his jacket straight, and together they left the room. Mark Lewis was slumped in the chair, grey-faced, wrung-out, looking sixty-five if he looked a day.

*

Striding along the corridor towards the viewing room, Tennison stabbed the air. 'We want bank statements, address books, phone numbers, fax numbers. We want names of his clients. We want tax payments, VAT payments – we'll throw the lot at that seedy, revolting pervert and do his place over tonight.'

Haskons strode along with her, keeping pace, just. He'd seen her in this mood before, when they'd worked together on a murder case. She was like a woman possessed. She bloody well was possessed, Haskons thought, by whatever demon it was that drove her.

The room was full, the reflected light from the screen showing up the thick wreaths of smoke hanging near the ceiling. The men were enjoying it, laughing uproariously and shouting out lewd remarks. There were high-pitched squeals, effeminate ooohs and aaahhs, as they mimicked the participants in the cheap, tawdry drama that had been shot by shaky hand-held camera in Super VHS PornoScope.

Boys' night out, Tennison thought sourly, standing in the doorway. All they were short of was a bar, and later on a blond striptease act with forty-four-inch tits. Superintendent Halliday was there, she saw, sitting near the front. From this angle she couldn't tell if he was laughing too, or even enjoying it. All in the line of duty.

Some of the men noted her presence, but it didn't inhibit them. Probably gave the whole thing an extra charge, that snooty bitch with the cast-iron drawers watching this filth.

But Tennison wasn't shocked by the images, nor even disgusted. She was simply, and very deeply, saddened by them. That boys and young men should do this to make money was enormously dispiriting; that others should pay to see it, and get pleasure out of watching it, was even worse. She herself felt grubby and demeaned at witnessing this joyless, miserable, pathetic shadow play.

She signalled to Dalton. A general moan went up as he stopped the VCR and a snowstorm filled the screen. The fluorescent lights flickered on. Tennison moved to the front.

'Could just the officers directly concerned in the Colin Jenkins inquiry please remain. Everyone else . . . show's over.'

Chairs scraped as the men filed out. Halliday, staying where he was, crooked a finger. Tennison ground her teeth, hoping it didn't show. She looked attentive.

'I'd keep a record of all these tapes,' Halliday said gravely. He looked at her from under his brows. 'Don't want any to go walkabout.'

Tennison's sober expression matched his. She leaned closer and said confidentially, 'I'd like you to listen to the Mark Lewis interview.'

Halliday nearly smiled and immediately stood up, pleased that his new DCI was inviting a second opinion.

Tennison watched him leave, metaphorically dusting her hands. That's got rid of him.

The team settled down to watch the Connie video. 'What we watchin' then?' asked Haskons as Dalton started the machine and stepped back beside Tennison's chair.

'*Gone With the Wind*, what d'you think, pratt?' came Otley's reply.

They all waited as the screen jumped and buzzed. Tennison looked up and said quietly, 'You know, Brian, if you need to talk, there's always me, or there's a very good counsellor.'

Dalton didn't move, though it seemed, Tennison acutely sensed, as if he was withdrawing tightly into himself. Both his hands were clenched, the bandage on his right hand vivid against the bloodless skin. A muscle twitched in his cheek. He stared straight ahead at the screen, fragmented pictures starting to form.

Tennison turned away as the film proper began.

A desolate, windswept children's playground. Pools of water on the cindery ground. A row of swings, some with broken seats, creaking to and fro on rusted chains. The shaky camera panned to the left, picking up a slight, red-haired figure in a padded red-and-black baseball jacket and sand-coloured chinos. The wind ruffled his curly hair as he sat down on one of the swings and gently rocked. The camera moved in close until the boy's face filled the screen. He had a sweet shy smile. Fringed by long auburn lashes, his brown eyes sparkled. He had a fair complexion and skin soft as a girl's. He giggled, biting his lower red lip with small white teeth.

'Hi! My name is Connie. I am fourteen years old, and . . . '

Again the infectious giggle.

'I'm sorry, I'll start again.' He straightened his face. 'Hi! My name is Connie . . . '

He couldn't keep it up. He covered his mouth. 'This is stupid.' He pointed off camera. 'It's Billy's fault, he keeps on pulling faces at me!'

A cross-eyed Billy appeared, features contorted in a dreadful grimace. It was too much. Connie had broken up, hanging on to the swing, helplessly wagging his head from side to side. Someone's hand whisked Billy out of sight, but it was past saving, Connie had had it.

'Get Billy Matthews brought in,' Tennison said quietly, face set.

The video went off and then started again as they tried for another take. This time a straight-faced Connie, his eyes still moist from laughing, gave it his best shot.

'Hello. My name is Connie' – the same shy, sweet smile filled the screen – 'and I'm fourteen years old . . . '

*

Otley and Hebdon had St Margaret's Crypt, Haskons and Lillie the Bullring, WPCs Kathy Trent and Norma Hastings the underpass next to Waterloo Bridge.

It was a fine night, with a pleasantly mild breeze blowing off the river. The waxing quarter-moon rose up behind the distant towers of Canary Wharf, a dusty orange-red scimitar seen through the haze of the capital.

The chances of finding Billy Matthews were slim. Just one punk kid among the hundreds sleeping out on the streets, dossing down in shop doorways, huddled on the concrete walkways and beneath the brick archways on the South Bank.

Norma hated it. To the drunks and dossers, she and Kathy were two respectable, well-dressed young women, and as such fair game. They got the lot, and had to endure it. The obscene invitations and suggestions, the grimy faces jeering at them from the shadows, the beggars and buskers accosting them at every corner. Down by Cardboard City, at the tea wagon run by two middle-aged women, they came across a gang of kids with a skinny dog on a bit of string. The kids took off as they approached them, scattering in all directions. One of the boys stumbled, and Kathy managed to get near him, a fresh-faced lad with a ragged blond fringe, his face showing signs of a recent beating.

'Do you know Billy Matthews? Have you seen him?'

Fear in his eyes, Alan Thorpe picked himself up and

stumbled off past the cardboard and wood shacks lining the viaduct walls, ducking out of sight in the labyrinth of shantytown.

Kathy looked hopelessly at Norma. They both felt like giving up. Drunken voices sang, argued and swore in the darkness. On a tinny, crackling radio, Frank Sinatra boasted that he'd done it his way. A busker with an out-of-tune guitar sang 'She said, Son, this is the road to hell,' while a reeling drunk clutching a bottle of Thunderbird yelled out in a hoarse voice that boomed and echoed under the viaduct, 'Oh, when the saints ... Oh, when the saints ... Oh, when the saints go marchin' in ...'

Keeping close together, Kathy and Norma moved along the slimy, littered pavements. A head was thrust out on a scrawny neck, its front teeth missing. 'Hello, girls! This way to the National Theatre, have yer tickets ready – pul-ease!' He cackled with insane merriment.

Norma evaded his clutching hand, and bustled on quickly, shuddering. She touched Kathy's arm, having had enough, about to retreat from this underworld of the damned – to hell with Billy Matthews – and there he was, lying against the wall, wrapped in a filthy sack. He was in a terrible state. They weren't even sure, at first, if he was alive or dead.

Kathy felt for his pulse. 'Radio in for an ambulance, Norma!'

Norma came back to herself, fumbling for her radio. She was sick to her stomach. Along the pavement, the busker with the broken guitar was singing her song.

'This ain't no upwardly mobile freeway—
Oh no, this is the road to hell.'

Jessica Smithy didn't give the Sierra Sapphire time to stop before she was out from behind the wheel of the black BMW, switching on the tiny microcassette recorder and holding it concealed in her gloved hand. Carl, her photographer, was a few paces behind as she crossed the quiet tree-lined street, thumbing the auto flash on the Pentax slung around her neck.

Jessica reckoned she deserved this break. She had waited over an hour, since 9.45, listening to *The World Tonight* on Radio 4 and the first five minutes of *Book at Bedtime*. At last she had been rewarded. She flicked the long tail of her Hermès scarf over her shoulder and patted her knitted ski hat down onto her razor-trimmed, slick-backed hair. Tall and athletically slender, she had a sharp, fine-boned face and quick, darting hazel eyes. Intelligent and tenacious, she never let a good story escape her grasp, and she scented that this one was high-yield plutonium.

'Excuse me, Inspector Tennison? Are you Detective Chief Inspector Tennison?'

Tennison locked the door of her car. She turned

warily, eyeing the woman and the bearded man with the camera with deep suspicion.

'I'm Jessica Smithy. I have tried to contact you, I wondered if you could spare me a few minutes . . . ?'

Evidently, Tennison couldn't. Briefcase in hand, she marched around the back of the car to the pavement. They pursued her.

'Can you give me an update on Colin Jenkins?'

Tennison pushed open the wrought-iron gate. Without turning, she said, 'There was a formal press conference yesterday. I have no further comment.' She banged the gate shut and went up the short path to her front door.

'But is his death still being treated as suspicious or accidental?'

Jessica Smithy hovered at the gate as Tennison let herself in.

'Are you heading the investigation?'

The door was firmly closed.

'Shit.' Jessica Smithy kicked the gate viciously and switched off the recorder.

At 10.35 p.m. Billy Matthews was being rushed along a corridor towards the emergency resuscitation section. The red blanket was up to his chin. Eyes closed, a dribble of blood-streaked saliva trailing from his open mouth, his pale peaked face was drenched in sweat. His hands clutched the edge of the blanket, as a child seeks to cuddle up warm in the comfort and security of a favourite fluffy toy.

Trotting alongside, the nurse leaned over him anxiously. Billy opened his eyes, blinking away sweat.

'I'm okay.' He smiled up at her. 'I'm okay. I'm okay.'

Chapter Nine

That bloody woman again! Did she never give up? Tennison had unlocked the door of her car, tossed her briefcase inside, mentally preparing herself to do battle with the early morning gridlock, and there she was – climbing out of a black BMW across the street next to the park railings. The bearded guy with the camera was with her.

'Chief Inspector Tennison!'

Did the damn woman never sleep? Even before Tennison could get in and zoom off, she was hurrying across, the heels of her high brown leather boots clicking, coat flapping around her.

The photographer nipped in and a flashlight went off.

'Hey – what is this?' Tennison demanded angrily. 'What's he taking pictures of me for?'

Jessica Smithy wafted her hand. 'Go back in the car,

Carl.' She gave Tennison a warm friendly smile, all sweetness and light. 'I'm sorry, but I just need to talk to you.' She held up a press card, a passport-size photograph sealed in plastic. Tennison's eyes took this in, and also the pocket recorder partly concealed in Jessica Smithy's other hand.

'Is that on?'

'You're not interested, are you?' Jessica Smithy's face hardened, the smile evaporating like morning mist. 'Why? Because he was homeless? A rent boy? Doesn't he warrant a full investigation?' She was holding up the recorder, quite blatantly. 'You are the officer who brought George Marlow to trial—'

'Is that on?' Tennison repeated, getting riled.

'I'm writing an article on the boy that died in the fire, Colin Jenkins. You see, I met him a couple of times, and my editors really want pictures ... he promised me an exclusive.'

'I'm sorry, we have no pictures of him,' Tennison said, clipped and precise. She was looking at Jessica Smithy with renewed interest.

'They must have taken some when they found him, surely?'

'How often did you meet him?'

'Just a couple of times. I have been very willing to come in to discuss my entire interaction—'

'An exclusive?' Tennison interrupted. Jessica Smithy frowned; the interrogator had suddenly become the interrogated. 'You mean Colin Jenkins was selling his story, yes?' She pointed. 'Is that tape on?'

'He was prepared to name his clients, including a high-ranking police officer,' Jessica Smithy admitted.

Tennison jerked back, bumping into the side of the car. A spasm tautened her stomach muscles. 'Did you record your interview with Colin Jenkins?' she asked, pointing at the recorder.

'Yes, and I'm willing to let you hear the tapes, but I want an exclusive interview with you.'

Tennison had a nasty streak. Jessica Smithy got the brunt of it.

'I want to interview *you*, Miss Smithy.' She thrust her wrist out, glared at her watch. 'You be at my office – with the tapes – at nine o'clock. That's official.'

Jessica Smithy smiled, holding up her hands. 'Hey, I'll be there! I've been trying hard enough to get to you . . .'

Tennison slid behind the wheel.

'Thank you very much, Chief Inspector!'

Tennison said frostily, 'It's Detective Chief Inspector, Miss Smithy,' and slammed the door on her.

DI Ray Hebdon pushed through the black curtain, blinking in the light. 'Nothing in the darkroom.' His expression sagged dejectedly at the sight of the thick albums, several piles of them, on the coffee table. 'We got to go through every one of them?' he asked Brian Dalton.

' 'Fraid so.' Dalton's mouth twisted in his tanned face. 'Sickens me. I don't understand it – I mean, there's thousands of them ...'

'Of what?' Hebdon hoisted one, riffled through the pages.

'Poofters,' said Dalton, with repugnance.

Hebdon kept turning the pages, saying nothing.

The caretaker shuffled in from the passage leading to the studio. Tufts of white hair sprouted from under a greasy flat cap and his baggy cardigan almost reached his knees. The unlit stub of a cigarette was welded permanently into the corner of his mouth.

'You goin' to be much longer? Only I wanna go out. I do the place next door. You want the keys?'

'Need you to stay, sorry,' Dalton said, though he didn't sound it.

'Only the uvver blokes 'ad 'em.' The caretaker sniffed. 'Larst night.'

Hebdon frowned at him. 'Somebody was here last night?'

'Yers ...' The caretaker nodded, waving his hands around in circles. 'Took a whole load of stuff out. Police.'

Hebdon pushed past him to the phone.

Vera's friend with the tight firm buttocks, Red, stood in the sitting room of Mark Lewis's flat, smoking a cigarette in an ebony holder. He wore a silk kimono with purple

dragons and fluffy high-heeled silver slippers. His eyebrows had been shaved off and redrawn with an artist's
flourish, and his lips were glossed a pale pink.

Head back, he blew a graceful plume of smoke into the
perfumed air, watching Haskons rooting through the
drawers of the gilt escritoire. From the bedroom came the
sound of closet doors being opened and banged shut as
Lillie conducted a thorough search.

'If I'd known I was having so many visitors I'd have
waxed my legs,' Red mused, addressing no one in particular.

He swanned across to the long low Habitat sofa and
dinked the cigarette in the frosted lead crystal ashtray. He
sat down, crossed his smooth bare legs, and with a little
sigh began filing his nails.

'You could help us,' Haskons said accusingly. Not yet
eight-fifteen in the morning, and already he was frazzled,
frustrated, and thoroughly pissed off. 'Where's his diary?
His address book?' Red shrugged, shaping his thumbnail
to a point. 'What about his tax forms? VAT forms?'

'I don't know, unless they took it all,' Red said placidly.

Haskons straightened up, flushed. 'Who?'

'They said they were police, and that Mark was being
held in custody. I mean' – his painted eyebrows rose in
two perfect arcs – 'there's not a lot you can say to that.
Nobody even asked me about him, you know.' He gave
a little plaintive sigh. '... Connie, he was a sweet kid. Not

all the time – he was quite an operator – but then, he had the equipment.'

Haskons raised his hand to Lillie, who had appeared from the bedroom, telling him to keep quiet.

'Connie . . .' Red said pensively, propping his chin on two fingers. 'He wanted to be a film star. There's a lot of famous stars that pay out to keep their past secret. That's life. Whatever you do catches up on you.' He gazed down sadly at his feet. 'Tasteless slippers, aren't they?'

The day hadn't started well, and by nine o'clock Tennison was in Halliday's office, spitting mad. Commander Chiswick was there, his portly bulk framed in the window, neat as a bank manager in his blue and white striped shirt and pinstripe suit. Halliday, across the desk from Tennison, was in one of his twitchy moods. But he was determined not to be bulldozed by this harridan.

'Both Mark Lewis's flat and studio cleaned out!' Tennison stormed. 'And supposedly by police officers.'

'I'll look into it,' Halliday said.

'I hope you will, because it stinks.'

'I said I will look into it. But we have to abide by the rules,' Halliday insisted, 'we have to get the warrants issued.'

Tennison rapped her knuckles on his desk. 'There isn't a single piece of paper with his name left on it, let alone any of his clients' names. What's going on?'

Beneath the level of the desk, Halliday's fingers dug deep into the leather armrests. His pale blue eyes bored into hers. 'Chief Inspector, check your transcripts of Mark Lewis's interview. He was allowed to make a phone call. Maybe he arranged for someone to clear his place out, and it had nothing to do with delays in issuing bloody search warrants!'.

'Don't go casting aspersions around – or they'll come down on your head,' Chiswick boomed, his fleshy jowls quivering with indignation. 'We are just as keen to get a result as you are!'

Tennison half-raised her hand in a gesture of apology. She was so fired up, she'd overstepped the mark. What with missing tapes, not-so-subtle warnings, and officers she didn't altogether trust, it was easy to get paranoid around here. Or was she simply paranoid about being paranoid?

Chiswick loomed over her. 'May I remind you that you inferred that an arrest would be imminent!' He had her on the defensive and was taking full advantage of it. 'How much longer do you require four extra officers to assist your inquiries?'

That was rich, Tennison fumed inwardly, when she'd made no such request for extra manpower in the first place. It had been foisted upon her. However, she let it ride.

'I can't put a time on it. You've seen those videos,

there're kids in them . . .' Tennison looked from one to the other. 'I got a breakthrough today, from a journalist. I've not interviewed her yet, but she met the victim, taped Colin Jenkins for an exclusive. He was selling his story, and prepared to name his clients.' She checked the time. 'In fact she should be here now.'

Silence. Both men seemed taken slightly off guard by this. Chiswick cleared his throat loudly.

'What's the journalist's name?'

'Jessica Smithy.'

He rubbed the side of his face, then gave a curt nod, indicating that she was free to go. Tennison went.

Halliday waited. He jumped up. 'Don't cast aspersions! Coming down on whose head?'

Chiswick rounded on him. 'Whose idea was it to bring her here! We've got a bloody loose cannon now, and we're both going to be in a compromising position if it gets out.'

'I warned her off, all right?' Halliday said, low and angry. He pushed his chair aside and stalked over to the window, massaging the back of his neck. 'But now there's this journalist . . . we can't tell her to back off.'

'I know what she said,' Chiswick snapped. He took a breath, trying to calm down and think straight. 'So give her twenty-four hours. If she's not charged Jackson, she's off the case. Get Dalton on this journalist woman.'

Halliday stared at him for a moment. He returned to

his desk, twitching, and picked up the phone and asked for the Squad Room.

There were three butts in the ashtray, ringed with lipstick. Jessica Smithy added a fourth, grinding it down with a vengeance. She looked at her watch, yet again, and let her arms flop down on the table.

'Am I going to be kept waiting much longer? She asked me to be here by nine o'clock. It's already—'

'Chief Inspector Tennison is caught up right now,' DI Hall said, 'but as soon as she's free . . .'

He went back to gazing out of the window, at the tiny patch of blue sky he could just see between the buildings opposite, daydreaming about Lanzarote. Three weeks to go. Roll on.

Tennison switched on the tape recorder and sat down. She gestured to a chair, but instead Otley perched himself on the corner of her desk. She noticed he hadn't shaved this morning, and it crossed her mind that he might be drinking again.

Clicks, mike noises, rustlings, and then Jessica Smithy's voice came out of the twin speakers.

'I'm going to put this on – is that okay? Only I don't have shorthand. This always makes my life easier.'

Cups and saucers rattling, Muzak playing, background noise of traffic. Café? Restaurant? Wine bar?

'Is there any other place I can contact you? I called the advice centre ...'

'I told you not to do that! I said I would contact y*ou*!'

Tennison looked at Otley, who nodded. Connie.

'We got to first agree on what you will pay me.'

'I can't say we will pay you this or that amount of thousands, without first having at least a bit of information.'

'I'll take it elsewhere ...'

Tennison tightened her lips in annoyance as Dalton and Haskons came in. She jabbed the STOP button and glared at Dalton. 'You're late. We've got tapes of Colin Jenkins.' On her feet now, she jerked her thumb to Halliday's wall, and lowered her voice. 'This is to stay with us until I say otherwise. This woman said that Connie was selling his story – that he was going to name a high-ranking police officer.'

Deliberately not looking at Dalton when she said this, nevertheless she saw his reaction to it in the droop of his eyelids, the slight stiffening of his jaw.

Tennison went on, 'And two, a Member of Parliament.' She gave each of them a searching look. 'If a name comes up it stays with us, understood? Because we could be opening up a big can of worms, and we will need hard evidence to back it up.'

The three officers pulled their chairs forward as Tennison restarted the tape.

Dalton was leaning forward, wearing a frown of concentration. 'Sorry I'm late, but when did this come up? Who brought this in?'

Tennison shushed him. Dalton dropped his head, staring down at his injured hand, now heavily bandaged and secured with tape.

The Muzak and traffic noises seemed worse than before. They had to strain to distinguish the voices from the irritating background clutter.

'Just telling me that you have important names isn't good enough. I mean, what if this is all a lie? Just to get money out of my paper?'

'I told you I had names – very important people, high-up people. An MP, a police officer, a . . .'

The three men flicked glances at one another.

'I have to go to my editor, Connie. I have to sell him the story too, you know.'

'I want big money.' Tennison recalled the sweet, shy smile in the video. But this was the hard-faced Connie, the calculating hustler out for everything he could get. '. . . Because if they found out I was doing this, then they'd kill me. There's a guy called Jimmy Jackson, he's real crazy.'

Tennison clenched her fist, looking around triumphantly. Bingo – first name! She craned forward with the others.

'I want at least twenty thousand quid . . .'

The rest was drowned out in scuffling footsteps, a door opening, the sound of traffic suddenly swelling.

Impatiently, Tennison looked at her watch. From her desk drawer she took out a small Panasonic tape recorder, slipped it into the pocket of her dark blue jacket, and stood up.

'Get the dialogue transcribed and see if the tech boys can clear off the background noise,' she instructed Haskons. 'We want names, and as fast as possible.'

She gave Otley the nod to follow her outside. In the corridor she paced, turned, paced again, on a real high. At last they were getting somewhere. It was the best buzz she ever got, when the pieces started coming together. Beat an orgasm hollow.

She stabbed her finger in Otley's chest. 'Get someone to keep tabs on Jackson. If he knew about those tapes, he wasn't looking for Connie because of any money.'

Otley went off at the double. Dalton came out. 'I had to go back in for the blood tests,' he said with an apologetic shrug, and tapped his bandaged hand.

Tennison faced him. 'Yes, I know, and I'm sorry. I didn't mean to sound off at you in there.' She turned to go.

'I'll get the results this week. In the meantime I just have to wait,' Dalton continued as she walked off. '. . . Can I sit in on the Jessica Smithy interview?'

Tennison paused and looked back at him. Her name hadn't been mentioned in there, and yet Dalton knew. He'd asked who brought the tape in, and all the time he knew that too.

What she knew was that somebody was playing silly buggers, for sure. She nodded. Dalton trailed after her.

'I had two meetings with him. We met once on the tenth in Mr Dickies at Covent Garden, and on the fourteenth in the Karaoke K bar.'

'How did he first contact you?'

'He called the office.'

'But how did he know to get to you, specifically?'

'Maybe he reads my column.'

'So – if I called your office at the paper and said I had a hot story, you would drop everything and meet me in the middle of Covent Garden?'

'You get to have a feel for a story, intuition.'

'And you had a feel for this one?'

'I just don't understand your attitude.' Jessica Smithy puffed on her cigarette, eyes rolling at the ceiling. She said tartly, 'Unless you don't want an investigation into Colin Jenkins's death.'

'I'm not sure what you mean,' Tennison said, though she had a pretty good idea.

'But then – if what Connie told me is true, it would make sense.'

'What exactly did he tell you?'

'That one of his clients is a high-ranking officer within the Metropolitan Police Force.'

'He told you that?'

'Yes. That is why I wanted to talk to you. Being a woman ... if there was a cover-up.' Jessica Smithy stared hard at Dalton, his crime being that he was the only male present, and possibly a pederast into the bargain.

'You had two sessions only with Connie, correct? Just two, and both of them taped?'

Jessica Smithy blew a gust of smoke out in a long sigh. 'Yes!'

'Did you make any further tapes?'

'No, I did not,' she stated, enunciating each word separately.

Haskons came in and leaned over to whisper in Tennison's ear. She listened, nodding, and scribbled on a notepad, tore it off and passed it to him. He went out. Watching every detail of this interaction with her restless, darting eyes, Jessica Smithy smoked furiously. Her long pale cheeks were hollowed as she sucked in, held it, suddenly let go.

Tennison wafted the air. 'Have you tried the patches?'

'What?'

'To give up smoking.' Jessica Smithy flicked ash, ignoring her. 'You had only two meetings with Colin Jenkins ... ' She carried on ignoring her. 'And on both these occasions you recorded the entire conversation between you and Colin Jenkins?'

'Yes.' Token answer, bored to tears.

Tennison ploughed steadily, resolutely on. 'You said that

Colin Jenkins first contacted you directly at your office. How did you get in touch with him the second time?'

'I left a message for him at an advice centre. In fact I even went there, it's the one in Soho, and I knew it was a big hangout—'

'What date?' Tennison cut in.

'—for rent boys. It would have been the twelfth of this month at three-fifteen – p.m., not a.m.'

'When you went to the advice centre did you interview any other boy?'

'This is bloody unbelievable,' Jessica Smithy snorted, stubbing out her cigarette in a cloud of ash. 'No, I did not. I didn't interview anybody.'

'Did you speak to anybody?'

'Edward Parker-Jones. He runs the centre.'

'What did you tell him?'

'I didn't *tell* him anything.' She dusted her fingertips. 'I just asked if he knew where I could contact Colin Jenkins.'

'Did he know who you were?'

'Look, I'm a journalist, okay, and I have to sometimes . . . ' She spread her hands.

'Lie?'

Jessica Smithy's lips came together primly. 'No. He presumed I was a social worker and he was very helpful. But somebody must have told him who I was, and he asked me to leave, in fact he got quite abusive. If I'd wanted to interview any of the kids there he wouldn't have let me.'

'So Mr Parker-Jones knew you, a journalist, were looking for Colin Jenkins?'

'*YES!*' Jessica Smithy might have been trying to get through to an imbecile. 'So now what?' She leaned forward eagerly, eyes alight. 'Is he a suspect?'

Tennison was distracted by movement in the small square window of the door. Haskons was talking to someone, and a moment later she saw Halliday's baby blues peering inquisitively in. Hell and damnation. She might have known he'd be lurking about, nose twitching, quick as a shithouse rat.

'Why aren't you trying to find out which MP or which police officer used him?' Jessica Smithy said angrily. 'Maybe even killed him! He was murdered, wasn't he?'

Tennison regarded her calmly. 'Who else did you speak to at the centre? Another boy maybe?'

'I've told you,' Jessica Smithy said wearily. 'I didn't speak to anyone, because Parker-Jones wouldn't allow me to. He asked me to leave ...'

Haskons was beckoning. He pushed open the door as Tennison went across. They stood together in the doorway, having a murmured conversation. Glaring at them, Jessica Smithy rose, snatching at her shoulder bag, slinging it on. Tennison leaned in.

'Please remain seated, Miss Smithy.'

Jessica Smithy sat down again, drumming her fingers on the table. She opened the cigarette packet, found it empty, and crushed it and tossed it away. Tennison came in and collected her things. Haskons sat down in Tennison's vacated chair.

Thinking she was free to leave, Jessica Smithy got up again, and to her intense annoyance was waved down again. She sat there fuming, fists clenched on the table.

'One more thing,' Tennison said. 'How much did you pay Colin Jenkins for the tapes?'

'I didn't,' Jessica Smithy replied, a shade too quickly. 'That's why I was looking for him. I'd been given some money by my editor.'

'How much?'

She hesitated. 'Few hundred. But I don't see that is of any concern of yours.'

'Few hundred?' Jessica Smithy nodded, and then nearly jumped out of her skin when Tennison thrust her head forward and barked, 'Exactly how much, Miss Smithy? How much were you going to give Colin Jenkins, Miss Smithy? I can call your editor.'

'Five hundred . . . '

Tennison leaned nearer, intimidatingly close. Her voice sank to a lethal whisper. 'Did you meet Colin Jenkins and give him the five hundred pounds?'

'I—' She nearly blurted something, and checked herself. 'No, I did not.'

Tennison looked her straight in the eye. Jessica Smithy turned away. First time she'd been caught out. Tennison knew it, and so did Jessica Smithy.

Haskons said formally, 'We will, Miss Smithy, be retaining the tapes you made of your two meetings with Colin Jenkins, as evidence. You will be asked to sign a legal document which bars you, and your paper, from using any information—'

Jessica Smithy tried to interrupt.

'—appertaining to the said tapes.'

Jessica Smithy was wild eyed and furious. 'What? This is crazy! You can't stop me from printing.'

Tennison opened the door. 'We just did,' she said, going out.

'You tell her—' Jessica Smithy pointed a trembling finger after Tennison, turning her furious face to Haskons and Dalton. 'When my story gets out, she won't want it in any scrapbook!'

Otley was outside, propped up in his usual indolent slouch, hands stuffed in his pockets. He nodded towards the interview room.

'Anything?'

'Yes.' Tennison indicated they should move on, and they walked along together. 'Parker-Jones knew Jessica Smithy was a journalist, knew she was looking for Connie.' Tennison threw a backward glance. 'She's also lying. I think she met Connie. She had five hundred quid, same amount found on his body. I think she paid Connie.'

'Maybe I should run a check on Parker-Jones's credentials,' Otley suggested.

'I already have. Mallory, Chicago University don't exist, and the rest are a load of cobblers.' She gave Otley a big smile. 'I'm getting closer, we've got a motive!'

'For Jackson?' Dalton said, right behind her.

Tennison looked around quickly, not realizing he had been following. She nodded. 'Until I get back, keep the pressure on breaking those kids' alibis,' she told the two of them.

'You want me to come with you?' Dalton asked.

'What, to my doctor's?' Tennison grinned and set off. She halted. 'Oh, one more thing. Halliday wants the transcripts of the Smithy tapes.' She narrowed her eyes at Otley. 'But nobody gets them before me, understood?'

And then she was striding off, a jaunty spring in her step.

Dr Gordon said, 'I'll make an appointment for you to have a laboratory sensitive test, and then we'll get the beta sub-unit hormone measured.' He completed the note in her medical records and looked up and smiled. 'All very advanced technology now!'

'But are you positive?' Tennison said, fastening the top button of her blouse.

'I think so,' Dr Gordon said, smiling. 'You're pregnant – just!'

Tennison needed the edge of the desk to support herself.

She gulped hard. She couldn't believe it. This wasn't happening.

Things like this never happened to her. Then she realized they did, and had, and she started to smile.

Chapter Ten

One hour later, Tennison was back in the thick of it. On the return journey she did something she'd never done before. She bought a pound of seedless white grapes and ate them at one go, sitting in her car in the underground car park of the Soho police station. It didn't occur to her till afterwards that she'd always associated grapes with illness and convalescence. But she wasn't ill – she was pregnant! She knew of the hormone cocktail her glands were even at this moment manufacturing, and of the cravings it gave rise to. But so soon? Was her body trying to tell her something? Or was her mind so shell-shocked that it had flipped a circuit and caused her to wolf down a pound of grapes in secret – some kind of bizarre Freudian ritual? Puzzling.

She went directly to the Squad Room, where Haskons gave her the first news, which wasn't good. They'd drawn a blank on the Jessica Smithy tapes. Haskons had listened to the cleaned-up version over headphones and no further names were mentioned.

Tennison felt frustrated. She had really believed, hoped, that this was going to be the breakthrough. It was one step forward, two steps back. As per bloody usual with police work.

She was with Dalton at the board, getting an update on Operation Contract, when Otley arrived. He didn't come over, but instead gave her a private look. Get over here and don't bring Dalton.

'This just came through.' Otley was holding a thick bunch of faxes. He moved around so that his back was to the board. 'I've been doing a bit of digging after a tip-off . . . 1979. A Mr Edward Parker was accused of molesting a boy in his care when he ran the Harrow Home for kids, Manchester. Case dismissed for lack of evidence.' Otley plucked out another sheet. 'Anthony Field. 1983. Indecent assault on a minor. Case dismissed. Same Mr Edward Parker again, this time running the Calloway Centre in Cardiff, another home for kids.' Next sheet. 'Jason Baldwyn . . .'

Tennison held up her hand. She glanced around. 'Are you saying what I think you are, that this Parker . . .'

Otley nodded, pinching his nostrils. 'Could be Parker-Jones. I've got the addresses of both kids. I can be up in Manchester and back by tonight.'

'Manchester?'

'Cross over to Cardiff – be nice to have something on Parker-Jones, and if I can get some dirt on him . . . !' His eyes gleamed.

'I'll do it,' Tennison said. 'I'll go.'

'What? You go?' Otley was choked. 'I'd have thought you'd want to be here.'

'No, it'll give me a chance to talk to Dalton.' Tennison was already moving off, oblivious to Otley's glare. She called the room to attention. 'Can I have a word!'

She waited at the board for the team to gather around.

'I don't bloody believe it,' Otley said bitterly, as Hebdon and Lillie joined him. 'I do all the leg work and she gets the day away.'

'Okay, quiet down. I didn't have time this morning to have a briefing, so let's do it now, and crack on. I want us to keep on those kids. Jackson only needed ten minutes from that centre to Vernon Reynolds's flat.' She looked to Kathy. 'Have we got a tail on him?'

'No, we haven't found him yet.'

'Brilliant.' Tennison smacked her fist into her palm. 'Go back to his hunting ground, the stations, that's where you picked him up the last time.' Somebody was mumbling, but she carried on. 'We want to break down these alibis. We now have a strong motive for Connie's murder . . . ' Her eyes raked over them. 'And we all know it isn't robbery.'

Slouched against his desk, head bowed, Otley was muttering to DI Hall, 'I checked out his credentials. Now I got not one but two possible child abuse cases against him.'

Hall frowned, not a clue what the Skipper was nattering on about. But Tennison, senses like needles, had caught some of it.

'What was that, Bill?'

Otley scratched his armpit, eyes shifting away. He shrugged. 'I was just saying, pity we got nothin' off the Smithy tapes.'

'They're useless,' Haskons broke in. 'Connie never named anyone! Apart from Jackson, just some clubs where he met his clients.'

'No addresses yet,' Lillie said, reading from a sheet of paper, 'but clubs are: Bowery Roof, Lola's, Judy's, and somethin' that sounded like "Puddles".'

'"Poodles",' Ray Hebdon said. 'It's called Poodles. The last two are gay bars, but the Bowery Roof Top is pretty exclusive. Lots of drag acts, transexuals, transvestites, but most members are homosexuals – city types, professionals, not the usual low-life punters.'

Grinning broadly, Lillie gave him a dig. 'You're pretty well informed, aren't you? I've only just got 'em.'

'I'm a member,' Hebdon said quietly.

Lillie's loud laugh faltered and dwindled into the general dead silence of the room.

Tennison said, 'Ray, are you joking? Because it isn't funny.'

Hebdon didn't seem to think so either. 'I know it isn't,' he said, his face quite serious, composed. 'That's why I thought it was about time I came clean.' He spread his arms, eyes wide and frank, and looked around. 'I'm gay!'

Tennison sipped her coffee. She put the cup down, shaking her head, more in sorrow than in anger. 'You took your time in telling us! It's your private business, Ray, but considering the—'

'I'll leave,' Hebdon said.

'Let me finish, will you?' Tennison leaned her elbows on the desk. She was trying to assimilate this revelation. She also had a vague, as yet unformed notion that something positive might come of it. 'What I was going to say was that it was a pity you didn't have the confidence to tell us sooner.'

'Chief Inspector, I have never hidden what I am. Most of us don't go with underage kids.'

'I know.'

'I feel as repulsed as anyone on the team,' Hebdon said with feeling, 'but I do know the gay scene. I only proffered the information because it might be of some use.'

Tennison nodded. It had never crossed her mind that he might be gay, but now that she knew he was, she thought she could detect certain telltale signs. He grew his dark, rather unkempt hair long, over his collar. He seemed edgy at times, and was prone to blinking nervously. He didn't mince, yet he was light on his feet, his movements quick and alert . . .

All this was bullshit of course, and well she knew it. These weren't telltale signs at all, merely her fanciful imagination. Label anyone gay, and you'd soon invent the evidence to support it. Ray Hebdon's characteristics were those of a human being, nothing more, nothing less.

Put that aside and forget it. Down to business.

'So, which one of these clubs would be likely to be used by, say—'

'Judges, MPs, barristers, solicitors, lawyers . . . top brass?'

'Police officers!'

'The Bowery,' Hebdon said at once.

'You well known at the Bowery?'

'No. It's very expensive. I've only been twice.' He pointed his finger at her. 'But I do know one thing . . . asking questions with that lot in tow!' He jerked his head to indicate the rest of the team. 'One, they'd never get past the door. Two, word would leak, you'd never get to the top bracket, let alone get them to talk to you.'

'What about access to their membership lists?'

'No way. Most of them use false names, or coded names, even though what they're doing is perfectly legal. But if they are going with underage kids, it ups the ante even further on cloaking their identity. I mean, they'll really have to protect themselves. So who they are would be very hush-hush. One hint of a leak and they'd close ranks.' Hebdon's sober expression suddenly cracked in a smile. 'Unless we get the lads dragged up – get in that way – nobody pays any attention to them.'

Tennison smiled with him. 'I'd pay money to see that!'

Superintendent Halliday came in, wanting a private word. He had the Jessica Smithy transcripts in his hand. Hebdon got up to leave.

'Go and get some lunch,' Tennison said, and glanced at her watch. 'If you see Inspector Dalton, tell him to get his skates on, we've got a train to catch.'

He went out and Halliday closed the door. He waved the transcripts, looking like the cat that ate the cream. 'Only one name off the Smithy tapes, but it's your man. It's Jackson.'

'Yes, I know. Lets you off the hook then, doesn't it?' Tennison said glibly. She saw Halliday flush, and got in quick. 'Just a joke . . .'

Halliday sat down, adjusting the knife-edge crease in his trousers, trying to appear mollified when actually he wasn't. Damn woman was too clever for her own good. A loose cannon, Chiswick had called her. More like a loose bloody tank battalion.

Tennison was anxious to have her say before he did.

'This might not be the right time, Jack, but it has to be

obvious to you that this case is opening up and treading right on Operation Contract's heels. It is my honest opinion that we should cut our losses ... Concentrate solely on the murder investigation.' She met his stare with a laser beam of her own. 'Because the information I am getting goes much deeper than a cleanup of the street kids.' She spelt it out. 'I think Connie was murdered to silence him, because he was about to name the men involved in a paedophile circle.'

'And you think Parker-Jones is involved?' Halliday said after a moment, probing.

Tennison tried to shrug this off. 'He is being very cooperative and very helpful,' she said carefully. It sounded weak to her, but she hoped it convinced him. 'I don't have a shred of evidence to link him to any paedophile circle, but the advice centre, along with a number of other venues—'

'What about Jackson?' Halliday insisted. He had the feeling he was being bamboozled, and he wanted to keep it neat and simple.

'I still think he killed Colin Jenkins, but ...'

'But?' Halliday said sharply.

Tennison dropped her eyes. 'Nothing.'

'You'd better reel in Jackson then.' He wasn't asking, he was telling. He went to the door. 'You've a very impressive career. Don't blow it. Charge Jackson, bury everything else.'

When he'd gone she sat thinking for a while. Why was her career in danger of being ruined if she didn't nail Jackson, and what else lay buried at the bottom of this crock of shit? She could have cheerfully murdered for a cigarette.

Haskons unzipped his pants and breathed out a sigh of relief. He looked at Otley, two stalls along. 'You've not said anything, Bill. What d'you think?'

'About him being an iron? Doesn't worry me.' Otley gazed with hooded eyes at the ceramic wall. 'Iron' was Cockney rhyming slang: iron hoof = poof. 'We had one at Southampton Row, he didn't last long.'

He zipped up and turned away. Ray Hebdon was standing by the washbasins. Otley walked straight past, ignoring him, and went out. Haskons finished, and made a studious effort at looking everywhere but at Hebdon. He fastened his jacket, giving a little furtive smile, and went to the door. 'See you in the pub ...'

Hebdon washed his hands and wiped his face with his wet hands. In the mirror he saw Dalton come in.

'Is it true?'

Impatiently, Hebdon propped both arms against the basin. 'What, that I'm gay?'

He sighed heavily and went to dry his face on the towel.

'I just don't believe in this day and age, everybody

making such a big deal of it.' He returned to the mirror, and started combing his hair. Dalton hadn't moved. His face bore a sullen expression.

'What you looking at me like that for?' Hebdon asked.

'I just don't understand. I thought I knew you.'

'You do,' Hebdon said.

'Why?' Dalton was angry and mystified. 'Ray ... why?'

'Why? Are you asking me why I'm gay? Because that's the way I am. I've always been.'

'Queer?' Dalton said, blinking painfully as if recovering from a kick in the stomach.

Hebdon rammed his comb into his top pocket. 'Yes! Queer, poofter, woofter, screamer, screecher – yes, they're all me. I'm gay, I don't apologize for it, I just don't feel I need to broadcast it – for obvious reasons.' He raised his hands, clenching and unclenching his fists helplessly. 'Look at you! The other two will come out with infantile, puerile cracks from now on ... '

'I don't believe it,' Dalton said, squinting at him. 'Do you live with a bloke?'

'Do you?'

Dalton exploded. 'Of course I bloody don't!'

'What difference does it make? My private life is just that. I don't poke my nose into yours, what gives you the right to ... '

Dalton grabbed him by the lapels and shook him.

'Because I work with you!'

Hebdon dragged himself free. He pulled his jacket straight, breathing hard. 'I was gay when we first met, did I start touching you up? Propositioning you? Did I? I respect you, why don't you fucking respect me? Now back off!'

He stormed to the door, but then stopped. When he turned he was still white in the face, but he was smiling.

'I was a great rugby player, what I got away with in the scrum . . . ' He held up his hands. 'Just joking! Look, Brian, I know you are probably going through it, I'm referring to the bite, okay? I just want you to know that if you need to talk to someone, a lot of my friends have been tested and—'

'Piss off.'

Dalton barged past him. Left alone, Hebdon stared at his own reflection, and the look on his face was transformed as the bravado crumpled.

15:00. Manchester Piccadilly. Platform 6.

Tennison and Dalton ran across the concourse of Euston Station and reached the barrier of Platform 6 just as the train was pulling out.

'Shit!' Tennison stood there, panting and fuming. She'd never been able to figure out how British Rail got their trains to leave dead on time and arrive late.

'What time is the next one?'

'An hour's wait,' Dalton said, looking at the timetable.

'Okay, go and ask the station master if we can use the Pullman lounge. Might as well wait in comfort.'

'What's that?'

Tennison said with tart irritation, 'It's the lounge for first-class ticket holders. Go on, I'll meet you there.'

On the main concourse she glanced up at the departures board to make sure of the next train. 16:00. Manchester Piccadilly. Platform 5. No chance of missing that one.

Passing behind her, not twenty feet away, Jimmy Jackson was carrying a plastic holdall belonging to a young girl of about twelve years of age. She had pale blond hair, pulled back into a ponytail, and the healthy look and ruddy cheeks of someone brought up in the country. She seemed nervous and lost, gazing around at the milling crowds, her first time in the big city.

'So where you from?' Jackson asked, a broad friendly grin plastered across his face.

'Near Manchester.'

Jackson was hugely surprised. 'Well, there's a coincidence!'

Tennison hoisted her briefcase and turned, heading towards the Pullman lounge.

'You from there?' the girl asked him.

'No, but I was waiting for a mate, he must have missed the train.' Jackson pointed to the sign: Passenger Car Park. 'You want a lift?'

The girl hesitated for a second, and then she nodded.

Reaching the glass-fronted entrance to the Pullman lounge, Tennison dumped her briefcase and looked around for Dalton. She couldn't see him, but then she froze. She stood on tiptoe. Jackson and a girl. Walking towards the steps leading down to the underground car park. Lugging her briefcase, Tennison weaved in and out through the crowd, fumbling for her portable phone. Jackson and the girl were turning the corner at the bottom of the steps as she reached the top. She set off down.

Returning from the station master's office, Dalton got the barest glimpse of Tennison's blond head as she disappeared down the steps. He legged it after her.

The girl was giggling at Jackson's chat-up line, Tennison saw, which must be good, whatever it was. She watched from a distance, peeking around a concrete pillar, and saw him take out a bunch of keys and approach a car. He looked up, and Tennison slid out of sight. She couldn't see Dalton, who was scuttling between the parked cars, ducking and diving to get a look at the number plate.

Tennison cupped her hand around the mouthpiece. 'It's a dark blue Mercedes, old four-door saloon. I'll get you the number ... but is there a car in the area? Suspect is James Jackson. Do not apprehend, just tail to destination.'

Dalton returned, panting slightly, and eased in beside

her. He had the number written on the back of his hand. Tennison passed him the phone. 'I told them to look for him at the station exit.'

Over the speakers, booming in waves through the concrete cavern, came an announcement.

'THE TRAIN ON PLATFORM FIVE IS THE MANCHESTER PULLMAN EXPRESS. WE ARE SORRY TO INFORM YOU THAT THERE WILL BE NO BUFFET CAR FACILITIES ON THE FOUR O'CLOCK TRAIN TO MANCHESTER DUE TO STAFF SHORTAGES. BRITISH RAIL APOLOGIZE FOR ANY INCONVENIENCE ...'

At the wheel, Hall kept a sharp lookout on his side of the street while Otley did the same on his. They were somewhere north of Euston – Camden Town, Chalk Farm – Hall wasn't sure where exactly; he was lost in the maze of streets. He pulled into the kerb and stopped behind a rusting Skoda with both rear tyres flat to the ground. The dark blue Mercedes was parked on the opposite side of the street. Otley pushed his nose up to the windshield to get a good look at the house.

It was four storeys with cracked and peeling stucco showing red brick underneath. The windows that weren't boarded up were swathed in thick dark curtains. The entrance porch was supported by one stone pillar, the other a crumbling stump. On the surviving one, the numerals '22' could just be made out in faded black paint.

Hall reached for the radio handset. 'See if we can get more info on the house.'

A light went on in one of the third-floor windows, visible through a chink in the curtains. 'He's still in there,' Otley said.

Hall was patched through. 'Kathy? You got anything on the Langley house yet?'

Seated at the computer in the Squad Room, the phone cradled in her shoulder, Kathy was scrolling through column after column of names and addresses.

'Getting nothing from the polling lists ...'

'Come on, come on,' Hall's impatient voice said in her ear.

'I'm going as fast as I can. I'll call, soon as I have anything.'

She hung up and kept searching. Norma came in with two plastic cups of coffee. She put one in front of Kathy and sat down at her own desk. 'Where's her Ladyship today?'

'Up north – doing what, I do not know!' Kathy took a sip and grimaced at the taste. 'But she took Dalton with her.'

'Did he get cleared – his hand?' Norma said, shaking her head and tutting loudly. She smacked herself on the forehead. 'Shit – Billy Matthews. Guv wants him requestioned about the Connie video.' She found the number and dialled. 'It's all very well her saying arrest him, but he had four court appearances last year alone. They didn't want to take him, you know, said he'd only just been in a few days before—'

She broke off. 'Charing Cross Hospital, emergency ward.' She waited for the connection. 'What was that nurse's name at the hospital?' she asked Kathy.

'Mary Steadman.' Kathy blinked her eyes at the screen. 'Shit, I still got nothing on this Jackson address. It isn't listed under the name Jackson.' She went down the lists, mumbling, 'Twenty-two, Langley Road ... Islington, Kentish Town, Camden ...'

Norma got through to Mary Steadman. 'This is WPC Norma Hastings. I brought in a Billy Matthews ... yes.'

Kathy let out a whoop. 'Got it – property owned by an Edward Jones. Two sitting tenants. First floor, Maureen Fuller, and basement, Abdul unpronounceable. It's flatlets.' Beaming, she reached for the phone.

Norma banged the phone down. She looked sick.

'Billy Matthews discharged himself an hour after we left him there!'

At six-twenty that evening Tennison was sitting in the back of a patrol car outside a pebble-dashed late-Victorian house with bay windows in one of the posher areas of Salford, trying without much success to get through to DI Hall on her portable. She'd had him once, and then he'd gone, lost in a blizzard of static.

She wound the window down and spoke to the uniformed driver, standing on the pavement. 'Is there any way I can get my batteries recharged?'

The PC stared at her.

'For my portable phone, officer. What did you think I was referring to? A vibrator?'

Inspector Dalton was speaking to Mrs Field on the doorstep, a white-haired woman in her sixties, casually yet smartly dressed in a cardigan and pleated skirt, a single string of pearls around her neck, several gold rings on her fingers. She smiled diffidently and shook her head. Dalton came down the garden path and put his head in the window.

'Ma'am?'

'Just a minute,' Tennison said shortly, hearing Hall's scratchy voice coming from Mars. No food on the train, nothing to drink, and no bloody batteries. 'Hello? Can you hear me? Hello? Ruddy phone.' She gave it a shake. 'Hello . . . ? Listen, you can gain entry even on the suspicion that a minor is being held there.'

Face screwed up, she was straining to hear.

'*I'm* reporting it, okay? She's already been with him for more than four hours. God only knows what's happened to her . . . *Hello?*'

Dead and gone. She pushed the aerial in.

'Er, his mother's home,' Dalton said, nodding to the white-haired woman, 'but she said he was working late . . . can we come back?'

The door hit Dalton's leg as Tennison thrust it open.

'Sorry, and no we can't come back,' she said, getting out.

As soon as they stepped inside the front door it was clear that Anthony Field's mother was very houseproud. The smell of furniture polish was like incense. The living room was obsessively neat, not a speck of dust anywhere, and bedecked with shining brass ornaments. It was almost a sacrilege to walk upon the thick Axminster carpet.

'Would you like a cup of tea?' Mrs Field had a rather refined voice, and Tennison suspected she was the kind of woman who thought herself a cut above her neighbours, even if she wasn't.

Tennison nodded and smiled. 'That would be really nice.'

As Mrs Field went out there was a creak from the room above. Tennison folded her raincoat and placed it on a chair, not wishing to wreck the symmetry. She sat down and crossed her legs. Another creak from above. She looked up at the ceiling.

'Come on down, Anthony. There's a good boy . . . '

Dalton's eyebrows shot up. 'Is he in?' Tennison nodded. 'How do you know?'

'Because I saw him at the window.'

A few minutes later Mrs Field returned with a tray of tea things, which she set down on a low table that had a nest of smaller tables underneath. She fussed about, sorting out cups and saucers. 'It isn't about the bank, is it? Only Anthony is sure to be made assistant manager.'

Just then, the would-be assistant manager himself breezed in. He was a tall, lithe young man, clean-cut and good-looking, in a V-neck lemon sweater and natty bow tie. Not as affected as his mother, he spoke fast, running thoughts and sentences into each other.

'Sorry to keep you waiting, but I only just got in. Is the kettle on, Ma? Well, when it whistles I'll hear it – don't miss your programme.'

His mother patted his arm, gave him an adoring smile, and went out.

'Sorry, I got cold feet as you were late,' Anthony said brightly, standing in front of the gas fire, briskly rubbing his hands. He grinned boyishly. 'I didn't expect you to arrive in a patrol car, bit embarrassing ...' He darted to the door as the kettle whistled.

'Excuse me.'

Dalton's gaze shifted sideways to Tennison. He said out of the corner of his mouth, 'Another one, isn't he? Gay?' Tennison looked away, expressionless.

Jackson stood halfway down the staircase, one hand gripping the banister, the other pressed flat against the wall, barring their way. Otley and Hall stared up at him from the second-floor landing.

The entire place reeked as if ten tomcats had saturated

the threadbare carpets. Black plastic bags, ripped open, spilled rubbish and putrefied food over the floor.

Otley put one foot on the bottom step. 'We don't need a warrant, we have reason to believe you are holding a minor. You were seen leaving Euston Station accompanied.'

The anaemic glow from the bare dusty bulb made a yellowy snarling mask of Jackson's face.

'Bullshit. I know my rights. Now – piss off.' He aimed his finger at Otley, right between the eyes. 'You got no warrant. You are on private property, and I have a right as a citizen to defend my property!'

Hall moved along the murky passage and knocked on a door. He tried the handle. Locks, bolts and catches were undone, and a frail elderly woman peered around the edge, grey hair trailing over her bleary eyes.

'Are you Mrs Maureen Fuller?'

Jackson let out a cackle. 'Hey, is that the juvenile I'm supposed to have prisoner?' he jeered at them.

Otley moved up another step. He shouted to the floor above.

'HELLO? IS THERE ANYONE UP THERE? THIS IS THE POLICE.'

Jackson came down, fist raised. Otley ducked under his arm and scrambled up the stairs. As Jackson turned to grab at him, Hall went up fast, grappling with him, and got an elbow in the teeth. Stunned, he fell back against

216

the banister. Jackson dragged him down to the landing, twisted his elbow behind him in an arm lock, and butted Hall's head into the wall. He yelled up at Otley.

'You want me to break his arm? Now get the fuck out of here!'

Otley started to come down, very slowly. 'Jimmy, this is crazy . . . we just want to see the girl. Just let us see she's okay.'

A shadowy figure appeared on the landing above.

'She's up here,' Vera Reynolds said.

Jackson's eyes glittered. His fleshy lips drew back against his teeth. 'You're dead, Vera,' he said, icy calm. Savagely, he swung Hall around and pushed him into the banister post and charged down the stairs, his thudding boots making the house shake.

Anthony had made the tea. Tennison and Dalton drank, both watching the slender young man standing at the glass-fronted bureau full of china figurines and cut glass knick-knacks. He picked up a black-and-white photograph in a gilt frame from several on top of the bureau and showed them.

'This was my dad, my little sister. They were killed in a car crash when I was five. After that, Mother . . . ' He looked to the closed door. 'She had a mental breakdown. That's why I was sent to the home.'

He spoke without any emotion whatsoever.

Tennison said carefully, 'Can you tell me about the court case, Anthony? I know how difficult it is.'

'Really?' He stared at the photograph.

'I need to know about the man who ran the home, Anthony. You see, I believe that the man who assaulted you is still . . .'

She hesitated, trying to choose her words.

'At it?' Anthony said. He replaced the photograph and turned towards them, drawing in a deep breath. 'His name was Edward Parker, and my case never even got to court.'

Chapter Eleven

Otley sat on the edge of the narrow bed, his hand resting gently on the shaking mound under the smelly grey blanket. There were three other beds crammed into the small back room. A teddy bear with only one arm, the stuffing sprouting out, lay on one of them. Otley got another blanket and pressed it around Billy Matthews's shivering little body. The boy was burning up with fever. His wet face was buried in the grimy pillow, spiky hair sticking up over the blanket.

'I'm okay, I'm okay, I'm okay . . . ' It went on and on, a meaningless dirge. He whimpered suddenly – 'Don't leave me on me own. Please . . . please.'

'Billy?' Otley said, patting the blanket. 'Billy? I'll stay with you.'

Hall appeared in the doorway. 'I called an ambulance.

The other kids are being taken in now.' He looked along the passage. 'And Vera asked if she can go.'

Billy's hand crept out and fastened tightly around Otley's fingers. His head came up, eyes drugged and filled with a vacant terror. He wouldn't let go of Otley. 'Don't leave me ...'

Vera came in. She looked dowdy and defeated. There was a deadness in her eyes, as if nothing mattered anymore and never would again.

'I'm doing the club tonight, can I go? Doin' the cabaret.'

She looked at Billy, hanging on to Otley like grim death, and slowly shook her head. 'You won't get any sense out of him, he'd tell you anything just to stay here.' In a flat, weary voice she started to sing, '"Life is a cabaret, my friend ... come to the cabaret."'

'I'm okay, I'm okay,' Billy said, staring at nothing. 'Everythin' okay.'

Vera sighed drably. 'No, you're not, Billy love. You're not okay at all. Can I go?' she asked Otley, who nodded.

Vera went along the passage and down the stairs, high heels clacking. Otley put his arm around the shaking mound of grey blanket, hugging it. He turned his head to Hall. 'Where's the bloody ambulance?'

'They said there was about a fifteen-minute delay.'

'I'm okay, I'm okay,' Billy insisted in a voice so thin it was barely a mouse's squeak. 'I'm okay.'

It took twenty-five, not fifteen, minutes for the ambulance to arrive. They put Billy Matthews inside and off it went, lights flashing. Otley walked over to Hall, who was leaning against the bonnet of their car. It was growing dark, and there were spits of rain in the air.

'I'm just going for a walk,' Otley said. He patted Hall on the shoulder and carried on walking.

'Jackson's car's gone.'

'He won't get far.' Otley turned on the pavement. 'Vera's at the Bowery Club, isn't she?' His eyes were narrowed slits in his craggy, gaunt face. 'Get somebody watching the place.'

Hall watched him amble off in his unmistakable round-shouldered slouch, hands stuffed in his raincoat pockets. Was he going to get pissed out of his skull? He'd shown no emotion over Billy Matthews, but Hall wouldn't have been surprised if the Skipper got rat-arsed.

'It hurt, and I screamed, but he put his hand over my mouth. I bit him once, really bit his hand, but it didn't make any difference. I was very small for my age, and he had a special name for me. He said that when he used that special name it was a code, that was when he wanted me to go to his room.'

Sitting very straight in the armchair, feet together, knees pressed tight, Anthony Field recounted his experience at the children's home. His tone never varied,

never betrayed any feeling; it was a nightmare, permanently fixed in his head, endlessly repeating itself, that
had numbed him into this mechanical retelling. He
was pale, however, and his long thin fingers were never
still.

Tennison prompted him after a moment's painful
silence.

'How long did this abuse go on for? Before you told
anyone?'

'Three years. There was no one to tell.' Anthony's
dark-lashed eyes were downcast. He had shapely dark eyebrows, his brown hair brushed and neatly parted in the
approved bank employee manner.

'He always said that if I told anyone, I would have to
eat my own faeces. I got a letter from my mother, she said
she was much better, so I ran away.' He blinked once or
twice at the carpet. 'I went to the police station, they
called in a probation officer. A woman. I had to tell
her . . . it was very embarrassing.'

Tennison again waited. 'How old were you then?'

'Eight, nearly nine. They took my statements, and then
a plainclothes police officer came in to question me.'

His hands clasped, released, clasped, released. He was
leaning forward slightly, his body hunching tighter and
tighter.

Tennison waited. Smoothing her knees, she said quietly, 'I really appreciate you telling me this, Anthony.' And

quieter still, 'Can you go on?' When he nodded, she said, 'Thank you very much.'

Anthony breathed in a long quivery breath.

'This police officer. I never even knew his name. He asked me if I knew what happened to boys that – that—' His hands were jerking, writhing in his lap. 'That tell lies. I said I was not telling lies.' His voice went abruptly harsh. '*Well-he-said-We-will-soon-know.* And he undid my pants. And he did it to me. He said that if I told anyone I would go to prison.' Anthony stared at the carpet, his face drained of all colour. 'Hard to tell what would be worse, eating your own shit or going to prison.'

'This police officer penetrated you?' Tennison said. He nodded, head bowed. 'At the station?' He nodded. 'Was anyone present?'

Anthony shook his head. He shuddered. He was close to breaking. Tennison was calculating how much more he could take, and praying to God she hadn't underestimated.

'So I said I was – that I had been telling lies. Case dismissed. And they sent me back to the home. I was there for another two years. Then Mother collected me.'

'After you left, you didn't tell anyone?'

Anthony straightened up and looked at her. He shook his head.

'Can I ask you why not?'

'My aunt told me that Mother was still in a very nervous state, so how could I tell her? I love my mother very much. I always felt that if I upset her in any way, I ran the risk of being sent back. So I never told anyone, and . . . ' He gave a listless shrug. 'I just got on with my life.'

'I am sorry to make you remember, Anthony,' Tennison said, feeling the pain with him. But he looked at her as if she'd said something incredibly stupid. He stood up, and almost imperceptibly he thrust out his hip in a tiny flick of campness. *I know what I am, and I don't care that you know it too.*

'Oh, I never did forget, Inspector,' he said softly.

Tennison took in Dalton's expression, which was looking distinctly uncomfortable. She said in a quiet yet urgent tone, 'Anthony, I sincerely believe the man responsible for the assaults against you is also—'

'I am not interested in what you believe, I am only concerned with my life and career.' Fists clenched by his sides, the controlled icy anger came spitting out of him. 'Whatever happens to him is no longer my concern. I refuse to let him destroy my life.'

'But you'll let him destroy others?'

'No – you let him.' The room was suddenly filled with his awful glacial rage, for years bottled up inside, festering.

' . . . I don't care about anyone else. If there was a court case, if – then I would be forced to relive what that bastard did to me! I would be on trial. My private life now would be made public – I don't want that – I only agreed to see you on the condition you didn't want me to go to court. I won't testify, you can't make me, I'm all right now, I'm all right now . . . ' His face crumpled and a strangulated sob came from his chest. 'Or I was, I was, before you came, so go away, just go away.'

He closed his eyes, his dark brows very vivid against his white face, fists clenched with the knuckles showing through. 'Leave me alone . . . please.'

Red delved into the rack of evening gowns in the bedroom closet. He lifted one off on its hanger, and lips pursed, head tilted, gave it a critical, searching scrutiny. With a tiny vexed shake of the head he put it back, and chose another. This was fractionally more demure, in midnight blue lace, its upper half studded with diamantés, split up one side as far as the knee. With an approving smile he laid it out on the bed.

He opened a drawer and took out a corset.

Dressed in a silk kimono, Detective Constable Lillie sat before the dressing-table mirror, gazing with interest at the beautiful and expert job Red had done on him. Powdered and rouged, with lipstick, blue eye shadow and false eyelashes, his cheeks seductively shadowed, he was mesmerized by his own gorgeous appearance. He wore a short silvery blond wig, a few artful strands teased over his forehead. He couldn't get over the transformation. It was bloody amazing.

Detective Sergeant Haskons, also made up, was struggling into the corset Red had found for him. His wig, a rich glowing auburn swept up to masses of curls, was on a stand on the dressing table. Red had chosen the midnight blue lacy job for him, while Lillie's was a full-length shimmering lamé dress in puce, set off by a huge flouncy ostrich feather boa in blush pink.

Ray Hebdon stood at the door, observing all this, trying mightily and just failing to hide the glimmer of a smile.

Corset on, Haskons was perspiring as he bent down to try on different pairs of shoes. His square, chunky jaw still showed a trace of blue shaving line even after Red had plastered on dark base and powdered it over four or five times. He was complaining bitterly, already regretting the whole daft episode.

'I still haven't found a pair to fit – or ones that I can even walk in!'

'Cuban will be the easiest. These' – Red pointed down at his own blue satin stilettos, rolling his eyes – 'Killers. It's not just the high heels, but the pointed toes.' Flawlessly made up, he was done up to the nines in a tight, flesh-coloured, sequined evening dress, two long ropes of purple beads hanging down, and matching purple globes dangling from his ears.

'You know it's way after ten,' Hebdon said.

'Oh, don't fuss.' Red fluttered his hands in a shooing gesture. 'Nothing starts until midnight anyway.'

Haskons squeezed his toes into a pair of spangled turquoise slippers with square heels and stamped his feet into them.

'My wife's never going to believe this. I told her I was off duty, then I had to tell her I was on; now, after midnight?' He blew out his glossy red lips in annoyance. 'It's Friday night!'

Lillie draped the feather boa over his shoulders and preened at himself in the mirror. 'You remember that film, *Some Like it Hot*? Jack Lemmon and—'

'Tony Curtis,' Red snapped. 'It was dreadful! Silly walks – they'd never have got away with it. Anyone could see they weren't female.'

Lillie thought this was being pedantic. 'That wasn't the point though, was it? It was a comedy.'

'Well, for some, dear, being in drag is the only time they feel right,' Red told him tartly, smoothing his hands over his hips. He cast a sidelong look at himself in the mirror. 'And they very rarely fancy anyone but themselves – it's not funny at all.' He arched an eyebrow at Hebdon. 'Is it?'

'I wouldn't know,' Hebdon said stiffly, and jerked away into the sitting room.

Haskons, feeling as though he had a couple of hairy spiders glued to his eyelids, caught Lillie's warning expression in the dressing-table mirror. Like treading on thin ice, they silently agreed. You had to be careful what you said to people of this persuasion. Touchy, touchy.

The patrol car drove up the corkscrew ramp to the main entrance of the Piccadilly Hotel in the centre of Manchester. The plateglass doors whispered open and Tennison and Dalton trudged wearily into the lobby. It was gone 10.30 and they were both thoroughly knackered.

'Do you want to have some dinner?' Dalton asked.

'Thanks, but no, I'll order room service.' Tennison summoned up a fleeting smile. 'Sorry I've been a bit snappy . . . better when I've had a large whisky and soda.'

Dalton looked at his watch. 'I'll go and find an all-night chemist. Do you need anything?'

'Oh – toothbrush, toothpaste. Thanks.'

She watched him walk back across the lobby and through the doors, and then she asked for her key. She was dead on her feet, yet there remained things to be done. A policewoman's lot is not a happy one, Tennison thought sourly.

Otley sat alone in the viewing room. He had the remote control in one hand, a can of Red Stripe in the other, watching the videotapes of Connie that had been seized from Mark Lewis's studio. A half-eaten ham and pickle sandwich was on the arm of the chair. At this late hour the station was quiet. A vacuum cleaner could be heard from the Squad Room down the corridor, whining in the lower register as it practised its scales. From somewhere in the vicinity of Regent Street, a police siren wailed off into the distance.

Otley had a house, but not a home, to go back to. If he was there now he'd have been sitting in an armchair, can of beer in hand, watching some old crackly movie on TV, the remains of an Indian take-away in a polystyrene tray at his feet. Same difference. Except here he had a reason and a purpose, or anyway the illusion of having them.

The video was very amateurish. Wobbly camera work, hollow soundtrack, pathetic acting. It was set in a school classroom, half a dozen boys in ties and blazers at old wooden desks, a schoolmaster in mortarboard and gown, wielding a cane. He didn't look like a schoolmaster, more like a barrister, Otley reckoned, or maybe a senior politician. He had snow-white hair and bulging watery eyes with heavy bags, a slightly misshapen nose that looked as if it had been broken when he was a young man, its bulbous end reddened by threadlike blood vessels.

The 'schoolmaster' whacked the desk with the cane. 'Any boy who disobeys me will be severely punished!' Booming fruity voice, the vowels of the privileged public school class.

Otley zapped back and reran the sequence. Connie was

in the front row, looking very innocent in his school blazer and striped tie, his mop of red curls cascading over his forehead. Behind him, and partly hidden, was Billy Matthews. Alan Thorpe, with the ragged blond fringe, was sitting farther back.

'Any boy who disobeys me will be severely punished!'

Otley pressed a button, holding the picture in freeze-frame. He rolled it on, held it on Connie's face. Rolled it on and held it. Billy Matthews. Rolled it on and held it as each of the boys' faces came in view.

There was a quick tread in the corridor and DI Hall poked his head in. 'Skipper . . . Billy Matthews.'

Otley looked at him in silence. 'Is he dead?'

Hall came in, shaking his cropped head. 'He's got a bronchial infection. He's back at Charing Cross Hospital where the nurse – real old battle-axe – pointed out they would not or could not take responsibility for him as he persistently discharged himself. Once on the seventeenth, again last night, and . . .'

Otley gave a snide smile. Hall frowned. 'Did you hear what I said?'

On the screen, the 'schoolmaster' was standing in front of Connie, hand held out, demanding his homework. Otley's face had the ghost of a smile as he watched it.

He said softly, 'Seventeenth? Night Connie died? Right?' He nodded slowly. 'Discharged? Discharged him-self? What time? So he couldn't have been at the advice centre, yes?' He stuck his thumb up, pointed his index finger at Hall. 'Yes! Lovely ... Edward Parker-Jones was very specific about our Billy.'

Otley freeze-framed the picture and pointed. 'Alan Thorpe! He was too drunk to remember – so we got to find those other two lads and Jackson's screwed!' He bounced up, clapping his hands. 'Fancy a hamburger?'

Hall pulled a long-suffering face. 'Hey, come on, Skip. You know what time it is? I came off hours ago ... '

Otley was bending down, changing the tape. He said cheerfully, 'On yer bike, then. See you tomorrow!'

Hall went. Tomorrow was less than an hour away. He speculated idly whether the Skipper curled up in the chair or bedded down on the carpet.

Tennison sat with Detective Chief Inspector David Lyall in the grill room of the Piccadilly Hotel. The excellent dinner they had just consumed was on Tennison's expenses, so Lyall hadn't stinted himself. He didn't stint himself on anything, so far as Tennison could see: prodigious drinker, heavy smoker, and he'd gobbled up the mints that came with the coffee as if frightened they'd melt in front of his eyes.

He was rather handsome in a seedy way, with a fine head of greying hair, but of distinctly dishevelled appearance. His dark grey suit was speckled with cigarette ash, his tie pulled loose, shoes scuffed and unpolished, and his fingernails were a disgrace. Tennison wouldn't have cared if he had BO and farted like a brontosaurus providing he came up with some answers.

She took a document file from her briefcase. It contained the faxes Otley had dug up on the two boys in the children's homes, Anthony Field and Jason Baldwyn.

'I suggested to Halliday this morning that Operation Contract should be quietly put to bed. You worked on it for six months, didn't you?'

Lyall lit up, nodding through the smoke. 'I worked for six months, doing surveillance on all the areas we targeted, right. On the night earmarked for the big swoop, we got no more nor less than on a usual busy Friday night.'

He had a phlegmy smoker's voice, and she thought she could hear his chest wheezing. Lyall drained his glass of wine. He made a face, but went on to refill it to the rim.

'Don't like the vino ...' He took a deep slurp and wiped his mouth on the back of his hand. 'Anyway, three clubs were empty, apart from the hostesses. Course there was a leak, where the fuck, excuse me, where it came from, inside or out, I honestly can't tell you, and I was' – he elbowed the air – 'out faster than a greyhound.' He looked moodily at his wine. 'I prefer a Scotch.'

'Did you target Parker-Jones personally?' Tennison asked.

Lyall chewed on his cigarette, gulping in smoke. He

found something on the tablecloth to interest him. 'Why do you ask that?'

Tennison tapped the file. 'I know it was you sent the faxes to Otley about this case up here and one in Cardiff.' She watched him closely.

'Look, I'm going to be honest with you.' Tennison automatically took that to mean he was going to lie through his teeth, but DCI Lyall surprised her by reaching into his battered briefcase and putting a thick file down on top of hers. His gruff voice dropped to a growling mutter.

'I photocopied these before I left, just more or less to protect myself, if there was any shit ...' He gave a half shrug. 'Sorry, but I didn't want to shoulder the entire blame, right? There's some kind of cover-up — now, I don't know who it's connected to, and to be honest I don't want to know.' He sucked hungrily on his cigarette. 'Dig into these. I think it goes way back maybe before me. Halliday's a bit of a puppet.' His streaky grey eyebrows went up. 'Chiswick pulls the strings.'

It only rubber-stamped what she already knew. The warning signs were all over the Soho Vice Division, big as billboards for anyone with eyes to see. 'So there is a cover-up,' Tennison said, leaning in.

Lyall looked over his shoulder. The fact that the restaurant was almost empty didn't encourage him to say any more. Tennison thought of an inducement that might.

She signed the bill, and ten minutes later she was handing him a miniature bottle of Whyte & Mackay from the mini bar in her room. Seated in one of the low leather chairs next to the teak table, Lyall accepted it with undisguised relish.

'Ah, that's more like it, ta.' He poured the entire contents into his glass. Tennison sat down with her own glass of Scotch, tempered with a little soda. Lyall took a healthy sip and smacked his lips, watching her over his glass.

'I've heard very good things about you. That you're not scared into backing off anything. Well, I am.' He wasn't shamed by the admission; a small shrug and that was all. 'They'll be demoting lots of us in our rank, and I happen to know there's a Superintendent vacancy coming up. So, you take this.' He nodded to the file. 'I'm sorry, but I'm lookin' out for my future. This Sheehy inquiry's gonna put the flutter around.' He drank, and stared into his glass. 'Only ones safe will be those with thirty years' experience. I don't fancy being demoted. Worked hard enough for the DCI rank as it is.'

The hard drinking and general scruffiness didn't mean that he wasn't a good copper, Tennison thought. Her gut feeling told her that he was a good 'un. Plus, he wouldn't have been shunted up north if he was a gutless pushover or plain incompetent.

Lyall's head whipped around as someone knocked.

Tennison went to the door and opened it. Dalton held out a small plastic bag with a chemist's logo on it.

'One toothbrush, paste – and I thought you might need this.' He shook the bag. 'It's make-up remover.'

'Oh, very thoughtful. How much do I owe you?'

She stepped back to get her purse, pushing the door wider.

'Receipts are in the bag. It's the type my girlfriend uses,' Dalton said, pointing to it. He looked up and saw Lyall. 'The remover ...'

Tennison gestured as Lyall rose to his feet. 'This is Detective Chief Inspector David Lyall. This is Detective Inspector Brian Dalton.'

The two men acknowledged one another from a distance. Tennison counted out change and handed it over. 'Your room okay?' She smiled, holding up the bag. 'Thanks for this!'

Dalton hovered in the doorway, waiting to be invited in. 'Room's fine ... er ...' He raised his hand in a little wave. 'Nice to meet you.'

There was no use waiting, because Tennison closed the door on him. She didn't see Dalton's blink of surprise, though Lyall did. On her return she tossed the bag of toiletries onto the bed. 'I didn't expect to stay overnight.' She sat down, hands laced around her knees, leaning forward. 'There was a leak, wasn't there?'

Lyall's answer was a cool, rather ironic smile.

'How did you get on with Bill Otley?' Tennison asked.

'Good man, one of the old school, hard worker.' Lyall drained his glass and set it down. 'He tell you that?'

'Yes.'

Lyall took out a cigarette. He offered the packet. 'You smoke?'

Tennison shook her head, which turned before she knew it into a nod. She took one and accepted a light. Lyall's faint ironic smile was still in place. 'I reckon I've done my favour.' He tapped the file and got up, holding out his hand. 'So, good luck to you.'

They shook hands, and Tennison walked him to the door.

'Where, just as a matter of interest, is the vacancy?'

Lyall chuckled throatily. 'Want in on the fast track, do you? I'd get your skates on.' He prodded her gently on the shoulder. 'Area AMIT, one of the eight. Everybody can't go up, but I'm gonna give it my best shot. Good night, love.'

Eight Area Major Incident Teams in the London Metropolitan region, but which one? Lyall wasn't saying.

Clutching his battered briefcase under his arm, trailing smoke, he went off. Tennison slipped the chain onto the door. She stood there thoughtfully for a moment, and then went to the phone by the bed and dialled room service.

'Room forty-five. Could I have a pot of coffee and ... do you have cigarettes?'

She went over to the table and picked up the thick file, holding it in both hands. From experience she knew there was about four hours' solid reading here. She hung her suit jacket over the back of a chair, switched on the free-standing domed lamp, settled herself, and dived in.

The doorman wore a red plush uniform with gold braid epaulettes. Behind him stood two heavyweight characters in white dinner jackets, arms folded in the regulation manner, guarding the lift entrance to the Bowery Roof Top Club. Looking like a million counterfeit dollars, Red sashayed towards them across the marble-floored lobby, hips swivelling, the purple globes swinging from his ears like miniature golf balls. Haskons and Lillie followed, accompanied by Ray Hebdon, who appeared insignificant and nondescript in his dark suit alongside their plumage and finery.

As one of the Bowery's artistes, Red got the royal treatment. The doorman thumbed the button, the bronze-coloured doors slid open, and a moment later the four of them were on their way up to the top floor.

Red adjusted his wig in the smoked glass mirror wall of the lift. 'Well, that part was easy,' he breathed in a quivery sigh. He dabbed his shiny nose with a tissue. 'Now it's the third degree – I must be out of my mind, I'm sweating.'

Inside his tight corset, so was Haskons. He stared at

himself in the mirror. All that he recognized were his eyes, gazing back at him in a kind of stricken glazed terror. Completing his midnight blue ensemble, he wore long satin gloves up to the elbow, with large flashing rings on his gloved fingers. A dinky gold shoulder bag with thin gold straps dangled at his waist. His feet were killing him.

Lillie's face was lost in fluttering ostrich feathers. The rest of him was a shimmering vision in puce lamé, a V-split up the back of the dress almost to his panty line. His short blond wig kept slipping over one eye, and it was the devil's own job trying to tug it straight, the false red nails getting snagged and entangled. Also, he was dying for a piss. He suddenly wondered how, with these bloody pointed nails, he was going to manage that simple act. He might do himself a serious mischief.

'It doesn't stop on any of the other floors,' Red said, pointing to the indicator panel.

'I know,' Hebdon said, giving him a surly look.

Haskons had already had second thoughts. He was on about his fourth or fifth. 'Red – if we want to leave, is this the only way?'

But Red was more preoccupied with the appearance of his two protégés, inspecting them critically, a pat here, a tweak there.

'Well,' he observed crisply, an eyebrow raised, 'I doubt if you'll pull anything, but that said, I think it's a good job.'

'How do we work it then?' Haskons asked, dry-mouthed.

'I won't be on until about twelve-thirty. Then I have another show – at Lola's, two o'clock.' He wagged a finger. 'But I will need the wigs back, so I've left the main front door key under the old scraper thing ...'

'Don't you have a spare set?'

'No, I'm not a permanent fixture,' Red said tetchily. 'But I'm working on it.' He groomed himself in the mirror with little fluttery movements, and moistened his lips. 'I'm also really nervous. Why I said I'd do this ...' He shook his head at himself. 'Names – what are you calling yourselves? And voices, don't put anything on ... we don't ...'

'What you calling yourself?' Haskons asked Lillie.

Red pointed to Haskons. 'You be Karen. You ...' He frowned at Lillie. 'Jackie'll do. Remember, this is my life. This gets out, and it won't be worth living. Don't fiddle with the wigs.'

The doors opened. Red straightened up, head high, shoulders back.

'Here we go, eyes and teeth, luvvies.'

Queenlike, he sailed out into the foyer, Karen and Jackie traipsing behind like two dowager duchesses.

Tennison's resolve had been busted wide open. She was halfway through her second pack already, the room a blue mist of smoke, the ashtray spilling over onto the table. Two silver coffeepots, one empty, one half full but nearly cold, were on the tray with two dirty cups.

Crouched over, a cigarette sticking out of her mouth, she was frowning with concentration as she listened to Connie's voice on the headphones. These were the conversations Jessica Smithy had taped, which Tennison had heard a dozen times before. But in light of the information supplied by DCI Lyall she was hoping desperately to make new connections, ferret out some tiny fact that until now had seemed obscure or unimportant or both.

'. . . no, I mean top brass – there's judges, barristers, Members of Parliament.' The innocent little voice that had the impervious quality of a six-inch steel nail driven through it. 'I know them all, but I'm not stupid, Miss Smithy. I need some guarantee.'

Tennison flipped back over several pages of scrawled notes. She searched on the table among the scattered photocopies. Checking, cross-referencing, matching Connie's assertions with the file that Lyall had hoarded and kept locked away as his own insurance. It was here somewhere, she was convinced, in these tapes and documents. The clean, clear, direct line that connected Connie and Vera Reynolds and Mark Lewis and Jimmy Jackson and Edward Parker-Jones and . . . and who else? *Who else?*

Tennison lit a fresh cigarette from the stub of the old

one. She leaned forward, eyes shut, listening to that young-innocent-old-cynical voice.

'I got the names of high brass, Miss Smithy, they're all in it. Young boys, kids ... they only want really young kids.'

Chapter Twelve

'Brian! Have you missed me?'

Arms held wide, fingertips all aquiver, Red floated across the foyer to the handsome receptionist with the slicked-back ponytail and Vandyke beard, gelled to a glistening point.

Red posed before him, one hip thrust out. 'Now, I've got one member, this youngster ...' He indicated Hebdon with a graceful wave of the hand. 'And two from Hampstead Garden Suburb.' He giggled and fluttered his eyelashes coquettishly. 'No, we're old friends ... is it okay?'

Brian wasn't too sure. He was giving Haskons and Lillie a close, gimlet-eyed examination.

To divert attention, Red was practically doing his stage act right there in the foyer. Twirling around, high-pitched to the point of hysteria, he squealed to Hebdon, 'Show your member, darling.' He leaned forward over the desk, trying to cover his jangling nerves with a breathily confidential whisper.

'Now, I know this is naughty, but these are very old friends of mine. And, Brian, daahhhling, we've only got one member!' He rolled his eyes theatrically under azure lids. 'Oh, I'm so tired of that gag.'

'Members sign,' Brian said, handing the pen to Hebdon. He stared hard at Haskons and Lillie, who were hanging back, attempting to merge into the wallpaper. 'Are they for the cabaret?'

Red let out a little trill of amusement. 'No, dear, but they just want to learn from me! Don't they all? You remember that bitch that came up with me a few months ago – she's only ripped off my act!'

Brian checked Hebdon's signature against his membership file on the computer screen. He gestured the party to go through, but he still needed some convincing about Karen and Jackie. His eyes never left them. 'There's no table free, not until after one, but there's a booth, far side.'

Red linked arms with Haskons, sweeping him on, and ushered Lillie quickly forward. 'Booth will be fine, we're not staying long, just until my act's over . . . '

He pushed the two of them on ahead, towards a doorway swathed in red velvet, and leaned back to Brian.

'Anybody in I should know about? Film producers?

Casting agents? I need exposure.' Brian shook his head. 'Back room busy?' asked Red, but Brian's attention had switched to some new arrivals emerging from the lift.

Haskons and Lillie stood just inside the red velvet curtain. The club was dark and smoky, and Haskons was having trouble with his false eyelashes. He had to keep looking down, about three feet in front of him, to see where he was treading as Red led them past the crowded tables and up a short flight of steps to a small balcony on the left-hand side of the stage, which at the moment was empty. The cabaret was due to start in a few minutes.

Haskons was half blind, but Lillie was taking it all in. The clientele was certainly an exotic mixture. The bar area, to the rear of the club, was favoured by groups of elderly, distinguished men, most in lounge suits, but a few in evening dress. Ostensibly chatting with their cronies, Lillie could see them casting glances to the tables in front of the stage. This was the unofficial 'stage show', where the young boys sat with their companions and the transvestites congregated, drinking champagne and shrieking with laughter. The butch boys wore white T-shirts and leathers, one or two in Marlon Brando leather caps. The more overtly gay were elegantly dressed in velvet jackets and frilly shirts, long shiny hair draping their shoulders in the style of Lord Alfred Douglas, Oscar Wilde's bosom chum.

The transvestites and transexuals were fabulous creatures. Lillie felt dowdy by comparison. All, without exception, were tall and willowy, with masses of either blond or red hair tumbling down. They wore glittery evening gowns slashed low to reveal shaved chests and the sensuous slant of their backs, curving to tiny waists and slender, non-womanly hips. The make-up of each one was in itself a work of art. Lillie, contrary to what he had expected, was fascinated rather than repulsed. It wasn't in the least a threatening experience, just endlessly engrossing.

Having got them seated, Red went off on a circular tour, flitting like a vivacious gadfly from one group to another. Vera Reynolds had seen Red come in with the others. Furiously, she tried to attract Red's attention. What the hell was the stupid bitch playing at? The management weren't thick. They'd have a blue fit when they found out – as they soon would – that the fuzz was around. And not only would the management find out; that was the least of it. Vera's blood ran cold when she thought of the consequences of what the crazy queen had done, bringing them in here.

It was Vera's spot any moment now, and she only had time for a quick, explosive word in Red's startled ear as she headed backstage to prepare for her act.

Hebdon brought drinks to the table. Luridly coloured cocktails in long-stemmed glasses. Haskons had all but given up trying to peer into the gloomy depths of the club. 'I can hardly see myself, never mind clock any faces,' he complained morosely. The blue shadow on his square jaw was even more evident now. He had the horrible feeling that the straps in his corset had gone. Would this fucking living nightmare never end?

Finger extended, Lillie took a dainty sip of his drink. 'How much did these set you back?'

'A lot – buy a bottle for the price of one,' Hebdon replied. 'Knock 'em back, you both look like you need something . . . ' He turned his head. 'Here's Red now.'

Red leaned over the table, his eyes hot and agitated. Vera's word in his ear had got him seriously rattled. 'I've not much time before I'm on, so let's make it snappy.' Haskons and Lillie started to rise.

'One at a time,' Red hissed. He cast a nervous glance to the private members' bar behind the curtained door. 'I don't know if I can get you in the back bar, it's jammed in there. Maybe you can work it yourself.'

Haskons and Lillie stared miserably after him as he went off. Left to their own devices, their chances of getting in there were zilch.

Two spotlights stabbed through the smoke, and there was a spattering of applause as the compere came on, a comically stocky figure in a leather bomber jacket and leather pants cut off to reveal fat, hairy calves. He grabbed the mike off its stand.

'It's cabaret time! And we have a great favourite, a truly beautiful, talented act. Please welcome – Vera Reynolds!'

Taped music started up. A twenties-style dance orchestra with muted cornets and plunkety percussion. Vera's tall, lithe figure glided on, clad in a high-necked flesh-coloured costume speckled with sequins, the spotlight making a dazzling halo of her platinum-blond wig. Her red-tipped fingers caressed the microphone suggestively.

'I wanna be loved by you, just you, and nobody else but you ...'

The breathy voice was uncanny, the luscious pouting lips a perfect replica. It was Marilyn to the life.

Thinking of Jack Lemmon and Tony Curtis, alias Karen and Jackie, Haskons kicked Lillie under the table. 'Well, we got the whole cast now!'

'I wanna be loved by you alone ... boo-boo-bee-doo ...'

Down by Waterloo Bridge, Otley was on his own private one-man patrol. He'd had no luck in the Bullring, drawn a blank at St Margaret's Crypt. At the hamburger stall, in the shadow of the iron trelliswork, he caught up with Alan Thorpe. The boy was sullen and uncooperative. Otley didn't blame him. These kids lived on a knife edge. As young as fourteen and fifteen, they had to fend for themselves, keep body and soul together, survive in a hostile, uncaring environment.

'I just want to buy you somethin' to eat. Have a talk, Alan.' Otley put his hand on the boy's shoulder, as much to reassure him as restrain him.

'Leave me alone!' Alan squirmed away. He pointed to his right eye, puffy and shiny purple. 'I got this 'cos I talked to you before!'

'Nasty,' Otley said. 'So who did that to you, then?'

'It's always questions wiv you, innit?'

'You want a hamburger or not?'

Alan jerked his thumb to the group around the smouldering fire.

'What about me mates?'

'You hungry?' Otley called to them. He put a tenner on the counter.

Alan Thorpe stared down at the cindery ground. He said bitterly, 'Jackson done me, Sarge. Okay?'

Vera came storming into the dressing room. She tore off her wig and flung it down among the pots of cream, tubes of glue, foams and sprays. 'Are you crazy? Why?' She thumped Red in the chest, hard. 'Why did you do it?'

'Because they asked me to!'

'Well, I'm out of here – and if you'd got any sense you'd leave too.'

'But you've got another spot—'

'You do it!' Vera was throwing her make-up into her vanity case.

'But I haven't done my own yet!' Red protested.

'They stick out like a sore thumb,' Vera snorted, grabbing her wigs off their stands and ramming them into plastic bags.

'They don't . . .' Red said uncertainly.

'*Yes they do!*' Vera turned on him in fury, arm outstretched, pointing. 'They're asking everybody bloody questions! That's why I clocked them.' Her lips thinned. Her eyes were large and fearful. 'You don't know, you just don't know . . .'

Red lowered his voice to a husky whisper. 'About Connie – yes, I know, that's why they're here. I wanted to help. I thought you cared. Somebody killed him, you know it, I know it.' He was on the verge of tears. 'Well, you might be able to stomach what goes on . . .'

'*Me?!*' Vera shrieked. 'You live with that slime-bag, Mark Lewis, not me! I have never been involved in it all, I've never wanted to know.' She wrenched her outdoor coat off the hanger and dragged it on over her dress.

Red gripped her arm. 'But you are involved, aren't you?' His tone was low and venomous. 'You lied to me. I covered up for you. But this other stuff with the kids and Jackson . . .' He shook his head in disgust.

Vera pulled her arm free, struggling into her coat. 'I am shacking up at his place because I got nowhere else.'

The mask slipped, and behind it was a trembling, abject creature terrified half out of her wits. 'He won't leave me alone until this all blows over, and now you've gone and got the cops in here.' Vera said hoarsely, 'He'll think I done it – not you – me!'

The door was pushed open and Brian, the receptionist, came in. Vera slammed her vanity case shut, picked up her wig box, and barged past him into the corridor. Brian yelled after her.

'You've got another spot, Vera!'

'I'll do it.' Red was sitting at the dressing table, shoulders slumped, toying with a hairbrush.

Brian leaned on the back of the chair, looking at Red in the mirror. 'Those two queens – I've just had a complaint. They'll have to go.'

Red sighed heavily and started powdering his face. 'Oh, all right, I'll come clean. I don't know them. They latched onto me at Lola's club, gave me a few quid to get them in.' He met Brian's accusing stare in the mirror. 'It's the truth, I swear before God! Now can I have some privacy – my tits need readjusting!'

A chill wind with a flurry of drizzle hit Vera in the face as she stepped into the street. She blinked, looked quickly up and down, and set off at a trot. The blue Mercedes ghosted around the corner behind her, with just its sidelights on. Vera started to run, hampered by the small cases she was carrying. The Mercedes speeded up, Jackson's head sticking out of the window.

'Hey! YOU! Vera!'

Vera kept running. The Mercedes came alongside and mounted the pavement. Its brakes squealed, and Jackson was out, pinning her against the wall, his hand gripping her by the throat.

'I've bloody protected you, slag, and you . . .' He gave her a stinging slap with the flat of his hand. 'You bring the filth to the house!' He slapped her again, back of the hand. She felt his ring snag her cheek. 'Why did you do that, Vera?' Jackson snarled, fingers digging into her throat, forcing her head up.

'*It wasn't me*. I swear before God, Jimmy, it wasn't me.' Vera was gasping and choking, spittle running down her chin. 'I wouldn't, would I, I wouldn't . . .'

Jackson eased back, releasing his grip. 'What?'

Vera massaged her throat, trying to calm him, talk him down.

'I need you, why would I tip off the law about you?'

'Who is it to do with, then, Vera?' He gathered the front of her coat in his bunched fist and drew her closer. 'Is it Red? How much does he know?' He shook her. 'Where's Red? Eh? *Eh?*'

It came out in a gabble. 'I dunno, she's not on tonight, she had a cold. She's stayin' at Mark Lewis's.' Vera let out a long quivering moan. 'It's the truth, Jimmy, honestly . . . that's how she knows everything.'

Jackson looked back along the street. A taxi was standing outside the wrought iron, glass-domed entrance to the club. Two figures came out, tripping across the pavement in their high heels, hurrying to avoid the thickening rain. One of them wore a red wig. They climbed in.

Jackson let go of Vera. She dodged past him, staggering in a blind panic, banging into the wall.

Half-stunned, she heard the car door slam. Jackson drove off the pavement and did a U-turn, blue exhaust fumes billowing up. Vera leaned her head against the wall, watching his tail-lights disappear, feeling the trickle of blood on her cheek.

Otley had gone the whole hog and taken the lot of them to a greasy spoon diner two blocks along from Waterloo Station. Leading the ragged-arsed, snot-nosed, filthy, stinking tribe in, he felt like Fagin, devious mastermind of London's poor dispossessed youngsters, the forgotten underclass.

Alan Thorpe he knew well, most of the others he knew by sight. He made it his business to put names to faces. Tennison might have muscled in on his graft in uncovering the kids in Manchester and Cardiff, but Otley was confident that there was more than one way of skinning a cat. This sorry, scurvy bunch held the key. Otley was about to turn it.

He bought burgers and fries all around, with plenty of Cokes, milk shakes, and tea to wash them down. They occupied two tables, set at right angles, in a corner next to the steamy window. He told them to keep the noise down, but with food inside them, fags lit, they were a rowdy, foul-mouthed lot. More than once, Otley saw the manageress casting a disapproving look to their corner. But with their bellies full, he'd got them relaxed, got them talking, and the last thing he wanted was to start throwing his weight around by showing his ID. So he held tight, hoping there wouldn't be trouble.

Otley reared back, hands raised defensively, as another kid sidled in and sat down.

'Hey, what is this! Think I'm made of money, do you?' The kid's two grimy fists rested on the scratched Formica table. 'S'okay – here!' Otley tossed a fiver. 'Get what you want, and a cuppa for me.'

The kid, whose name was Frankie, scurried off to the counter like a starving rat.

Alan Thorpe went on with his tale. 'So how it works – he, Jackson, picks yer up from the station, right?' He squinted up at Otley with his one good eye. 'Wiv me? An' that 'ouse – one you was at – he takes us there, like, an' he—'

'He never done me!' Disco Driscoll boasted, tapping his chest. He looked about twelve but was possibly fourteen, a half-caste kid in a torn green baseball jacket. Filthy matted hair hanging over his eyes, mouth smeared with ketchup. 'I got me own gaff!'

'No, you 'aven't, yer fuckin' liar!' Thorpe shot back.

Otley half-covered his face, looking over his hand at the other customers. It was after one in the morning, but it was still pretty busy, with overspill trade from the station.

'I'm not,' Driscoll said, pulling a face. He turned to Otley, and said fiercely, as if it was a matter of real pride, 'He done 'em all, but he ain't done me, he done 'em all.' He gave a defiant nod.

A pug-nosed boy named Gary Rutter said, 'He keeps yer there, like, gives yer stuff. He gives yer gear, so, like, yer don't mind stayin' – know what I mean?'

Frankie returned from the counter with a cheeseburger and fries, a raspberry milk shake for himself and tea for Otley, slopped over into the thick saucer. He plonked the change down onto the greasy table, strewn with mashed chips and ketchup.

'The woman behind the counter said you can't take the cup out, and that you're a pervert!' he chortled, giving Otley a gap-toothed grin.

'Know what that means, do you?' Otley asked Frankie.

'Him? He don't know nuffink,' Alan Thorpe said derisively.

A middle-aged man and woman got up from a nearby table and went out, muttering darkly and shaking their heads. Otley huddled over the table, keeping his voice low.

'Did you all know Connie?'

'Nah, we don't know him – pervert!' Alan Thorpe jeered.

Otley cuffed him lightly on the back of the head. 'You know what pervert is – I've seen you in a film with Connie ...'

Alan Thorpe went a mottled pink as the table erupted with raucous laughter. Hooting loudly, the lads started throwing chips at him.

'He's a pervert, he's a pervert!' Frankie chanted.

Incensed, Alan Thorpe reached over and belted Frankie on the side of the head. It was getting out of hand. Otley waved his arms.

'Come-on-now! Cut it out, or we'll be thrown out.'

Alan Thorpe wasn't through. He swung another punch at Frankie, then grabbed a fork and tried to stab him with it.

Otley pushed him down, fingers splayed against the bony chest, and slumped back into his own seat. 'What am I?' he asked wearily. 'The pied piper?'

Lillie turned the key in the front door and let himself into the gloomy passageway leading up to Mark Lewis's flat. He passed the key back to Haskons, who slid it into its hiding place under the outdoor rubber mat.

Across the street, Jackson drew up, and killed the lights. He saw the shadowy figure in the dress and red wig stooping to replace the key. So Red was sick, was he? Too ill to do his act. That bitch Vera had lied again. It was all fucking lies.

In the dim streetlight he watched the figure straighten up and totter inside, lifting the hem of his dress. The door closed. Jackson patted the pocket of his leather coat, just to reassure himself. A light went on in the flat above. Jackson lifted the handle and the door clicked open.

The manageress had the phone in her hand. She peered around from the kitchen doorway, keeping a beady disapproving eye on the gang in the corner. Ten of them now, not including the bloke, flocking in like wasps around a honey pot. She set her jaw and started to dial.

Fag in his mouth, Alan Thorpe was on a boasting streak. Not yet fifteen, he was a forty-a-day lad, when he had the money. 'I done arson, robbery, indecent assault and . . .' He frowned into space. 'Can't remember the other, I got four though,' he bragged.

Otley needled him. 'Not as many as Connie.'

'Connie? Huh! All he ever done was dirty old men.'

'That wasn't what I heard.'

'When he lived at Jackson's he went out more'n any of us,' Alan Thorpe confided, looking up through his fair lashes. 'He liked it.'

'That's true, that's true,' Disco Driscoll said. Probably high on lighter fuel or something, Otley suspected, which accounted for his slurred, rapid speech. 'That's true – he went for whole weekends, didn't he?'

'Yeah! That film I did was nuffink!' Alan Thorpe stubbed out his cigarette on a paper plate and stuck it upright in the sugar bowl. 'I just got me arse tanned – me dad gimme worse. Connie was doin' the nobs.'

The heads around the table nodded. Connie had been chosen for better things, moved in higher circles. Several of them – Thorpe, Disco Driscoll, Kenny Lloyd, Gary Rutter, Frankie Smith – at one time or another had served time at Jackson's place, observed Connie's comings and goings. None of them liked him, stuck-up little poofter.

Disco Driscoll fixed blurred eyes on Otley. 'He wasn't like us, different you know, always sniffin' around, lookin' for fresh meat, I reckon he got a back hander ...' He tilted his matted head, seeking Otley's ear. 'You know Billy OK Matthews? Well, when he first came up, he was, what ...?' He looked to Alan Thorpe. 'Ten? Yeah, he'd be about ten. His mother's bloke raped him, so he's a bit – you know.' Driscoll screwed his finger into his head. 'Connie nabbed Billy fast, didn't he?' he said, gazing blearily at the others.

'You think Connie was paid for finding young kids then?' Otley said casually. Inside, he felt the opposite of casual. His nose twitched. He could almost smell it, he was that close. He'd got their confidence, and they were spilling the lot, only they didn't know it. To them it was just shop talk.

Alan Thorpe nodded, lighting another cigarette. He sucked in the smoke like a seasoned professional, which was what he was. 'Yeah, for the films like . . . '

'Who was the bloke in the mortarboard?'

'The what?' Kenny Lloyd said, sniffing up a greenish candle drip from the end of his nose.

'The gown,' Otley said, plucking at the lapels of his raincoat. 'He had a cane.'

Kenny despised them, and his pale young face showed it, mouth twisted. 'He's a pervert, they're all perverts. Big posh 'ouses, lotta dough – dirty bastards!'

Otley's heart was trip-hammering. He kept his eyes hooded as he looked around at them, shaking his head disbelievingly, grinning his snide sceptical grin.

'You scruffy buggers were never taken to posh houses – who you kiddin'?'

Haskons knelt on the mat, leaning into the bath, soaping his face and hair. The shower curtain hung down, obscuring his upper body. The red wig was balanced on the edge of the washbasin, a bedraggled ferret of a thing after Haskons had sweated into it all night. He still wore his dress, open down the back, the half-undone corset straining at its straps.

He groped for the shower head on its flexible stem. The water was too hot. Blindly, he spun the taps, adjusting the mixture. The water hissed out and gurgled down the drain, covering the creak of the door as Jackson came in sideways, bringing his hand out of his pocket, the click as the knife sprang open also lost in the hissing and gurgling, and in Haskons's grunt as he bowed his head into the bath.

Slowly, Jackson reached out to the plastic curtain. Drag it down over the bitch. Wrap it around her and in with the knife, clean and neat and quick. His fingers gripped the edge of the curtain. The plastic rings clinked and jostled on the rod.

Haskons raised his head, soapy water running down his face. 'Can you untie the ruddy corset strings! I can't get it off . . .'.

He heard the plastic rings clash and ping as Jackson tore the curtain off the rod. Blinking wildly, trying to clear the soap from his eyes, Haskons saw the gleaming blade. He twisted his body, half leaning into the bath, his feet churning at the mat as he tried desperately to get out of this exposed and vulnerable position. From the corner of his eye he saw the blade swoop. Tensing his body against the impact, he swung out his right arm in a helpless reflex action, and in the next instant had the breath knocked from his body as Lillie hurled himself at Jackson. Tangled together, the three of them

259

crashed to the tiled floor between the bath and the washbasin.

Lillie had hold of Jackson's knife arm, but he wouldn't let go. Haskons struggled to get up, feet slithering. He grabbed out for support, hitting the shower head, which spun around, spraying water everywhere.

Lillie got a handful of Jackson's hair and held him still while he punched him in the face, really laying into him. Jackson bucked and squirmed, boots flying. Lillie hit him again. 'Drop it!' A boot whacked into Lillie's ribs, making him gasp. 'Get the bastard's legs!' he yelled at Haskons.

Together they pinned Jackson to the floor, Haskons hanging on to his legs. Jackson tore his head free from Lillie's grasp and butted him in the face, making blood spurt. This made Lillie mad. He cracked Jackson across the mouth. He dug his thumbs into Jackson's wrist, jerked it viciously, and the knife went skittering away. This time he got two handfuls of hair and banged Jackson's head against the tiled floor. Then for good measure smacked it sideways into the washbasin pedestal. This seemed to work, so he did it again, twice more.

'That's enough,' Haskons panted in his ear. Lillie did it again.

'HEY – THAT'S ENOUGH! Get off him!'

'It's my blood,' Lillie said. He was trembling all over. He still had Jackson's spiked greasy hair entwined in his white-knuckled fists. 'And I'm not gettin' off him,' he snarled. 'Tie his legs.'

Otley wasn't altogether surprised when, behind Disco Driscoll's tousled head, he saw the red and blue stripe of a Panda car sliding in, its blue light casting a ghostly aura through the steamy window.

They all trooped out, Otley leading the way, and stood on the wet pavement, the lads jostling one another and sniggering. The two uniformed PCs were from south of the river; they didn't know Otley, and he didn't know them. He took one of them aside and produced his ID. The other policeman, barely out of his teens himself, kept watch on the motley bunch of giggling boys.

Alan Thorpe grinned up at him insolently, nodding towards Otley. 'He's a copper, you stupid git!' The lads hooted, loving it.

The young policeman made a grab at him.

'Leave him alone, he's with me,' Otley said, coming over.

'See, what did I tell you?' Thorpe chortled, and gave the young PC the finger.

Otley beckoned. Alan Thorpe and Kenny Lloyd followed him a few paces. 'You two want a ride around in a Panda? Take me to that posh house? Yeah?' He slid his hand inside his jacket. 'Tenner in it – what d'you say?'

The two lads exchanged looks. Thorpe nodded. 'Okay.'

They had only a hazy idea of where the house was – 'Somewhere just off the Heath,' according to Kenny. With the two uniformed officers in front, Otley and the boys crammed in the back, they drove up through Highgate and circled the northeast fringe of Hampstead Heath. Up here, the large detached houses stood safe and secure behind tall hedges and wrought-iron fences. The red ruby eye of a burglar alarm glowed from each one. When they'd covered Cranley Gardens, Muswell Hill, and Aylmer Road north of the golf course, Otley was growing impatient. 'Now, come on, this is the fifth road. Is it here or not?'

The Panda car turned into a secluded tree-lined avenue, and Alan Thorpe sat forward and pointed. 'That's the one – 'as it got a big double front door with stone animals? Connie said they was lions.'

The house was set back behind a thick hedge of trimmed conifers. It had a steeply gabled roof and white-leaded windows. The house itself was in darkness, but the frosted globe of a security light shone down on the gravel driveway.

The older of the two policemen got out to take a look. He peered in through the gates, saw the studded double doors and the two lions flanking it, and nodded back to the car.

Otley grinned and ruffled Alan Thorpe's hair. 'Good boy . . . remember any more?'

The policeman came back and leaned in the window. He was shaking his head. 'I think the lad is pulling your leg, Sarge! This is Assistant Deputy Commissioner Kennington's home.'

Otley slowly sat back, staring out, pinching his nose.

Chapter Thirteen

Tennison had phoned ahead and there was a car waiting to meet her and Dalton at Cardiff Station. The driver was a young WPC, Bronwen Webb, who'd dug Jason Baldwyn's file out of Records. Tennison skimmed through it while they drove to the estate.

It was a dismal day, an unbroken sheet of murky cloud scudding in from the Severn Estuary. What with the late night and the early call at six-thirty, Tennison wasn't feeling her best. Her first sight of the estate did nothing to lighten her mood. It was a huge grey barracklike place, ten-storey tower blocks with balconies and draughty walkways. Some humorist had named the bleak crescents after trees: Sycamore, Birch, Cedar, Oak. Much of it was boarded up, graffiti everywhere, gutters choked with uncollected rubbish. Wrecked cars rested on their axles, leaking pools of oil. Tennison gazed out on the depressing scene, feeling more depressed by the minute. Welcome to the armpit of the universe.

The car stopped outside a tower block, and she sat there for a minute, summoning up the resolve to move. Dalton was reading the file, quizzing Bronwen about Jason.

'You say he's known to the locals?'

Bronwen unfastened her seat belt and half-turned, leaning on her elbow. 'He's more than known – he spends more time in the cells than out!' There was only a trace of the singsong Welsh accent. She gave a little resigned shrug. 'He's a nice enough bloke when he's sober, but he's a nightmare when he's not. Been had up for assault, petty crimes. Has a lot of marital troubles – she's always calling us in, but then withdraws the charges.'

Bronwen's eyes widened, as if to say, *What can you do?*

She got out and went to open the rear door just as Tennison's phone beeped. Bronwen stood with Dalton on the crumbling pavement while Tennison spoke to Halliday. The driver's window was open an inch, and Dalton tried to listen in, none too successfully, except it was apparent that the Super was giving her one hell of an earful.

Tennison was nodding, trying to get a word in edge-ways.

'I can't really do anything about it from here, Guv . . .' More nodding as she looked out at the estate. 'Yes. Well, as I just said, I can't do anything right now, hopefully by twelve, yes . . . '

She finished the call and zapped the aerial back in with a vengeance. She got her briefcase and pushed the door slightly open with her foot. She looked at Dalton. He didn't get the coded message, and it was Bronwen who jumped to it, sweeping the door wide for the Detective Chief Inspector to get out.

Belatedly, Dalton tried to assist. Tennison buttoned her raincoat and glowered around. Dalton looked at her expectantly.

'The bad news is not worth discussing, Haskons and Lillie got themselves dragged up.' Dalton's jaw dropped. '*Don't* even ask. But the good news is, they brought in Jackson, and this time we can hold him,' she said with grim satisfaction.

'You serious, they got dragged up?' Dalton said with the glimmering of a smile.

Tennison was not amused. 'I said I don't want to talk about it. But we've also another alibi down. Driscoll this time!' She seemed more ferocious than triumphant. 'He's admitted he lied because Jackson threatened to beat him up.' She turned to Bronwen, waiting patiently. 'Thank you. It's number – what?'

'Sixty-three.' Bronwen pointed up to the third-floor balcony. It was reached by a concrete walkway that zig-zagged several times, so you had to walk five times the distance to get where you were going.

'Do you want me to come up with you?' Bronwen asked. 'It's a bit of a warren in there.'

'No, thanks. Judging by the look of the place, you'd best stay with the car.' She gave a nod, squared her shoulders, and set off with Dalton up the ramp. 'Jackson physically assaulted Lillie and Haskons, and Larry Hall, all in one night.' She stumped upward, eyes fixed straight in front of her. 'Just let that oily little brief try for bail . . . !'

Dalton didn't know what effect Tennison had on suspects, but in this kind of storming mood she scared the shit out of him.

The girl who let them in – not more than eighteen – had a baby in a shirt but no nappy balanced on her hip, and she was about seven months pregnant with the next one. She had a hollow-cheeked wasted look and lacklustre eyes. She led them through the tiny hallway, where they had to squeeze past a pram, into the living room. It was oppressively hot, with the close dank smell that comes from clothes drying in a sealed room. The source was woollen baby clothes steaming gently on a wooden frame in front of a gas fire that was going full blast. Fluffy toys and plastic building bricks were strewn everywhere, along with empty beer cans and dirty cups and plates, strategically located to make it odds on that you'd step onto or into something. The few sticks of furniture looked like the remnants of a car boot sale on a bad day.

Jason came in from the kitchen. He was tall and very thin, with straggling hippie-length hair, and to Tennison's consternation he was exceptionally good-looking. Over ragged blue jeans he wore a striped pyjama top. The buttons were missing, showing his ribs and flat, fish-white belly. He was barefoot, the nails long and curved, grime between his toes.

'She's no need to be in on this.'

'Not unless you want her to be,' Tennison agreed.

Jason jerked his head. 'Go on.'

The girl went out with the baby. Jason heeled the door shut.

'I'm Jane Tennison, and this is Brian Dalton. Can we sit down?'

'Sure. Sorry about the mess.' He pushed both hands up into his hair and flung his head back.

Tennison sat down in the lumpy armchair, shifting to avoid the spring. Dalton chose a hard-backed chair, well away from the fire. Jason semi-reclined on the arm of the settee, one knee pulled up to his chin. 'You want tea or ...?'

'No, thanks,' Tennison said politely. That was the second surprise. He had a lazy, low-pitched voice, easy to listen to. What had she been expecting? she asked herself. Grunts and slobbering growls? She glanced at Dalton, making sure he was taking notes, and smiled at Jason. 'So, where do you want to begin?' He was studying his thumbnail. 'You're from Liverpool originally, aren't you? How old were you when you went into the home?'

'Which one?'

'The home run by Mr Edward Parker.'

'Ten.' Jason flicked away something he'd found under his thumbnail. 'I was sent there from a foster home. I got into a bit of thieving, so they got shot of me.'

'Would you be prepared to act as a witness for the prosecution?'

'Sure.' Jason twitched his thin shoulders in a listless shrug.

'Would you tell me when the sexual abuse started?'

His eyes flicked towards her, and quickly away. He had thick, dark lashes any woman would have been proud of. And any woman would have fallen for the full-lipped mouth with a slightly sullen droop to it.

'Second or third day I was there, Parker just called me into his office and that was it ... started then. And you couldn't say anything, or do anything about it – like he was a law unto himself. And it wasn't just me, he was having us all. He'd give you a certain amount of fags, like five say, for a blow job. Always knew when one of the kids had gone the whole way with him, they were flush with fags. Have you got one, by the way?'

Tennison reached into her briefcase. 'I have, as a matter of fact. Here, keep the packet, I've given up.'

Jason uncoiled from the arm of the settee and knelt

down to get a light from the gas fire. Tennison rummaged for matches, but he was already lit up. He stayed where he was, long legs stretched out on the tatty hearth rug. The pose was overtly sexual, the pyjama top falling open, the tight jeans displaying the bulge at his crotch. It made Tennison unsure whether he was behaving naturally, unselfconsciously, or trying it on, deriving some secret amusement from the situation. He was a very disconcerting young man.

'I'm grateful that you're being so frank with us,' Tennison said. The heat of the closed room was making her perspire, and she was sorry she hadn't taken off her raincoat when she came in. Now didn't seem the right time.

'No other way to be, really, is there?' he said, dribbling tiny puffs of smoke from his mouth.

'What made you report him?'

'He shortchanged me on some fags, so I thought – screw him. So I went to the probation officer. Stupid bitch, I think she fancied him – he used to get it off with women, too. Anyway,' Jason said in a long sigh, 'she went on and on at me, did I know what I was saying, what it meant? I said, "Oh yeah, you know what it fuckin' means to me?" I said, "If you don't do something, I'll go to the cops."'

'And how old were you?'

'Twelve or thirteen.'

'And did you go to the cops?'

'Yeah . . . ' Jason rolled onto his stomach, flicking ash onto the carpet. 'Well, he wouldn't leave me alone, and she wasn't doing anything about it. So I went to the police station, made a statement, and then – sort of everybody run around, like, asking me all these questions. Then a doctor examined me, and . . . ' He dragged deeply, letting the smoke trickle out. 'Oh, yeah. This copper. He gets me into his office.'

'And?' Tennison leaned forward. 'What happened then, Jason?'

'He said that if I said I was lying, that he would make sure I had it cushy – you know, money, cigarettes. Things like that. And that they'd move me – somewhere nice.'

He shook his hair back and looked up at her. He had beautiful eyes, but their expression was opaque, a deadness deep down.

'Do you remember this police officer's name?' Tennison asked quietly. 'Was he wearing a uniform?'

'Nah! He was a friend of Parker's. They worked it between them.' His tone was dismissive. That's how the world operated. Those with power and influence dumped on the great unwashed below. Fact of life. 'So they sent me back,' he went on, and laughed without humour. 'They never got around to moving me, and I became a very heavy smoker.'

Jason took a last drag and stubbed out the cigarette on

the tiled hearth. He sat up and favoured Tennison with a sunny, beaming smile.

'That's it.'

Tennison nodded. 'Do you remember the name of the doctor? The one that examined you?'

'Be no help if I did. He died of cancer, nice guy. Think his name was something Ellis.'

Dalton made a note.

Tennison said, 'Was it all the boys, Jason? Or specifically the very young ones?'

'The little 'uns, he liked the little ones.'

'Do you have a job?'

'Nope. No qualifications. A five-year-old kid reads better than me. I do odd jobs around the place, fix up cars.' He smiled in a simple, childlike way. 'I get drunk, and sometimes I get angry.'

'And then you get into trouble?' Tennison hesitated. 'Have you ever told somebody about your past, Jason?'

'There's no point.' Again the offhand dismissal. 'I just have to live with it.'

Tennison fastened her briefcase and sat with it across her knees, her hands gripping the sides. She said softly, 'I will do everything possible to put this man away. I promise you.'

Jason stared at her, as if she might possibly mean it, and then he laughed harshly. 'You haven't even got him, have you?'

She couldn't find it in her heart to lie to him. She shook her head, and Jason laughed again, harsh and angry.

He led them out, past the pram in the hallway, and stood on the concrete balcony in his bare feet. A short flight of steps led down to the walkway, littered with broken bottles and crushed beer cans. The breeze ruffled Jason's pyjama top. A change had come over him. He followed after them, speaking in a mechanical monotone, telling them a tale, his breathing rapid.

'One night at the home we was watching a documentary, Nazi thing. This guy ran a concentration camp, you know what they are?'

Tennison and Dalton had paused to listen. They both nodded.

Jason leaned back, his shoulder blades pressed against the concrete wall. 'Yeah, well, this guy was called the "Angel of Death", right? And after the war, he escaped, right? He was never hanged, nobody arrested him, nobody brought him to trial ... ' He gave a peculiar croaking giggle. 'Just like Parker. He did me for eight years, he did every boy in his care. You know what we used to call him? We called him "The Keeper of Souls".' He grinned down at them.

Tennison put her hand out. 'Go back up the stairs, Jason. There's glass on the stairs, you'll hurt yourself ... '

Jason's fingers tore at the pyjama top. He ripped it off and flung it down the stairs. 'You want to see what the "Keeper" did to me?'

He staggered down the steps towards Tennison. Dalton tensed, about to dive up, thinking he was about to attack her. But Jason turned around, showing the pale scars on his skinny back. Tennison touched his shoulder, and moved her hand gently down the hard ridges of puckered flesh. 'I will make him pay, Jason, I promise you . . .'

Jason slowly turned, and Tennison could barely tolerate the terrible desolate anguish in his eyes. The buried pain, the torment of those years, was even worse than the horrible scars. His lips trembled, but he couldn't speak. He bowed his head and nodded mutely, his hair hanging down over his bare white shoulders.

Tennison went down. Hunched inside, her throat dry and tight, she heard his agonized whisper, swirled by the breeze down the concrete stairwell. '*Keeper of Souls . . . Keeper of Souls.*'

Bronwen stood by the car, the rear door open. 'We'll only just make your train.'

Drained of all energy, Tennison tossed her briefcase inside. She turned, holding the door, taking one last look back at the godforsaken place. She clutched her throat. Jason was balanced on the edge of the balcony. His arms were spread wide, exposing his ribcage, the narrow chest. He swayed forward.

'Jason! No!' Tennison's cry was shrill, almost a screech. '*NO!*'

He fell, a pale blur, turning over in the air, and they heard his body hit the ground, a soft moist sound, hidden behind a concrete parapet. Dalton raced forward across the scrubby patch of mud and scrambled over the wall. Tennison, in her heeled boots, struggled up the slope. She gripped the wall and craned to see over. Dalton was kneeling by the crumpled body, feeling for his pulse. He lifted the eyelids, searching for a reflex. Very gently he cupped Jason's head in his hands, and looked towards Tennison.

Badly hurt, but he wasn't dead, Tennison knew that, because the boy was weeping. She could see the tears streaming down his cheeks from his closed eyes.

She closed her own eyes and rested her forehead against the rough grey concrete. Tears smarted her eyes, but she wouldn't cry. She refused to cry. She held on to the emotion, hoarding it, needing it like a fix, feeding her the strength for what she had to do.

Tennison sat at one of the three computer consoles in the Records Department of Cardiff Police Station. It was 12.35 p.m., and the train had long gone. Bronwen stood with arms folded, looking over her shoulder. Tennison scrolled the list of addresses up the screen. She took a mouthful of lukewarm coffee and made a *Yuck!* face. She jotted an address down and held up the pad.

'Is there any way you can do a cross-check on this for me?' Bronwen hesitated, rubbing her palms. 'It's lunchtime. Come on, see what you can do.'

Bronwen took the sheet and went out, almost colliding with Dalton. Tennison looked up anxiously.

'He'll live. Broken leg and hip bone.' Dalton shrugged out of his raincoat, giving Tennison a straight look to reassure her. 'He's okay.'

'You've been a long time.'

'Yeah, he . . . he wanted me with him.' Dalton cleared his throat. 'He was crying, kept on saying he was sorry . . . sorry for crying.' Dalton gave a wan smile. He was still badly shaken. 'His wife and kid, I sent a cab for them.'

'There's another train at two twenty-five,' Tennison said, glancing at her watch. Already she was back studying the screen, concentrating.

'Jason and Anthony, it's too much of a coincidence.' She chewed her lip. 'If Edward Parker-Jones moved on, maybe so did the same police officer.'

She was watching the screen, but even so she could feel Dalton's unease. She'd let him go his own sweet way, allowed him into her confidence. Sooner or later he would have to pay for the privilege. She judged the time was ripe.

'Any developments on Jackson?' Dalton asked. He blinked several times when she looked at him. 'You said he'd been picked up . . .'

'No. What about you? Have you heard from the hospital yet?'

Involuntarily he touched his bandaged hand. 'No, not yet,' he said stiffly. 'Still waiting.'

'How long does it take?'

'Don't know.'

There was a silence. Tennison sat back in her chair and gave him a cool level stare. Dalton fidgeted, then shoved his hands in his pockets in a weak show of indifference.

Yes, the time was definitely ripe.

'Why don't you tell me what a high flyer like you is doing attached to this investigation?'

'What do you mean?' Dalton blustered.

'You're from the Fraud Squad, university educated, you're hand-in-glove with Chiswick, you report back to him.' Tennison swept her arms wide. 'For God's sake, when are you going to come clean! You're my mate, come on!'

Dalton stared at the floor, no doubt hoping a yawning chasm would appear and swallow him up. He wagged his head back and forth. 'I have to report back to Commander Chiswick if – only *if* – your investigation crosses another investigation.'

Tennison waited.

'Yes? And? Come on, now you've started.' Tennison's eyes bored into his, whenever he had the nerve to meet them. 'You have to report back to Chiswick. About what exactly?'

Dalton was a deeply unhappy man. His usual tan was

looking none too healthy. 'It's about the blackmail of an Assistant Deputy Chief Commissioner. He was or had been on enforced leave for eight months. Six months previous to the blackmail threats.'

Tennison stared at him. She snapped her teeth together. 'I don't believe this.'

'One of the most senior officers ever to be subjected to disciplinary procedures. The matter was passed to the Home Office from Scotland Yard . . .'

'So who the hell is it?'

Dalton jumped as if her bark had bitten him. 'Assistant Deputy Commissioner John Kennington.' It only just crept out.

'What was going on before the blackmail? Eight months is a long time. It must have been something big.'

'His possible connection to a paedophile ring,' Dalton said.

Tennison rested her forehead on her hand, shaking her head to and fro. She was thinking that she must have porridge for brains. Not even an inkling until now. And it was so obvious – all the incestuous spying and rumours and heavy hints. Where had she been *living*? Disneyland?

Bronwen came in. She was smiling.

'Margaret Speel. She's now based in—'

'London!' Tennison said, jumping up. 'Thank you very much!'

*

'Kennington vehemently denied all the allegations of wrongdoing, which also included bribery and handing out favours, and he cooperated in a full inquiry. My department was brought in, we examined every log book, letter, document in his entire career file. We checked his associates outside the police – receipts, hotel bills, airline tickets.'

Tennison and Dalton sat on a bench seat, platform 4, waiting for the London train. The rain had held off, but there was a nasty gusting wind, shuffling the cigarette packets and sweet wrappers at their feet, piling them in corners.

Unable to stomach British Rail coffee, Tennison was drinking hot chocolate from a plastic cup. She was still getting to grips with what Dalton had told her. She felt numbed by it, the double-dealing and duplicity going on all around while she was busting a gut, doing her level best to conduct an honest, professional investigation. Her anger, like the other violent emotions, was seething under the surface.

'And at the end of this big investigation, what was the outcome?'

'One and a half million quid later we were no farther in proving otherwise.' Elbows on his knees, Dalton was leaning forward, smoothing down the tape on his bandaged hand where the edge had come unstuck. 'And no evidence that he was involved in any perverted sexual activity.'

Tennison frowned to herself. Something here that didn't make sense. As yet she couldn't quite put her finger on it.

'Kennington was reinstated, but moved to a different department,' Dalton continued. 'The entire investigation made everyone really jumpy, especially if it ever got leaked to the press.'

'Well, of course,' Tennison said caustically, 'and they put a lid on it.' Put a lid on her, too.

'But it all opened up again.' Dalton peered at her from under his brows. 'About six months ago, of his own voli- tion, Kennington ...'

'Admitted it?'

Dalton shook his head. 'No, this time he was being blackmailed. He wanted to press charges. But I suppose under pressure he withdrew. He resigned. No case was ever brought.'

Tennison's anger bubbled up dangerously. 'And who was doing the blackmailing?'

'I don't know. I was off the case by then.' He caught the full impact of her flat disbelieving stare, and insisted, 'I really don't know. But I would say, whoever it was, must have some connection with your investigation, otherwise why would they have brought me in?'

'Are you expecting me to believe that Kennington was prepared to bring charges of being blackmailed but never named who was doing it to him?'

'If he did, I was never told . . . '

Tennison decided she couldn't stomach British Rail hot chocolate either. She got up and chucked the half-filled cup into the basket. She paced up and down, scarf whipping in the chill gusts. She stopped in front of Dalton.

'Did Edward Parker-Jones's name ever come up? Was there any connection proved between him and Kennington?'

'The Fraud Squad discovered there had been several charitable donations from Kennington to Parker-Jones.' Dalton held up his hand to forestall Tennison's fierce nod. 'But they were all legal, all documented. The advice centre was only one of a number of organizations Kennington donated monies to. They found nothing incriminating.'

The smell of all this was positively reeking now.

'Could that be why Chiswick wants me to back off Parker-Jones?' Dalton made a vague gesture. Tennison pressed him. 'There has to be some reason unless . . . was it Parker-Jones doing the blackmail?'

'No way. As I said, he was checked out.'

'Who do you think it was? Oh, come on, you must suspect somebody,' Tennison said, losing patience.

Dalton looked up at her. 'It could be Jackson.'

'Yes, there's always Jackson.' Tennison paced, pushing her wind-ruffled hair back from her forehead. 'Let me try this on you.' She was trying it on herself as much as on

Dalton. 'Kennington had been investigated and came up smelling of roses. He must have been very confident, but then he's forced to resign. Connie was selling his story to Jessica Smithy, right? Claiming that he was prepared to name names – one a high-ranking police officer. What if it was Kennington? Connie was just a rent boy, swat him like a fly. He was just a kid, no parents, nobody to even identify his body.'

Tennison stood in front of Dalton, pushing her hair back, staring down at him. Dalton was intent on his hand, pressing the tape flat with his thumbnail.

The minute Superintendent Halliday walked into the Squad Room, Otley picked up the warning signal. He was in one of his twitchy moods. He kept squirming his neck inside his collar and rubbing his throat as if undergoing slow strangulation. Most of the Vice team were there, busy at their desks. Ray Hebdon looked to Larry Hall, who in turn glanced at Haskons and Lillie. Norma stopped typing.

The room quieted. Halliday tapped his watch. It was late in the afternoon, going on for five.

'Is there anyone in this building who can tell me where Detective Chief Inspector Tennison is?'

'She's on her way from Cardiff, boss, expecting her any moment,' Otley called out.

Halliday nodded, lips tight. He turned to leave, and

turned back, seething. He pointed at Haskons and Lillie, available targets to vent his spleen on.

'And you two, as far as I am concerned, have behaved in what can only be described as an utterly farcical manner – one which would, if ever it were made public – put not only myself but also this entire department in jeopardy.'

Lillie coloured up, while Haskons looked defiant. Otley turned away to hide a grin.

Commander Chiswick pushed open the door and said to Halliday, 'In your office,' and went out.

'Just tell me – what in God's name possessed you to do it?'

'But we brought Jackson in, sir!' Haskons protested, rising to his feet. 'He is still the main suspect for the murder of Colin Jenkins.'

The door opened again, and Chiswick's stern face appeared.

'Sorry, I'll be right with you,' Halliday said. He strode to the door, rubbing the back of his neck. He whipped around. 'DS Haskons, DC Lillie – you will return to Southampton Row as from tomorrow evening. DI Ray Hebdon will leave today. That's all.'

He pushed at the door, and something caught his eye. A doll was pinned to the notice board, golden curls and a frilly pink dress with pink satin slippers. The block printing above it read: 'DI HEBDON. FAIRY OF THE WEEK.'

Halliday's nostrils twitched. 'Get this crap down!' He slammed out.

The door squeaked to a stop, and in the silence everyone looked at one another. Otley leaned against the desk, hands in his pockets.

'Just a passing thought, but does anybody have any idea where she is?' He nodded to the clock. 'She should have left Cardiff hours ago!'

Chapter Fourteen

On arrival in London, Tennison deliberately hadn't reported in. She'd sent Dalton off to pick up a car while she took a cab to the Islington Probation Department, with instructions for him to meet her there. It was after five o'clock, and she was afraid that Margaret Speel might have gone, but she hadn't. She was writing up reports in a tiny cluttered office that had a look of impermanence about it, as if she were in the process of moving in or moving out, Tennison couldn't decide which.

However temporary her office, Margaret Speel's sarcastic manner was firmly in place, exactly as before. There was something about the cynical slant of her mouth that was extremely irritating. In her petite bouncy way, she reminded Tennison of a chirpy strutting sparrow with an attitude problem: however smart you think you are, I know I'm smarter.

285

'Now what can I do for you, Chief Inspector?' she said world-wearily, gesturing to a chair. Her mouth slanted. 'You want any more boys off the streets?'

Tennison sat down. She placed her briefcase on the faded carpet and sat up straight. She was all through with taking crap, especially from a cheeky sparrow with an irritating smirk.

'You were at one time working in Cardiff, yes?'

Margaret Speel rocked back in the chair. She recovered quickly. 'Yes, and Liverpool. And I've also worked in Birmingham.'

'Was Edward Parker-Jones also working in Liverpool and Birmingham?'

'No.'

'Well, we can be thankful for that, can't we?' Margaret Speel's eyes narrowed under her dark fringe; she was a mite uncertain now, getting edgy. Tennison kept up the barrage. 'Do you know Anthony Field?'

A hard glare, and a frown.

'No? What about Jason Baldwyn? He was a resident at—'

'Yes,' Margaret Speel interrupted. 'Yes, I remember Jason.'

'Do you have a relationship with Edward Parker-Jones?'

'I don't think that is any of your business,' Margaret Speel said in a quiet, outraged voice.

'But it is. It is very much my business.' Tennison leaned

towards her. She stared her full in the face. 'Jason tried to kill himself this afternoon, right in front of me, Margaret. He's prepared to make a statement that when he was in the care of Parker-Jones he was sexually abused, for a period of six years. You were at that time his probation officer!'

Margaret Speel's hand jerked to her throat. Her fingers plucked at a necklace of jade beads. Her pale neck was taut and strained.

'You were Jason's probation officer, weren't you? Jason Baldwyn's probation officer.'

'Yes, yes I was,' Margaret Speel said in a barely audible whisper.

'Do you have anything to say about these allegations? Were you aware of them when you were working in Cardiff?'

Margaret Speel was struggling to take this in. Her chirpy sarcasm was gone, shocked out of her. She made a valiant, desperate effort that only came out sounding weak. 'Jason was always telling lies, he was a compulsive liar—'

'Ten-year-old boy, Margaret, and you refused to believe him, and he had six more years of abuse,' Tennison went on relentlessly.

'This isn't true!' She shook her head, almost in pain. 'This is terrible . . . if I had believed, for one moment . . . '

'Believe it, Margaret. What do you know about Connie – Colin Jenkins – Margaret?'

'I was telling you the truth! I swear I didn't even come here until eighteen months ago. Edward contacted me. He even tried to renew our relationship . . . ' Her head dropped. Tennison let her stew. She believed that Margaret Speel was genuinely distraught, she even felt sorry for her, but Tennison's bottled anger fuelled a passion to cut straight to the rotten heart of this, to ruthlessly expose it to the light, no matter who got hurt along the way.

'Are you sure?' Margaret Speel asked, feebly grasping at straws. 'You know, these young boys make up stories, and I remember Jason—'

'Margaret – do you also remember if a doctor examined Jason Baldwyn?'

'Yes, of course he was examined.'

'Margaret, do you recall a police officer? Someone who would have known Parker-Jones in Cardiff?'

'Do you mean John Kennington?'

Tennison's face remained calm, she didn't so much as move a muscle. She felt as if she had been struck by a lightning bolt. With scarcely a pause she said blithely, 'It could possibly be John Kennington. Do you recall what rank, or if he was uniformed or plainclothes?'

'Er, yes, um . . . ' Confused, still in a state of shock, Margaret Speel rubbed her forehead. 'I think he was – Superintendent. I never saw him in a uniform. He lives in London now.'

As if it was of minor interest, Tennison said casually, 'Do you happen to know if John Kennington and Parker-Jones are still in touch? Still friendly?'

'Yes, yes I think so.'

Tennison thanked her and left. On her way out she heard Margaret Speel sobbing at her desk. She didn't like the woman, though she did pity her.

Tennison sat in the driver's seat outside the steeply gabled house with white-leaded windows, a dense windbreak of conifers shielding it from the road. Dalton, very subdued, sat woodenly beside her. Tennison clicked the door open and looked across at him. He knew what she was about to do, and what the consequences were, and both of them knew where it put him. Between a rock and a hard place. Anyway, his decision, she thought. He was a big boy now and she certainly was no wet nurse.

'You can stay in the car if you want!' Tennison said bluntly.

Dalton clenched his jaw, bit the bullet, and reached for the door handle.

A middle-aged housekeeper with a foreign accent showed them into the large L-shaped drawing room. French windows gave a restful evening view of a flagged patio with stone urns of flowers, and beyond a stone balustrade a lawn sloped down to a grove of beech trees.

A grandfather clock, genuine antique to Tennison's inexpert eye, ticked solemnly in the corner, emphasizing the silence. There was a baby grand on a small platform, a Chopin étude on the music stand. Two long wing-backed sofas covered in rose silks faced each other across a coffee table that was bigger than the kitchen table in Tennison's flat. The fireplace was white lacquered wood inlaid with gold leaf, and displayed on the mantel were family photographs in ornate silver frames. Tennison went over for a closer look.

'Well, he didn't buy this on wages,' was her considered opinion, after giving the room the once-over. 'This place must be worth a packet.'

'It happens to be my wife's.'

John Kennington stood in the doorway. He came in, tall and distinguished, with silvery hair brushed back from a high tanned forehead. As a young man he must have been stunningly handsome. Even dressed in a buttoned fawn cardigan and dark green corduroys, with soft leather loafers, he gave the appearance of fine taste and casual elegance. He was totally at ease, charming, and rather patronizing.

Tennison had never met him before. She'd seen him from afar, once, at a grand reception for a delegation of European police chiefs. At the moment she was a bit unnerved, both by him and the surroundings, but she was damned if she was going to show it.

She said formally, 'I am Detective Chief Inspector Jane Tennison, and this is Detective Inspector Brian Dalton.'

Kennington didn't invite them to sit. He looked from one to the other, and negligently scratched an eyebrow.

'What seems to be the problem?'

'I am making inquiries into the death of a young boy, Colin Jenkins. Do you know him?'

Kennington shook his head. He strolled over to the fireplace.

Tennison turned to keep facing him. 'Do you know a James Jackson?'

'No.'

'Do you know an Anthony Field, sir?'

'No.'

'A Jason Baldwyn?'

'No.'

'Do you know Edward Parker-Jones?'

Kennington hesitated before shaking his head. 'No, I can't say that I do.'

The grandfather clock ticked on in the brief silence.

'You were at one time stationed in Manchester,' Tennison said, 'and previous to that, Cardiff, is that correct?'

'Yes.'

'Did you at any time meet a Miss Margaret Speel?' She watched him closely. 'A probation officer?'

Kennington shook his head again, this time more abruptly. 'I'm sorry, I don't recall the name.'

He was good at stonewalling, and this could have gone on all night. Tennison didn't have time to waste.

'Your recent resignation, sir – you were about to initiate charges which due to your retirement—'

'What exactly is this inquiry about, Chief Inspector?'

His tone had sharpened. He no longer held the rank of Assistant Deputy Commissioner, but he retained the gravitas of past authority, the prestige of office that demanded a certain respect.

'I should be most grateful if you would answer the questions, sir,' Tennison persisted, refusing to be bullied or patronized.

'I have no inclination to answer anything else, and I would appreciate it if you left my house.' He made a brusque gesture of dismissal. Dalton shuffled his feet. He looked to Tennison, a mute agonized plea in his eyes.

'Colin Jenkins also used the name Connie,' Tennison said, standing up straight. 'Do you recall ever meeting him? He was fifteen years old, about my height, with pale red hair. He was, sir, a practising homosexual . . .'

Mottled spots of red had appeared in Kennington's cheeks. He was nearly a foot taller than Tennison, and he came forward, using it to intimidate her.

'I'd like you both to leave. Now.'

Dalton was already halfway to the door. He wanted to physically drag Tennison with him, but the woman hadn't budged. She stood her ground, gesturing to the silver frames on the mantel.

'It was just that I noticed ... you have a number of photographs of young—'

'They are my sons,' Kennington said, his outrage giving his voice a harsh rasp. 'Please leave my house NOW!' He stood over her, trembling, fists clenching and unclenching.

'Was Colin Jenkins blackmailing you? Was Parker-Jones attempting to put pressure on you? Which one of them was blackmailing you? Were you aware Colin was selling his story to the newspapers?'

Kennington raised his fist as if he might strike her. He dropped it as an attractive, middle-aged woman came briskly in, her streakily grey hair cut short in a young style that actually suited her. She passed Dalton and looked around, smiling vaguely.

'Oh! I'm sorry ... ' She looked to her husband. 'John?'

Tennison stepped forward, holding out her hand. 'Mrs Kennington, I am—'

Kennington grasped her by the elbow and started pushing her. Tennison pulled her arm free and stood back, holding up both hands.

'Please!' She smoothed her sleeve straight. 'Mrs Kennington, your husband was just answering some questions. I am investigating the death of a young rent boy, fifteen years old, and I'm—'

Mrs Kennington's eyes widened in alarm as her husband bodily propelled Tennison across the room. Leaning forward, face carved out of stone, he thrust her ahead of him into the hallway, and kept on going.

'His name was Colin Jenkins, you may have read about it . . .'

Tennison's fading voice was interrupted by the sound of the front door being swung violently open on its hinges.

Dalton and Mrs Kennington looked at one another. It was hard to know who was the more shocked. Dalton gathered his wits and quickly went out.

Standing at the coffee table, Mrs Kennington reached down, and without looking took a cigarette from a black ebony box. The front door slammed shut. She held the cigarette between her fingers and slowly and deliberately crumpled it, her face frozen in a white mask.

Dalton beside her, Tennison drove into the yard at the rear of Southampton Row Police Station. This was her old division, before being shunted sideways to Soho Vice. Her old boss, Chief Superintendent Kernan, was crossing the yard to his car. Genuinely, or by design – hard to tell – he happened not to see her. She rolled the window down and stuck her head out.

'Buy you a drink?'

Rather reluctantly, he came over. 'Sorry, I'm late as it is.' His pouchy cheeks and heavy jowls always reminded her of a disgruntled chipmunk. She couldn't once recall him looking happy, except when he was pissed. He nodded to Dalton. 'Nothing wrong, is there?'

'What do you know about John Kennington?' Tennison asked.

Kernan sighed and stared off somewhere. He didn't hold with women having senior positions in the force, and that applied to Tennison in spades. She was a real ball-breaker. He bent down to the window.

'He just got the golden handshake. Why?'

'Is he homosexual?'

Kernan laughed abrasively. 'I don't know – why do you ask?'

Tennison opened the door and started to get out. Kernan backed away, making a negative motion. 'I've got to go, Jane ... '

Tennison did get out. Kernan's shoulders slumped as she confronted him. 'Mike, I need to know because I think he is involved in this murder, the rent boy—'

'I've nothing to tell you.' His face was a closed book.

Tennison gave him a hard, penetrating stare. She said in a low urgent voice that was almost pleading, 'They're young kids, Mike, some of them eleven and twelve years of age – your boy's age. All I want is the truth.'

Kernan glanced guardedly towards Dalton in the car, and moved farther off. He looked down on her, flat-eyed. 'Do you want me to spell it out?'

'Yes.'

'If you start digging dirt up again on Kennington,' he muttered, shaking his head, 'it'll be a waste of time. He may no longer be a big fish, but he'll have a hell of a lot of friends who still are. A whisper gets out, you'll tip them off and you won't get near them, and it won't help the kids, won't stop the punters. They'll all be still on the streets. You should back off this one, Jane.'

'Even if he was a high-ranking police officer,' Tennison said heatedly. 'Even if there are judges, politicians, barristers involved ...'

'Kennington's out of the force now,' Kernan said heavily, trying to make her see sense. 'Ignore it, that's the best, the only advice I can give you.'

Tennison nodded slowly, but it didn't fool him. She pursed her lips. 'There's a Superintendent vacancy up for grabs, you know which area?'

Kernan gazed at her for a moment. He held up his hand, fingers and thumb spread wide. Five. He gave a smirk and said out of the corner of his mouth, 'Becoming a player, are you?'

Tennison nodded. She got back in the car and slammed the door. She revved the engine and put it in reverse. Kernan stood watching.

'Good night!' he called out.

'Thanks, Mike,' Tennison said, backing up.

Kernan whacked his open hand on the car roof and she

shot off, through the archway to the main road. He shook his head wearily, puzzled and pissed off. If he couldn't stick the woman at any price – and dammit he couldn't – why did he so admire the bloody bitch?

Twenty minutes later Tennison dumped her briefcase on her desk, flung her coat over a chair, and scooped up the sheaves of reports, internal memos, and phone messages that had piled up in her absence. After twelve straight hours on the job she was fighting off bone-weary fatigue with pure nervous energy. Her nerve ends jangled.

Dalton trailed in after her. He had a limp, wrung-out look to him, the classic symptoms of bags under the eyes and pasty complexion, sweat trickling from the roots of his hair.

He stood, slack shouldered, making a great effort. 'Can I say something, apologize really, but I didn't have much say in the matter and I've . . . '

His voice trailed away when he realized she wasn't listening, too preoccupied as she scanned through the messages. The silence sank in.

'What? I'm sorry?'

'I'm sorry, and, well . . . ' His speech stumbled along. 'I dunno where I am. It's like I'm in some kind of limbo . . . '

Tennison paid full attention. Dalton seemed to be cracking up in front of her eyes. He wasn't able to look at her, too embarrassed or fearful or something, and it all came tumbling out in a flood, a dam-burst of raw feeling.

'I can't sleep and, well, my girlfriend, I haven't told her. I'm even scared to have sex with her because ...' He swallowed painfully. 'It's just hanging over me all the time. What if I have got AIDS?' His eyes suddenly filled with tears. He choked down a sob, standing there forlorn and pitiful. 'I'm sorry, sorry ...'

Tennison went to him and put her arms around him. She gave him a strong, comforting hug. She could feel him shaking inside. She stood back, holding his shoulders.

'Listen, anyone would feel the same way. And, listen – I think it'll be good for you to sit and really talk it all out ... and to someone who understands all the fears – and they're real, Brian.' She touched his wet face. 'You go and wash up. I've got the contacts here for you, okay?' She nodded to her desk. 'Maybe you and your girlfriend should go together.'

Dalton let out a shuddering sigh. 'Yeah, thanks. Thanks a lot.'

He wiped his face with the back of his hand and turned to leave. Tennison waited for the door to close. She pressed both hands to her face, covering her eyes. She held a deep breath for a count of five, and then snapped back into action, picking up her messages as she returned to her chair.

The door was rapped. Otley looked in.

'We've got Parker-Jones in interview room D oh three.'

'What?! He's here?' Otley nodded. Tennison glared at him. 'Whose bloody idea was that?'

'Mine,' Otley retorted, sauntering in. 'We got some kids that recognized Deputy Chief Commissioner Kennington's house. Plus, the property where we picked up Jackson, it's owned by him.'

'What?' Tennison was on her feet.

'Jackson's been living in a house owned by Parker-Jones. It's all there . . .' He made a flippant gesture to the desk. 'Full report.'

'Who's interviewing him?'

'Haskons and Lillie.'

Tennison swore under her breath as she scoured the littered desk for his report.

Otley's long gaunt face was looking distinctly tetchy. He'd worked his bollocks off on this case, and what did he get in return? Sweet F.A. Overbearing cow. 'And as you weren't here,' he said, not troubling to hide his sarcasm, 'and we couldn't contact you, I'm just trying to close the case.'

Tennison flared up. '*You?* I know what you're playing at, but you are just not good enough. Stop trying to demean me at every opportunity. This *isn't* your case!'

'I know that.'

'Then stop working by yourself. I didn't want Parker-Jones brought in yet.'

'You got a reason?' Otley said, insolent to the last.

She had half a dozen, but she'd be damned if she was going to rhyme them off, chapter and verse, for his benefit. She was in charge of this investigation, and Bill Otley had better wise up to it double quick.

'I'm not ready for him,' was the only reason she – Detective Chief Inspector Tennison – felt obliged to give the cheeky toe-rag.

Edward Parker-Jones, quietly casual in a dark check sports jacket, collar and tie, green suede shoes, sat in interview room D.03. Haskons sat directly opposite him, with a beautiful shiner of a black eye and a cut lip. Lillie had a bruised forehead where Jackson had butted him and a bandage on his chin over the wound he had dabbed with TCP cream.

'Yes, the properties are mine. I have admitted that they are, and I would, if you had asked, given the information freely. I have nothing to hide.'

He was one cool customer, Haskons thought. A real con artist, and he'd met a few. But, so far, Mr Parker-Jones was completely legit, and had to be handled with care.

'Do you have the books?' Haskons asked, raising his undamaged eyebrow. 'You are paid a considerable amount of money from not only Camden Council, but also Holloway and Hackney.'

'They are very large houses, and yes, if you wish to see

the books, then all you have to do is contact my account-ant. Taking care of the homeless is not a lucrative business, far from it. Laundry bills, heating, electricity, water ...' He looked pointedly at his watch, shaking his head and sighing. 'Is all this really necessary? Why exactly have I been brought in yet again? Why wasn't this all asked before? I have been perfectly willing, and cooperative ...'

The door swung open. It was as if an icy blast had swept in.

Lillie bent towards the mike. 'The time is six-thirty and DCI Tennison has just entered the interview room.'

Haskons took one look at Tennison's face and vacated his seat. She sat down in it. She wasn't afraid to let the silence linger as she settled herself, flipped open her note-book and unscrewed the cap of her fountain pen. She looked up.

'Could you please tell us about your relationship with Margaret Speel?'

Parker-Jones hooked a finger over one ear, pushing back a trailing strand of jet-black hair. 'She's my fiancée.' The question hadn't surprised him, or if it had he'd cov-ered superbly.

'Did you, in 1979, run the Harrow Home for boys in Manchester?'

'Yes.'

However closely Tennison scrutinized him, she couldn't detect a flicker of concern or unease.

'And in 1986 the Calloway Centre in Cardiff?'

'Yes.'

'Do you know Anthony Field?'

A half smile. 'Yes.'

'And Jason Baldwyn?'

'Yes, they were both in my care.'

Tennison pretended to jot something down. Eyes downcast, she said, 'Do you also know John Kennington?'

Parker-Jones eased back in the chair. His body language gave nothing away. He tilted his head slightly. 'Yes – not well, but I have met him.'

'Could you tell me about one of your employees, James Jackson?'

'I wouldn't call it employed, but he did on the odd occasion do some repairs – caretaking, that sort of thing.'

'How well did you know Mr Jackson?'

'As I have already stated,' Parker-Jones said, making it sound weary and pedantic. 'I did not know Mr Jackson on a personal or social level. He simply did the occasional odd job for me. Nothing more.'

Tennison leaned her elbows on the table. 'But he lived in a property owned by you, Mr Parker-Jones.'

Parker-Jones looked to the ceiling. He smiled very patiently, humouring her. 'Again I have admitted this. I paid Jackson only a nominal amount, and in return for his room he repaired the property. I have no reason to know or even be aware of what Mr Jackson did in his private life.' He spread his hands. 'I was also unaware if he lived there on a permanent basis, as he told me he had an elderly mother he took care of and spent a lot of time with.'

Tennison decided to pass on the elderly mother. She idly wondered why he hadn't bothered to mention that she was white-haired, crippled, and had multiple sclerosis as well. Instead she said:

'What other names have you been known under?'

'I have two houses in the name of Edwards, and one in the name of Jones.' Glib, straight out with it. As if he already knew the questions and had rehearsed the answers. 'I have on occasions used both.'

'Why did you use different names on the deeds of these properties?'

'I just did.' The half smile appeared. 'There is no law against it.'

She'd started off gentle, tossed him some easy ones, and he'd batted them back without breaking sweat. She now got ready to lob a few grenades. Her voice went up a pitch.

'Would you like to tell me about the two charges for indecent assault? The ones in Manchester, and Cardiff!'

Parker-Jones fiddled with his signet ring. 'Not really. In both incidents all charges were dropped.' His deep-set eyes returned her gaze, measure for measure. 'I can see no reason to discuss them.'

'Did John Kennington assist or advise you in any way concerning these two sexual assault charges?'

'I don't recall.'

'Have you at any time in the past months attempted to get monies from John Kennington?'

'What?' He blinked several times.

'Blackmail? Or extortion? Have you, Mr Parker-Jones, *attempted to get monies?*'

'Absolutely not.' He laughed at the idea. 'Ridiculous.'

'Were you aware that John Kennington was consider-ing bringing blackmail charges against—'

'I would obviously not consider attempting to extort monies out of someone who freely donated to my centre,' he said caustically. He tapped the table with his manicured fingers. 'I have, as requested, presented a detailed list of all those who forward charitable donations to the centre. I presume this information was passed on to you ...'

Tennison cut across him. 'Did you on the night of the seventeenth of this month call the emergency services?' she asked sharply.

He hadn't rehearsed this one, because he stared blankly at her for a second. 'I'm sorry?'

'Did you call an ambulance? On the night of the sev-enteenth of this month?'

'No.'

'Would you please state where you were on the night

304

of the seventeenth from eight-fifteen p.m. to nine-thirty p.m.'

'I have told you,' Parker-Jones ground out. 'I never left the advice centre.' He threw up his hands. 'This is really becoming ludicrous ...' He looked at Haskons and Lillie, as if they might help him in dealing with this raving mad-woman.

'You think so?' Tennison said, her voice as soft now as it had been sharp a moment earlier. Her tone implied that they hadn't reached ridiculous yet, never mind ludicrous.

'Do you know it is illegal to display false credentials?' While he was grappling with this change of tack, she switched again.

'We would like the names of the witnesses who you say saw you at the centre for the duration of the evening of the seventeenth.'

Parker-Jones slumped back.

Not *again*.

He was beginning to get an inkling of what lengths ludicrousness could get to. He started off, lips thinning as he repeated the old familiar litany of names:

'Billy Matthews ... Disco Driscoll ... Alan Thorpe ... Kenny Lloyd ... Jimmy Jackson ...'

The Squad Room was winding down. The last reports of the day were being written up. A skeleton staff would be on duty through the night, but most of the team had knocked off at seven.

Kathy was at the alibis board when Tennison wandered in. She looked dead on her feet. Hungry yet too tired to eat, she was hollow-eyed and ratty.

Kathy turned with a big beaming smile. 'I think I deserve a bottle of champagne because ...' She tapped the board with a felt-tip marker. 'Billy Matthews's alibi is now withdrawn. Billy was not at the advice centre or anywhere near it. He was in fact in hospital, taken there by ambulance on the night of the sixteenth. And this is the best part – from the advice centre ...'

Tennison stuck up a clenched fist. One more down. She looked at the list of names. 'Martin Fletcher dead.'

'... Donald Driscoll, alibi withdrawn,' Kathy went on. 'Kenny Lloyd ditto. Just Parker-Jones giving Jackson an alibi and vice versa. The only other one out of the entire list is Alan Thorpe, and he has admitted he was drunk! If we'd been able to keep Jackson locked up, we'd have probably got them to admit they lied earlier on.'

An aura of energy had transformed Tennison. Adrenaline pumping, she stared at the board, eyes gleaming.

'Where've they got Jackson?'

Haskons and Lillie had entered, and Haskons said, 'He's with the Sarge and Larry the Lamb, room D oh five downstairs.'

Without acknowledgment for Kathy's success, or even a word of thanks, Tennison did a smart about-face and marched to the door. A tight-lipped Kathy watched her go, hands on hips.

Passing Haskons and Lillie, Tennison said briskly, 'You two. Divvy up a bottle of Moët for Kathy, in repayment for that fiasco . . .'

She pointed. On the notice board next to the door were two photographs of the pair of them, dug out of the files and blown up, their lips daubed with red felt-tip, flouncy dresses sketched over their outdoor clothes. The caption read, 'FAIRIES OF THE WEEK.'

'Bloody hell, who put those up?' Lillie snarled, flushing pink.

The culprit, Kathy, giggled behind her hand. Tennison shot one look back and went out. From the corridor came her full-throated, uninhibited bellow of laughter.

Chapter Fifteen

'What did Connie owe you this money for?' DI Hall asked.

'He needed to get some photographs, he needed some new gear.' Jackson shrugged. 'Well, that's what he told me, so I lent him the dough.'

He looked up as Tennison came in. He nodded and smiled at her in a friendly fashion. For the record, Hall stated that DCI Tennison had entered the room, timed at 7.35 p.m. He went on to ask Jackson, 'How much?'

'Two hundred quid. Then he disappears. So, I go out looking for him.' Perfectly natural, nothing untoward, his tone implied.

Jackson's normally scruffy mop of spiky hair had been gelled and combed down. His face bore the signs of the previous night's fracas, but otherwise he looked quite presentable in a clean T-shirt inscribed with 'Happy

Mondays' and a brown suede trucker jacket. His jeans even had creases in them.

His brief, Mr Arthur, had made no such effort. If anything, he was even seedier than before. A small attaché case rested on the shiny knees of his trousers, its cheap leatherette scratched and torn, one of the clasps missing.

Otley said, 'You go to Vernon's flat looking for him?'

'Yeah, but in the afternoon. I spoke to Vera, she was there.'

'And she told you what?' Otley asked.

'That Connie wasn't there!' Jackson exclaimed, the obvious answer to a dumb question. 'I told you all this, I've said all this . . .'

Tennison had remained standing, next to the wall opposite Jackson, which meant he had to swivel his head as the interrogation switched direction. Her turn.

'Did Parker-Jones ask you to say you were at the advice centre?'

'I'm sorry, I don't remember.'

'You don't remember? Tell me about the money. Did you often lend Connie money?'

'No. He usually had enough. He was always pretty flush.' Jackson gave his thick-lipped smile. 'I mean, sometimes I borrowed from him.'

'When exactly did you give him the two hundred pounds?'

Jackson peered off into space, brow furrowed, in a

credible performance of thinking hard. 'Don't remember – I'm sorry.'

'Did Connie live at the house in Camden Town?'

'Sometimes left his gear there, but he'd not actually lived—' He cleared his throat. '—lived there for months.'

'Do you know where he was living?' Tennison asked. 'Say for the past few months?'

Jackson shook his head.

'Please answer the question.'

'No.' Jackson answered in a drab, long-suffering voice. 'I dunno where he was living.'

'So where did you give him the money?'

'At the advice centre.'

'But according to Parker-Jones, Connie hadn't been there for – quite a few months.'

'Yeah, well, I don't remember where I give it him!' Jackson said testily. He glanced edgily at Mr Arthur, and then his smile was turned on again, full beam. 'I'm sorry, really I am. Just don't remember . . .'

'How well do you know Edward Parker-Jones?'

'I work for him, pays me a few quid to look after his property.'

'Have you at any time attempted to extort money out of a man called John Kennington?' Jackson gave her a blank stare. Tennison moved nearer. 'Blackmail, Mr Jackson. Have you attempted to blackmail John Kennington?'

Jackson shook his head. 'No, I dunno him.'

'On the night Colin Jenkins died,' Tennison said quietly, moving closer, 'did you discuss anything with Parker-Jones?'

'Yes.' He paused, deadpan. 'Price of toilet paper. I get it in bulk for him.'

'And after the death of Colin Jenkins, did you discuss anything with Mr Parker-Jones? Not necessarily toilet paper.'

'Like what?'

'You have stated that Donald Driscoll, Billy Matthews, Alan Thorpe, and Kenny Lloyd all saw you at the advice centre the night Colin Jenkins was murdered, is that correct?'

'Yes, that's right.'

'You listed the exact same names as Mr Edward Parker-Jones – so I am asking you.' Tennison gripped the edge of the table and leaned over. 'Did you at any time discuss this with Mr Edward Parker-Jones?'

'No. No reason to.' Jackson slanted his body away, trying to maintain the distance between them. His heavy-lidded eyes flicked sideways towards her. 'They were there and so was he. So he's bound to say the same lads as I say, because I was there . . .'

Tennison straightened her back. 'You are going to be charged with the attempted murder of a police officer, Mr Jackson. You also refused an officer entry to the house in

Camden and physically attacked another police officer.' Jackson tried to interject, but she steam-rollered on. 'You were holding a fourteen-year-old girl against her will. You have been living off immoral earnings. You want more? Because we have more.'

'I didn't know they was coppers!' Jackson held up his hands, palms pressed against an invisible wall. 'On my life – I mean they just barged into the house and – that girl won't bring charges – she begged me to give her a place to stay – I didn't know she was fourteen!' He jerked his head, gulping. 'And that other thing. I thought it was Red, that stupid old drag queen, didn't know it was a copper . . . just mistaken identity.'

'Why did you want to kill her?'

'I didn't want to kill her, no way. I just wanted to . . . frighten her a bit.'

'Why?'

Jackson was thinking hard now, and it was no pretence. He suddenly found himself in a hole, and instead of digging in deeper and deeper, he wanted to dig himself out. He licked his lips. 'Well . . . Vera told me she'd been talking to the cops, and all I wanted to do was frighten her off.'

'Why?' Tennison said. 'Why did you want to frighten Rodney Allarton?' Jackson looked confused. 'Red?'

Jackson wanted the help of his brief. Mr Arthur had his head down, scribbling away on a notepad, using his attaché case as a desk. No help there. Jackson looked around, a bit panicky, and then said lamely, 'Because I did. Look, I'm sorry, really sorry about that, it was all a mistake . . .'

'You must have had a reason.'

'No, no, I didn't have a reason. And that is the God's truth!'

Tennison gave a little sigh, shaking her head sadly.

'Well, Jimmy, you are going away for a very long time – for no reason.'

Jackson made a wild gesture, at last attracting Mr Arthur's attention, who leaned over for Jackson to whisper in his ear. Mr Arthur sat back. 'My client is very tired, perhaps we can continue this interview in the morning?'

The punishingly long day had taken its toll on Tennison too. The lines around her eyes were etched in, the furrows in her forehead deeply ridged. She felt like saying, *Enough's enough, get this scumbag out of my sight*, but instead she merely nodded to Hall, who spoke into the tape, concluding the interview.

However desperately she might have desired it, the day was far from over.

They had Jackson running scared – no doubt about it – but he hadn't cracked, and until he did their case was long on suspicion, short on hard-clinching evidence. She was going to sweat that bastard and wring him out like an old dishrag.

Taking Otley along, she drove up to the house in Langley Road, Camden. From Otley's description of the place she knew what to expect, but it turned out to be even worse. The squalor of the poky bedrooms at the top of the house disgusted and depressed her. The smell made her nauseous.

They checked out the wardrobes and drawers, sorted through the kids' clothing and pitiful belongings. After ten minutes Tennison had had it. She slumped down on a narrow trestle bed, the one occupied by Billy Matthews, and picked up the physically challenged teddy bear and gazed at it with listless eyes. Some poor mite had clung on to this battered relic, seeking love and comfort. It felt damp, and she imagined they were a child's tears.

Otley slammed a drawer shut and looked at her over his shoulder. In a parody of Mr Arthur, he muttered in his sardonic drawl, 'My Guv'nor's very tired, perhaps we can continue this search in the morning!'

Scrawled into the plaster above the bed, in jagged cap-itals, she read: 'MARTIN FLETCHER LIVES HERE.'

Tennison rubbed her eyes. 'I met a friend of yours in Manchester, David Lyall.'

'Yes, I know, he called me,' Otley said, leaning on the dresser. 'I wondered why you were hot to trot to Manchester.'

'Good that I did ...' She gazed up at him, her hands

limp on her knees. 'It's like a jigsaw. I've got all the pieces and they just won't fit.'

'Best not to push them into place,' Otley advised, wise old sage. 'Got to have patience.'

'I've got that,' Tennison snapped back, nettled, 'just don't have the time.' She added resentfully, 'You jumped the gun with Parker-Jones – I wasn't ready for him.'

Otley didn't think that merited a response. Anyway, he didn't give one, just wandered off into the next room. After a moment Tennison levered herself up and followed him.

There was a TV set, video recorder, porn videotapes and magazines, a crate of Newcastle Brown, half consumed, and a 200 carton of Benson & Hedges, the cellophane broken, just one packet gone. Jackson's room, quite evidently. His long leather coat hung behind the door, and there was other masculine tackle scattered around.

Otley was rooting through the wardrobe, taking stuff off hangers, going through the pockets, feeling the seams and throwing it on the floor. 'They all stink, these rooms, used clothes, mildew . . . ' He sounded puzzled. 'If Connie stayed here, where's all the smart gear he was supposed to wear?'

Tennison rummaged through a chest of drawers, poking at Jackson's belongings with distaste. Otley was on his knees, feeling under the wardrobe. All he found was dust, so he moved along the linoleum to the smaller of the two beds. He lifted the corner of the stained eiderdown to look underneath the bed, and almost sneezed as the dust got to him.

'He must have had letters or a diary or something,' Otley said, sniffing and pinching his nose. Crouching, he craned his head. 'Hang on, what have we got here? If he was selling his story to that woman – what was her name?' Grunting as he reached under the bed.

'Jessica Smithy. That's what he said ...! And Martin Fletcher – "I can sell my story for a lot of dough."' Tennison straightened up. Something had just clicked. 'What if Jessica Smithy met him first, and Connie came second? Rent boys, not just one rent boy. She was writing an article on rent boys – plural.'

Bent double, Otley dragged a small brown suitcase from underneath the bed. It was locked. He took out his penknife, and after a couple of seconds' fiddling that got him nowhere, lost his patience and used brute force. The clasps sprang open. Tennison looked over his shoulder as he flung the lid back. The two of them stared down at the jumble of whips, knives, blackjacks, rubber masks, leather jockstraps, bondage gear, and sundry other exotic sado-masochistic gear.

'Nice little away-day assortment!' Otley commented.

He shoved the case aside and peered under the bed again. Frowning, he got to his feet and leaned over, looking closely at the wall against which the bed was pressed. Dark stains and splashes. He whipped the eider-down off the bed. The sheets were spattered with dried blood, and there were other discolorations that might have been vomit and diarrhoea, going by the smell.

Together, Otley and Tennison moved the bed away from the wall. A pair of soiled Y-front underpants came to light, an odd sock covered in fluff. More dark red splashes. And something else. Lower down near the skirting board, bolted into the wall, an iron ankle bracelet on a chain, its edges crusted with blood.

Tennison recoiled with disgust, wrinkling her face.

'We better get Forensic in here, check the entire house over! And I want it done tonight!' She went to the door, sniffing Givenchy Mirage from her scarf. She said with grim satisfaction, 'I don't think Jackson's brief's going to believe this – he's already worn his nasty little felt-tip pen out tonight, writing down all the charges!'

Outside, Tennison breathed in deeply, taking a lungful of wonderful evening air. She climbed into her car. Otley leaned in the window.

'I think we should have another go at our Vera,' he suggested. 'I mean, she's been living here.' Tennison nodded agreement. 'I'll hang around for the Forensic blokes, they could be a while.' He snapped off a mock salute. ' 'Night. Mind how you go.'

As the car moved off, Tennison gave him a look. 'This is my case, Bill. Don't jump the gun again.'

Otley's slitted eyes watched her drive off down the street. He wore his nasty little grin. 'Your case? Yes, ma'am.'

Ray Hebdon sat in the darkened viewing room, remote control in one hand, pen in the other, making notes as the tapes unrolled on the screen. Some of the stuff was pretty anodyne, some pure filth, and Hebdon wasn't watching by choice; he was forcing himself to sit here and endure it by an act of will, suppressing his repugnance.

He ejected the tape, stuck in another, and sat back in the chair, reaching for his lukewarm can of beer.

He'd seen this one before, but he watched it again. The classroom and the compliant pupils, the stern school-teacher whacking his cane on the desk. From its innocent, even quaint, beginning, it degenerated very rapidly to the teacher meting out punishment and demanding penance in the form of spanking, masturbation, blow jobs, and buggery. Other 'teachers' appeared on the scene, ready and willing to lend a hand, or some other part of their anatomy. Hebdon studied their faces and made notes.

'What the hell do you think you're doing?'

Hebdon turned. 'I'm almost through,' he said to Dalton, who had come silently into the room.

'What? Jerking off?' Dalton's expression was that of someone who's just got a whiff of a stale fart in a lift. 'Are you into this kind of thing?'

Hebdon started to flush from the neck up. 'Yeah, I'm off duty,' he sneered, his eyes burning into Dalton's. 'So shut the door when you leave, will you?'

Dalton hesitated, as if something was on the tip of his tongue and he couldn't bring himself to utter it. He coughed and turned to leave.

'G'night then.'

As the door closed behind him Hebdon swung around and hurled his can of beer at it. Hot-eyed, he stared at the screen, his skin prickling with rage, and jabbed savagely at the remote control, freezing the frame on Kilmartin receiving the favours of Connie, Alan Thorpe, and Kenny Lloyd.

The hot water felt so good she could have stayed in another twenty minutes, but then she noticed her fingertips getting wrinkly. She dried herself, chucked sandalwood talc everywhere she could reach, wrapped herself in her Chinese silk robe, and stretched out on the sofa in the living room, glass of red wine within easy reach. She thought of putting on a CD she'd bought recently – Albinoni's Adagio in G minor – and then decided not to. The silence was too beautiful, and the peace and quiet too precious. Tennison sighed and closed her eyes.

The doorbell rang.

On her way to answer it she looked at the clock and

saw that it was a few minutes after eleven. She pushed her hair back, still damp at the roots, tightened her robe, and opened the door.

'I'm sorry, I didn't wake you, did I?' Ray Hebdon said, genuinely apologetic.

'No, but I hope this is important.' Tennison's look could have penetrated galvanized steel at twenty yards. He followed her in. She gestured for him to sit. Her half-full glass of wine was on the coffee table. 'Do you want to join me?'

She went off to the kitchen and came back with a glass and a fresh bottle of wine. Hebdon had taken off his coat and was standing somewhat self-consciously rubbing his hands.

He cleared his throat. 'I suppose you know I'm going back to my station?' She nodded. He smiled. 'So I thought I'd do a bit of homework before I left.'

Tennison handed him the bottle and corkscrew. 'I've been watching the videos,' he said, peeling off the foil. 'You know Chiswick was after them? We've been shuffling them around until we'd had a good chance to check all the faces out. Maybe that's why the top brass want them!' He nodded behind him. 'Look in my coat pocket.'

Tennison picked up his coat from the back of the armchair. She found his notepad and flipped it open.

'Took me a long time, but I've listed all the faces I recognized. There's a judge, two MPs, a lawyer – big criminal lawyer, a barrister . . . '

'Any police officers?'

'None that I recognized.' Hebdon uncorked the wine. He topped up Tennison's glass and poured himself one. 'But that's quite a list!'

'Why?' Tennison was studying the names, frowning and shaking her head. 'Why do they do it?'

'It's what they're into.'

That didn't answer her question. 'But to risk every-thing, their careers – for what? I don't understand.'

'I think it gets to a point where they can't help it.' Hebdon shrugged.

'Can't help it?' Tennison said with a grimace. 'My God . . .'

Hebdon sat down. He sipped his wine and stared at the carpet, and struggled to explain. 'Because . . . there's also the power, like they're above the law, untouchable.' He looked at her. 'Maybe because they are the law.'

Tennison sat down on the sofa and reached for her glass. She said quietly, 'Ray, who do you think killed Connie? One of these men?'

'I don't think it's as big as them – I mean, they might have instigated it, but they wouldn't dirty their hands.'

'What about Parker-Jones? He's involved, that's obvious. Just as it's obvious he and Jackson cooked up their alibis together. But did he give Jackson the order to kill Connie?'

Hebdon drank, frowning into space. 'That could be why he's covering his tracks.'

'He'd also lose a lucrative business,' Tennison pointed out.

But it seemed she was off beam, because Hebdon was shaking his head. 'No, no, that's where you've got it all wrong. It's not the money.' He leaned forward, elbows on his knees. 'I think Otley and Co. have been off course – you know, looking for the money element. Those houses he owns – sure, they're cash in some respects, but it's not that. It's the power of being the supplier.'

'What do you mean?'

'Call in the favours. It's obvious he had to have connections to have got off not just one charge but two. Parker-Jones must have big contacts. It makes him ...' Hebdon pinged the rim of the glass with his fingernail. 'Untouchable. I doubt if he'd want to mess it up with murder – or blackmail.'

Tennison sloshed some wine into her glass and sat back on the sofa, grinding her teeth. 'So we're back to Jackson.' She took a swig and licked her upper lip. 'If Parker-Jones sticks to his story, Jackson will get away with murder – unless we break it.'

'Going to be tough, because that means you got to break Parker-Jones. If he ordered Jackson to kill Connie, no way will he back down.'

The wine was getting to Tennison. But instead of making her more relaxed, she was feeling uptight and jittery. She said, 'Do you have a cigarette?'

Hebdon shook his head and finished his wine.

'Time is running out on this one, isn't it?' Tennison brooded. She saw his empty glass. 'Have another one – you opened the bottle, for Chrissakes ...' Her tongue slurred over 'Chrissakes'.

Hebdon hesitated for a moment, and then refilled his glass. Tennison's head was back on the sofa, her eyes closed. She said slowly, almost mechanically, 'I want to tell you something.' Her lips felt numb. 'I need to tell somebody.'

Hebdon waited uneasily. He didn't know what to do, so he had another drink. He watched her, head back, eyes closed.

'I am pregnant.'

Hebdon blinked, and filled the silence with a muffled cough.

'Congratulations.'

'No, you don't understand,' Tennison said, opening her eyes. She looked at him. 'I am pregnant and I have absolutely no one I can talk to. I've tried, but ... you tell me. Should I have it?'

'It depends, really.' He shifted uncomfortably. 'Well, on whether you want it or not,' he added lamely.

'Would you, in my position?' The question wasn't just hypothetical, it was stupid. Tennison stared into her glass. 'Hell, I could be out of a job tomorrow!'

'What about the, er – the father?'

'There isn't one – well, obviously there is, but not . . .' Her voice dropped to a whisper. 'He doesn't know.'

'Will you tell him?'

Tennison didn't have to think. She shook her head at once.

'We lived together for a long time and almost got married. But then I got cold feet and he went away and found somebody else.' She threw the last of the wine back. 'He is a very nice man, and I would like to be his wife . . . but it wouldn't be right.' An expression of pain crossed her face. 'No, it would be right, it was always right, just me that messed it up.' She bowed her head, tightly clutching the stem of the wineglass in both hands.

Hebdon said cautiously, 'Well, I suppose it comes down to whether or not you want it. Do you?' She was hunched over, hiding her face from him. 'Do you want to be a mother?' he asked quietly.

Tennison's head came slowly around, her eyes bright and moist. A shy, radiant smile lit up her whole face. She said softly, 'Yes. Oh yes, I do, very much.'

Chapter Sixteen

Tennison was twenty minutes late arriving in the Squad Room. She had no excuses, except that she had a foul head and a thick taste on her tongue, and she wasn't going to offer those up in mitigation. When she finally made it, DI Hall had the 9 a.m. briefing under way. He had on a superb suit in dark olive green and a tie with so many swirling colours it made Tennison ill just to look at it.

She gave Hall the nod to carry on, while she took off her raincoat and tried to get her brain in gear.

'Parker-Jones owns a number of bed and breakfast stroke hotel stroke houses, under the company name "Protega". Mostly for children in local authority care.' Hall referred to his notes. 'As a registered charity he's got a staff of four, one administrator and two youth work-ers. Annual running costs of around one hundred and twenty thousand. He's on a number of grants, one hundred and sixty grand from Camden, another one from Westminster Council, that's for advice and support ...'

Dalton came over and stood by Tennison's elbow. With one ear on the briefing, Tennison said, 'They're still keeping you on, are they?'

'... he's also got another fat one from London Boroughs Grants Committee,' Hall was saying. '*Added* to all the grants, Parker-Jones receives from the local authorities a hundred and ten pounds per person. So far we've got eighteen registered to one house, another twelve in Hackney, and the one in Camden has eight.'

He carried on, giving more details, as the team made notes and asked for a point of clarification now and then. The PA *bing-bong* chimed out. 'DCI Tennison to Superintendent Halliday's office immediately, please.'

Tennison glanced up to the Tannoy, a strange fierce light in her eyes. 'This is it! I think it's charge or pull the rug time.'

Dalton put his hand on her arm. 'The doctor attached to the Calloway Centre, Cardiff. His widow, Joyce Ellis, two sons, aged fifty-two, in 1987 married John Kennington.'

Tennison gave him a crooked grin. 'What's this? Changing sides, are you?'

Bing-bong.

'DCI Tennison please return to her office immediately.'

Dalton also looked to the Tannoy. 'He doesn't know.'

'Thank you,' Tennison said, squeezing his arm. She headed to the door. Otley was there, beckoning urgently.

Tennison walked past him. 'I know, Halliday wants me.'

'Commander's with him!' Otley hissed.

She pushed through into the corridor, not waiting to see if he was relishing this or not, and caring even less.

Halliday was standing in front of her desk and Chiswick was sitting in her chair. The Commander had a crabbed look on his face, his small mouth tight and hard. He didn't give her time to shut the door.

'You have not one shred of evidence against Parker-Jones and his involvement in the death of—'

'Colin Jenkins?' Halliday edged out of the way as Tennison came forward, all fired up, ready for a show-down. 'No, I haven't got him to admit his involvement, but I know he's covering up for Jackson and possibly for John Kennington.'

'Drop it!' Chiswick said, icy quiet.

'Are you serious? In 1979 and again in 1986 both John Kennington and Edward Parker-Jones . . .'

Chiswick made a brusque sweep of the hand. 'I am fully aware of the cases you are referring to.'

'Then you should have made whatever information you had available to me!' Tennison said angrily. 'I have wasted a considerable—'

'Waste being the operative word, Chief Inspector. You were supposed to be investigating the murder of—'

She was sick of his interrupting. It was her turn.

'The murder of Colin Jenkins. But if – *if* – I also discover evidence that proves Edward Parker-Jones . . . '

The bastard did it again.

'*This is not the Colin Jenkins case.*'

' . . . is unfit to be awarded massive grants from four different councils, and is a possible paedophile . . . '

'Is this true?' Halliday asked Chiswick, but the Commander had no time for non-combatants. His sights were fixed on Tennison. It was a double-headed contest, two boxers slugging it out, attempting by sheer weight of punches to batter their opponent to the canvas.

'Chief Inspector Tennison, you give me no option but to warn you, that if you continue to investigate persons—'

'Persons?' Tennison was in like a flash. 'One Edward Parker-Jones?'

'—against specific instructions, then disciplinary action will be taken.'

Tennison took a deep breath and slugged on. 'You take it, sir, and I will fight you every inch of the way.' Her eyes flashed. She wasn't just angry now, she was blazing mad. 'I have been fobbed off with "stay clear of this or that person because of," and I quote, "repercussions to this department." Well, this department has blatantly attempted to cover up my investigation into a murder, which has direct links to a paedophile ring – members of that said ring, and one member, John Kennington, who has been under a full-scale internal inquiry!'

'John Kennington was reinstated,' Chiswick said, his voice trembling as he struggled to retain his composure.

'Yes – but six months later he's being blackmailed! The case never even got to court. What happened, everybody get cold feet, so retire him?' Tennison was filled with contempt. She was cutting in deep and raw, but what the hell, these were spineless excuses for officers charged with enforcing law and order. She thumped the desk, and Chiswick visibly jerked back.

'Retire him,' Tennison raged on, 'pay him off, and when another investigation touches on it ... John Kennington is still alive, Colin Jenkins is dead.'

'Just calm down,' Chiswick said, raising his hand. 'Look at it from our side, my side, the investigation into John Kennington—'

'Failed ... and to the tune of over one and a half million. Next, Operation Contract!' Tennison shook her head, smiling bitterly. 'How much did that set the Government back? You knew there was a leak – well, was it John Kennington?'

'Be very careful what you are insinuating,' Chiswick warned her solemnly, playing the Senior Figure in Authority card.

Tennison closed her eyes for a second, breathing in deeply. She pressed her palms together. 'All I want is to find the killer of Colin Jenkins. If it touches on Parker-Jones or anyone else, then that's the way it's got to be.' She faced him squarely, looking him straight in the eyes. 'You can lay it all on my shoulders. I take full responsibility. But I will not be anybody's scapegoat, and if you pull me off this case now, I won't go quietly.'

Chiswick stared balefully at her across the desk. 'Don't make threats, Detective Chief Inspector.'

He rose ponderously to his feet and jerked his head to Halliday, indicating that the interview was at an end. As they reached the door, Tennison said coolly:

'I'd like to be put forward for the Superintendent vacancy on the AMIT Area Five. I am very confident that I'll make an arrest for the Colin Jenkins murder this weekend, and therefore, with the case closed, it will be unnecessary for me to continue any further investigation into John Kennington's connection with Colin Jenkins.'

The two men were standing stock-still. They were both trying, as best they could, to take on board what Tennison had said.

Commander Chiswick opened the door and went out, stooping, not looking back. Halliday went meekly after him, pausing for a look at Tennison that was both guarded and puzzled before quietly closing the door.

Tennison heard them enter the next door office. She heard the rumble of voices through the wall. She closed her eyes and slowly sank back, needing the solid desk to support her.

Vera extended her tongue, delicately picked something off it, and wiped it on the handkerchief in her lap. She puffed on her cigarette and batted the smoke away. With soulful, heavy-lidded eyes she watched as Tennison took the packet of cigarettes, extracted one, and put it between her lips.

'You got a light?'

Vera struck a match and Tennison leaned towards the flame.

'Did James Jackson kill Connie?'

Close to her, Tennison saw the twin match flames reflected in Vera's eyes. She saw fear there, deep down. Deeper yet, stricken terror. She resumed her seat, breathing smoke through her nostrils. 'He can't hurt you, Vera, he's going to be behind bars for a long time. So, tell me ...'

'I don't know,' Vera Reynolds said huskily. She bowed her head and smoked, looking down into her lap.

'Do you know a John Kennington?'

Vera shook her head.

Tennison sighed. 'Vera, look at me. Come on, help me. Why was Jackson looking for Connie that night? He says Connie owed him money.'

'Connie didn't need to borrow money from Jackson. He always used to have money.'

'Did you know any of his clients?'

'No.' Vera raised her head. She looked past Tennison to Otley, standing near the door, his arms wrapped around the shoulders of his wrinkled suit. She took a breath. 'No, he was very secretive about them. Well, you give one kid a name, next minute they're offering themselves. You think he was just gay, don't you?' she said, a faint smile hovering. 'Why do you think we got on so well?'

'I don't know how well you knew him,' Tennison said gently. 'Why don't you tell me?'

Vera swallowed, the prominent Adam's apple jerking in the long white throat. Above it, her make-up ended in a smudgy tide-mark. Her blond wig wasn't on straight. She looked defeated and pathetic.

'He was the same as me. He'd go with gays, but he liked straight men better. He wanted money, needed a lot for the operation. They do the best in Rio. He would have had to pay for it, you see, there's no way the NHS would have given him the operation, he was too young. As it is you've got to go through six months of interrogation, analysts, and God knows what else, and then you're on a waiting list that'll take years ... I know.'

She took a deep drag, right up to the filter tip, and stubbed it out in the ashtray. She looked pensive.

'Always been my dream. I've been on the hormone tablets, but they're so expensive, and then I've got to buy costumes, pay rent. I just never had enough – but Connie, he felt ready.' She tightened her lips suddenly, as if she was about to cry, turning her head away. 'He was very beautiful, and ... sometimes we'd talk, and ... he understood ... because we were alike, we were the same.'

'Was one of his clients going to give him the money for the operation?' Tennison kept to her gentle tone.

'No.' Vera's finely arched eyebrows went up. 'Ten grand? More. You need a lot of after-care treatment.'

'So Connie needed a lot of money – maybe ten, fifteen thousand pounds, yes?' Vera nodded. 'How was he going to get all that? Blackmail?'

'Connie was capable of anything.'

'Blackmail, Vera?' Tennison said more insistently.

'Yes, well, I think he was trying it on a few people – the famous ones. But I don't think he got very far. I think he got scared off.'

Tennison jotted something down. Her cigarette smouldered in the ashtray. She mashed it out. 'Do you know a Jessica Smithy?' Vera nodded. 'Connie was selling his life story?' Vera nodded. 'And?'

'I think she kept stringing him along, promising big money – he used to brag about it. But she wanted evidence. Names, photographs. Photographs.'

'And Jackson knew about this?'

'Yes. He knew Connie had got a sort of file. You know,

to show this reporter. He found out, because Martin Fletcher stole some things from Jackson and gave them to Connie.'

Vera fumbled for a cigarette. Tennison waited. Otley shifted onto the other foot. Vera picked something imaginary off her tongue and wiped it on the handkerchief.

'That's why Jackson was looking for Connie. Not just to get back his things, but because he knew if Connie was selling his story, then he'd be in it. Connie had been one of his boys, you see, early on. Not lately, of course.'

'Jackson got Connie on the game?' Tennison said. She made a note.

'Yes.' Vera was nodding slowly. Her eyes were very sad. 'He got him so young. He was only ten years old when Jackson found him.' She looked at Tennison from under her eyelids. 'But you got to understand, Jimmy was an abused kid himself. Didn't make any difference to him if they were eight or eighteen. They never stay with him long. Not once they get the hang of it.' Her voice had become drab, lifeless; her whole behaviour was subdued.

'Did you see what Martin stole from Jackson? What he eventually gave to Connie?' Tennison asked.

'No, I didn't see them, he just told me.' Vera patted her chest, indicating that Jackson had concealed something in his jacket. 'Probably pictures, photographs, maybe letters, I don't know. I never saw what Martin nicked from

Jackson. But that's why Martin got beaten up. Because he stole the stuff from Jackson.'

'If Connie told you about the "stuff" Martin had taken from Jackson, told you about the press connection, did he also mention who he was going to blackmail with it?'

Vera shook her head. 'He never told me, but he was kind of excited – you know, very pleased with himself. Said he'd get the money for his operation. He was very certain.'

Tennison made a note and closed her notebook. She reached over and touched Vera's hand, a light firm pressure.

'Thank you, Vera.'

Tennison stood up. Vera sat there, eyes clouding with confusion.

'You can go,' Tennison said. She went to the door, pausing by Otley. 'You doing anything lunchtime?' He shook his head. 'See you in my office.' She went out.

In her haste, getting to her feet, Vera had managed to drop her handbag, tipping most of the contents onto the floor. She got down on her knees, shovelling in lipsticks and tubes of make-up. Otley's face appeared beneath the table. 'Get your handbag, Vernon, and you're out of here,' he drawled.

Vera scrambled to her feet, clicking her handbag shut. She was palpitating, her eyes a bit wild. 'That's it . . . ? I can go?'

Otley jerked his thumb.

She scurried to the door, heels clacking, clutching her handbag.

'Vernon!'

Vera skidded and pitched forward. She whipped a frightened look over her shoulder.

Otley was dangling a hairbrush by its handle. 'This yours?'

Alan Thorpe stood in the mustard-tinged gloom of the advice centre, idly glancing over the contacts board. He had a full carton of Rothman's King Size under his arm, and he was leisurely lighting up from the packet he'd just prised out of the cellophane wrapper. It was a little after 10.15 a.m. It was quiet, no one in the games room or the TV lounge.

Quiet for the next ten seconds until Margaret Speel came clattering down the stairs and barged through the door, frizzy black hair bouncing on her shoulders, her mouth taut as a steel trap.

She marched past the reception counter, did a smart right turn, and banged her small fist on the door marked 'E PARKER-JONES. PRIVATE.'

Parker-Jones opened the door. He stepped back and smiled, gesturing her in.

Margaret Speel didn't move. Her voice had a rasp to it.

'This won't take long. I intend to report you, get you blacklisted with every council, every government-run scheme that you have abused.'

Parker-Jones had spotted Alan Thorpe, who couldn't help but overhear. He moved farther back, trying to draw her in. 'What's brought this on?' he asked, quiet and steady, no histrionics.

'I trusted you, I may even have helped you – that is what is worst, worse than any of the lies you have told me.' Her shoulders were hunched with the strain, fists clenched at her sides. Her usual pale colouring was now white as chalk. 'I don't care if I lose my job—'

'Who's been talking to you, Margaret?' Parker-Jones asked, keeping his voice low. He reached for her hand.

'DON'T TOUCH ME!'

He swayed back, spreading his arms defencelessly. 'Come in, at least talk this through.'

Margaret Speel wore a bitter smile that made her pert face ugly.

'She knows everything – about you, and about John Kennington. And when I've finished you'll go to prison.' Spittle flew from her lips.

Parker-Jones reached out and grasped both her wrists. 'You don't know what you're talking about, Margaret. This is from that policewoman, Tennison, yes?' His face showed pain and bewilderment. He tugged beseechingly at her wrists. 'Oh, Margaret, don't you understand? Please . . . just calm down.' His hand touched her cheek. He implored her softly, 'Just come in a minute. Let me explain.'

She took a swift decisive step backward, pulling herself free. 'Yes, I do. I do now.'

And then she was striding off, past the reception counter. Alan Thorpe stared at her. She spun around, glaring at him, making a sudden grab for his arm.

'Don't come here anymore. Do you hear me? Don't come here. This is closed. *This is closed down!*'

Under the force of this onslaught Alan backed away from her. He wasn't scared, just bemused. Margaret Speel pushed him aside and started snatching down the letters and cards on the contacts board. She tore them off and ripped them up, scattering the pieces, and then she tried to drag the board itself off the wall. One corner came loose and she attacked it in a frenzy, bringing the whole thing crashing down.

Parker-Jones came around the corner from his office. He leapt towards her, face livid, his hand grappling for her shoulder. Margaret Speel pivoted on her heel, her arm swinging, and caught him smack across his face, a stinging slap that split his lip. Her shoulder bag had come off. She swung it back on and stormed up the echoing wooden stairs.

From his breast pocket Parker-Jones took out a clean white handkerchief and dabbed his lip. He returned to his office, picked up the phone and dialled, dabbing his lip and looking at the spots of blood on the pristine white linen.

The connection came through.

He held the receiver close to his mouth, feeling the sluggish warm trickle on his chin.

'Mrs Kennington? It's Edward Parker-Jones.'

Jimmy Jackson was bent double in the chair, his hands locked across his head, tufts of hair sprouting through his fingers.

'All right. I never lent him any money!'

Mr Arthur sat close by him, knees firmly together, fingers laced beneath the threadbare cuffs of his overcoat.

Tennison went on, 'You were told by Martin Fletcher where Connie was. You then went to Vernon Reynolds's flat.'

'I didn't – I've admitted I was looking for Connie, but I wasn't the only one.'

'Who else? Who else was looking for Connie on the night he was murdered? Jimmy, it's just five ... ten minutes there and back from the advice centre.'

'I never killed him. I couldn't have.'

Otley put his hand on the back of Jackson's chair and leaned right over. 'But you had to silence him, didn't you? Connie was going to tell about the way you kidnap underage kids. The room at the top of the house. We've seen the chains, the weapons, the knives.'

'Did you torture boys up there?' Tennison said expressionlessly. She looked at his hands, the spiky hair sticking

339

through. 'Is that why we have, to date, fifteen separate blood samples, from walls, floorboards, bed sheets? What were you doing to those children?' She glanced at Mr Arthur, and then inspected her fingernails. 'Mr Jackson, I would really try to be as helpful as possible. The charges against you . . .'

'Look, I did go to the centre, right?' His head came up, eyes bulging at Tennison, lips red where he'd been chewing them. 'I told Mr Parker-Jones I couldn't find him, right?'

'Edward Parker-Jones,' Tennison said, looking at Otley.

Jackson nodded. 'Yeah . . .' He sounded short of breath. He twisted around to Mr Arthur, and twisted back again, plucking at his T-shirt where it stuck to him, one boot agitatedly thumping the carpet. He said hoarsely, 'Martin Fletcher took my stuff out of the house . . .'

'What stuff?'

'Things, photographs . . . I wanted them back, right?'

'Photographs of you?'

'Some of them,' Jackson said cautiously, 'but Connie had nicked them, he got Martin to get them for him from Camden, right? You with me?'

'Who else was in the photographs?'

'I can't remember,' Jackson said too quickly.

'You almost kill a boy for them,' Tennison said, her voice brittle with disbelief, 'and you can't remember who they were of? Who was in the photographs?'

Jackson shakily lit up. He dragged deep, crouched forward, elbows on his knees, blowing smoke at the carpet.

'Was Parker-Jones in these photographs?' Tennison said.

'No.'

'How about a John Kennington? Was he in any of these photographs?'

Jackson tried to shrug it off. 'Just kids, blokes dressed up . . . bit porno, that's all. Anyway, it got to about eight, bit later, an' I told Parker-Jones that I couldn't find Connie, an' he said go and get Martin Fletcher, he'd know where he was.' He stared at her sullenly from under his thick brows. 'So I did. Ask Martin Fletcher, he'll tell you.'

'Martin is dead, Jimmy.' Tennison allowed the silence to hang heavy. 'So Parker-Jones wanted the photographs – why? If as you have just stated he wasn't in them, why would he want them?'

'I don't know. All I know is he wanted them, but so did I.'

'But you were in the photographs.' Tennison pointed her finger. 'Are you sure there weren't any of Edward Parker-Jones?'

'I didn't have any pictures of him,' Jackson said through his teeth.

'Was John Kennington in any of these photographs?'

'No! I told you before, I don't even know that bloke . . .'

341

'So they were just photographs of you? And you wanted them so desperately you were prepared to kill for them?'

'Look, when that fire started ... I was over the other side of Waterloo Bridge.' He waved his arm, indicating a vast distance, the back side of the moon.

Tennison rubbed the nape of her neck, trying to ease the hangover that was thudding in the base of her skull. Red wine was lethal bloody stuff. She felt rotten.

Otley saw her close her eyes for a second. He said, 'So, who was at the centre when you were there?'

Jackson half-turned to him. 'I was only there two minutes, no more,' he said irritably. 'Then I come out.'

'Anybody else?' Tennison asked. 'Did you speak to anyone else apart from Parker-Jones?'

'Yeah.' Jackson sounded weary. 'Vernon Reynolds.'

Tennison and Otley exchanged looks. Vera? Since when was she at the centre that night? First they'd heard of it.

Head hunched down between his bony shoulders, Jackson stared miserably at his boots, blowing smoke at the carpet.

Tennison drove north along Highgate Hill, fuming at the traffic. Otley sat beside her, filling his face with a cheeseburger, a plastic cup of coffee held up in front of him to avoid spilling any. It was twelve-thirty. A soothing Brahms string quartet was on Classic FM, but it didn't help Tennison's temper any.

She swung the wheel, avoiding what she knew would be a totally clogged Archway and Muswell Hill, and took to the side roads on the eastern edge of Hampstead Heath.

'If Jackson is telling the truth, then he couldn't have done it,' she said, turning right unexpectedly, so that Otley had to concentrate like fury to save his coffee.

He stuffed in the rest of the cheeseburger, cheeks bulging. 'What about Vera, then? That was a turn up. I mean, she's never mentioned anything about being in or anywhere near the centre.' He swallowed and took a slurp of coffee. 'But she couldn't have started that fire – she was onstage at Judy's at nine-fifteen. She was bloody onstage.'

The Sierra Sapphire came into the tree-lined avenue of large detached houses. Tennison leaned forward, peering through the windshield.

'What's going on here?'

There was an ambulance outside the gates, its rear doors standing open. Two attendants were wheeling a trolley from the driveway. There was a humped shape under the red blanket.

Tennison stopped the car and hurried forward. Otley took a peek through the gates, seeing the Panda car outside the front door.

'What's happened?' Tennison asked, showing her ID.

The attendants were about to lift the trolley into the

ambulance. She turned back the blanket. It couldn't be, she told herself, it couldn't be, but she was wrong. She clenched her jaw.

'It's John Kennington. Shit.'

Otley glanced towards the house. 'We'd better leave it,' he advised, 'must have just happened.'

He looked around for her, but she wasn't there.

'Guv!'

Tennison was walking through the gates, heading up the gravel drive.

'Guv!'

Chapter Seventeen

Tennison stepped through the open front door into the parquet-floored hallway. To her left she could see a cluster of uniformed police in the study. There was a plainclothes officer kneeling on the carpet. Somebody else was taking flash photographs. She moved across the hallway towards them, and then stopped. The door to the drawing room was open. Mrs Kennington was sitting on the sofa, her head downcast, a cigarette in one hand, a crumpled lace handkerchief in the other. A crystal tumbler, filled nearly halfway with Scotch, was on the coffee table in front of her. An open bottle of Macallan's Malt stood next to it.

Tennison put her hand on the doorjamb. 'Mrs Kennington? Could I speak to you a moment?'

The woman didn't move or look up as Tennison came in and eased the door shut behind her. The room contained an unnatural quietness, the stately ticking of the grandfather clock portioning out the silence.

'Are you all right?'

Mrs Kennington stirred. 'He shot himself, not me,' she said, vacant and subdued. She turned her head. 'You were here the other night, weren't you?'

'Yes.' Tennison moved up to a winged armchair, set at an angle to the sofa. 'I can leave if you want ...'

'But then you'll want to come back, so ask whatever you want. Get it over with.'

She happened to notice she was smoking. The cigarette was nearly done, and she took another from the box and lit it from the stub, very ladylike, little finger stuck out. She then noticed the Scotch, and drank a mouthful, little finger out. Tennison sat down. She put her briefcase by the side of the chair and folded her hands.

'I was in the front bedroom,' Mrs Kennington said. 'We sleep in separate rooms. There was a phone call, I put it through to John's study. About half an hour later I heard the – well, I didn't know what it was, to be honest. I thought it was the plumbing. It's been making extraordinary noises. Obviously it wasn't. John had shot himself.'

She blinked at Tennison, as if making an apology for some unfortunate social gaffe. She had bright, intelligent eyes, a striking light blue. Even under stress she maintained her poise, and Tennison was able to understand what an asset she must have been to her husband in furthering his career.

'Do you know who the call was from?' Tennison inquired after a decent interval.

'Oh yes, I know who it was from. His name is Edward Parker-Jones.'

She didn't notice, or paid no attention, as Otley slid into the room. He moved behind Tennison's chair.

'At least this saves me getting a divorce.' Mrs Kennington smiled faintly, gazing at nothing. She delicately wiped the corners of her mouth with the wisp of handkerchief. 'There have been obstacles in the way for almost a year . . . '

'I know about the investigations,' Tennison said.

'Oh, do you?' Mrs Kennington remarked, cool to the point of half frozen to death.

'You were a doctor, weren't you? Do you still practise?'

'No. My first husband died. We worked together, or in the same practice.'

'In Cardiff?'

'Yes, in Cardiff. Why do you want to know about my husband's practice?' She peered closely at Tennison, frowning. 'Why are you here?'

'When you were in Cardiff, Mr Parker-Jones was running . . . '

'The Calloway Centre.' Mrs Kennington was now paying full, complete attention. She looked at Otley and then at Tennison, quite perplexed. 'Why are you asking me these questions?'

'Did you examine a young boy called Jason Baldwyn? It was a sexual assault charge.'

'Which was subsequently dropped. No, my husband examined the boy—' Her mouth fell open. 'Oh, my God,' she gasped. 'You think I had something to do with that? My husband was critically ill, he was very sick, I had two small children, and ...' She faltered, rubbing her forehead distractedly with the wadded handkerchief. 'He had cancer, I only remember it because, because he died. Then there was this investigation about ...' She stared, trying to recall the name, and failed. '... This boy. But there was so much confusion about whether his reports were stolen, or just mislaid, I really don't know.'

The facade had cracked a little, and to repair it she took a drink, finger out, and was careful to put the glass down without making a sound. She dabbed her lips. 'My first husband was a very decent human being. I can't say that about my second, I wish to God I had never married him. But I did,' she added under her breath.

Tennison said, 'Do you know if young boys were ever brought here?'

Mrs Kennington rose and went to the white mantel. With her back to Tennison, she murmured, barely audibly, 'Do I know if young boys were ever brought here?'

'Perhaps when you were away,' Tennison said. She opened her briefcase and took out a photograph. 'There is one boy I am particularly interested in.' She got up and crossed over. 'His name was Connie, Colin Jenkins.'

Mrs Kennington slowly turned. Her eyes were fixed on Tennison. They drifted down to the photograph. They flicked back, icy blue, sharp as needles.

'Get out of my house,' she said, low in her throat, under iron control.

'Please look at the photograph,' Tennison said quietly, equally controlled.

A shudder passed through Mrs Kennington's whole body. She averted her face and stared at the row of silver-framed photographs on the mantel with a force that was almost manic in its intensity. Two fair-haired handsome youths progressed from grinning schoolboys to young adults with darker hair and engaging smiles.

'There were many young boys brought to this house, whether I was here or not.' Her chin trembled. 'I was at least able to protect my own sons.'

Tennison slipped the photograph into her briefcase and snapped it shut. She nodded to Otley, and followed him to the door.

'I hope for their sake that you did,' she said.

Tennison pushed through the double doors into the corridor, unwinding her scarf, and headed towards her office.

As she reached the door, Halliday came out of his office and beckoned to her urgently.

'Have you got a moment?' He glanced up and down. 'I want this kept very quiet, it's not official yet, but—' His voice dropped to a murmur. 'John Kennington committed suicide this morning.'

Tennison took a full pace back. 'Good God!'

Halliday nodded darkly. He squinted at her: 'That vacancy by the way, for Superintendent. It's Hammersmith, Commander Chiswick knows the Chief there; in fact they're playing golf.'

Tennison widened her eyes, blinking owlishly. 'I'd better charge Jackson then, hadn't I?' she said.

Halliday strode off and she entered her office. She tossed her briefcase down and hung up her coat. There was a mound of paperwork on the desk, and she contemplated it, spirits sinking.

First, though, she had a call to make. The call. But no joy. The receptionist promised to pass the message on immediately after Tennison had emphatically insisted.

Five minutes later there was a tap on the door and DI Hall looked in, dark eyebrows raised inquiringly. 'You wanted Jessica Smithy? She's just arrived – and, was it correct you wanted Vernon Reynolds brought back in, only we just released her.'

'Yes. And you keep your eye on Alice in Wonderland – Miss Smithy to you. Put her in interview room D oh two.' The phone rang. She waved Hall out and answered it. Decision time. Now or never.

'I'm sorry to disturb you at home, Dr Gordon, but I wanted to talk to you as soon as possible.'

'I can make an appointment for tomorrow if nothing's wrong.'

'No, it's just that I would like to arrange a termination,' Tennison said. She heard her own voice, and marvelled at its brisk impersonality. It was like listening to someone else, some other woman, strong and confident, without the slightest qualm.

'Are you sure?' Dr Gordon asked after a pause. 'This is a very big decision.'

'Yes, I am aware of that.' How calm, how collected! 'It is a very big decision, but . . . '

'Obviously it is yours, Jane, but I think you should consider, or come in and discuss it with me.' He wasn't hectoring, and she was glad about that, because she wouldn't have stood for it.

She toyed with her fountain pen. 'I know it's a big decision, and I have obviously given it a great deal of thought.' She pressed the nib into the blotting paper, testing it not quite to breaking point. 'I want an abortion.'

'It could also be a very final decision . . . considering your age.'

'Yes, I know.'

The door opened, Otley rapping with his knuckles

when he was already halfway in. He hovered on one foot, motioning whether he should leave her alone. Tennison shook her head. She said into the phone, 'I'll call you next week, to arrange a time and date.'

'Think on it,' Dr Gordon advised her. 'Goodbye.'

'Goodbye.'

Slowly she replaced the phone and sat staring at nothing. She took a sudden sharp breath, drumming her fingers on the desk. 'I told Halliday we're ready to charge Jackson' – brisk and businesslike once more.

'You know something I don't?' Otley muttered, eyes narrowing suspiciously.

Tennison opened her mouth to reply, but nothing came out except a pitiful choking sob. Otley was totally transfixed, torn between embarrassment and disbelief. Numb with the shock of it, he watched as she burst out crying, tears pouring down her cheeks. She put her hand over her eyes, shoulders heaving, fumbling blindly for a tissue from the drawer.

'I'm sorry ... sorry ...' Tennison blew her nose, making it difficult for herself by shaking her head at the same time.

Otley stood like an empty sack of clothes, his face like a stunned rabbit's, arms hanging limply by his sides. For once his snide cynicism had deserted him.

Tennison wiped her cheeks. 'I just feel as if I'm hitting my head against a brick wall.' She sniffed hard, making a contemptuous gesture towards Halliday's office. 'Get no help from him!'

'I could get the screwdriver, take off a few feet of his office and give it to you if it'll make you feel better,' Otley offered helpfully, giving a gaunt ghost of a smile.

Tennison tried to smile with him, but this only brought on more floods of tears. Muffled behind a bunch of tissues, she croaked, 'I have never done this before, I'm sorry . . .' She sucked in a deep shuddering breath. 'He knows Kennington's dead.'

'Good news travels fast,' Otley remarked glibly. He gave a little uncomfortable shrug, hands spread. 'Look, I can handle this afternoon.'

'No!' Tennison wadded the tissues into a sodden ball and threw them viciously in the basket. 'I give you an inch and you'll take a mile.'

Otley sighed. 'Do you want a cigarette?'

'No, I don't want a bloody cigarette!'

'Coffee?'

'No.' Tennison straightened her shoulders, sitting upright in the chair, combing her hair back with her fingers. 'Just . . . just give me a few minutes on my own.'

She felt mortified. Not only about breaking down, but breaking down in front of Bill Otley, of all people.

Ye Gods, get a grip, woman.

When he'd gone she sat drained and empty, the muscles in her belly still quivering. Her chest ached, and she had to fight with all her strength to stifle the sobs that at any moment might engulf her.

But twenty minutes later, a transformation. Hair brushed, face washed, fresh make-up applied, she was in fine fettle for Vera. The momentary loss of control had somehow cleansed her, swept all her doubts and depression away, given her a steely, hard-eyed resolve.

She smashed the table with her fist, making Vera's hunched form jump and jerk, her stifled sobs turning into strangulated hiccups.

'And you *lied* to me – you never at any time even mentioned you were near that advice centre. Why? Why, Vernon?'

'You've always called me Vera,' Vera wailed, raising a tear-streaked face, her eyes filled with childish hurt.

'Stop playing games with me!' Tennison barked. She spun around as Otley came in. 'I said five minutes, Sergeant.' She glared at him and bent towards the microphone. 'Sergeant Otley has just entered the interview room at three-fifteen p.m.'

Norma looked up from her pad, casting a hooded glance at Otley as one foot soldier to another; she's breathing fire and brimstone, keep your head down if you don't want it blown off. Otley leaned indolently against the wall and folded his arms.

'Did you or did you not see Jackson on the night

Connie died?' Tennison demanded, returning to the attack.

'Yes,' Vera said miserably.

There was a commotion outside in the corridor. Otley crossed to the door and half opened it. The strident tones of Jessica Smithy could be heard as Hall hustled her along.

'Just how long am I expected to wait? I've been here nearly an hour . . . she's doing this on purpose!'

Otley wafted them on and firmly shut the door.

Tennison paced up and down. She yanked the back of her jacket straight and without warning swept the file sheets off the table with such force that Vera cowered in her chair.

'You know what really sickens me about you?' Tennison rasped, leaning forward on her knuckles, face thrust towards Vera's. 'That you said you liked Connie, understood him, that he was like you.'

Vera ducked her head as Tennison leaned even closer, inches away.

'He wasn't though, was he? He wasn't like you. Because he was twenty years younger than you.' Her voice was scathing, pitiless. 'And he was going to get everything you always wanted, wasn't he? *Wasn't he?*'

Vera wriggled, her face collapsing in on itself, biting her lip to hold back the tears. Tennison resumed pacing. She stopped at the window, staring out. 'What time did you get to the advice centre?'

'About eight-thirty.' The answer barely crept out.

'Eight-thirty?' Tennison revolved slowly on her heel. '*Eight-thirty*?' She moved nearer. 'Where was Connie?'

'In the flat.'

'Alone?'

'Yes.'

Tennison bent down to retrieve the scattered sheets. She dropped them any old how on the table. She folded her arms. 'Well, your friend Red is now in trouble. He swore on oath that you were at his friend's studio at . . . '

Vera quickly jumped in. 'Six-thirty – I was. He never knows the time, and I left to go to the club, just as he said.'

'When you left your flat,' Tennison said with ponderous deliberation, 'was Connie there?' Vera nodded. 'Suspect nodded his head.' Tennison leaned in. 'Alone?' Vera shook her head, eyes downcast. 'Suspect shook his head. Who was with Connie when you left your flat at six-thirty?'

The Adam's apple bobbed in the long white throat. Vera's heavy-lidded soulful eyes came up, brimming with moisture.

'A journalist.'

Tennison felt a jolt in her spine. She stared at Vera.

Jessica Smithy sat on the edge of the table, smoking, tapping her cigarette ash on the floor. Beside her were two empty cups of coffee and a half-eaten sandwich on a paper plate. With unconcealed impatience she was watching DI Hall, who a moment before had answered the wall phone. He was nodding. 'Yes, she's still here.'

He cradled the handset and turned to her, a deprecating smile on his lips, fidgeting with his tie.

'Choose them yourself, do you?' Her slender leg in its Gucci shoe swung to and fro like a relentless metronome.

Hall fingered his tie. 'No, my girlfriend does,' he responded brightly, beaming.

Jessica Smithy's hazel eyes flashed, sliding off somewhere. 'I'd get rid of her.' She blew smoke in the air, tapped ash on the floor.

'I tried – I told you – gave you all the clues. It was me that said the advice centre, even said Parker-Jones's name, and it was me that told you about Jackson, me who told you about the press . . . '

Vera scrabbled in the box for another tissue. She discarded the sodden one and noisily blew her nose. She discarded that one too and wrenched out a handful to wipe her damp face.

'I went back to the flat because I'd forgotten a sequined choker.' The tears welled up again. 'Connie was still there, talking – talking. I just listened for a second, I didn't want to interrupt, but I could see them, the door was just ajar, and he was showing her my album.'

Vera gazed up beseechingly at Tennison. 'She was looking at my photographs . . . you don't understand, do you?'

Her arms folded, Tennison looked down at her watch.

'There were some loose pictures of me before, before . . . of my mum and dad, private pictures, no show business ones, just my mum and dad, my brother.' Vera's face crumpled. She talked on through her crying. 'I hurt them enough . . . I don't ever see them, so the pictures are very special. After all I had done for him, he was selling me, too.'

She wiped the tissues under each eye, one at a time, and with a loud sniff straightened her back. Smoke trailed up from the cigarette in the ashtray but she didn't pick it up.

She said huskily, 'I didn't want to make a drama, not in front of the press woman. I just called him out of the room, said I wanted to talk to him. He swore to me he wasn't letting her have a single picture. She left a few minutes later, and I went in to check my album. He lied. There were a lot missing, so I confronted him. He swore he hadn't given her anything, he said she must have stolen them, but he was such a liar, and, and . . . and I got hysterical. I hit him. With an ashtray, I think. I didn't mean to hurt him, but he fell down, I helped him to the sofa. And he – he gave me that smile of his, he had such a sweet smile. And, then, he closed his eyes, and I couldn't feel his pulse. He was – he was dead.'

Silently, without expression, Vera stared in front of her,

tears rolling down her cheeks and dripping onto her lemon yellow blouse.

'Did you call an ambulance?' Tennison asked.

'No, my phone's not working. I told Mr Parker-Jones and he said he would . . . ' She trailed off.

'What? Do what?'

'Take care of everything. Call the ambulance.'

'Did he?'

'I don't know,' Vera said, and in the same dead voice, 'I want to go to the toilet.'

'We are terminating the interview at three-forty-five p.m. in room D oh five as Mr Vernon Reynolds has asked to use the bathroom.'

Tennison switched off the tape and looked to Otley. 'Take him with you.'

Vera stood up, very tall and slender. 'I was put in prison when I was not much older than Connie. That's what I am scared of. Inside they're all Jacksons. I was raped every night, that's what I've been so scared of.' She clutched her handbag under her arm and went to the door. 'I've wanted to tell you, but I was just scared.'

She turned and looked at Tennison with large reproachful eyes.

'You're horrible. You just pretended to like me. Why can't you take me to the ladies?'

She followed Otley out.

*

Otley stood at the washbasins, attempting to flatten the recalcitrant points of his shirt collar. She was taking her bloody time. He sighed, glancing at his watch.

'Come on, Vera, love!'

A toilet flushed and Halliday emerged from one of the cubicles, buttoning his jacket. 'Who's in there?'

Otley looked to the cubicle door, Vera's high-heeled shoes visible underneath it. 'Sorry, Guv, it's Vernon Reynolds ...'

He drew Halliday aside, speaking from the corner of his mouth.

'He's admitted that he struck Colin Jenkins. We just finished questioning him.'

Behind them, beneath the cubicle door, a thick pool of blood was forming, spreading around Vera's spiked heels.

'So it wasn't Jackson after all,' Halliday said, raising his eyebrows.

Otley turned. He snarled, pushing Halliday roughly out of the way, and dived for the cubicle door. 'Get someone up here fast!'

Halliday dithered, old woman that he was, and looked around helplessly.

'She's cut her wrists!' Otley yelled, putting his heel to the lock.

Spurred on at last, Halliday slammed through into the corridor. By now he was running. 'GET SOMEONE IN HERE ...!'

He ran on as Tennison came out of the ladies toilet.

Hurtling into the gents she came upon a bloody scene. Vera was propped in a sitting position against the tiled wall, legs stuck out, one shoe off, limp as a rag doll. Blood was spurting from both wrists. The front of her dress, her legs, the floor, were soaked in it. A smeared red trail led from the cubicle where Otley had dragged her.

Tennison grabbed the roller towel and gave it a fierce, frantic jerk, pulling the end loose from the machine. She kept pulling, unreeling a long white tongue, as Otley ran water in the basin.

Tennison knelt at Vera's side, her knees in the pool of blood.

'Vera, hold on! It's going to be okay – listen to me, can you hear me?' The blood was pumping out. She gripped Vera's upper arm, squeezing with both hands. 'Hurry, she's losing an awful lot of blood . . .'

Vera's head lolled from one side to the other, her wig slipping askew. 'Sorry, I'm sorry,' she kept mumbling.

'Vera, listen to me! Can you hear me? You didn't kill Connie, do you understand?' The eyes were glassy, unfocused. 'He was still alive.' Tennison stared into the ghastly white face, streaked with blue mascara. 'The fire . . . *it was the fire*.'

Vera looked at Tennison, eyelids drooping shut, and her head flopped forward onto her chest. Otley dumped the soaking roller towel onto the floor and began binding it tightly around Vera's arms.

Halliday barged in, heaving for breath. 'There's a fif-teen-minute delay on the ambulance call out . . .'

Tennison snapped, 'Then get a car organized—'

She whipped her head around as it sank in what Halliday had just said. Fifteen Minute Delay. Her lips thinned. 'And one for me.'

She looked to be grinning, but it was fixed in place, frozen to her lips, icy and implacable.

'I am bringing in Parker-Jones personally.'

A furious Jessica Smithy marched along the corridor, Hall in close pursuit. 'Half past two – I have been here since half past two!' she raged. Hall grasped her by the elbow and she gave him a withering look that would have scorched asbestos. 'I want to go to the ladies.'

Hall coloured up and released her.

Jessica Smithy's eyes sparkled dangerously as she spied Tennison coming towards her. She plonked herself in Tennison's path, taller by several inches, her expression haughty and indignant.

'You have no right to waste my time,' she stormed, tossing her head imperiously.

Tennison, her blouse and jacket cuffs, the hem of her skirt and knees caked in blood, let her have it. 'I have every right, and I will hold you for as long as I want. You have lied. You have withheld vital evidence – and you have wasted my time.'

Tennison swept past her, saying, 'You wanted the ladies room, Miss Smithy, follow me.'

She pushed open the door into the female staff locker room, and didn't hold it for Jessica Smithy, who nearly got her face battered. They went inside.

Otley appeared through the double doors at the end of the corridor, running. 'Where the hell is she?'

'Toilets,' Hall said.

Rubbing his face, Otley stood panting and fuming.

Tennison flung her soiled blouse into her locker and took out a short-sleeved navy shirt with breast pockets. She hadn't a matching jacket, so she had to make do with a double-breasted blazer in dark red with gilt-buttoned cuffs. No spare skirt or hose, dammit, she'd have to soldier on with what she had.

She ran water in the washbasin and was rinsing the blood from her hands when the toilet flushed and Jessica Smithy came out of the cubicle. There had been a subtle change. There was a dent in her haughty demeanour, her quick darting gaze not as brashly confident in the face of Tennison's grim single-mindedness of purpose, her firm authority.

Nevertheless, for the sake of appearances, she tried to rekindle her righteous indignation. 'How long am I going to be here for? I am supposed to deliver copy for this evening's—'

'For as *long as I want*!' Tennison didn't need to raise her voice. The lethal sting in it was enough. 'You were at Vernon Reynolds's flat the night Connie died – did you make a third tape?'

The journalist had a sullen pout. 'No.'

Tennison gave her a searching look in the mirror and went over to the roller towel. Jessica Smithy's lean cheeks were slightly flushed. She stared at Tennison's back. 'No, I only made two tapes. I swear before God, just two tapes. I never mentioned before' – clearing her throat uncomfortably – 'I mean, I know I should have told you about me being at the flat . . .'

Tennison finished drying her hands. She picked up her shirt and shook it out. 'Did you remove anything from Vernon Reynolds's flat?' She slipped the shirt on. 'Did you?'

'Yes. They were just some snapshots – nobody famous. Just a few black-and-white photographs and drag acts. Nobody famous,' she repeated anxiously.

'So, apart from these photographs you took, did Colin Jenkins give you anything?'

'Nothing, nothing . . . just some story about being picked up when he was ten or eleven. But I'm beginning to think he made that up.' Her face had a strained, pinched look. 'Oh God, it isn't the way it sounds – I didn't do anything!'

Tennison buttoned her jacket. 'Oh, yes, you did. You

stole photographs that meant a lot to someone, meant so much that Colin Jenkins died for them.' She spared her nothing. 'That's what you did, Miss Smithy.'

Otley's head peered furtively in. Tennison gave her appearance a final check in the mirror and went over. 'Kathy said you wanted to see me?' Otley murmured. 'Something about an ambulance?'

'Yes.' Tennison shot a look at Jessica Smithy. 'Follow me.'

She led the way to her office, Otley bringing up the rear. He could tell from her walk that she was a transformed woman, another person entirely from the one he'd seen weeping less than two hours ago. It was incredible. He couldn't fathom her. He didn't understand women as a species all that well, but Tennison absolutely baffled and amazed him.

Jessica Smithy was contrite, sitting in a chair, puffing nervously on a cigarette. 'I tried to contact you, you know I did, it's not as if I didn't attempt to see you.'

'Just stop the Doris Day act, it's getting on my nerves,' Tennison said shortly, eyes narrowed. 'Martin Fletcher?'

DI Hall came in and spoke over Jessica Smithy's head. 'Car's ready and waiting, Guv.' Tennison acknowledged him and beamed her attention back on the woman.

'He was the first boy I approached, and he introduced me to Connie.' She gulped down smoke. 'Then it seemed obvious to me that, well, Connie would make a better story. We were worried that Martin was too young and—'

'Martin Fletcher is dead, did you know?' Tennison said brutally.

Jessica Smithy's eyes rounded with shock. She felt she was being battered from all sides. The tough shell of blasé cynicism was falling to pieces, exposing a frightened woman floundering out of her depth.

Tennison looked at her watch. She was in a hurry to get on. She snapped her fingers, and Otley imagined he could practically see an aura of sparks coruscating around her head.

'So you drop Martin Fletcher and now offer Connie money, yes? Did you give him the money in Vernon Reynolds's flat?'

'Yes.' Jessica Smithy nodded numbly. 'He put it in his pocket, said it wasn't enough, he wanted more.'

'Then what happened?'

'I said I couldn't give him any more, not until I at least saw what he had to offer . . .'

'And did you?' Tennison demanded impatiently. 'Come on, Miss Smithy, did he show you anything? Give you any names?'

'No.'

Tennison looked again at her watch. 'So then what happened?'

Jessica Smithy stubbed out the cigarette and wiped her fingers. 'He left the room for a minute and there was this album on the coffee table. I'd just paid him five hundred pounds, so . . . ' She blinked fearfully at Tennison. 'I opened the album and just – I just took some of the loose photographs, and a few others . . . '

'Vera Reynolds's album? Yes?'

'They were just photos of a family,' Jessica Smithy protested. 'Couple of somebody in drag. They were no use, they meant nothing.'

Tennison stood with her hands on her hips. 'Wrong, Miss Smithy. They meant an awful lot to somebody, enough to . . . ' She reached for the ashtray. 'Make him pick up a heavy glass ashtray and hit Colin Jenkins with it.' She emptied the ashtray, banging it against the side of the metal basket. 'You have a lot to answer for.'

Pale and stricken, Jessica Smithy licked her dry lips.

Tennison looked to Hall. She flipped her hand. 'Take Miss Smithy and bring her back with Vernon Reynolds's photographs.'

Jessica Smithy rose slowly to her feet. 'Are you going to charge me with anything?' she asked tremulously.

'I'll let you know,' Tennison glowered, wafting the bloody woman out of her sight.

There was a real buzz around the place. Everyone could feel it. Something big was going down.

Haskons and Lillie, infected like everyone else, hurried along from the Squad Room, in time to see Otley emerging from Tennison's office.

'Hey, Sarge, what's going on?'

Otley went past them. 'She's picking up Parker-Jones,' he said, not breaking his stride.

Hall came out and escorted Jessica Smithy to the main staircase.

Otley had halted, midway along the corridor, as Kathy rushed past him. She came up breathlessly, meeting a steely-eyed Tennison head-on as she marched out of her office.

'Emergency services have said there was a fifteen-minute delay that night, and all callers were informed that—'

Tennison punched the air. 'I've got him! And this time I am ready for him.' All fired up, she shouted to Otley, 'Let's go!'

Chapter Eighteen

Otley went first, holding the door for Tennison to walk through into the reception area. She was alerted; it seemed unusually quiet. It was the dead time of the afternoon, but even so ...

The door to the office was ajar, and Tennison peeked inside. The normally neat desk was a muddle of correspondence and document files spilling their contents, papers strewn everywhere. The desk drawers were open, and so were several of the filing cabinets, as if someone had been hastily rooting through them.

'Looks like he's about to do a runner,' Tennison observed. 'You think he's been tipped off?'

Otley stepped over the torn-down notice board. He gazed around at the address slips and contact cards, ripped up and scattered over the dank green carpet. He opened the door to the TV room and looked in. Empty. He turned back to Tennison with a shrug.

A sudden crash made Tennison jump. She spun around to find Parker-Jones looming over her, the door to the kitchen swinging shut behind him. He stared down at her, the black curtains of hair framing his sneeringly handsome face.

'Well, I hope you're satisfied. As you can see, the place is empty.'

Tennison snapped erect. 'Mr Edward Parker-Jones, I am arresting you for questioning regarding the murder of Colin Jenkins. I have to warn you that anything you—'

'I want to call my lawyer,' Parker-Jones said brusquely, striding on to his office. But then he turned in the doorway, all silky charm with a contemptuous edge to it. 'Please continue, Inspector, you seem to like the sound of your own voice!'

Seething inside, Tennison followed hard on his heels. She gave the nod to Otley, who repeated the caution. Parker-Jones ignored it, his tall figure moving swiftly around the desk and reaching for the phone.

Tennison beat him to it. Her hand came down on the phone.

'We can do that at the station, sir.'

A muscle twitched in his taut cheek. His long jaw was rigid with anger. Tennison stared up unflinchingly into the deep-set eyes. She beckoned Otley forward, there was a flurry of movement, two sharp clicks, and a moment later Edward Parker-Jones was blinking down in amazement, stunned and incredulous that these stupid thick morons had the nerve to slap the handcuffs on him. *Him!*

Halliday saw him being brought in. Standing outside his office he had an uninterrupted view the full length of the corridor to the double doors at the top of the main staircase. Two uniformed officers led the handcuffed Parker-Jones through. Even from this distance Halliday could see the dark glittering eyes, the suppressed manic fury in his stiff-legged stride.

The officers guided him towards one of the interview rooms in the adjoining corridor and he passed from view.

Halliday headed for the Squad Room. His shoulder blades felt clammy. He ran his finger inside his collar, clearing his throat as he pushed through the doors. Almost everyone was there, yet the room was eerily quiet. A telephone drilled through the silence and someone quickly answered it. Tennison was standing at her desk, calmly sorting through her interview papers. Damn woman was made of titanium. Halliday went over.

'Parker-Jones's brief is in reception.' His voice became low and terse, a bit ragged. 'You all set?'

'Yes, sir.' Tennison's hand was nerveless as she slipped the sheets inside the document file. 'Some developments this afternoon warranted my bringing in Parker-Jones.'

'I know,' Halliday said. He touched her arm, causing her to look up. 'But you'd better nail him.'

'I intend to.' Tennison pushed her hair back over her ears, smoothed the front of her jacket, picked up the document file and snapped it smartly under her arm. She was ready.

Flanked by Halliday and Otley, she marched through the hushed room to the door. It was as if everyone was holding one huge collective breath. Eyes swivelled, watching the neat compact figure, seeing in the set of her shoulders and her raised head a ruthless compulsion, a chilling determination.

Nail him, Halliday had said. And by Christ she would.

Haskons stood near the door. He moved aside. 'Good luck, Guv!'

Tennison gave a tight curt nod and went through.

The handcuffs had been removed. Edward Parker-Jones sat straight-backed in the chair, his manicured hands resting some distance apart on the table. If not relaxed, he seemed rather more at ease, the angry glitter in his eyes replaced by an opaque self-concealment, his face an expressionless closed book.

Perhaps the presence of Joseph Spelling, his lawyer, had worked the trick. Spelling exuded probity and restraint, from his starched collar and tightly knotted dark green silk tie to his pinstripe trousers and highly polished black shoes. His pearl-grey homburg hat rested on his briefcase on the table, the initials J.D.S. stamped in gold in the burnished leather.

He regarded Tennison with a faintly quizzical air, prepared to tolerate her even though she was a mere woman doing a man's job. Seated next to his client, he leaned forward attentively, his bony beak of a nose in the deeply lined face thrust in her direction as she spread the papers out and unscrewed the cap of her fountain pen.

Tennison slowly lifted her head and gazed directly at Parker-Jones.

'On the evening of the seventeenth of this month you have stated that you were at the advice centre, Soho. Is that correct?'

Parker-Jones's face stayed impassive. 'Yes.'

'Could you please give details of who else was there on that night?'

Parker-Jones closed his eyes. How many more times? 'Billy Matthews,' he began wearily, preparing to repeat them all again, *yet again*, but got no farther.

'Statement withdrawn.' Tennison's voice was quiet, devoid of emphasis or emotion. 'Matthews denies being at the advice centre.'

'Donald Driscoll ...'

'Driscoll has withdrawn his statement and denied being at the advice centre.'

'Alan Thorpe, James Jackson ...'

'Alan Thorpe has stated that he was, on the night of the seventeenth, at the centre.' She paused, seeing in the depths of Parker-Jones's eyes a mocking triumph. She went on, 'He was not only intoxicated from alcoholic beverages, but was also suffering from other substance abuse, and was, in his own words, unable to remember if he was actually there himself.'

'James Jackson,' Parker-Jones repeated steadily, his heavy dark brows knitting together as his eyes bored into her.

Tennison glanced down at the sheet in front of her. 'Mr Jackson made a statement this afternoon contradicting an earlier statement. He now states, under caution, that he was at the advice centre but for no more than two or three minutes.' She raised her eyebrows. 'Do you, Mr Parker-Jones, have any other alibi witnesses that you wish at this stage to be noted?'

Erect in the chair, hands spread on the table, Parker-Jones was an edifice of cold contemptuous arrogance. He tilted his head as Spelling whispered in his ear. They conferred. Tennison tapped the table with her pen. Halliday and Otley, standing side by side against the wall, waited and watched.

'My client will answer,' Spelling said finally, leaning back.

'I realize I have been very foolish,' said Parker-Jones smoothly, and Tennison marvelled at how his change in personality could be switched on and switched off at will, in a trice. Now he was conciliatory.

'I can only apologize . . . but I was trying in some ways to protect Vernon Reynolds. Vernon was at the centre on the seventeenth.'

'Did you speak with Vernon Reynolds at all?' Tennison asked.

'No comment.'

'But you do admit that Vernon Reynolds was at the advice centre on the seventeenth?'

A tiny hesitation. 'I have just said so.'

'Did Vernon Reynolds ask you to call an ambulance?'

'No comment.'

Tennison looked thoughtful for a moment. She allowed her eyes to slide up from the desk to his face. 'Mr Parker-Jones, we are in possession of a tape recording made on the evening of the seventeenth, and it will be very simple for us to match the voice on the tape with yours. Did you or did you not call an ambulance?'

Tennison was lying through her teeth, and both Halliday and Otley knew it. They had such a tape, yes, but despite the best efforts of the technical people it hadn't been possible to identify the voice. Too much static and distortion. She was way out on a limb.

Parker-Jones was half turned away, whispering in Spelling's ear. Spelling replied, Parker-Jones nodding, and then he turned back.

'Yes, I did. Vernon's phone was disconnected and he was in a dreadful state. Said that Colin Jenkins and he had argued, and that Colin, Connie, needed a doctor. So, I did place a call to the emergency services . . .'

Halliday and Otley exchanged relieved looks. She'd gambled and it had paid off. Yet her face betrayed not a flicker, not the slightest sign, and she carried on imperturbably, 'What did the emergency services tell you, Mr Parker-Jones?'

'That an ambulance was on its way.'

'Anything else?'

He shook his head carefully. 'No, I don't think so.'

'Why didn't you leave your name?'

He smiled, somewhat ruefully. 'To be perfectly honest with you, the advice centre has had to – on a number of occasions – place emergency calls. Some of the boys, well, they get deeply disturbed when they are diagnosed HIV positive. It's fear, you see, and then they refuse to go to hospital.' He turned his hands, palms uppermost on the table, a gesture appealing for her understanding. 'So I was afraid they might not be willing to respond—'

Tennison cut in, impervious to his smarm.

'Were you informed that there would be a fifteen-minute delay?'

He switched again, face stiffening when he realized she wasn't buying his bill of goods. 'I can't recall.'

Tennison was all patience and reason as she spelt it out. 'But if you were informed that there would be a fifteen-minute delay, it would make sense, as the advice centre is only a few minutes' distance from Vernon Reynolds's flat, to ...'

They were conferring again. Tennison sighed. She gazed at the ceiling, tapping her pen.

Parker-Jones faced her confidently. 'I was unaware of any delays.'

'Why didn't you call a doctor?' Tennison pressed him. 'Or make that short journey?'

He had his answer ready. 'At no time did he – Vernon Reynolds – make it appear there was a dire emergency, that Connie ...'

'... was possibly unconscious?'

'I was asked to call an ambulance or arrange for one to be sent. I have admitted that I did lie – or did not give you the information when I was asked before about this ambulance call out.' Parker-Jones was back to being reasonable again, doing all he could to help the police with their inquiries. No doubt the influence of his lawyer, urging temperance and moderation. 'I apologize, but surely you can understand my reasons – I simply did not want to get Vernon Reynolds into trouble.'

It was neat and plausible and Tennison had no idea how to break through and expose his story for the pack of lies it was. This man was a filthy sadist, a vampire preying on the children entrusted to his care and leaving behind a wreckage of young lives. He'd been doing it for years, in different parts of the country, using Kennington and Margaret Speel and possibly countless others to aid and abet him and cover his tracks. He was a cancerous growth in society that long ago should have been cut out. Tennison was the surgeon, but it was as though the scalpel in her hand was blunted, or had been whipped away the moment she started to operate. He was a devious, clever, calculating, lying, perverted bastard with an impregnable sense of his own superiority. He had friends in high places, money to buy the services of a good lawyer, and sufficient power to put the frighteners on anyone who might be tempted to blow the whistle. He was above the law, that was the contemptuous opinion of Edward Parker-Jones, and Tennison had a horrible, gnawing suspicion in the pit of her stomach that he might be right.

The silence in the room stretched on and on. There was just the rustle of papers as Tennison sorted through the file. Halliday eased his chafed neck inside his collar, his pale blue eyes loose in their sockets. Spelling cleared his throat ponderously. He leaned forward, his quizzical expression making his forehead a maze of corrugations.

'Do you have any further questions you wish to put to my client?'

'Yes, I do,' Tennison said at once. 'Mr Parker-Jones, you have apologized earlier for lying. You lied about the presence of four witnesses that you said saw you on the evening of the seventeenth. One of these witnesses was Billy Matthews, is that correct?'

'Yes, but you must understand,' he said loftily, in a patronizing drawl that infuriated her, 'there are a number of them on any given evening . . . '

'But you were most specific about Billy Matthews,' Tennison butted in. 'You said you recalled him being at the advice centre because he was ill.'

'Yes.'

'But as it now transpires, Billy Matthews was not at the advice centre, he was in actual fact in Charing Cross Hospital.'

He brushed it aside. 'I'm sorry, I was simply confused as to the exact evening.'

'Really? Even though you called an ambulance for him? That would be the evening of the sixteenth,' Tennison stressed, and was charged with exhilaration to see, for the tiniest split second, a shadow of uncertainty flicker in the deep-set eyes. 'On that occasion you did leave your name, and on that occasion you were informed that there would be a fifteen-minute delay. Is that correct?'

'It's possible.'

'Possible.' Tennison seized on this. 'So it would also be possible that when an ambulance was called on the following evening you were fully aware there would be a delay.' She stared him out. 'Giving you perhaps even more time to leave the advice centre and go to Vernon Reynolds's flat. Did you? Did you go to Vernon Reynolds's flat?'

He was in a corner, but there was a simple way out, and he took it.

'No, I did not.'

Back to bloody stalemate! She couldn't shake him, couldn't budge the arrogant bastard. They could sit here all night, her lobbing questions and accusations, and they would just bounce off that smug stone wall, that sneeringly superior shell he had built around himself. He was fucking fireproof. She felt like screaming and yelling and leaping across to tear out his eyes and rip the lying tongue out of his mouth.

Tennison was furious with herself. Not a snowball's chance in hell of nailing this shit if she allowed her emotions to veer out of control. By an act of will she quelled them. She looked up, her eyes cold, her voice without a tremor as she asked, 'Mr Parker-Jones, are you aware of the existence of certain compromising photographs that belonged to James Jackson?'

Parker-Jones leaned towards Spelling, but they didn't confer. The lawyer merely gave a long slow blink. Parker-Jones straightened up, wearing a smirk that Tennison wanted to smash from his face.

'No comment.'

'That in many of these said photographs you are pictured with the deceased, Colin Jenkins?'

'No comment.'

'That you were also photographed in various poses with a number of juveniles, and these photographs were taken from your home in Camden Town?'

'No comment.'

'I think you knew of the existence of these pictures, and knew that Colin Jenkins intended to sell them.'

'No comment.'

'On the night of the seventeenth you had James Jackson searching all over London, desperate to track these photographs down.' Her tone became thin and cutting as she replayed the scenario, telling the real story to his face, making him know that she *knew*. 'To track Colin Jenkins down, but you just couldn't find him, could you?'

'No comment.'

'And then Vera, Vernon Reynolds, came to you in, as you have said, a dreadful state . . .'

'No comment.'

' . . . telling you that the very person you were looking for was not only *in* her flat, but unconscious, alone, and with the said photographs.'

'No comment.'

'You said you would arrange everything. You would even call the ambulance—'

On his lips she saw the words forming and leapt up, slapped her hands flat on the table, her body arched tautly towards him.

'*No comment?*' Tennison hissed. 'NO COMMENT AGAIN? Mr Parker-Jones, you have admitted you were aware of the emergency services' delays during this period—'

'No comment.'

'—You used that fifteen minutes to hurry from the advice centre, run over to Vernon Reynolds's flat. He wasn't dead, was he? Connie was still alive. And so you made sure, made sure he would never be able to tell anyone about you, Mr Parker-Jones. *You* and your friends. It was so easy, wasn't it? He couldn't fight back, couldn't make any attempt to stop you as you set light to him . . . left him to burn to death.'

She knew, at last, she had him. She was certain she had him, because he said nothing, his long face smouldering and sullen. Then he folded his arms, the corner of his mouth curling up in a little smirk, and she knew sickeningly that she hadn't.

Tennison stood outside the interview room. She felt so weary that she could have stretched out on the carpet in the corridor and gone fast asleep.

She looked away as Parker-Jones came out. 'Good night, Inspector Tennison.' His smiling glance passed over her dismissively. He turned to Otley. 'Which way is it?'

Otley led him towards the main staircase. Tennison leaned against the wall. Spelling came out, carrying his briefcase and homburg, followed by Halliday. She watched the lawyer hurry along briskly to join Parker-Jones, who patted his shoulder and pumped his hand. Otley pointed the way and they went off.

Tennison sighed tiredly, rubbing her eyes. 'I had to try, Jack.'

Halliday nodded. She was drained, both physically and emotionally, he could see that. He said, not unkindly, 'Supposition, intuition, really are worthless. Without hard evidence you didn't stand a chance in hell. Without a witness who actually saw person or persons unknown set fire to that flat, you will never have a case – especially not against someone like him.'

She looked up at him with a strained mocking smile. 'Does this blow my chances? Superintendent?'

'No. You'll get it. No strings.'

'Guv!' Otley came up. 'Jessica Smithy's back.' He jerked his thumb towards Tennison's office.

Tennison touched Halliday's arm. He'd told her what she wanted to know. 'Thank you,' she said. She smiled at him, and kept smiling all the way back to her office.

Jessica Smithy handed over a buff-coloured envelope. Tennison delved inside and looked at the snapshots of Vernon Reynolds and his family: little Vernon in short pants with his mum and dad, standing on a sunny promenade, the holiday crowd surging around them. Vernon as a lanky teenager in the back garden, one arm clasped around his mother's shoulder, both of them smiling. Other family snaps – school speech day, weddings, day trips, picnics – and three or four of Vernon, now Vera, as a very young man in a primitive drag outfit he must have compiled from jumble sales. Tennison slipped them back in.

'Is Parker-Jones going to be charged?' Jessica Smithy was anxious to know. She examined Tennison closely, keyed up, smoking rapidly with short little puffs.

In contrast, Tennison felt calm, wearily peaceful. 'Still after the scoop, Miss Smithy?' she asked nonchalantly.

'I'm paid to expose the truth. It's my job, a bit like yours.'

'No, Miss Smithy,' Tennison corrected her, 'your job is not like mine.' And as if to demonstrate the truth of this, she opened a file crammed with statements, photostats, photographs, lists of names and addresses, phone memos and faxes, nearly three inches thick.

'But it is criminal that a man like Parker-Jones is able to gain access to young innocent boys,' Tennison mused sadly. With her thumb she riffled through the contents. 'All with the blessing of the social services.'

Jessica Smithy turned her head to exhale smoke, but her eyes never left the file that Tennison was idly leafing through. Tennison detached a black-and-white photograph of Jason Baldwyn, holding it up.

'"Keeper of Souls." This young boy said that was his nickname – good headline! Nice turn of phrase for a sick pervert ...'

Tennison let the photograph slide from her fingers and drop onto the open file. She looked at her watch, and then reached behind for her shoulder bag. 'Would you excuse me for a moment?' She came around the desk and went out, picking up the buff envelope on the way.

Her footsteps receded down the corridor.

In the silence Jessica Smithy slowly edged around the desk, craning her head. She nudged the corner of the file with her thumb, aligning it more directly into her field of vision. With a swift glance to the door and back, she took hold of the photograph and stared at it.

Several minutes later the door opened a crack. Tennison peered through. Her back to the door, Jessica Smithy was bent over the file in a cloud of smoke, micro-cassette recorder close to her mouth, sifting through the thick bundle of papers.

Tennison eased the door shut and released the handle from her clammy palm.

She was heading for the staircase when Otley emerged from the Squad Room, his wrinkled raincoat draped over his shoulder. He cocked his head. 'You off then?'

Tennison nodded. 'Miss Smithy's in my office. Give her another fifteen minutes, then get rid of her.' She held out the buff envelope. 'Oh, and would you make sure these photographs get delivered to Vernon Reynolds?'

'Yes, ma'am.' Otley tucked them under his arm. His head went back, watching her through slitted eyes. 'Superintendent next, is it?'

'I think so,' Tennison conceded, cool and poised.

'I guess my mate didn't have the right strings,' Otley said. He made it sound casual and indifferent, but she could feel the bottled-up force of his resentment, the boiling anger.

'No, he just didn't know whose to pull,' she told him.

'You live and learn.'

'Not always the best man wins,' Tennison responded glibly, matching his cliché with one of her own.

She walked on, feeling his stare burning holes in her back.

'Good night,' she called out, not turning.

Otley's lips moved, spitting out volumes of silent abuse, calling her every stinking name under the sun, and he knew plenty—

Tennison whipped around, catching him in the act, a huge exuberant grin spread across her face. She crouched, aiming her finger at him, cocked her thumb and shot him dead. She blew smoke off the barrel and bounced down the stairs.

SIMON &
SCHUSTER

Lynda La Plante

The Legacy

For three people 'The Legacy' was a curse . . .

Hugh, hard drinking lion of the Welsh valleys. His
daughter Evelyne – who lost her heart to a travelling
gypsy. And handsome prizefighter Freedom – saved from
the gallows to do battle for the heavyweight
championship of the world.

From the poverty of the Welsh pit valleys to the glories of
the prize ring, from the dangers of Prohibition America to
the terrors of Britain at war, Lynda La Plante delves into
the lives of a remarkable family and its fortunes, and the
curse that forged their names.

'A torrid tale of love, intrigue and passion' Daily Express

Paperback ISBN 978-1-47110-024-6
Ebook ISBN 978-1-47110-026-0

**SIMON &
SCHUSTER**

Lynda La Plante

She's Out

**They locked her up in Holloway for murder . . . but
now she's out, she has unfinished business to attend to.**

After serving a lengthy sentence for shooting her husband
at point blank range, Dolly Rawlins is set free from prison,
with only one thing on her mind – the six million in
diamonds she stashed prior to her imprisonment.

Waiting for Dolly is a group of women who all served time
with her. They know about the diamonds and they want a
cut. Also waiting is a detective sergeant in the Metropolitan
Police. He holds her personally responsible for the death
of his sister in the diamond raid ten years earlier.
And now he wants her back inside.

Dolly Rawlins has other plans: to realise the dream that
kept her going for years in prison. But against such
determined opposition, the fantasy soon turns into
a very different, tragic and violent reality …

**Paperback ISBN 978-1-47110-027-7
Ebook ISBN 978-1-47110-029-1**